I0637111

Rescued by Her Cowboys

Cowboys Online, Volume 8

Jan Springer

Published by Spunky Girl Publishing, 2024.

Also by Jan Springer

Standalone
A Touch of Menage Boxed Set
Shades of Menage Boxed Set
Naughty Girl Desires Boxed Set
Nice Girl Naughty
Sinderella Sexy
The Biker and The Bride
The Fire Within
Bared to Him
Pleasure Bound : A Futuristic Adult Romance Boxed Set
Merry Menage Kisses Boxed Set
Inner Girl Rising
Stripped Naked
Risqué Girl Delights Boxed Set
A Holiday Menage
Ménage À Trois
A Hitman for Hannah
Billionaire Boyfriend
Edible Delights
Vampira
Toygasm
The Dark Side

Watch for more at www.janspringer.com.

Rescued by Her Cowboys

Moose Ranch #7 ~ Cowboys Online #8
Jan Springer

Jennifer Jane (JJ) Watson has spent ten years in a maximum-security prison.
The last thing she expects is to get an early release, along with a job on a remote Canadian cattle ranch serving dinners to three of the sexiest cowboys she's ever met!

Rafe, Brady, and Dan thought they were getting a couple of male ex-cons to help out around their secluded ranch, but instead they get an attractive and very appealing female.
In the snowbound wilds of Northern Ontario, female companionship is rare.
It's a good thing the three men like to share...

When JJ embarks on a solo flight to the city for a fun-filled surprise wedding shower for a pilot friend, her trip is shattered when she's caught in a violent storm. She has no choice but to land upon one of the many desolate lakes in the unforgiving wilderness of Northern Ontario, Canada. After securing shelter on land, she teeters on the brink of despair when her float plane disappears on the lake of many bays.

Has her plane sunk? Or is it floating out there somewhere? JJ will have to tap into newfound courage in order to protect her unborn baby and survive while grappling with the uncertainty of rescue.

Rafe, Dan, and Brady are thrown into a desperate rescue mission when the woman they love doesn't come home. With the help of their pilot friends, they'll leave no stone unturned in their search. With little sleep and ongoing dangerous weather hindering their search, each cowboy must face their own fears about the possibility of life without JJ and the baby she is carrying.
Will they ever find out who the father of the baby is? Will JJ and her unborn baby make it out of the unforgiving wilderness? And can her three cowboys hold it together as they race against the elements to bring her home to her young daughter and back into their hearts once again?
Find out in Rescued by Her Cowboys.

Copyright

License Notes

This book is licensed for your personal use only.

Author Note

This is a work of fiction. Characters, places, settings and events presented in this book are purely of the author's imagination and bear no resemblance to any actual person, living or dead or to any actual events, places and/or settings.

Cowboys Online Series

Book One ~ Cowboys for Christmas – Moose Ranch
Book Two ~ Cowboys In her Pocket – Moose Ranch
Book Three ~ Loving her Cowboys – Moose Ranch
Book Four ~ Cowboys in Her Heart – Moose Ranch
Book Five ~ Always Her Cowboys – Moose Ranch
Book Six ~ Her Forever Cowboys – Snowy Creek Ranch (Milena's story)
Book Seven ~ Claiming Her Cowboys – Moose Ranch
Book Eight ~ Rescued by Her Cowboys ~ Moose Ranch
Book Nine ~ Wrangling Her Cowboys ~ Moose Ranch

Next story in this series:

Wrangling Her Cowboys
Is it a boy or a girl?

A tumultuous Thanksgiving wedding, a birthday and holiday dinners are upon Moose Ranch, and a very pregnant JJ finds herself playing hostess galore!

When Christmas draws close, an unexpected snowstorm strands her three men and its up to JJ to wrangle her cowboys together just in time for her to give birth. Now that we know who the baby daddy is...will JJ have a baby boy or a baby girl?

Find out in Wrangling Her Cowboys.

Chapter One

Moose Ranch
Present Day ~ July

J J blew out a tense breath and wiped the light perspiration from her forehead with the back of her hand, then returned to folding the last towel and placed it onto the laundry pile.

Mercy, but it was warm in the laundry room. Even with wearing her light cotton sundress, she felt hot.

Late afternoon summer sunshine streamed in through the array of open windows illuminating the bright colors of the loads of clothing that she'd folded earlier and placed onto the nearby table. Overhead, a ceiling fan hummed noisily and from outside she could hear a woodpecker cracking its beak against one of the towering pine trees in the immense forest that surrounded their wilderness cattle ranch.

Taking care of three men and a baby, sure did produce a lot of laundry. But she wouldn't change it for the world. It beat rotting in prison like she'd done for years, and she absolutely loved her hardworking cowboys, and adored her beautiful seven-month-old daughter.

JJ placed her hand over her swollen baby bump. And she loved her unexpected pregnancy.

She was now just a little over four months along and thankfully her morning sickness was gone. Physically she was feeling good but there were a couple of concerns.

One of them being, she just wished that she knew who the father of her baby could be. Not knowing didn't seem to bother the men, unless they were acting, just like she was acting.

When she'd first found out she was pregnant again so soon after Chrissy, the paternity hadn't taken priority. She'd also heard in the past that those tests could cause harm to the baby, but her doctor had recently reassured her that there were non-invasive tests.

Truth be told though, she now wanted to have a non-invasive pre-natal paternity test done. According to her midwife, all that it entailed was a blood test from the mom and cheek swabs from each of the men. She just didn't know how to broach the subject with the guys.

She gazed at the clock and frowned. She hadn't realized it was already almost supper time. She still had to set the table, get some lettuce from their garden, whip up the salad, and check on that roast beef she'd stuffed into the oven earlier.

She'd just have to put away the loads of laundry later. Much later.

First, the roast.

The savory scents of the cooking meat had her mouth watering as she made her way down the hall into the kitchen.

Surprise washed over her as she noted the table had already been set and she spied a couple of large bowls of green leaf lettuce salad on the countertop. Dan must have realized she'd lost track of time and had gone out the back door and picked the lettuce from the garden while she'd been folding the laundry.

The salad looked so yummy she couldn't resist but snap up a piece of lettuce and nibble on it. The crisp green literally melted in her mouth. The lettuce had been washed and all it needed was the dressing.

From her vantage point in the kitchen, she spied her daughter, Chrissy, laying on her back, fast asleep in her playpen. And Dan was laying down on the sofa right beside her. He was fast asleep too.

Quietly, she went over to the pen and gazed down at her baby girl.

This morning JJ had dressed her in a cute summer outfit that made her smile every time Chrissy wore it because it made her look like a bright bundle of sunshine.

It was a sleeveless V-neck, lemon print dress with a puffy yellow bow at the chest and because Chrissy was growing so fast this was probably the last time the cute dress would fit her.

With a touch of anxiety, she stared at her daughter's chest willing it to rise and fall. When it did, she sighed in relief. A pacifier dangled from between her cherub shaped lips and her tiny hands were clenched into fists at her sides as she slept.

Getting pregnant again had increased JJ's anxiety and panic attacks. That was her other concern.

According to her midwife, it was JJ's hormones preparing her to protect her child. Knowing the reason for her amplified anxiety didn't do much to alleviate the attacks though, especially since her worries had overflowed to her men.

Not too long ago, Dan had gotten his foot caught in a rusted animal trap and he hadn't been able to break free. He'd been out working on clearing the trails after a violent storm and they hadn't realized he was missing for some time. He'd gotten hypothermic, but thankfully they'd found him in time to save his foot and his life.

Will, the new bush doctor for the area, had said Dan was lucky as things could have been much worse. The doctor had also warned them to keep an eye out for blood clots and other possible medical emergencies where Dan was concerned and since then she'd been hypervigilant in keeping an eye on him.

Just like she was now as she tiptoed over to Dan and studied him. She waited for his inhalation of breath and found herself relaxing when it came.

He was so adorable when he slept. The harshness of working on a wilderness ranch always disintegrated from his face when he was asleep, replaced by an innocent, boyish appearance. Except for that scruffy five o'clock shadow hugging his face which reminded her that Dan was all prime grown-up male.

She swallowed as her pussy clenched in remembrance of last night and how wonderful he'd felt when he was thrusting his shaft into her eager vagina as he kissed her so tenderly.

While Brady and Rafe had kept the ranch running, Dan had been ordered to stay here and help her out while his foot healed.

The past couple of days and nights while Brady and Rafe had been away tending to the cattle, she and Dan had had some hot sex during the days as well as the nights. She wished he was awake so she could suggest they have a nice little quickie before Rafe and Brady returned and Chrissy woke up.

Yeah, some naughty fun in the afternoon would certainly take the edge off her nervousness.

As she contemplated leaning over and kissing him awake, the far-off puttering of approaching all terrain vehicles whipped through the open windows, making JJ hurry into the kitchen.

The men would be hungry.

In more ways than one.

WHEN MOOSE RANCH CAME into view, Brady's, excitement just about overwhelmed him.

Inside that ranch house was the woman he loved and who might be carrying his child and his beautiful baby daughter.

He brought his all-terrain vehicle to a stop in the front yard and his heart hammered as he spied JJ at the kitchen window. She was waving at him. He waved back and then she was gone, most likely getting dinner ready.

A moment later, Rafe pulled his vehicle in behind him. Brady quickly turned off the ignition and joined Rafe as he hurried toward the ranch house.

"I am starving! I can smell that roast from here," Rafe chuckled as he hurriedly stomped up the stairs. He held the mud room door open for Brady, and once they were inside, they quickly removed their work boots.

"Who cares about the roast. I just want JJ on my menu tonight," Brady growled in a low voice as he grabbed his black cowboy hat off the nearest peg and headed down the hallway, catching a glimpse into the laundry room and the piles of folded laundry.

He wasn't about to give her any time to do all that work. Not with what he had planned for her tonight.

Rafe laughed, obviously thinking he was joking about JJ on his menu.

Truth be told, he was not kidding. He seriously wanted to make love to JJ and the cowboy hat on his head should have tipped Rafe off as to what he wanted, which was a few minutes of alone time with JJ. He'd been wanting her the entire time Rafe and he had been away. He always missed her when he was away from her, whether it was an hour or whether it was days.

"You go on ahead, I'll catch a quick shower," Rafe said as he slipped into the bathroom when they were halfway to the kitchen.

"You son of a bitch. You want me to make a bad impression on her because I haven't showered, eh?"

"You got it," Rafe replied with a laugh as he quickly shut the door.

Brady smiled. Rafe was using the excuse of a shower so Brady could have alone time with JJ. The cowboy hat *had* tipped him off because they all knew that JJ loved it when one or all of them wore their cowboy hats.

Since day one when she'd arrived here, fresh out of prison, on an icy cold winter night, drunk as a skunk and drugged up on meds to keep her anxiety in check, she'd confessed to him she loved a man wearing a cowboy hat.

He grinned at the memory. He'd been so smitten with her right from the start that he'd been pissed off at how his body had been reacting to her. But he wasn't pissed off anymore.

He was in love.

From the end of hallway Brady could see that his daughter was fast asleep in the play pen in the living room and his heart clenched with love for her. He couldn't wait for her to wake up so he could kiss her pudgy little cheeks and let her know that he was back home. She was always delighted to see him, and it made his heart swell with pride that JJ and himself had made such a beautiful little girl.

His gaze flew to Dan, who appeared to be fast asleep on the couch.

Bonus. Definitely some alone time with JJ.

Yeah, it felt so good to be back.

A moment later he burst into the open concept living room / dining room / kitchen area and found JJ bent over in front of the open oven, about to pull out a roasting pan.

"Let me get that, baby doll," he said.

He took the towel she'd been about to use, and he watched as she straightened, giving him a view of the swell of her baby belly. Man, he swore that little baby bump had grown since he'd been gone.

"Welcome back. Where is Rafe?" she asked as she eyed his black cowboy hat.

"Shower," he answered.

Using the thick towel, he grabbed the heavy roasting pan, relishing the spicy heat blasting against his face. When the roast was clear of the oven, she closed the door, and he placed the pan on the large wood chopping board on the counter.

He turned around to find her studying him with the cutest smile.

"What's up with the hat?" she teased as he suddenly could do nothing but stare at her.

"Just let me look at you," he whispered, feeling the emotion of love spring thick and raw in his chest. Man, she became more beautiful every time he looked at her.

She was smiling so hard that dimples popped in her cheeks, making him catch his breath. She hadn't smiled like that in quite some time, especially with everything that had gone on this year.

Her postpartum depression following the birth of Chrissy, his brother-in-law's unexpected death, Dan's accident, JJ's surprise pregnancy, which had shocked all of them.

But none of that mattered at the moment. He just wanted to focus on his woman.

She had the longest eyelashes, the cutest pert nose, and he ached to run his fingers through her velvety brown hair. Too bad she had strung it up in a ponytail. But he didn't blame her, it was blistering warm outside today, and the ceiling fans just weren't doing their job because he felt fever hot, and he knew that JJ was the only one who could put out the liquid fire that burned through him.

"Brady?" she asked softly.

"Baby mama, I have missed you too much," he whispered.

He just kept staring at her, soaking in her bright brown eyes, the light-coloured freckles sprinkled across her cheeks and her luscious mouth that he ached to kiss.

He could barely breath because of his overwhelming emotions, but he could smell her fresh scent. She smelled of a delicate floral perfume. That fragrance always made his cock spring to attention, hardening and growing thick and powerful, just like it was doing now.

"That cowboy hat is really turning me on," she whispered and gave him an eyebrow wiggle.

"That is the idea," Brady replied.

He reached out with one hand, grabbed her by her waist and pulled her against him. He felt her tremble as both her breasts flattened against his chest and the baby bump pushed against his lower abdomen. He heard her moan as with his other hand he reached up and feathered his thumb against her lush lower lip until her lips parted.

He looked into her eyes, and he could see her excitement flaring like flames in those brown depths.

This is how it was for him when they were alone. Like time stopped. Like nothing in the world mattered. He also realized it was getting increasingly difficult for him to leave the ranch because of this magnetic pull she had over him. She just made him feel...safe and loved, for lack of better words.

He could hear her every inhalation and sensed her breaths were quickening because she knew his intent.

The mesmerizing moment broke as she suddenly reached up and knocked his hat back a bit with the flick of a finger to the brim.

"Kiss me hello, you fool," she demanded in a husky voice.

He didn't wait another moment. He lowered his head and claimed her lips.

Her mouth was lush and yielding, and he closed his eyes as he felt her warm hands curl over his shoulders and slip against the nape of his neck. She pulled his head closer.

Desire poured through him as she kissed him back, and he let her know just how much he wanted her by pressing his erection harder against her curvy body.

He could feel himself losing control in his need for her. Could feel himself wanting to bring her to a bedroom, lie her down on the bed, strip off their clothing and make mad, passionate love to her. Or simply bend her forward over the kitchen countertop, lift up her pretty sundress, pull down her panties, if she was wearing them, and take her from behind.

He groaned at those thoughts and moaned as she ground her body against his engorged cock, causing arousal to pour into his penis and make hunger roar inside him.

"Oh, come on, man. Get yourselves a room," Dan's sleepy voice felt like a bucket of ice-cold water being dumped on Brady's head.

Then suddenly Chrissy was sobbing for attention and Brady sensed she'd seen that he was back home, and she wanted him to pick her up to say hello.

Damn, alone time was already done.

Reluctantly, Brady broke the kiss and JJ whimpered her disappointment.

"We've got tonight, baby," he said softly as he looked into her bright eyes.

She nodded jerkily and licked her lips.

Yeah, they had tonight. They wouldn't be alone, though. Dan and Rafe would be joining them.

It was an arrangement they had. When one or two or all three of them were away overnight and then they were all back together again, they would share JJ their first night back. She had said she wanted it that way. To have all her men with her that first night they were together again before they began to go to her bed separately for their one-on-one nights together.

It could have been a complicated relationship, sharing the woman he loved. But Rafe and Dan loved her too and he felt good to know if something happened to him, the guys would take care of her and Chrissy and the new baby, whoever the daddy turned out to be.

"How was everyone while we were away?" he whispered.

"Fine," she whispered back.

"I took very good care of your two girls, Brady. My foot is also getting better very fast. I can get back to work now."

"Not until the doc gives the okay," Brady said as he let go of JJ, swooped up his cowboy hat from the floor, brushed off a bit of dirt, then plopped it onto her head.

The hat was a bit too big on her, but she kept it on and laughed as she focused her attention to the salad bowls.

He headed to the playpen where his girl was gazing up at him with complete adoration. Her blue eyes bright and sparkling.

Man, she was so damned cute! He bent over and swooped her into his arms. Holding her tight, but not too tight, and planting a bunch of kisses upon her warm pudgy cheeks until she was giggling.

As he bounced her up and down in his arms he focused his attention on Dan, who was now sitting up on the couch, watching Brady with an excited gaze. He'd bet a million bucks his friend and partner was aroused watching Brady and JJ kissing. Hell, he got aroused himself when he sometimes watched Rafe or Dan kiss her or make love to her.

He also knew Dan wanted Brady to say that they wouldn't wait for the doctor's final clearance so he could get back to working on all the chores that needed doing, but Brady wouldn't do it.

Dan was too important to put his life in that kind of danger. Just before Rafe and Brady had left to go and work in the northwest quarter of the ranch, the three of them had had a big argument in the barn, away from JJ's ears, on that subject.

Dan knew where they all stood and his comment about his foot getting better made Brady realize they would most likely have another argument on the matter when the time was right.

"I would think you might have enjoyed yourself way too much lounging around here," Brady said and winked at Dan so he would get his meaning.

"Dan was a perfect gentleman," JJ said from where she was pouring the dressing onto the salads. But he could hear the laughter in her voice.

Could see the satisfied smile whip across Dan's lips.

"I bet he was," Brady mumbled as he gazed into Chrissy's eyes. Eyes that reminded him of his mother's eyes. Always cheerful and so blue that he'd always liked looking into his mom's eyes, just like he enjoyed looking into Chrissy's eyes.

"Hey, I am starving! Where's the food!" Rafe suddenly whipped around the corner.

He wore a bathrobe and was towel drying his hair. But within a second, he'd bunched up the towel and shot it at Dan's head. But Dan easily caught it.

"Ha! Missed!" Dan laughed.

Rafe ignored him as he moved in to kiss Chrissy on her cheek.

"Hey, squirt," he said with a chuckle.

She giggled and kicked her feet into Brady's belly with such force, he swore she was going to be one strong little girl.

"Better cover Chrissy's eyes. I'm about to kiss her mamma," Rafe warned.

Brady strolled to the living room window with Chrissy now squeezing his nose as he pointed to a squirrel that was scampering through the back yard.

Rafe then quickly moved in behind JJ. He settled his warm hands upon her hips, and she giggled as he nuzzled her neck, the five o'clock shadow rasping her tender flesh.

A moment later, he twirled her around to face him and then his hot mouth melted over hers in an intoxicating kiss that literally made her toes curl and her pussy cream with excitement.

Oh my gosh, first she'd almost lost her self-control with Brady and now Rafe was testing her willpower of not having sex with all three of them right now.

"Oh, come on, get a room already," Dan and Brady said in unison from the living room.

JJ whimpered her disappointment as Rafe broke the kiss leaving her feeling way too hot and bothered.

Suddenly she knew exactly how their ménage night was going to begin.

But until then, it was time to eat.

Dan studied JJ as she brought the large dish of steaming sliced up roast beef to the table where they all sat. Her cheeks were flushed pink, and her eyes twinkled with cheerfulness. It was clear that she was happy everyone was back under one roof. He was glad too.

Beside Brady, seated in her highchair, Chrissy smiled happily as her gaze flew from Rafe to Dan and to her father. The kid was glad all her dads were home too. All was good in her book.

He smiled to himself thinking about how Brady had reacted earlier when he'd told him his foot was getting better and he was ready to get back to work.

The man had tensed right up, and anger had flared in his eyes. Dan had hoped Brady had changed his mind about letting him get back to work. It's why he'd hit Brady with the comment when he'd been tired after a full day of work, hoping Brady would melt. But he hadn't buckled. Not one inch.

Truth be told, he felt pretty guilty in not helping them out with the cattle and the ranch. He knew JJ appreciated him being around and helping her with the household chores and babysitting Chrissy, but he was an outdoor guy not a house husband type.

And he really should be getting off his ass and help her bring the rest of the food to the table, but he was just enjoying watching the family way too much at the moment.

Besides, she had everything under control. She was like that. Organized and a damned good cook.

Everything smelled so good, and his mouth was just watering. The spices from the steaming roast beef wafted under his nose almost making him moan out loud at the delicious scents. He could even smell the sweet potatoes drenched in butter, the maple glazed carrots, and the honey Dijon brussel sprouts.

He ignored Rafe and Brady's talk about what they'd done over the last two days as they began helping themselves to the food and he concentrated on studying JJ's swelling belly.

Man, there was just something so sexy about her being pregnant. When the guys had been gone, he'd enjoyed running his hands over her swollen baby bump. Her skin had been velvety soft and firm, full of life beneath his fingers. He'd relished her pleasure moans as he'd made love to her in the garden when she'd come to him wanting sex yesterday morning.

So, he'd led her over to the nearby laundry line post and made love to her right there, pushing her up against the post, removing her clothing out in the open for all the birds, chipmunks, and squirrels to watch. Then he'd taken her, hard and fast, her gasps and moans filling the warm summer air.

Last night, when he'd made love to her, he'd gone slow and gentle, just because he'd wanted to take his time and pleasure her properly. He'd been greeted with those sultry moans of arousal again and he'd savoured the sexy sounds she made.

"So, what do you think, Dan?" Rafe's gruff voice broke into his thoughts about JJ.

"Huh?" he answered, not hearing anything of what they'd been talking about.

"He wasn't listening. Was keeping his attention on JJ," Brady broke in.

He was smiling at Dan, obviously enjoying that he'd been caught watching her.

"Well, shit, I don't blame him. She *is* the most beautiful woman in the world," Rafe replied.

Dan felt his face warm as JJ fixed her gaze upon him.

"There will be plenty of play time later. Now focus on the ranch talk and eat your supper," she admonished him with a wink.

He was glad the guys didn't make more fun of him as they began ranch talk again. He tried to focus on it, truly he did, but his mind just wasn't on work at the moment.

His mind and his throbbing cock were on JJ and their upcoming ménage tonight.

He could hardly wait!

RAFE GAZED DOWN AND checked one more time to make sure that Chrissy was fast asleep. Her eyes were closed, her breathing calm and her cherub shaped lips had stopped moving on the pacifier.

Being satisfied that she was fully in slumber land, he stood up from the rocking chair beside the open window, where he'd been gently rocking her and softly singing to her and quietly carried her over to her crib.

Every so gently, he lowered her warm little body and placed her on her back upon the mattress. Then he repositioned the soother in her mouth, quietly lifted the sheet over her tiny body, leaving it just below her chin.

Man, she was such a cute little thing. His heart always burst with love when he looked at her or thought about her.

"Good night, sweet baby angel," he said quietly.

He turned off the nursery light but kept the ceiling fan going on low to help alleviate the warmth in the room and then slipped into the hallway.

Brady had wanted to put his daughter to bed tonight, but Rafe had been selfish and urged him to grab a shower so they could get started sooner on their evening with JJ.

Truth be told, he'd wanted to spend a bit of time with the little girl himself, especially since her dad had been hogging her all evening; playing peekaboo with her, taking her down to watch the sunset off the dock by the lake and then coming back up and playing with her some more.

The little girl's giggling had made Rafe wish for a little girl of his own with JJ. Sometimes he wondered if he would have said yes had she come to him to ask him to father her first child, instead of going to Brady. At the time, he'd thought he wasn't dad material and that he wasn't ready, but now he realized he was ready to be a dad. He treasured his time with Chrissy, just as he had enjoyed it tonight.

He had cleaned and then changed her little squirming bum into clean diapers and gotten her into her summer nightie. Then he'd held her little body snuggly against his chest while she'd gazed up at him with her adoring sleepy blue eyes as he'd rocked her in the rocking chair by the open window, singing softly to her until she'd drifted off to sleep.

Now with baby girl down for possibly eight or more hours, it was time for the adults to play.

He crossed the hall and peeked into JJ's room. It was a nice room. They'd decorated it with handmade pine furniture and red and brown décor. It had its own fireplace for when the power went out. And its own bathroom with a shower.

He'd fully expected to hear her in the shower, and had planned on joining her there, but he frowned when he spied her bathroom door open and no sign of JJ. He walked back into the hallway just in time to see Brady stroll out of the room where they usually had their foursomes.

His hair was damp, and he wore just his pyjama bottoms and quite the erection tenting those pants.

Rafe grinned. JJ was in for a good time tonight.

"Do you know where JJ is?" Brady asked.

"No, figured she was in her room. But she isn't there," Rafe answered.

Brady frowned.

"Thought she might be waiting for us in the bedroom we all share, but nope. She's not in there."

"Maybe, she's with Dan?" Rafe suggested.

Brady chuckled.

"Maybe she joined him in his shower. Let's go crash the party," Rafe suggested.

Brady eagerly nodded and they moved in unison toward Dan's room, but then Dan suddenly stepped out into the hallway from his bedroom.

Obviously, he'd taken a shower as he was wearing just his pyjama bottoms and was towel drying his hair. Rafe couldn't miss the fact that Dan's arousal was pushing boldly against his cotton threads.

"JJ in there?" Rafe asked, his hopes soaring.

Dan gave him a funny look.

"Would I be out here with you two, if she was in there?" he answered.

"He's got a point," Brady chuckled.

Great, three aroused men and no JJ.

"When was the last time anyone saw her?" Rafe asked.

"She said she was going to put away some of the laundry just before I came up to shower," Brady answered.

"Okay, then let's go help her," Rafe suggested.

His excitement grew as the three of them raced down to the main floor. When they reached the laundry room, the piles of folded laundry were still there on a table.

But no JJ.

Huh, where had she gone?

The water danced against JJ's pussy as she moved further away from the baby monitor that she'd placed on the shoreline when she'd come down from the ranch house. Now that Chrissy was fast asleep, JJ had turned up the volume to full blast so she could hear if her baby woke up.

Earlier, she'd planned on putting the laundry away but then she'd realized it could wait, she couldn't. At least not for too much longer.

She was dying to have all three of her cowboys come down to the lake and make love to her. She felt so feverish, like she was on fire. Of course, the heat of the day hadn't helped either. But the heat was doing nothing to diminish her cravings for sex.

It had been wonderful distraction eavesdropping on Rafe while he sang to her daughter as she'd listened on the baby monitor while she'd washed herself and then shampooed her hair.

He had such a soft voice; she hadn't realized he could actually sing.

It was funny too because until he'd begun to sing to Chrissy, JJ had listened with amusement as Rafe had talked to her, trying to bargain with the seven-month-old by promising her a bunch of mama's scrumptious chocolate chip cookies for tomorrow's breakfast if she'd just hold still while he gave her a bath. Which Chrissy didn't do because JJ had heard tons more splashing and giggling.

That was followed by more bargaining from Rafe. Promises of bringing her a heaping plate of pancakes drenched with her pappa's delicious homemade maple syrup for breakfast while Rafe had struggled to get diapers onto her tush. But her daughter had just kept on laughing, and JJ suspected wiggling too.

Then when he'd started singing softly to her, Chrissy's giggling had stopped, and JJ hadn't heard another sound. She'd probably been mesmerized by Rafe's singing voice, just as JJ had been.

And then all had gotten quiet and after awhile she'd heard Rafe whisper goodnight. That meant Chrissy was asleep.

But that had been a little while ago.

So, where were her cowboys?

Before heading out, she'd left a note on the kitchen countertop, grabbed the baby monitor from the living room, swiped some soap, a washcloth, shampoo, and a towel from the downstairs bathroom and came down to the lake where the air seemed a bit fresher, although still humid.

The full moon was high in the east, casting a beautiful silvery hue over the calm water. To her left, she spied the silhouette of their long, wood dock that stretched far out into the lake, as well as her bush plane, which was moored on the other side and near the end of the dock. All were bathed in the glitter of moonglow.

Overhead, heat lightning flashed white from stray cloud to stray cloud, which slowly stalked toward the moon. But there was no thunder, so she figured she was safe.

The water was mild, and it felt quite delicious smoothing against her hot flesh.

She was so lucky to have courteous men who helped her with the ranch house chores and with Chrissy. Their assistance kept her from getting overtired, which in turn, put her into a really good mood for sex.

And since the men weren't in a hurry to pleasure her then she may as well get started without them.

She lifted her hands over her breasts and began rubbing her nipples with her palms.

She inhaled sharply at the raw sensations zipping into her breasts.

Goodness, her nipples were ultra sensitive and felt so engorged. She moaned as she began to tug and pinch them, closing her eyes, enjoying the arousal shimmering inside of her.

"Hey, baby, don't get started without us," Rafe's thick voice spoke from immediately behind her.

"Yeah, sweetheart, we can take care of you," Dan murmured.

JJ smiled.

Finally!

She turned to find Dan and Rafe.

Both men stood no more than three feet from her. Water lapped at their knees. Both men were naked, their cocks at full mast.

JJ smiled. They wore their cowboy hats. Their muscular chests, and hard-looking stomachs were tanned but as her gaze dropped, their flesh gave way to lighter skin, which was usually hidden by their pants.

But their intimate parts weren't hidden beneath pants now. Now, she spied washboard abdomens, the thick thatch of dark hair, which adorned their groin area and their heavy, swollen scrotums, which held their seed and would, she hoped, produce more babies for her in the future.

She trembled as excitement rolled through her at the thoughts of having more babies with the three men she loved. She wanted a big family. A happy, joyful brood of children.

But that idea vanished as she became mesmerized while the two men held their cocks with one hand, and with the other they massaged their thick erections with slow, sensual strokes.

Her pussy and ass clenched with anticipation at having their cocks thrusting into her, bringing her the much-needed pleasure she craved.

"Do you like what you see?" Rafe whispered.

"Are you ready for us?" Dan asked.

"More than ready," she breathed, feeling sexual tension snap through her like live wires.

She watched as they continued to caress their cocks. Their erections grew thicker and elongated and looked deliciously hard.

The sight of their aroused shafts heated her blood and made the breath back up in her lungs.

Mercy, she'd been aroused already, but watching them touching themselves was causing all her nerve endings to fire up.

Where's Brady?" she whispered, suddenly barely able to speak.

Anxiously, she peered behind them and saw no sign of him.

Disappointment rolled through her as her need mounted. She wanted all three of her men here with her. Wanted all three of them touching her, kissing her, loving her.

"Right here, doll," Brady's voice erupted from right behind her.

JJ spun around to find Brady standing no more than two feet away from her.

Droplets of water cascaded over his naked chest. He wore his black cowboy hat and his eyes sparkled with want in the moonlight.

It appeared he had quietly swum over here, in order to sneak up on her.

"Now that all your cowboys are here, let's pick up where you left off, shall we?" Brady said with a sexy grin.

"Turn around. Let them pleasure you," he instructed.

JJ trembled as she turned back around to find Rafe and Dan had moved closer and were now just inches away from her. Their scents crashed into her. Rafe was wearing her favorite cologne and Dan smelled of lavender from the soap he'd used.

Both men suddenly grabbed their cowboy hats off their heads and flung them like Frisbees toward the shore.

"Come on, sweetheart, don't be shy. Let's give us a nice view of your pretty breasts," Rafe urged as they returned their attention to her.

She realized she was still covering herself with her palms and immediately dropped her hands.

Their hot gazes focused upon her chest and both men nodded their appreciation. She didn't miss that their tongues were peeking out from between slightly parted lips.

"Your breasts are bigger than the last time I saw them," Rafe said.

JJ wished she could laugh at Rafe's comment. He'd seen her naked just before he and Brady had left a couple of days ago. But she couldn't laugh. She was way too tense awaiting their next move.

"Much bigger and much juicier," Dan commented.

Well, he would know. He'd loved sucking on her nipples when they'd been alone and the other two had been away.

Instinctively she threw her shoulders back, making her breasts jut out some more. This would get her cowboys moving. Their hot stares were torturing her.

"Oh yeah, baby, that's what we want to see and what we want to taste," Rafe murmured.

The two men didn't waste any time as they reached out and cupped her breasts with their hot hands. Their palms scorched her flesh as they held her mounds like they were a treasure.

"Let the suckling begin," Brady whispered from behind her.

Dan and Rafe lowered their heads, and she moaned as each man took a sensitive nipple into their hot, beautiful mouths shooting fire through her entire body.

Brady's body heat flowed against her back in shimmering waves as he moved in closer. His hands settled like hot brands on her waist.

Slowly, with the two men latched to her nipples, she leaned back against him, knowing instinctively what he wanted to do to her.

"I missed you like crazy, baby," Brady cooed into her right ear.

She didn't answer. Couldn't, actually.

The feel of hot mouths tugging and sucking on her nipples was making her breathe too fast. She couldn't even answer him to tell him she'd missed him like crazy too. Heck, she didn't even want to answer.

She just wanted to *feel*.

She spread her legs and his calloused hands slid down over her hips.

One hand stayed on her hip, the other slid beneath her pregnant belly and slipped between her open thighs.

She shuddered as his finger and thumb found her dangling labia. He pulled softly on her folds, and at the same time he kissed the sensitive area between her neck and her shoulder. She turned her head toward him and his hot, lush lips melted over her mouth.

Wonderful sensations shimmied through her, and JJ kissed him back, loving the rough-skinned finger that found and then gently rubbed her ultra sensitive clitoris. Pleasure shot into her as he massaged the sensitive bundle of nerves.

She shuddered at the feverish imprint of his thick, long penis as it pushed against the top of her buttocks.

His hot kiss and the pressure of his big shaft was an exquisite promise of more pleasure to come.

This is what Brady waited for every time he was away from JJ. To come back to her and slide his hands over her soft, supple flesh. To feel her tremble beneath his touches and to listen to her sultry moans as two men suckled at her breasts.

He'd never felt this way about another woman. This insistent need to be around her. To share her. To be inside of her.

Even his cock had a mind of its own pressing intimately against her backside. Yeah, every time any body part of his touched hers, it was a challenge to his self-control. Just like it had been when he'd come home earlier today and found her in the kitchen.

Just like it was a test now.

Her sweet, moist lips surrendered beneath his demanding mouth, and having her submit, always gave him a pleasurable high because he knew she enjoyed his strength. Knew she adored the pleasure he gave.

He kissed her harder, loving the bold way she kissed him back. Treasured the sultry way she parted her lips and allowed his tongue to thrust into her mouth. Her mouth scalded his senses. Her lips were perfectly shaped and the instant his tongue touched hers, sparks ignited throughout his body, and arousal rumbled through him like rolling thunder.

Her hand came up and cradled the back of his head pushing him harder against her mouth. He enjoyed the satiny feel of her fingers against the nape of his neck. Relished the erotic press of her body against his throbbing cock.

The desire for her roared deep within him like an untamed beast, and he almost lost it. Almost slipped his shaft deep into her ass because he wanted to feel her snug tightness envelope him. But he knew he needed to hang on to his tenuous self-control because her pleasure came first. It was their rule, albeit sometimes he was selfish, and he couldn't hold back.

But not tonight. Tonight, she was his top priority.

Chapter Two

As Rafe suckled on JJ's engorged nipple, his hand gently squeezed her breast, and he struggled to reign in his need to take her.

Man, he had just about lost it when JJ had bared her luscious full breasts to them. He swore every time he saw them, they were plumper. But that's because she was pregnant. It was so amazing to watch her body change as the baby grew inside of her.

He'd always felt an attraction to pregnant women. Had always been fascinated at how a woman's body changed as her pregnancy developed, but with JJ it was so much more. It was different with her. So extremely intense.

Maybe because she could be carrying *his* child?

Hell, he'd felt such an incredible attraction to her while she'd been pregnant with Chrissy, and he had *known* the baby was Brady's that time. Yet somehow this time, it seemed different.

Just looking at her had all his senses on full alert. He wanted to protect her from harm. Wanted to pleasure her in every way a man could please a woman.

He wanted to be inside of her and bring her the desires she craved.

He could feel her trembling as Brady worked his magic between her thighs and Dan and himself nibbled on her enflamed nipples. The nipple he sucked on was so hot and hard. It felt like smooth, silky glass, unyielding.

Sometimes he bit ever so gently into her hot flesh, and she moaned sexily in response.

Yes, he enjoyed listening to her pleasure.

He enjoyed it a lot.

EXCITEMENT POUNDED like a drug through JJ's bloodstream. Her nipples were hardening in the men's mouths, becoming extremely sensitive. They sucked with firm pressure, sometimes nipping, gently whipping pleasure pain through her.

They tortured her and she loved it.

Between her legs, her pussy felt so hot and swollen as Brady massaged her clit. Then he would let go and pull on her labia, stretching and rubbing. Then he'd release her labia and stalk his fingers toward the entrance of her vagina making her tense with anticipation.

But then his fingers would return to tease her clit again; kneading and stroking ever so gently until she tried to undulate against the hands that held her.

They must have known she was on the edge of losing control. They must have known exquisite sensations were tearing through her.

How could they not?

She was moaning into Brady's mouth while he was literally devouring her lips, his wicked tongue lashing hers like a whip.

The pleasure the three men created was rising within her like a volcano about to erupt. Fire lanced her pussy, making it drop and feel deliciously heavy. Pleasure pain rushed through her breasts in wicked waves, destroying any semblance of thoughts.

Her mind was fragmenting and the only thing she could do was feel the hunger raging, the need for penetration that consumed her.

Everything inside of her was going molten hot. She was quickly becoming too sensitive, impatient to be taken. She was like that when she was pregnant. Like fireworks ready to go off at the slightest source of heat.

She ripped her mouth away from Brady and gasped for air.

Instinctively, she began to writhe harder between the men, needing to orgasm.

"Easy, baby, we've got you," Brady murmured.

"I need...now," she begged. Her voice sounded throaty and demanding, not at all sounding like her own.

"You heard her, gentlemen. Let's get her close to the dock so all three of us can take her," Brady growled.

All three. She trembled at his words.

Suddenly, the luscious lips tormenting her nipples were gone.

She managed to open her eyes, but barely because she could hardly see due to the sexual haze or maybe it was because of the swirling white mist that now surrounded them. As the men led her into shallow waters, the silhouette of her float plane glared ominously at her and for the briefest of moments, a tinge of anxiety snapped through her as she stared at it.

Signals of danger swept through her, and she swore she was going to fly into a panic attack and then just as quickly the warning of impending doom vanished as the men brought her right up beside the dock.

Water splashed noisily as Dan hoisted himself onto the dock. He sat down right at the edge and spread his legs wide making her inhale at the serpent like cock aimed at her. He stroked his immense jerking length as he watched her, his eyes dark with desire, his lips parted as he panted.

From where he'd positioned himself it would be easy to take him into her mouth when the time came.

Reluctantly she tore her gaze from Dan as Rafe had her stand sideways in the water close to Dan.

Behind her, she heard slurps of lube shoot through the quiet night air. Her breath halted. She knew that Brady was preparing himself with waterproof lubricant.

Then without warning, Rafe's hot hands heated over her waist and his scorching mouth melted over hers in a kiss so sharp that it destroyed her senses. His tongue dove into her mouth like a heat seeking missile, his muscular body pressed against hers, and best of all, his rock-hard shaft slid into her quivering vagina.

She moaned her appreciation, reached out and clasped her hands upon Rafe's hips, holding herself steady.

A moment later, Brady's hands slid over her hips, and he held her tight as he pressed his lubed cockhead slowly inside.

She moaned as both men penetrated her, and she heard Brady groan as her anal muscles stretched, quivered, and clenched around him in welcome.

Rafe growled into her mouth as he powered into her, creating sharp bursts of pleasure inside her vagina, which in turn made her pussy spasm and tighten around his shaft.

Intuitively she bucked between the two men, her movements sending both cocks deeper into her channels.

"You're incredibly tight," Brady murmured near her left ear as he nuzzled his stubbled chin against the apex of her neck and shoulders.

She would have laughed out loud at his comment, stating what else did he expect with her having two delicious cocks throbbing inside of her?

But she could not speak with Rafe's delicious mouth making love to hers.

Rafe's hands tightened on her waist, and JJ's thoughts swirled as both men withdrew.

Then Rafe slipped his shaft into her vagina again, kissing her even harder.

Flames of heat whipped pleasurable sensations around her as he plunged deeper, his swollen length igniting her nerve endings with pleasure.

Rafe quickly withdrew.

Then Brady entered her. She keened as his big, swollen cockhead parted per sphincter, and his hard, velvet encased shaft stretched her sensitive muscles to the point were they hugged him tight and pulled him in deeper.

"That's it, baby," Brady moaned.

Then he withdrew.

JJ cried into Rafe's mouth as both men entered her at the same time, filling her wonderfully.

Oh wow, she was so close to coming but she needed one more thing before she could reach her release.

Dan.

She needed to have Dan inside of her to make this pleasure complete.

She ripped her swollen mouth from Rafe and turned her head sideways.

Dan had been anticipating what she needed because his cock was right there, an inch from her face. She opened her mouth, and he slid his cockhead between her lips. He guided his shaft in slowly and she nodded when he touched her tonsils. He withdrew about an inch, and she watched his other hand drop down and wrap around his shaft right by her lips. She knew what he was doing. He was placing his hand there to prevent his cock from going down her throat when he lost control.

Suddenly everything was now perfect. All her men were inside of her. Claiming her. Loving her.

Gosh, she felt so heady.

She began to bob her head, sucking Dan's cock and relishing the guttural male groans as all three of her cowboys began pistoning into her. She tightened her lips around Dan's shaft giving him a really nice tight seal. As Dan thrust, she caressed his hard flesh with her tongue until he was moaning.

As he drove between her lips, his velvet-encased steel-like shaft bruised her mouth in a beautiful way. She enjoyed the burning of his flesh against her lips. Loved the feel of three cocks plunging into her and taking pleasure from her.

As the three men pistoned, her breaths came faster, and her openings clenched around their fierce penetrations. Then without warning the fire of an oncoming climax crashed into her with such an intense speed that before she knew what was happening, she was exploding into a writhing sensual uncontrollable mess.

She shuddered within the waves of spasms as the men made love to her. Moaned around Dan's cock as she gyrated and bucked between Brady and Rafe's hard, muscular bodies.

Pure pleasure seared her. The erotic fervour burned so deep she shattered, losing all control of her body and her senses.

Bliss pummelled her and for a while she had no idea who she was. She was just a ball of agony and a tangle of pleasure melding into something spectacular.

They thrust harder and faster, making her fly higher and writhe harder as they quickly pushed her into a second wicked climax.

She trembled and keened and loved the burn of their hot swollen cocks filling her with the exactness she'd been craving all day. As she took their pleasure, and listened to their moans, she vaguely heard the dull roll of thunder from somewhere and she knew there was a storm brewing outside as well as inside of her. Knew they should stop and go indoors.

But this ecstasy was just too good to stop, so she allowed herself to become wrapped up by a third rocking orgasm. It zipped at her with lightning speed, cradling her body with searing convulsions and snapping through her mind like a terrific whirlwind, making her sense every sizzling spasm and every clenching muscle that powered pleasure into her.

Oh wow, this was just so wicked and intense. She wished she could ride it all night long and she did for awhile, loving everything, the spasms, convulsions, and the pleasure. Slowly her body released all that luscious tension that had been building inside of her all day and she knew she'd sleep really good tonight.

DAN GRINNED AS LIGHTNING flashed at the bedroom windows illuminating JJ who slept soundly. She was cuddled between Rafe and Brady's naked bodies. Both men snored softly, smiles on their faces. And JJ smiled too in her sleep. Probably dreaming about last night.

He grinned too as outside the open window, thunder roared with a crackling that would raise the dead. Not one of them stirred from the noise.

The storm had come upon them suddenly last night while they'd made love to JJ in the lake.

Heck, they might have made it an all-nighter for her in the water, she was coming so quickly and so many times. The thunder had finally chased them indoors, but not before grabbing the baby monitor from the shoreline, their clothing and retreating into the ranch house. A quick check on Chrissy had reassured them she was fast asleep.

After the three of them had made love to JJ once again in the king-sized bed they'd all fallen asleep. But Dan had awoken an hour ago when he'd heard the rumblings of another storm brewing and he'd lain quietly while listening to the rain pummel the metal roof and watched the flashes of white lightning blink at the windows while the thunder roared.

Now it was six a.m. and dawn had arrived awhile ago. But he debated whether he should wake everyone or just let them sleep in.

His thoughts turned to how JJ's dark eyes had glimmered hungrily last night while he'd been on the dock, and she'd looked up at him expectantly while she was sandwiched between Rafe and Brady. That she had two men penetrating her and she'd wanted him too, made him feel electric with excitement. He couldn't stop thinking that he'd never met a woman like her.

She loved all three of them equally and it was amazing that he felt no jealousy or threat to his manhood as he watched the two men make love to her. He knew their relationship was unique. Realized not too many women might want three men in her bed.

He considered himself to be one lucky son of a bitch and he was suddenly wishing really hard that the baby JJ was carrying belonged to him.

Speaking of babies, he'd best go and check on Chrissy. Maybe she was awake with all this stormy commotion, and he could start her day by changing, dressing, and feeding her.

Funny, because just yesterday, he hadn't been able to wait to get back to working out on the ranch and yet today he felt nicely domesticated. Maybe it had something to do with the rain and not wanting to go outside to work and get wet?

He chuckled to himself at that thought. Nah, he wasn't that shallow.

An inner happiness bubbled inside of him as he quietly slipped out of the bed from where he'd been lying beside Brady. He rummaged through the clothing they'd brought up from the lake until he found his pants. He slipped into them and headed out of the bedroom and down the hall toward the nursery.

He'd really bonded with the little girl. She was such a sweetheart and he found himself wanting to do things for her more and more.

Like preparing different types of foods for her to try, taking her down to the lake to swim, and making funny faces to make her laugh.

Quickly he checked in on her and disappointment shot through him when he found her still sleeping, despite the roar of thunder overhead. She was lying on her side with her thumb stuck in her slightly open mouth and her breathing was slow and relaxed. He had the feeling she was going to be sleeping for awhile longer.

Man, she was so cute, he just wanted to lift her up into his arms and cuddle her.

Oh well, he'd grab a quick shower, change into clean clothes, and then go downstairs and get the coffee started.

JJ AWOKE TO FIND THE bed empty and rain drumming upon the roof. She smiled as she remembered last night in the lake and then afterwards when they'd rushed back to the ranch house due to the oncoming thunderstorm.

She'd been so high on her orgasms that she'd let the men tie her down on the bed, her legs spreadeagled, her wrists and ankles secured while each of her cowboys made love to her again.

Whew, she felt so hot and flushed just thinking about all the sex she'd experienced last night and then throughout the night in her dreams. She had to be some kind of crazy nymphomaniac or something. Or all those years locked up in prison had buried her sexual arousal to a point where it had come out in abundance when she'd arrived here.

The scent of coffee teased her nostrils, and she could hear the men laughing downstairs. Such a cheerful group, her cowboys were. She wondered if Chrissy was up or if they had let her sleep. JJ had noticed Chrissy liked to sleep in on cloudy rainy days. She'd been like that herself when she'd been younger.

Before her mom had married her evil stepfather, her mom would let her sleep in on stormy mornings like this, if it was during the summer holidays or weekends.

But that had changed when her mom had married her cop stepdad. When he got up at six to go to work, her mom would have to get up and make him breakfast and he'd come into JJ's little room and yell at her to get her lazy ass out of bed or he'd beat the crap out of her. So, she learned fast to obey him.

JJ shivered with revulsion as she remembered her stepfather, the man she'd murdered.

The creepy way his eyes narrowed when he got angry had always made her tummy hollow out in a bad way, which alerted her to impending danger. When he got mad at her or at her mom if they didn't do something fast enough for him or the way he wanted, which had been often, he would fly into a rage. The man had been some kind of sadist or power-hungry nut.

He hadn't been horrible at first though.

When her mom had been going out with him, he'd appeared kind and loving toward her, professing she was the perfect woman. The only woman in the world for him. Mom had said he was her knight in shining armor and that he was just too good to be true.

He'd been nice toward JJ too, bringing her toys and candy.

But once her stepfather had gotten that wedding band on her mom's finger, things had slowly deteriorated to the point where JJ was getting screamed at or locked in closets by her stepfather while he'd yell and beat on her mother.

As she got older, he'd beat on JJ too.

When she was a teenager, her stepbrother would sometimes drop by for a visit. He would show an eerie interest in her to the point where her instincts warned her to stay away from him as much as possible. She'd find some excuse, usually a made-up homework assignment to spend time at the library or stay at a friend's place.

Her mom had sensed something off about her stepbrother too because she wouldn't leave JJ alone with him. She'd also secretly instructed JJ to place a glass on the inside doorknob of her room or lean a broom against her bedroom door so there would be noise if someone snuck into her room at night. Because of that JJ had learned to be an early riser so when her stepfather came in to wake her up in the morning and call her lazy, he wouldn't realize she had a warning system in place.

Man, all that trauma she'd gone through when she'd been young. No wonder she had anxiety, panic, and claustrophobia issues.

Thankfully, most of that horror was behind her, but her anxiety did rear its ugly head despite her being liberated from that hopeless life, free from prison, and now enjoying scrumptious menages with her three delightful cowboys.

She shifted away the unease the memories her stepfather and stepbrother brought to her, climbed out of bed, and grabbed a robe from the closet. After donning her robe, she strolled toward one of the bedroom windows to peer outside.

Thunder rumbled far off, and lightning blinked in the rolling grey clouds. Rain fell in silvery sheets from the sky and drenched the nearby pine trees. From here she could see the lake.

It looked dismal and gray, but she smiled when she spied her white float plane safely moored at the dock. For a split second she remembered having that doom and gloom feeling last night when she'd looked at her plane through the mist.

It must have been some kind of fluke of her pregnancy hormones that the aircraft had given her a sense of foreboding because she absolutely loved her plane. She treasured the sense of freedom when she soared above the dark green forests and enjoyed peering down at the brilliant patches of sparkling blue lakes and meandering rivers and the luscious meadows as she flew toward the city to pick up supplies for the ranch.

Not far beyond the plane she caught sight of two black loons bobbing on the moving waves as they hunted for fish. Even in the rain they had to work for their breakfast.

JJ smiled as warmth enveloped her. Despite the wet weather, she had a daughter and three sexy men to take care of. And there was plenty of work for her to do too in order to keep the ranch house running smoothly, so she'd best get to it!

ONE WEEK LATER...

"Plane coming in!" Dan called from the ranch yard where he was weeding in the vegetable garden about twenty feet from the open living room window.

"I hear it!" JJ called back.

Earlier she'd removed some bacon chocolate chip cookies from the oven and stuffed some broken pieces of pretzels into the hot dough. The cookies were cool now and she'd just been setting a platter of them on the windowsill to tease Dan with the scintillating scents when she'd heard the plane.

Lately she'd been craving salty and sweet, so for tonight's dessert she'd combined the two into baking bacon chocolate chip cookies, a recipe she'd found on the Internet. She hoped Dan liked them because she'd certainly enjoyed taste testing the ingredients.

As the drone of the plane drew closer, JJ quickly gazed over at Chrissy who had just fallen asleep in her playpen. Her daughter was sucking her thumb, a habit she'd gotten into.

Making sure Chrissy was breathing, she then did a scan of the playpen to ensure there were no dangerous items in there, not that there would be any, but she was just hypervigilant like that these days.

She let Dan know she was going to greet the plane and hurried down the hallway and into the hot mudroom. Looking out the array of mudroom windows, she spied sunshine glinting off a bright blue float plane splashing down in the glass-like lake.

Blue plane meaning Blue, a pilot friend of hers, from North Country Air. She was probably coming with their mail. It was that time of the month.

It was early afternoon and yet another scorching July day.

As she opened the door, a furnace blast of hot air greeted her. The air smelled of baking pine needles from the nearby forest and the humidity almost took her breath away as she ambled down the steps. The heat from the sweltering sun that hung high in the sky shot shimmering waves along the trail and beat upon her body as she walked toward the grey planked dock where Blue was now angling her float plane.

As she strolled toward the lake, she wondered how Dan could stand the hotness while weeding. She also thought about Brady and Rafe who were working outdoors in this hot temperature. They'd left a couple of days ago and they would be away for another few days driving the cattle to different meadows in order to prevent overgrazing.

She missed her men when they were away.

Lately, the guys had been talking about hiring some help to be in charge of the north area of the ranch. Maybe putting a man or two in that cute little cabin they'd built up that way. Then the guys wouldn't have to do so many overnighters anymore and she'd have them in her bed more often.

She inhaled as she remembered the guys making love to her in the king-sized bed in the room they used for their threesomes and foursomes. That last ménage they'd had down at the lake last week had certainly relieved the intense cravings for sex she'd had building inside of her, and Dan was doing a wonderful job keeping her satisfied while the other two men were away. But yeah, the cravings for another ménage were brewing deep inside of her again. She wanted all three of them back in her bed and soon.

By the time she reached the dock, she was sweating. Perspiring from the memories of her cowboys taking her individually on the king-sized bed after their tryst in the lake and of course sweating from the heat.

Blue had already secured her plane and was walking toward JJ with a bulk of mail in a dark green pouch.

Even in this heat, Blue looked fresh, slender, and relaxed. There wasn't a blonde hair out of place and her pretty blue eyes glittered with cheerfulness. It was as if she had not the slightest care in the world, which for some odd reason irritated JJ and she wished she knew why. Probably her silly hormones acting up.

"Got time for a coffee?" JJ called out, pushing away the unwanted emotion.

Blue grinned and nodded with excitement. Within a minute she joined JJ.

Blue smelled nice. Like flowers. It was a pretty scent and she'd have to ask the name of the perfume, but then again maybe not. She didn't want the men to smell JJ and think of Blue.

Good heavens, she couldn't believe there was a smidgen of jealousy rolling through her at this moment of her cowboys maybe looking at another woman. Again, it had to be her pregnancy hormones playing with her!

"That would be awesome. Thank you. I'll carry up the mail for you. Don't want you straining yourself with the little one you're carrying."

JJ laughed as she hooked her arm with Blue's elbow, and they strolled up the trail toward the ranch house.

On the way up they chatted about the hot weather and how they couldn't wait for the coolness of autumn. When they got inside, JJ asked Blue to leave the mail on the living room table while she put on a pot of coffee for them.

"Oh, she's so adorable. She's grown since the last time I saw her," Blue gushed in a low voice.

JJ warmed as she turned around and saw Blue peering into the play pen at a sleeping Chrissy.

"We need to schedule a play date so she and Ivy can play together," JJ suggested.

Ivy held a special place in JJ's heart because she had assisted Rafe in delivering the baby in Kelly's plane out on the ice after Kelly had brought Blue here while she'd been in labor.

"That would be lovely. I still haven't brought her up in my plane though. There just never seems to be enough time, with me being a single mom. Ivy doesn't get to hang out with little ones too much. My babysitter is an elderly lady in the same apartment, and she doesn't have any grandchildren, but she does take Ivy to the apartment's playground for an hour each day," Blue explained as she came around into the kitchen and stood beside JJ at the counter while the coffee made its way through the coffee maker.

"Chrissy is going to be so lucky because she'll have a baby brother or sister to play with. Do you know the sex of the baby?" Blue asked.

"No, not yet. We just may wait and see when he or she is born," JJ replied.

"I bet Brady is so excited having another baby," Blue said as she clasped her hands to her chest.

JJ hesitated for a moment struggling to find an answer.

"He is," JJ replied as unease whispered through her.

How in the world was she going to handle questions in the future if the baby turned out to be Rafe's or Dan's? This certainly was going to be a dilemma, wasn't it?

"I'm glad you invited me up. I would have posed my question down on the dock, but having coffee with you makes it just a bit more special, so I'll ask you when we sit down to coffee," Blue said.

She seemed cheerful and it made JJ wonder what her pilot friend was going to ask.

"I'm sorry we don't have it cooler in here for you. We don't have air conditioning. Just the overhead ceiling fans."

"No worries, my cockpit is airconditioned, so getting a little warm is good for me," Blue replied with a smile.

JJ gazed at the carafe which was already full and the scent of the coffee drifting through the air made her remember the cookies she'd made earlier.

"Well, the coffee is done, and you have perfect timing because I've got a fresh batch of yummies. Have a seat and I'll bring everything to you in a minute," JJ replied as she collected a couple of mugs from the cupboard.

She hoped Blue wasn't going to think she'd lost her mind when she saw the cookies she'd baked. She waited until her visitor was seated before grabbing the second plate filled with cookies she'd had cooling on top of the fridge.

A moment later they were both seated at the homemade dining room table and Blue was staring with an amused expression at the plate of sweets JJ had placed in front of her.

"I knew you must have been baking because it smells so nice in here. And I'm not sure what to say about these cookies. I've never seen pretzels stabbed into cookies before," Blue said as she picked up a cookie and examined it with a curious expression.

"Try it. I'm dying to know what you think," JJ admitted.

Blue grinned and took a tentative bite.

Instantly her expression changed to one of delight.

"Hey, these are actually good," she exclaimed and began to take more bites.

JJ sighed in relief. She'd worried that maybe her pregnancy cravings had seriously screwed up her taste buds and when Blue took a bite out of her second cookie and began leisurely sipping on her coffee, JJ relaxed.

Blue squinted her eyes, held up the cookie and closely examined the sweet.

"And is this bacon in here?" she asked, disbelief quite evident in her voice.

JJ nodded, feeling kind of embarrassed.

Blue beamed.

"Well, that's kind of cool. These really are awesome. I always love coming here because you've always got something delicious on the go. Speaking of delicious, where are all your sexy smexy cowboys today?"

JJ wanted to answer by saying damned right her cowboys were sexy, but she couldn't quite do it. The only ones she'd confided with about her lifestyle here at Moose Ranch had been to her midwife and to her good friend, Milena. She didn't want to tip Blue off that naughty stuff was going on beneath this roof.

"Brady and Rafe are mustering cattle and Dan's out back in the vegetable garden," JJ replied.

Blue shook her head and reached for a third cookie.

"I guess working on a ranch means no days off. I'll have to get used to that if I ever get a lamb ranch started. I've always loved sheep, and since helping your far away neighbour, Jane Sunflower, with her lamb ranch, I know that's what I want to do with the rest of my life. But starting one up, or even buying one, takes a lot of money."

"How about taking on partners, like Brady, Dan and Rafe did? There is strength in numbers," JJ said.

Blue frowned.

"Not sure if I can do that. I tend to keep to myself, and I like to be the one in charge. Which brings me to the something I'd like to ask you, JJ."

Blue's eyes twinkled with enthusiasm, and JJ suddenly gushed with pleasure.

That Blue was thinking about asking her something made her feel happy.

"Ask away," she said as she took a bite out of her cookie.

Sweetness and salt splashed against her tastebuds in a spectacular bouquet of flavors. Oh yes, these cookies would hit the spot for her cravings, and she'd probably pack on a bunch of pounds too if she weren't careful with them.

"I'd like to invite you to a wedding shower that I am throwing for Kelly. Would you come? It's two weeks this Saturday over in Thunder Bay. We can play games and stuff and I'm having it catered at a hall, so all you need to do is to just bring a present. I can email you the details of the time and where as well as a wedding registry to give you an idea for gifts. Do you think you can be free that weekend? Maybe we can make it a ladies weekend out? Do some shopping and eat out and stuff?"

"Of course she'll go. JJ would love to accept your invitation, right JJ?" Dan's voice boomed from nearby as he peered through the open living room window, the same one where she'd placed the other batch of cookies.

"She needs to get out more often and JJ you're killing me with these delicious aromas drifting out the window. If this screen weren't here, I'd be chowing down a bunch of your cookies," Dan said with a chuckle.

JJ smiled at Dan as she watched him staring back at them.

Gosh, he was shirtless, and her lower abdomen clenched with awareness as his tanned muscles bulged in his shoulders and chest as he lifted a water bottle and began to drink.

"Come on in and have some cookies and some coffee, Dan," Blue invited.

"Nah, it's okay. I'll let you ladies chat. I just had to see what was causing this nice smell. Dessert is going to be awesome tonight, JJ. Have a nice chat, ladies. Safe journey, Blue if I don't get a chance to say goodbye. Back to work for me," Dan called out and then he was gone.

Dessert is going to be awesome tonight.

JJ certainly knew he meant more than the cookies. Her face warmed as Blue was suddenly staring at her with a strange expression on her face.

Almost a knowing expression?

But there was no way she *could* know about her sleeping with all three of her cowboys, was there? She doubted Milena would say anything, especially since she was so shy about doing the same with her cowboy bosses. And her midwife had said anything JJ told her was strictly confidential.

Unless...

Something niggled at the back of her mind. Blue *had* slept over here at Moose Ranch; besides the night she'd spent after giving birth to her baby. It had happened last year when Dan had been missing and Blue had stayed over to help with the search.

Rafe and Brady had made love to JJ right here in the middle of the living room during a violent thunderstorm in the predawn hours while trying to distract her from her worry about Dan.

Gosh, she had forgotten about that. It had been her first summer here. It turned out that Dan had been attacked by her stepbrother who'd knocked him unconscious and stranded him by disabling his vehicle out in the wilderness, that's why he hadn't come home.

JJ blinked as a weird hollowed out feeling hit her in the gut.

Had Blue seen Brady and Rafe making love to her that time? She knew she was noisy when she orgasmed, and they'd hoped the storm would conceal any sounds. But what if it hadn't? What if Blue had come down and seen?

No way. But she did look at JJ as if she *knew* something. Or maybe it was JJ's paranoid imagination?

Blue's expression swiftly changed, and it left JJ wondering if she was mistaken.

"So? What do you say? Will you join us? I've already invited Kayley, Layla, and Milena. A few other ladies that you don't know are coming. They're women pilots from North Country Air. You could do some shop talk about planes. I would ask if you could give Milena a ride in and back since you two live so close? I've still got a couple more women to ask too. They're on my mail route and they know Kelly."

"What about Jane Sunflower? I could pick her up too. I have yet to meet her."

"Unfortunately, she's already declined. She doesn't like leaving her lambs. So, will you come?"

JJ smiled and nodded.

Her thoughts were already turning to what in the world could she get for Kelly and her fiancé, Jay.

It did appear she was going to a wedding shower!

BLUE WAVED FROM THE cockpit at JJ as she started the engine.

Gosh, JJ looked absolutely radiant in her pregnancy. She'd put on a bit of weight, and she was looking so happy as she waved back to Blue. It was a stark difference from the thin, shy woman, fresh out of prison when Blue had first met her.

Man, she was one lucky woman to be living out here on a prosperous ranch and having her pick of cowboys to bed, with no one around to judge them.

She had seen Rafe and Brady having sex with JJ that certain stormy night she'd stayed over. She'd observed the pleasure snapping across all three faces as lightning had blinked at the windows.

To watch two men making love to her like that, the men's hands holding her, their muscular naked bodies pistoning against JJ with her writhing between them making all kinds of naughty aroused noises had been like something out of an erotic fantasy.

The few times she'd seen all three cowboys and JJ together, like at the Christmas party and earlier this year at the spring barbeque she just *knew* that all three cowboys loved JJ. It was in the way they looked at her and in the way she looked at them.

She also had no doubt that JJ was bedding Dan too. The aroused look splashing across JJ's face when she'd seen Dan, shirtless, at the window was a dead giveaway.

Blue blew out a tense breath, feeling the heat of her imagination cascade through her body.

Oh boy, if she ever got a chance to have sex with two or more hot looking men like those on Moose Ranch, she would jump at the opportunity.

Moments later, she was airborne, and she watched JJ as she kept waving to Blue from the dock.

Yeah, JJ was one lucky woman.

Chapter Three

"So, what do you want most? A boy or a girl?" Dan asked as he watched JJ stroll from her bathroom where she'd finished showering moments earlier.

He'd already tucked himself into her bed and was eagerly awaiting their evening together, especially with little Chrissy fast asleep in the nursery.

JJ looked so adorable with her hair wrapped in a pink towel and her luscious body bundled in her terrycloth robe.

Even devoid of makeup, she was a natural beauty. Not that she wore makeup much. Just sometimes if they were expecting company, or if she was heading into the city on Moose Ranch business.

He watched as she pondered his question, nibbling cutely on her lower nip while she unwrapped her hair and then began to towel dry it.

She stared at him with her brown eyes, not answering.

Such a beautiful woman and she belonged to him, at least for a couple more nights. His cock was already hard with anticipation of sleeping with her tonight.

Hell, he pretty much had a permanent hard-on were she was concerned.

"I have thought about it. I've wondered if it would be best if Chrissy had a sister or a brother this close in age," she finally replied.

"But what do *you* want? Girl or a boy?"

"Not sure. I don't know. I just pray the baby is healthy."

Dan grinned. She was hedging the question.

"Well, that goes without saying."

"What would you like the baby to be?" JJ suddenly questioned. Her eyes were bright with curiosity.

"I asked you first."

Besides, he couldn't even fathom answering because he wasn't even sure if he was the father. But sometimes he did think about it, and he did know what he wanted. But he would keep it a secret. Until he knew if he was the dad. But even then, he might just keep it to himself.

"I've never had siblings, so I'm not sure which would be better for her," JJ mused.

Frustration gnawed through him. There she went again. Thinking of others, instead of what she wanted. Not that he faulted JJ for wanting the best for her little girl, he just wished he knew what *she* would want.

"You had two sisters that were close in age to you. How did you like that?" JJ prodded as she kept towel drying her hair and staring curiously at Dan.

"Well, I was the youngest. So, they pretty much treated me like a baby. I remember them dressing me up all the time in baby clothes when I was really young and pushing me around in a stroller like I was a doll, until one day I just had to tell them no more of that nonsense. I was thankfully starting to walk and talk by then and so they had to listen. But yeah, having two sisters to play with was cool. They got along really great together. They're best friends to this very day. But having sisters got even better when I became a teenager, and they brought their hot girlfriends over."

"Oh? So, you're into older women are you?" JJ asked.

He saw the teasing glint in her gaze.

"I'm into you, baby. Only into you," he whispered.

Those teenage girls had nothing on JJ.

She must have noticed his voice was sounding thick and hoarse because she finally tossed the towel onto the nearby table, turned to face him, and then she let her robe drop to the floor.

JJ loved the way Dan's eyes widened as she dropped her robe. Well, this was one way of getting him to shut up.

He was lying in her bed, stretched out on his side, gazing up at her with those gorgeous green eyes that always reminded her of a forest. When he lifted the sheet that covered his torso in a bid to welcome her into bed with him, lust snapped through her, making her tremble.

He was nude. She'd known that he would be. But it always surprised her at how intense her sexual need flowed through her when she saw one or all of her cowboys naked. And tonight, she felt incredibly needy.

Dan's cock was thick and long, and quite erect and she couldn't help but lick her bottom lip as she remembered taking his hard flesh into her mouth that night the four of them had been in the lake. She'd loved the way he'd pulsed in her mouth, the bruised feel of her lips afterwards.

"Looks like you got started without me," she teased, nodding to his bold erection as she slipped into bed with him.

He chuckled as he enveloped her beneath the sheet and then gathered her into his hard, muscular arms, his warm body pressing intimately against her. She hissed as she felt the outline of his hot heavy cock push against her thigh. He didn't say a word as he leaned toward her.

Instinctively she closed her eyes, and he kissed her so passionately that she swore brilliant stars floated inside her brain and electric pleasure cascaded into her very soul.

His fingers curled through the damp strands of her hair, holding both sides of her head captive as he deepened the kiss. His lips sensually licked her lips and then his tongue stroked into her eager mouth, clashing against her tongue like a powerful warrior. Their tongues met and mated sending shivers of delight coursing all over her body.

She slid a hand downward until she found his swollen cock and she whimpered as it throbbed with promise against her palm. Slowly she rubbed the length of his shaft, and he kissed her harder until she literally felt her toes curl.

Then his mouth moved away, and he peppered her neck with delicate, flaming kisses that made her moan as her sensitive nerve endings fired up at his every touch.

Oh yes, he knew what he was doing, and he always did it so perfectly.

His lips moved lower, and he cupped one breast, then sipped delicately on her erect nipple, destroying her thoughts, pushing her toward pleasure.

He suckled and licked and lapped until her taut bud was as hard as crystal and throbbing with exquisite pain. Then he moved his hand and cupped her other breast, taking her other nipple into his mouth. The heated warmth of his suckling arrowed arousal to parts south and she felt a gush of warm cream zipping along her vagina.

Soon he let go of her breast, his mouth dashing sexy kisses along her tummy and over the rise of her abdomen.

He whipped aside the sheets, scrambled away from her, and then repositioned himself until he was nestled between her spread-eagle thighs. His shoulders were pressed intimately against her inner thighs and his head was lowering.

She could feel his hot breath tease her swollen clitoris and then she cried out as his mouth seared over her pussy like an ultra-tight suction cup. His bristly tongue circled her clit like a naughty vulture, making hunger surge within. Then he dipped his tongue into her slit and his lips sucked, and she could feel the cream leaving her body, could hear him slurping and lapping.

She reached up and smoothed her hands over her breasts, massaging her mounds and tweaking her sensitized nipples while he lay between her legs dining on her. Tension was swiftly building; her thighs were tightening as her arousal increased.

Leisurely he slurped from her vagina, creating trembly pleasure and she shuddered as she fought for control. When his tongue began smoothing over her sensitive clitoris, fashioning exquisite desire, she couldn't stop herself from keening her warning to him. She wasn't sure she could hold off too much longer, the need to orgasm became so incredible and came so fast that it overwhelmed her.

As if sensing her distress, Dan let go of her throbbing pussy. Then he was swiftly moving over her. His big muscular body descending, his long cock stabbing out from between his thighs like a rock-hard sword aiming for her pussy.

Desperately she reached up and grabbed his shoulders, pulling him down upon her, his chest melting against hers.

She moaned as his swollen penis entered her in one quick thrust, his iron length going nice and deep, hitting all the spots that needed hitting. Then he withdrew and he began pistoning until mere seconds later she exploded into a frenzied ball of convulsions.

He kissed her neck and then nibbled her flesh there, his teeth like daggers, his mouth an exquisite suction, bringing a brilliant burst of pain and she knew he'd given her a hickey.

But that was okay, it just added to the pleasure zipping through her like searing tentacles. Tentacles that wrapped around her body, making her convulse and writhe as Dan kept thrusting into her. Sensations lashed her, their brutal force exploding her every sensitive nerve ending, setting her on fire until she was trembling inside the pleasure burn of spasms so hard, she wondered if it would ever end. Not that she wanted it to. She loved being wrapped inside pleasure. So beautiful. Such bliss.

Her head thrashed back and forth on the pillow as she cried out and he kept pistoning, filling her body with incredible sensations. She stayed within the waves for as long as she could and too soon her orgasm began to ebb, but Dan kept stroking into her, firing up another climax.

She could feel it building, could sense this was going to be an even bigger one than the first. And then it was here, untamed, harsh, and beautiful. She came apart on a scream that Dan captured in his mouth. She tasted herself on his lips, but it didn't bother her. She was used to her taste, and she knew Dan was kissing her to quieten her so she wouldn't wake the baby.

But she couldn't help but be noisy. When she orgasmed, she was just so out of control.

Vibrations flooded her and tremors snapped her muscles as if she were being electrically powered, and in such a wonderful way.

Sweet mercy! Dan was so good!

She could hear his every groan as he penetrated her and his every grunt as he withdrew. She felt every contraction of her vaginal muscles around his throbbing shaft.

Oh yes, very nice.

The pleasure raced through her, and she loved it, embraced it, and went with it.

After awhile, her climax began to recede and that's when Dan stopped kissing her and then he came inside of her. She could feel the spurts of his semen and then eventually he went still. She could hear him breathing hard and happy and her breaths mingled with his.

When he came down from his sexual high, he withdrew, tumbled off her and then gathered her to his side, embracing her as she snuggled against his hard length.

"Damn, that was good," Dan muttered into her ear as he nuzzled his chin against neck. His thick voice was laced with appreciation.

JJ smiled and she nodded.

Oh yes, incredibly good. Her orgasms had certainly hit the spot.

Her pussy continued to tremble with aftershock spasms, but they soon faded away, allowing her to listen to Dan's quiet breathing.

She smiled. He'd already fallen asleep.

And she wasn't far behind.

RAFE WAS FEELING PRETTY tired from being away from home for several days and he was seriously glad to almost be back now. Happiness brightened his heart as he began to catch glimpses of the buttery glow of lamplight flowing out of the ranch house windows as he passed the nearby pine trees that hugged the trail.

He was driving his atv leisurely instead of gunning it like he wanted to do because it was twilight. Toward evening there were more animals out foraging for their supper and they tended to use the trails. Over the past three-hour drive, he'd already caught sight of several deer, a couple of moose, a few beavers and a black bear strolling on the trails. The last thing he wanted to do was hit one of the creatures, so he'd stifled his impatience to get back home.

The glow of lights made him feel so welcome though and he hoped JJ wouldn't be too upset when he broke the news to her about Brady deciding to stay away another couple of days to tackle some chain sawing to clear the trail toward the roundup area of the railway that would transport their cattle to slaughter this fall.

Over the last few days, he and Brady had worked apart from each other, returning toward evenings to the roundup cabin they'd built last year, so they could cook themselves a decent breakfast and supper.

During the days, they'd each moved cattle in the middle quarter of the ranch to different meadows to prevent overgrazing. That part of the work was done for now. There were more cattle to be moved next month and more the month after and the big drive came late autumn when all the animals that were mature for the market would be moved closer to the railway tracks and loaded onto a commissioned train for such purpose of transporting cattle.

Sure, both of them could have stayed and chain sawed their brains out, but truth be told when Brady had suggested they pick straws for the deed, Rafe had wholeheartedly agreed. He'd hoped he could go home earlier and Brady, of course, was wanting the same thing. Despite Brady's crestfallen expression that he'd lost by picking the shortest straw, Rafe knew that the poor guy would get a hell of a homecoming from JJ for being away the longest.

He kind of wished that maybe he should have stayed back with Brady, but as he puttered his atv into the yard, he sighed his relief. Working alone for days was a tough job and he was thrilled he'd soon see JJ, Chrissy, and Dan.

In the yard, he shut off his machine, removed his helmet and listened.

No wind. All was quiet.

The silence was occasionally broken by the lonesome wail of a loon somewhere out on the lake. With the sun down, a half moon shone cheerful and white in the dark blue sky, and it reflected brightly on the glass-lake surface of the lake waters. Stars sparkled here and there but it was still hot, and humid and perspiration dripped off his forehead.

For a few brief seconds, he toyed with the idea of heading down to the lake and just diving into the water for a swim.

The memories of their last foursome tryst down in the water with the three of them making love to JJ spilled into his brain, zipping awareness into his cock which tightened painfully in remembrance.

Rafe sucked in a tense breath.

Man, that had been one hell of an awesome night and the last time it had rained too, come to think of it. Now that he was back he just wanted to be with JJ and gaze upon her perfectness and he wanted to play with Chrissy and see how Dan was doing.

Rafe smiled as he climbed off the atv.

Just then JJ's laughter spilled out from somewhere in the ranch house. She sounded really happy. Dan was probably amusing her with his jokes. He liked that about Dan. About him having a sense of humor where Brady and himself were a bit more on the serious side.

He was also glad that Dan was around to keep her company and to help her out with Chrissy and all the chores of running the ranch. But soon, Dan would get the go ahead from Dr. Willie that he could return to work, and then JJ, Chrissy and the newbie would be alone during the days and some nights once again.

That was life on a wilderness cattle ranch. Lots of work and when it was time to play, they made up for the challenging work by playing hard.

He sighed and nibbled on his bottom lip as thoughts of the unborn baby once again plagued his thoughts. Was the baby JJ carrying his child? That question was truly gnawing on him day and night now. Man, he could hardly wait to find out if he was the biological dad. Despite whom the father was, he would be the baby's dad just because he or she was a part of JJ.

He'd empty the trailer and put away the atv later. Right now, he just wanted to follow JJ's musical laughter and so he strolled quickly toward the ranch house.

He opened the mudroom door. His mouth watered as he smelled steak, and the spices lured him down the hallway and into the warm kitchen.

The lights were on, but no one was home.

Then came more laughter and he realized they were on the back porch. From here he could see past the screen door where Chrissy was sitting in her highchair. She was dressed in a transparent yellow cotton shirt and diapers, and her tiny fists were clenched as she playfully pounded on the tray of her chair all the while watching JJ as she set dishes onto the picnic table, and he spied Dan at the barbecue nearby, tending several steaks.

"Just in time! Want to shower first or eat first?" JJ suddenly called out as she caught sight of him. Her eyes sparkled with happiness as she gazed at him, and his gut twisted in a really nice feeling of seeing her again. He sensed she was about to come back inside to welcome him home with a kiss, but he didn't want her to smell his perspiration.

"Shower!" he called out and quickly headed up the stairs toward his bedroom before JJ could get to him.

A clean pair of clothes and a shower and then he'd be presentable in his gorgeous woman's company.

"YOU'RE AWFULLY CHEERFUL tonight, JJ," Dan said as he helped himself to his second steak and winked at Rafe. She was, of course, happy that at least one of her missing cowboys had returned.

"And you're awfully hungry tonight," Rafe commented as he sat across from Dan.

"Hey, just building my strength," Dan smiled back. Tonight, the two of them would be spending the night with JJ and sometimes he enjoyed teasing Rafe.

"Good. Because you'll need it with all the hard work piling up for you."

"Ouch," JJ said with a laugh.

"Ha, ha," Dan replied with a grimace. He hadn't anticipated that answer coming. Sometimes he just shouldn't kid a man who'd just spent days roughing it out in the wilderness.

Rafe wasn't one for joking around tonight, it appeared. He was most likely tired from working today and then from the long ride back home. But he certainly did look healthy and happy as he stared at JJ who stood beside Rafe with a bowl in her hand, scooping some more mashed potatoes onto Rafe's plate.

"Eat, I want you to build your strength for me too," she said softly.

Dan grinned as JJ gazed at Rafe with a sweet, seductive smile that promised a nice night in bed. He recognized that look as she'd given it to him many times while the guys had been away.

Pregnancy hormones was her excuse, but he knew better. She had a ravenous sexual appetite even when she wasn't pregnant. He sometimes wondered if it was because she'd been locked up in prison for so many years without a man.

"Baby, talk like that and I'll haul your pretty little ass upstairs right now, and give you hickeys like Dan gave you, except mine will be in places people won't see," Rafe growled as he looked at Dan and winked.

Dan chuckled. It appeared no matter how much makeup she put on that hickey he'd given her, it still shone through loud and clear.

"Promises, promises," JJ laughed.

Then she moved away to serve Chrissy another little dollop of mashed potatoes on her plate, since she'd pretty much stuck her fingers into the previous small batch and then wiped it all over her face without eating.

"Chrissy, your mouth is below your nose, not on your cheeks and chin," JJ chided cheerfully as she sat down beside Chrissy and attempted to spoon feed her. But Chrissy was having none of it, turning her face away and then dipping her fingers into the new batch of potatoes.

Dan stifled a laugh. He really should tell JJ that he'd fed Chrissy earlier when JJ had been upstairs changing the sheets on all the beds.

But he enjoyed watching her interacting with her baby. He'd confess in just a little while.

"So, what's been going on while I've been away?" Rafe asked between bites of his steak.

"Well, JJ's been invited to a surprise wedding shower for Kelly," Dan replied.

Rafe's dark eyebrows rose in surprise.

"Oh, really. How's that going to work? I thought Jay was planning a surprise wedding behind Kelly's back?" Rafe asked.

Dan shrugged.

"Three weeks to three months is the usual timeline for a wedding shower," JJ explained as she wiped the mashed potatoes from Chrissy's cheeks.

"So, that must mean Jay's got a date in mind for the wedding? I wonder how the hell he's going to pull a surprise wedding off, especially when he has such a skittish bride?" Dan pondered.

"And she turned down his proposal five times," Rafe replied.

"Yeah, the guy sure does have balls asking her so many times," Dan commented.

"Apparently he's a glutton for punishment. Probably figures she won't run if there are lots of presents to return," Rafe said with a laugh.

JJ giggled and shook her head as she gazed from Dan to Rafe and back to Dan again. Her sweet lips were uptilted in such a way that they looked like a Cupid's bow. Luscious lips that he suddenly wanted to kiss so bad that he actually physically ached from refraining himself.

"Look at you two gossipers go. And so, I may as well join in. Blue told me that Jay wants the wedding this October. On the Thanksgiving weekend. But they are still looking for a venue for the wedding and the reception," JJ said.

"What's that, about two months away? Talk about cutting it close. Don't people plan a year or two or more in advance? And won't she get tipped off that the wedding is going to happen sooner rather than later when the wedding shower is getting thrown...when is it?" Rafe asked as he reached for his coffee.

"Next weekend," JJ replied.

"Well, Jay is a man in love. Love does blind one. Maybe he's not thinking clearly," Dan said.

"I'll get more details from Blue when we meet up, and we can gossip up a storm when I get back" JJ chimed in.

Dan and Rafe laughed.

He was going to seriously look forward to having another gossip fest. This was actually kind of fun.

Suddenly the phone began to ring from inside the house.

JJ was up before Dan or Rafe could so much as put down their forks. He noticed how JJ's face had suddenly brightened even more.

"Keep an eye on our mashed potato monster while I get that, please," she said in a rushed voice, and she raced into the ranch house. The slam of the screen door quickly followed.

Rafe looked over at Dan, an amused grin on his face.

"Brady?" he suggested.

"Brady," Dan nodded in agreement.

"I bet she's going to tan his hide for not coming back home tonight," Rafe said with a wink. He stabbed his fork into a piece of steak and shoved it into his mouth, looking quite happy with himself.

A few minutes later, JJ's laughter rippled through the humid night air.

"Yup, she's really tanning his hide," Dan said.

They both laughed.

As Brady listened to JJ talking, his fingers tightened around the satellite phone they kept in the roundup cabin.

Man, why had he come up with that stupid idea of pulling straws to see who could go home early and who would stay and do the chain sawing? To tell the truth, he'd been convinced he'd win the straw pulling. Had convinced himself he'd be the one going home tonight and when it hadn't happened, his pride prevented him from getting out of the deal.

Besides, Rafe had been happier than a pig in...whatever pigs were happy in, and he just couldn't go back on his word.

But he missed her, and he missed his baby girl.

She'd told him about Chrissy playing with her mashed potatoes and had laughed because she looked like a snow monster with her face plastered with all that potato, then she'd let him know about being invited to a wedding shower and she sounded pretty excited about it which he liked to hear. He wanted her to have fun with female companionship and he wanted her to get off the ranch once in awhile, just so she could take a break from everything.

He just wanted her happy.

"So, what did you eat tonight?" she asked him.

"Cold, canned beans, and hard to chew dried up beef jerky," he teased.

He wanted her to feel sorry for him, probably because he felt sorry for himself.

"Brady, no. Tell me the truth," she prodded.

She sounded disappointed, which in turn made guilt sweep through him like a sledge hammer.

"Just kidding, sweetheart. I boiled up some potatoes, made a tuna salad, had a tin of corn, and a couple apples. For dessert I used that old manual labor hand beater and whipped up a chocolate pudding with condensed milk. Tasted pretty good. How about you guys?"

"Dan barbecued steaks. You should have come home, Brady. Playing silly straw games isn't going to get you into my bed," she said in a firm tone.

Brady frowned.

Shit. She seriously sounded pissed.

"Kidding," she laughed.

Brady smiled.

"How long are you going to be? I really miss you," she said softly.

Man, he had to be nuts to stay here.

"Should be back day after tomorrow. I figure close to a day chain sawing and then I'll start heading back, even if I don't get it done."

"Now you're talking. But go slow and please be careful. You need two hands to do the things I want you to do to me," she said in a husky voice.

Brady swallowed as he envisioned cupping her lush breasts in his palms and then lowering his head to sip on one of her pretty nipples. His cock hardened at the thought. He swore softly.

"Dan should be back to work soon, and things will go faster," she said.

He nodded. She was right. Things would go faster.

From outside the cabin, he heard a wolf howl somewhere nearby. The creepy sound sent shivers up his back. He hoped JJ didn't hear. It would freak her out.

When she said nothing, he figured she hadn't heard it. Now might be the time to cut the conversation. From past experience when one wolf howled, another would soon follow, and she would hear for sure.

Man, they really should hire someone to look after this area. It was desolate and the cattle up this way where the ones that were going to market. Someone keeping an eye on things year-round might be a promising idea. Maybe any workers could stay at this cabin to allow the four of them continuous privacy back at the ranch. He'd have to think on that angle.

"Do any of the guys need to talk shop?" he asked.

"Hold on."

She called out if someone wanted to talk to Brady. He heard answering murmurs but couldn't make out what was said.

"They said all is good, unless you need to chat. Rafe said he's heading out tomorrow to the west section to start haying there," she said.

Brady nodded.

"Good. Lots of haying to be done that way. No need to chat. Give our daughter a huge kiss and hug from me and tell her I miss her like crazy, and give the newbie a big hug too," he said as his grip on the phone tightened even harder.

A swell of emotions hijacked him just thinking about how much he loved JJ and his daughter and the unborn baby, even if he or she turned out not to be his kid.

"I will. And what about me?" she asked.

"What about you?" he teased.

He could barely keep himself from laughing and he could almost see her cute little frown burrow between her sweet eyebrows.

"Won't you miss me like crazy?" she asked softly.

"Woman, I will show you exactly how much I miss you the next time I touch you," he growled.

She squealed with delight.

"Now that's better. You hold onto that thought, my love," she said in a thick voice.

"I will. Good night, sweetheart."

"Good night Brady. I love you," she whispered.

"I love you too," he whispered back.

And then the line went dead.

He frowned. He should just pack up, get his ass on the atv, and go home. But the drive was over three hours during daylight, without breaks. At night, it would be even longer and more treacherous due to the animals crossing the trail, not to mention the dangerous terrain.

For several brief moments he almost did just about get up from the chair he was sitting in by the open bedroom window and start packing. But if he ran back to JJ every time he had the urge to see her and do some naughty things to her, this ranch wouldn't turn a profit.

He took a deep breath and listened as a second and then a third wolf joined in on the howling. It was so loud he knew JJ would have heard and most likely would worry to the point she wouldn't sleep.

He got up and walked into the kitchen where he'd left the propane stove on low keeping the kettle hot because he knew he'd want a second cup of coffee, despite it being blistering and muggy inside and outside.

Coffee kept him company on lonely nights like this one, and he sure was glad he was in a cabin with four sturdy walls tonight, instead of in a flimsy tent. Those wolves out there sounded mighty hungry.

Man, some nights he just hated his job.

WHILE DAN AND RAFE cleaned up the dinner dishes, JJ spent precious time with her daughter in the living room. She had sat Chrissy on her knees, facing JJ and held her pudgy hands clapping them together while her daughter stared curiously back at her with those baby blue eyes that reminded JJ so much of Brady. Her heart clenched with love for Chrissy and at the same instant in fear for Brady. She'd heard the wolf howl in the background and hadn't wanted him to think it had frightened her, so she'd said nothing.

But it did frighten her. He was surrounded by hundreds and thousands of acres of wilderness and who knew what kind of wildlife were lurking around outside that cabin he was staying in. It was a log cabin though. Sturdy and cute. But if some forest fire decided to suddenly pop up, Brady was screwed. Or if he got tired with the chain sawing and some freak accident happened, he could bleed to death out there. All alone.

She trembled at the ideas and forced herself to focus her entire attention on Chrissy. There was nothing she could do about it tonight. Tonight, he was safe indoors. He'd be home soon, and she could show him exactly how much she missed him.

Chrissy giggled as JJ kept clapping her hands together. Just yesterday she'd started grasping for toys that JJ was showing her, and she'd also noticed Chrissy's legs and arms were moving more.

Hmm, a little workout before she put her down, would be good for her.

JJ lifted Chrissy into her arms, then walked into the middle of the living room where she placed her on her tummy on a blanket on the floor.

To her shock, Chrissy suddenly placed her hands on the blanket and did a push up.

Her heart burst with excitement as her baby plopped down again.

"Oh my God! Did you see that? She did a push up!" she cried out and twisted around to see that Rafe and Dan had already turned their heads and were watching them from the kitchen.

"Yes, saw it. She'll be crawling in no time flat," Dan laughed.

Rafe grinned happily and suddenly winked at JJ.

"Keep your eyes on drying the dishes, Dan, or no dessert for you," Rafe grumbled.

Dan's mouth dropped open in mock horror as he turned and accepted the freshly washed dish Rafe handed to him.

"Listen to this guy. No dessert for me. You're the one who isn't getting any dessert tonight if you keep up this grumpy attitude. No more jokes for you and let that be a lesson to you for saving my ass out there."

"Too many rotten jokes. I guess I should have left you out there," Rafe replied with a chuckle.

JJ didn't like it when the two men spoke about Dan's close call with death regarding hypothermia while having his foot trapped, even if they were just teasing each other. She just wanted to forget about how dangerous it was for them to be working alone in the wilderness.

Anything could happen.

Thoughts about Brady popped back into her mind as she watched Chrissy do another push up and then plop back down onto her tummy.

She should be more excited. Her daughter was doing push ups. Soon she would be crawling and then walking and then getting into trouble. Then their newbie would be here and how was she going to handle taking care of three men and two babies? And all that worrying about the men working alone out there.

Anxiety swept over her, and her mind churned for a way to solve this situation before she had a full-blown panic attack right here and now.

The idea that they just might have to hire some help swooped to the rescue and she relaxed. But she didn't want to have strangers around Moose Ranch. Their privacy would be gone, and she absolutely loved afternoon sex with one of the guys outside in nature or the foursomes they had.

If they did hire extra help, the guys would be closer to home and safer too. It certainly would be a trade off.

But their safety was her main concern. She would discuss all this with the guys as soon as she mulled it over some more.

JJ smiled as Chrissy's head turned and her pretty blue eyes blinked up at her as if looking for approval. Gosh, she looked so much like Brady. She even had Brady's nose and mouth.

Her heart burst with love as her daughter's eyes began to close.

"Are you getting sleepy?" JJ asked as Chrissy's head dropped, and she began to rub her face against her pudgy clenched fists.

"Wouldn't blame her. She's been doing push ups all day," Dan said with a laugh.

JJ's happiness deflated.

"What? She has? How come you didn't tell me?" She felt hurt that she'd missed her baby's first push up. She'd thought the one she'd just seen was the first. Apparently not.

"You were busy. Didn't want to disturb you," he answered.

Hmm, maybe she should hire someone to help *her* out around here too so she could spend more time with her baby? But that thought was fleeting. She enjoyed taking care of her men and her daughter and they were one big happy family. Of course, she was going to miss some of her baby's first things but hey, at least Chrissy was healthy and growing at a normal speed.

She couldn't ask for more.

"Okay, let's go up and get ready for bed." JJ picked up her baby and Chrissy immediately snuggled against her chest, making another round of love course through her.

Her baby felt so warm and cuddly, and JJ couldn't help but squeeze her tight and kiss her velvety pudgy cheeks as she walked up the stairs.

Chapter Four

"She was busy? And that's why you didn't tell her about the baby doing something new? What the hell kind of answer is that?" Rafe asked Dan with a frown as they both made their way to the coffee machine.

They were like that, lots of coffee after washing and drying the dishes and of course coffee with a second helping of dessert as a treat for a job well done with the dishes.

"What do you mean?" And why was Rafe looking at him so damned serious?

"When the kid starts doing something new, like push ups! You need to bring it to the attention of her mother. Didn't you see the disappointment on JJ's face? You should let her in on developments concerning her baby."

It was Dan's turn to frown.

"I hadn't thought about that. Just figured she was busy, and I didn't want to bug her like every few minutes. I figured she would see it later again, anyway."

"You enjoy watching Chrissy do new things, right?" Rafe pushed.

Yeah, he did. It was an amazing feeling of watching new accomplishments that the baby could do. Guilt slammed through Dan, and he realized that Rafe was right. How could he have been so dense? He should be sharing his excitement with JJ right when it was happening.

Dan nodded as he poured himself a mug of coffee, then grabbed a piece of chocolate cake and set it onto a plate.

"So do her mother and her father. Keep her in the loop, especially if she's within calling distance. Brady's away, so he's excused."

"Well, I guess I've been told, haven't I?" Dan replied, feeling utterly dejected.

"Just saying."

Rafe's voice had turned soft as he sauntered over to the living room couch with his mug and cake.

Usually, they had a few card games while they had dessert, but maybe tonight wasn't such a good idea with Rafe being tired. He probably wanted to conserve his energy for time later with JJ.

Then an idea brightened Dan.

"Okay, I think I have a way of making it up to her, but I'm going to need your help."

Rafe shook his head and gazed over at Dan, his brown eyes twinkling with amusement.

"No way, man. You screwed up. You make it up to her."

Dan smiled. "Oh, I think you're going to enjoy my plan. But if you don't want to at least hear it?"

Rafe rolled his eyes and frowned.

"Okay, lay it on me."

JJ WAS STILL PERTURBED an hour later as she stepped into her shower under the pummelling spray of hot water. It felt good having her shoulder muscles massaged by the water jets and being in here alone gave her some time to think.

Chrissy was doing something new every day, and JJ was missing things like the push ups she'd done. But she also knew every working mom missed the first time for some things with her baby. Still, it would be nice to spend more time with her daughter and with her new baby when he or she arrived.

And it would be pleasant for the guys to all be home every night instead of being out in the dangerous wilderness tending to the cattle and other chores so far from home. Her thoughts flittered to when she'd first arrived here and had quickly fallen in love with all three of her cowboys.

She'd felt nervous about them being so far away from medical help if something bad happened to one of them. So, she'd secretly taken it upon herself to learn to fly a plane, with the idea that some day she would put a deposit down and buy one with her own money, so she could feel safe knowing they had a chance to get to a hospital if needed.

And she'd faced that challenge by learning to fly. It hadn't been easy having anxiety and panic attacks, but she had accomplished her goal and the guys had surprised her by buying a used plane for the ranch. For her.

Now she faced another challenge. Finding a way to keep her cowboys closer to home. It was something to ponder, especially with a new baby on the way. She wanted her children to know their dad or dads whatever the case may be.

She wanted her guys to come home every night like normal working dads. It would be nice too if they were around at lunch time and supper time. In order for that to happen, they would have to hire someone and since she preferred that they keep their privacy due to their unique relationship situation, she'd need to figure out where any new hires would live.

Movement just outside the glass shower door caught her attention. She turned and stepped away from the spray.

JJ smiled. She'd ponder upon her challenge another time.

Usually, the guys waited until she was finished showering, but hey, she was always in the mood for some nooky. She giggled as the shower glass door slid open.

Both Rafe and Dan stood there. They were completely naked, their bodies hard and tense and they were stroking their very erect cocks, staring at her with lust-filled gazes.

"Hey, babe. I'm sorry I didn't shout out to you today when Chrissy did something new. We've decided that you are in charge tonight. Your wish is our command. Is that okay?" Dan asked with a sheepish grin.

JJ feigned a pout before answering.

"Well, I'm not sure all is easily forgiven, especially when one has behaved so badly," she teased.

Dan's green eyes became stormy and lustful. She knew he enjoyed it when she became playful with him.

She couldn't help but smile inwardly at Dan's apology. She bet Rafe had had something to do with it as he gave her a quick wink. But there really wasn't anything to apologize for as she'd been busy, and Dan hadn't wanted to bother her. No apologies needed, but hey, if they wanted to play it this way tonight, she was all for it.

"Gentlemen, please step into my parlor," she said as a pounding gush of excitement grabbed her.

"How would you like us to proceed?" Dan asked.

"My nipples have been needy all day," JJ confessed.

She'd worn a padded bra to help protect her tender nipples, but they were just feeling so achy since she'd gotten pregnant, and her men always knew how to soothe them.

Dan smiled softly.

"Turn around," he instructed.

She did as he said, turning her back toward the shower spray allowing it to pummel her tense shoulder muscles once again. Oh yes, that felt good.

Dan slipped the bar of soap off the nearby soap holder and held it under the spray behind her.

"You are so beautiful when you're pregnant. I think we'll keep you pregnant all the time," Dan's voice sounded thick as he brought the wet soapy bar around to her front and swept it over her right taut nipple in whispery touches.

"Oh, and I get no say?" she breathed, hissing at the shockwaves that arrowed from her sensitive nipple right down into her pussy.

Dan chuckled and didn't answer.

She watched Dan hand the soapy bar to Rafe who'd squeezed in beside Dan. Rafe began to gently soap her other nipple. With the two of them touching her, she found her breathing coming faster and arched against them, needing more contact.

As both men continued to massage and soap her, JJ shuddered as incredible pleasure zipped through her body.

"Pretty little peaks aren't they?" Rafe complimented her nipples.

"Nice and plump, just the way I like them," Dan answered as both men tweaked and softly massaged until she was moaning.

Her entire body was becoming incredibly sensitive, filling her with awareness. She could feel her thighs tightening, her breasts feeling bigger, and her pussy and ass clenching with need.

Then they waited and studied her nipples with heated looks until the shower spray came over her shoulders and washed the suds away.

"It's a shame I have to cover my pretty perfect nipple with my mouth," Dan mumbled.

"Yeah, a big shame," Rafe growled.

JJ blew out a tense breath as both men lowered their heads.

She cried out as hot silky mouths enveloped her sensitive buds, and she watched as each one disappeared between luscious red lips.

Sensations quivered through her making her jerk as the two men began suckling.

Pleasure arrowed into her pillowy breasts and seared along her belly down her rounded abdomen and pierced deep into her needy vagina. She reached out and slapped her palms on each man's shoulders, digging her fingers into their muscles.

"That's perfect," she gasped and watched the two men at her breast.

She could feel their bristly tongues brush around her throbbing buds. Could feel the difference in how they suckled. Rafe a bit restrained and tender. Dan more forceful and needy. She enjoyed both ways as heat and arousal whipped her.

The men licked and lapped, making happy groaning noises as they drew their teeth over her sensitive buds, sending gasping shock waves spinning through her like a whirlwind. They continued their administrations until JJ's moans filled the shower enclosure and she was crying out.

"Sounds like you really enjoyed that, baby," Rafe muttered as both men finally released her trembling and tortured nipples from their mouths.

The two men stood in front of her, their heavy-lidded gazes giving away that they'd enjoyed themselves very much, just as she had. She looked down and spied their cocks were even bigger now, poking out from between their muscular thighs, engorged and pulsing. Just looking at them made her want their erections thrusting into her and bringing the pleasure she craved.

"I did, now I want you to make me come," she commanded.

Dan nodded and he stepped behind her. Rafe remained in front.

His sharp brown gaze promised plenty of pleasure as he lowered his head toward hers. She closed her eyes, felt his hands slide over her hips, and she eagerly moved into the brilliant sparkles as hot lips melted over hers in sultry possession.

From behind her came the slurp of lubricant as Dan used the tube of lube she always kept on a nearby shower shelf for such occasions.

She cried into Rafe's mouth as a moment later Dan's hands slid over her waist. She knew what was about to come and an instant later Dan's lubed erection pushed past her tight sphincter.

His engorged shaft easily slid into her and stopped when she felt the warmth of Dan's body press against her back. He remained inside of her while showering the back of her neck with delightful kisses.

Rafe pushed his cockhead against JJ's engorged clitoris and began a gentle massage, circling her clit, shooting more pleasure waves into her, which in turn made her heady with arousal.

She reached up and slapped her hands upon Rafe's hot shoulders and pushed her lower half against him craving a firmer contact upon her clit.

Instinctively JJ began to uncontrollably gyrate her hips, moving perfectly against Rafe's scorching hot flesh. It felt so good, having her ass impaled by Dan and using Rafe's cockhead as a clit stimulator.

As her arousal built quickly, she tore her lips from Rafe's mouth, gasping for breath and impatiently slid her hands off his bulging shoulders and down his arms. His muscles were smooth, hot, and taut and felt so good. She kept going until she clasped her hands into his and he intertwined his fingers with hers.

"Take me, now," she hissed, holding tight and feeling a rapturous climax rushing toward her at lightning speed.

Dan withdrew and Rafe wasted no time. He drove his shaft into her wet vagina, his iron length of throbbing flesh filling her beautifully.

She cried out as the two men began a rhythmic thrusting and she cried out again as Dan and Rafe entered her at the same time unleashing her orgasm. Pleasure assailed her senses.

Electrical lightning bolts sent her body into wild convulsions. Juicy spasms rocked her, and raw agony made love to her.

She lost herself in the incredible bliss of being sandwiched between two muscular male bodies. Vanished into the beauty of each shudder and fell into the spectacular release of all the pent-up needs that had accumulated throughout the day.

Dan and Rafe thrust harder and faster keeping her climax going endlessly.

She felt wild. Untamed. Loved.

Oh yes, it was all so perfect.

So wonderful.

This was exactly what she'd needed.

IT WAS GETTING DARK pretty fast tonight, and the air was so thick with humidity that Brady swore he could cut it with his chainsaw.

He knew better than to chainsaw when the sun went down, but he wanted to get this last tree cut up and pushed off the trail. He was working with his head lamp on now and the perspiration dripping onto his safety glasses obscuring his vision was pissing him off. Why couldn't they put little windshield wipers on these things anyways?

It was hotter than hell wearing all this protective gear and he couldn't wait to rip off his face shield, dump the irritating ear muffs that made his ears itch, ditch his sweaty clothes, jump into the nearby lake naked and get rid of the stench of gasoline fumes hugging his body.

Once refreshed he'd have a late snack and a couple cups of coffee at the cabin. Then he'd sleep his ass off with full intention of heading back toward the ranch at the break of dawn.

That was the plan anyway.

He'd been thinking about it all day while he'd worked.

He'd been chain sawing since sun up. The trails were clear now in this section of the ranch, and he would have been done much earlier had he not decided to check in on several herds of cattle in the nearby meadows while he was out this way, especially because of all that wolf howling he'd heard last night. Unfortunately, he'd found a couple of fresh calf carcasses. He'd buried what little had been left of them and felt pretty bad for their mothers who were mooing in a forlorn sound for their offspring.

The wolves were getting bolder. With so much easy access to cattle, the wolves would mate and multiply and there would be more kills. They would definitely have to get someone out here to keep an eye on things. Despite the wolf trouble, he still wasn't ready to get permission to kill them. They were magnificent animals who were hungry. He couldn't fault them for following their instincts.

He'd taken many breaks throughout the hot, hazy day too, drinking electrolyte water, which they usually kept on hand for days of challenging work like today. Electrolyte water kept him hydrated, and a couple of power naps under the shady trees this afternoon had helped keep his energy high. Now with what he hoped was only heat lightning flickering in the dusky sky, he could see the end of his job.

Relief began to pound through him as he sliced the blade of his chainsaw like butter through the last piece. He turned off the machine and lay it to one side so he wouldn't trip over it in the darkness. Then he rolled the remnants of the logs off the trail.

As he headed back to get the chainsaw, he let out a big happy whoop.

He was done! Damn it was a good feeling to have accomplished another job. He absolutely loved being his own boss out here in the wilderness. For years he'd truly enjoyed the solitude too, but more times than not ever since JJ came into his life, he wanted to be back home with her and his kid.

He grabbed the chainsaw and dropped it into the atv trailer he'd parked down the trail. Then he tore off his gloves, helmet with face mask and ear muffs, only to be greeted by the low rumble of thunder far off in the distance.

Well, shit, storm, or no storm he was going to take a swim anyways when he got back to the cabin. He removed his chaps and resisted the urge to lose the rest of his clothing, which clung to him like shit to a wet blanket. Not the best way to describe it, but that was sure as hell how it felt.

He tossed all the gear into the trailer and was about to get onto the vehicle when a whiff of smoke shot alarm bells through him.

Fuck! Forest fire?

He smelled the air some more. No, it was another smell. Like someone was cooking.

What the hell? The little cabin they'd built was about a ten-minute walk from here. Was someone squatting at their cabin?

If he returned with the noisy atv, he might scare off the perp or perpetrators, but then again, surely they would have heard him chain sawing, unless the sound didn't carry that far. He'd have to leave the atv and walk back just in case there was someone there. Hopefully though, it was just some well-equipped interior campers lounging on the shoreline of the lake, making supper.

Over head lightning flashed. He cursed and grabbed the rifle, setting it on the seat of the atv. Then he tied the plastic tarp he kept in the trailer over his gear and over the bearproof cooler which contained only a couple of drinks as he'd eaten everything he'd brought along. He tied a second tarp over the atv.

After that was taken care of, he checked to make sure the rifle's safety catch was on. It was and then his heart began to pound a mile a minute as he held the rifle in his hand and started to walk back down the trail. He would come back for the vehicle in the morning.

Blades of white lightning flashed illuminating the nearby dark
pine trees. A low rumble of thunder followed. His walk turned into
a jog, and he wiped sweat off his forehead, cursing the possible
intruders as he went.

He was glad his legs were doing okay. He hadn't had much
trouble lately. No more pain no thanks to the tetanus scare he'd had.
Every time he thought about how close he'd come to death because
of not keeping up with his tetanus shot, it made him uneasy. It
reminded him of the searing pains that had held his body hostage for
too long and sometimes he swore he got phantom pain too.

But he was okay now. He had to remember that and to focus
on the now because sometimes he could slip into anxiety mode
remembering about that horrible time. And when he got anxious he
thought about JJ and all the shit she'd had to endure through her
life with her anxiety and panic attacks and then getting locked up
in prison. In comparison to what she'd been through, his brush with
death was minor, in his opinion.

But just thinking about her made his momentary anger of
someone shacking up in the cabin dissipate. JJ was such a strong
woman. He admired her so much and loved her even more.

His thoughts about JJ vanished when the silhouette of the little
log cabin near the edge of the lake came into sight. Buttery glows of
lamplight shone unashamedly out of the windows.

His irritation about intruders returned. Obviously, they had no
clue that he was so close. When he'd left this morning, he'd made sure
to keep the place nice and tidy and he'd hung the food stash in a smell
proof plastic inside a knapsack high up on a branch behind the cabin
in an effort to keep any nosey animals from trying to break into the
cabin.

Whoever was cooking was going to draw bears and wolves to
the area from near and far because the scent was making *him* drool.
Despite the tantalizing aromas drifting through the night air, there

was no way he was bunking with a stranger or strangers as the case might be.

He wondered where they'd come from. This was private land, surrounded by public lands with many lakes. Someone could have portaged in from other lakes, or they could have come in here following the old railroad, which was rarely used. The railroad ran across their property at several points. Someone could have been following it, seen the clearings and corrals they used to hold the cattle that were to be shipped to the slaughter house and meandered along one of the atv trails and found the cabin.

The smell of smoke grew heavier the closer he got. Whoever was cooking, was doing a damned excellent job. His tummy was growling up a storm.

Despite that, he'd have to send them on their merry way. Well, maybe he'd kick them out after he ate some of their food.

Quietly he approached the cabin, sticking to the shadows and then he sauntered along the north facing wall and was able to peek into one of the front windows. Huh, the lanterns were lit, but the cabin was empty. No one was inside. Perhaps they were in the back bedroom?

He sniffed the air.

Barbecue. They were using the barbeque. It was behind the house near a picnic shelter they'd made.

Cautiously he crept around to the side of the cabin.

A moment later Brady jolted when he saw someone standing in front of the stone barbeque, puffs of blue smoke billowing upward.

No, not just anyone.

What the fuck?

"What the hell are you doing here!" Brady shouted.

JJ jumped at his shout and then she whirled around, fear plastered on her face.

When she saw him though, her face lit up like a beacon of happiness and he instantly regretted scaring her.

She let out a happy shriek and a moment later she flew into his arms. Automatically he embraced her and melted against her soft body, feeling her baby bump pushing against his lower abdomen.

"Brady! Oh my gosh! I've been here waiting for hours, hearing you chain sawing somewhere far off. I had hoped the smell of barbecued steak would lure you home and I was right!"

She planted a kiss on his mouth and any anger, irritation, and surprise he was harboring for intruders vanished as he kissed her back. She tasted so yummy. Fresh and flowery. Lush and ripe.

Her sweet body pressed against him, her warm curves melting against his intimate body parts, igniting naughty needs in all the right places.

Man was he ever glad she was here.

Brady was reacting big time to having JJ in his arms. His cock was engorging and pressing painfully against his pants. Heck, she was making him so hot, he was sure to explode.

He groaned in frustration and ripped his mouth away from hers. He gazed down into her pretty brown eyes that shimmered from the buttery glow of the gas lamp she'd hung on a hook beneath the roof of the picnic shelter, near the barbecue.

It was quite clear she was happy to see him and that gave him a great feeling.

"Wow, baby, with a welcome like that, I need to stay away more often," he growled.

JJ grinned.

"Rafe and Dan suggested I come out. They're babysitting tonight. You're all mine!"

"But I smell like a lumberjack. I'm going to need to change, or you'll run back home, and I don't want that."

"I love the way you stink," JJ laughed and pounded her fists against his chest, struggling to break free from his embrace.

"You see, you're trying to escape already," Brady complained with a laugh and let her go.

She hurried back to the barbecue and overturned the steaks, making a scrumptious sizzling sound ripple through the air. She flipped often when she barbecued, saying it prevented the steak from getting too crispy. But he liked it crisp. He also liked the way she made them.

He glanced at the nearby lake and spied JJ's white float plane moored at the dock. He'd been so focused on catching any hooligans squatting at the cabin, he hadn't even thought to look to see if maybe she'd flown out here. She must have come in when he'd been chain sawing and wearing his ear muffs, that's why he hadn't heard anything.

Right then, white lightning flashed over the lake, and he spied a roll of black clouds to the south. He bet it was already storming back at the ranch house. They were probably putting Chrissy to bed around this time too. His heart clenched with longing at thinking about his little daughter.

If he were back home right now, she'd be in her pajamas or just wearing a diaper because of the heat, her warm body sleepily snuggling against him as he put her into her little crib.

Man, he wished JJ had brought her along. He would have loved to bury his face in her fluffy baby hair and smell her baby scent. Would have loved to give her a goodnight kiss. But if the guys were babysitting, why be stupid and turn down such an opportunity to be alone with his baby mama?

"Brady, where have you been? I've been calling you to come over and get ready to eat," JJ said.

While he'd been dreaming about his daughter, JJ had returned.

"Just thinking on tonight," he said and wiggled his eyebrows at her.

She giggled and grabbed his hand, leading him back toward the picnic table which had been set with a red and white checkered tablecloth, white dishes, food inside containers with see through lids.

"You just peel off your clothes, and I will serve," she said and squeezed his fingers.

Brady laughed.

"I'll peel off mine, if you'll peel off yours," he teased, squeezing her warm fingers in return.

She wouldn't have much to take off as she was only wearing a maternity floral print cotton sleeveless sundress and a pair of sandals. And maybe panties. Or not. He certainly was curious to find out. She was also wearing her hair high up in a ponytail and he couldn't wait to let down her hair and run his fingers through her silky strands.

"Not until you've eaten. I want you full of energy tonight," she squealed.

She let go of his hand and returned to the barbecue and flipped the steaks on the grill again. He took the opportunity to see what she'd whipped up for their late supper. And he liked what he saw.

"Woman, you are after my heart tonight. Potato salad, Bean salad, chocolate cake and steak. All my favorites," he called out, feeling his mouth water in appreciation.

"I'm after more than your heart tonight," she called back.

Brady grinned and wished he had taken the time to throw himself into the lake and washed up before coming here. But peeling off his clothes was second best.

JJ TRIED TO PREVENT herself from observing Brady as he undressed. But she just couldn't. She always loved watching him taking off his clothes. He was like a magnet. He turned her on. Big time. And he didn't smell bad at all. Just some gasoline and a bit of perspiration. He was a hard-working man, and he had every right to smell.

He was just being self-conscious and sexy as hell as he tugged off his damp shirt, crumpled it into a ball with his large hands and tossed it toward the porch area. It ended up in the bushes.

Then he stripped off his pants, rolled them up and threw it toward the porch. It ended up sprawled on the railing.

"Your aim is off tonight, Brady," she teased as she forked the steaks off the barbecue grill and placed them on a plate.

"My aim won't be off when it's important," he hinted.

JJ laughed understanding his meaning. When it came to making love, he knew exactly where to aim in order to pleasure her to perfection.

Her mouth watered as she gazed at the steaks. Sizzling juice oozed from the delicious smelling well-done meat, and she almost dropped the plate when she looked up to see he'd removed the rest of his clothing and was standing there, watching her approach.

An abundance of tanned muscles bulged across his broad chest and his biceps but to her disappointment, he wasn't completely nude as she'd hoped.

He wore the old apron she kept at this cabin. The apron she'd placed on a bench seat of the picnic table earlier when she'd felt too hot wearing it over her baby bump.

Oh damn. What had she been thinking talking nonsense about feeding him first. All she wanted to do was rip off that apron and check out that enormous erection that was tenting against the material. But tearing off his apron would have to wait as he quickly seated himself and was opening the containers, scooping out food onto both of their plates.

It was obvious that he was hungry.

"Smells so delicious, and you do too," he chuckled as he glanced up at her, a teasing smile on his luscious lips. His blue eyes twinkled under the lamplight and her heart clenched with love, as it always did, when he looked at her.

JJ blew out a tense breath and placed the plate with their steaks in the middle of the picnic table.

Just then lightning flashed and thunder rumbled.

"Storm's getting closer," she muttered, a tinge of anxiety zipping through her. But she needn't worry as she had Brady here. She forced herself to relax.

She was about to head back to the stone barbecue to dump a bucket of water onto what was left of the glowing charcoals when Brady reached out and grabbed her hand.

"I'll do it, sweetheart. You sit and start eating. You'll need the energy for what I've got planned for you. Besides, that storm won't be here for at least another hour. It's a slow moving one from the sound of it."

JJ nodded and felt her pulse begin to pound at a most exciting speed. What naughtiness had Brady so quickly planned for her? But that would have to wait, because suddenly she was hungry too. And when Brady strolled past her, she got a good up close and personal look at his rock-hard bare ass. She couldn't help but let out a whistle of appreciation.

"You keep your eyes on your food," Brady called out.

JJ smiled and suddenly felt very happy.

Storm or no storm, tonight was going to be a nice night.

Chapter Five

"How's our baby girl doing?" Brady asked a few minutes later as they sat opposite each other at the picnic table, and he stabbed another forkful of steak into his mouth and made a succulent moan as he enjoyed the flavor of the meat.

Gosh, she loved the sensual way his lips were shaped, and she wanted to kiss him again. Bad.

But she also couldn't wait to share the exciting news where their daughter was concerned.

"She's actually doing push ups," JJ commented.

Brady stopped chewing; his eyes wide as he looked at her like she'd grown two horns.

"What? How is that possible? She's just a baby. She's only seven months."

"That's how they learn to crawl," JJ explained as he kept staring at her like he just wasn't understanding what was happening.

She didn't want to burst his bubble and remind him that Chrissy wasn't going to be a baby forever. She'd be moving into toddler territory in no time.

"Pretty soon you'll be helping her with homework and answering all kinds of questions about life and then there will be boyfriends..." She couldn't help but tease.

"Um, no. No boyfriends. She's too young. She's not having any boyfriends," Brady was adamantly shaking his head and frowning. He speared his fork into another piece of steak and shoved it into his mouth like he was furious.

Oh, dear Lord. Talk about protective daddy mode.

"I don't know how you can sit there all calm, JJ. You said she's doing push ups. Then crawling and then oh crap, we're going to have to home school her."

His frown deepened as he cut up another piece of steak, forked it and shoved it into his mouth. Then he stared at her as if he were suddenly having a light bulb moment realizing that their daughter wasn't going to be a baby forever. Worry snapped through his blue eyes.

"I have no idea how to home school a kid. Or kids. What if we do something wrong?" he asked as he took a sip of coffee and stared at her, his eyebrows raised as if he were expecting her to supply a perfect answer.

His eyes were sparkling in unison with the flashes of lightning behind him over the lake and despite his frown, she may have seen a fleeting upward tilt at the sides of his lips and then it was gone. Perhaps she had imagined it?

"Of course, we will make mistakes. We're humans. We'll get through it, sweetheart. Don't worry." She reached out and placed her hand over the back of his hand.

His frown deepened.

Wow, he was taking all of this so seriously.

"What if she wants to go to college or university? I can't prevent her from having boyfriends if she heads out on her own," he mumbled.

"Brady, she's just a baby. We've got time," she reminded him.

Maybe he'd worked too hard today. Maybe he was overtired and that's why he was talking so seriously?

Suddenly he cracked a grin.

"Had you going, didn't I?" he said and then he began to laugh.

JJ relaxed and shook her head. So, she hadn't imagined that slight upward tilt to his lips. He'd been teasing her and suddenly her heart felt full of smiles, and she was thankful that he wasn't overwhelmed.

"Damn right we've got time, baby mamma. I'll be teaching her everything she needs to know in how to protect herself from boys. There will be karate and self defence classes. I can learn them online and teach her. When she goes out into the world she'll be a wolf, not a lamb heading to slaughter. Don't you worry about that," he said with a firmness that made JJ believe he wasn't teasing anymore.

It was time to change the subject.

"I like this protective side of you, Brady. Very sexy."

He grinned, then took another sip of coffee.

"Sexy huh, I'd show you sexy right now, but I've got to finish dinner, take a bath in the lake, help wash the dishes. How is newbie anyway? I've been hogging the conversation about Chrissy, and I haven't even asked about how you and the newbie are feeling. Everything okay? The heat isn't bothering you?"

Concern flared in his gaze.

She didn't dare tell him that yes, the heat did bother her, especially since she'd been hovering over the barbecue. The temperature had felt like nasty blasts from a furnace. Sure, she could have produced a cold meal, but she knew he'd be ravenous after a grueling day of physical work.

Now she felt sticky, and the humidity made her anxious. But she didn't want him worrying. She would just drink extra water and stay hydrated. With a storm coming, she was sure things would cool off with a nice rain.

"I'm fine. All is good. And you are not going into the lake with lightning bolts shooting left, right and center. I will give you a sponge bath, after all the chores are done."

Brady chuckled.

"A sponge bath, eh? That's what I was planning to do to you, baby."

His voice had turned low and dusky, and his gaze was turning darker, like it always did when he wanted sex.

She bit her bottom lip. They were going to give each other sponge baths. How in the world was she going to be able to wait?

"Good thing we installed that new water tank with overflow pipe in the attic and the state-of-the-art water pump down by the lake earlier this Spring. I'll get it going after and pump up some fresh chilly water. That's why we put the water line in pretty far out and deep into the lake, so we can get cold fresh water on days and nights like this." He was eyeing her, looking for a reaction.

Oh boy, shop talk. She'd rather talk sponge bath now. And then an idea hit her.

"Would you be able to put a heater line in or around the water hose and put the pump in an insulated shed so it can be used in the winter?"

"Everything is possible. We'd have to get the hose deeper underground; beneath the frost line as where would you get power for a heater line. Solar panels on the roof would get you power, but if you run into a bunch of cloudy days you're in trouble unless you have a bank of batteries. There are other options, but why? Are you planning on having a tryst out here in the winter?"

JJ couldn't help but giggle.

"Now, who would I have a tryst with, when I have everything and everyone I need right at the ranch house?"

Brady's gaze narrowed, an amused expression on his face.

"Maybe you met a sexy hobo fresh off the railway tracks? He was irresistible and you wanted to give him all the comforts of home, without us knowing about him. Your own personal gigolo."

He did an eyebrow wiggle.

"You should have been a writer, Brady," she teased.

"I'll leave the writing for the writers, sweetheart. Why the questions? Are you thinking someone should be living out here keeping an eye on the cattle? Remember quite a lot of cattle are sold off in the autumn, so there wouldn't be that many to care for out this way during the winter months. It would be full-time work during the other months though."

Oh wow. That's exactly what she'd been thinking last night about having someone here. But she hadn't expected to be talking about it so soon.

"It would free up more time for you and Rafe and Dan," she hedged.

Brady inhaled a deep breath and nodded.

"Been thinking on the same thing, lately," he said.

"You have?"

Thank goodness!

He nodded again and helped himself to a large piece of chocolate cake. Then he poured some more coffee from the Thermos she'd brought along.

He certainly looked like he'd enjoyed his supper as the plate was clean and he appeared happy. She was always glad when one of her men was satisfied with a meal.

"Probably more than one person though for the three seasons. They can help with the castrating, insemination, haying, planting, and they could keep an eye on each other. Company for each other too. Not sure if there would be enough work during the winter for two people though," he said between bites of the cake.

"You could use Jenna's Cowboys Online program for inexpensive labor?"

"The place is isolated enough to qualify for someone having an early prison release through her program. But we'd need to bring the cabin up to a decent standard of living for them to stay. Running water. Generator. Fly in food."

"They could use the machines you already have out here to get to the cattle," JJ added. The men had built a big shed nearby where they housed all terrain vehicles, trailers, snowmobiles, and other equipment.

He nodded as he eagerly chewed the cake. Yes, he certainly was enjoying himself.

"We'd need to stay ahead of blizzards by making sure the cabin is well-stocked with food and fuel if we have someone here during the winter. Communication is sketchy out here in parts. Someone runs into trouble if a snowmobile goes on the blitz and they're far from the cabin; it could be deadly."

JJ's happy bubble burst and deflated.

Oh dear, that was true. It was the reason why she wanted her men closer to home, but to put another man or men at risk, the idea of having people out here in this seclusion suddenly wasn't as thrilling an idea anymore.

"What's with the frown?" Brady asked and took a sip of his coffee, squinting his eyes as he studied her.

"If something happened to someone because I want my men closer to home, I couldn't live with that," she admitted.

"We'll give Jenna a detailed description of everything that will be expected of the helpers. Only those who can stand seclusion will be considered. They'll be told it's a dangerous job. We won't sugarcoat anything, so whoever comes out will be tough as nails and will know exactly what can happen. And like any job of this nature, there are risks. None of it would be your fault. Just remember that."

Just hearing Brady say it wouldn't be her fault did make her feel a bit better.

"Do you really think it would be okay?"

Brady shrugged his shoulders.

"Well, like I said there is always a risk, right? There's a risk with any job of this kind. We give Cowboys Online all the gory details, and they can do the legwork to see who is a fit. No one will come out here with blinders on. Of course, we'll take the time to train them and that would cut down on the risks. The only problem is they wouldn't be allowed to handle firearms for self-protection. That would be a violation of the Cowboys Online program, I'm sure. But we can always try for permission. I'll talk to Jenna about our unfolding plans. See what she says."

Excitement began to pound through JJ again. Could something like what they were discussing tonight, actually happen? Would she be able to have her men back at the ranch more often? Oh, my goodness, it would be a dream come true.

"Of course, we'll bring Rafe and Dan up to speed on this going forward now. But I doubt they'd protest any freeing up time to be with you and our kids."

He stopped talking and frowned. He'd gone squinty eyed again as he studied her.

"What? What's wrong? Why are you looking at me like that?" he asked.

"Oh, Brady. You don't know how many sleepless nights I've had worrying when one or all of you are not at home at night."

To her surprise, Brady chuckled at her confession.

"Well, it's not like there are any other women out here."

JJ cursed and smacked his hand.

"Ouch! Such violence. Remind me never to cross you."

She felt like stomping her feet in distress. Why was he being so difficult tonight? She was baring her insecurities to him, and he was making fun.

"I'm serious."

Instantly he sobered.

"Oh, darling. I'm sorry. I expected you would have some worry, but it looks like it's been more than I thought. You're pretty good at covering your feelings."

It felt good confiding in him and now that they were talking about getting help onto the ranch, without their privacy being compromised, she felt incredibly relieved.

JJ nodded, feeling the sting of tears of relief burn her eyes.

Distress gleamed in his expression as he gazed at her.

"Hey, don't you go and start crying on me, baby mamma. I'll get everything in order. Worrying isn't good for you or the baby."

Thank God. He was listening to her.

"I'm fine. Just hormones."

Brady chuckled.

"Hey, I'm finished here. Aren't you having coffee and cake for dessert?" he suddenly asked.

JJ shook her head. She was stuffed.

"Okay let's clear off the dishes and then I'll run down to the lake and get that pump going so we have that nice cold water for our sponge baths."

"Just make sure you hurry. I don't want you to get hit by lightning."

As if the lightning was listening to them, it flickered, and a low warning growl of thunder followed. The sound sent a shiver of alarm through her.

"What? You don't like your men charbroiled like the juicy steaks?" he joked.

There he was again, toying with her feelings. And she knew she was being emotional, just like she'd told him. It was baby hormones. But she just couldn't seem to stop herself from feeling once again like he wasn't taking her seriously enough.

"Never kid about something like that, big guy. Or you'll be in big trouble," she chastised, stood, and began collecting the plates and cutlery.

"I like being in trouble. Means you'll have to find ways to punish me."

He winked at her and stood.

JJ just shook her head, and she was thankful that he quickly joined her to grab the food containers and the lantern and helped her to carry things inside.

It was warmer in the cabin than it was outside, and the humidity just about took her breath away as they placed the dishes on the counter. Brady quickly turned on a battery-operated lantern which doused the kitchen in bright white light.

She found herself really looking forward to something cold because when she opened the tap the water that came out into the sink was warm. She hadn't expected anything different because it would be quite hot in the attic where the water was being stored. At least she wouldn't have to heat it up on the propane stove to wash and rinse the dishes.

She was so glad too that they actually had a tap and a sink now, compared to the pails they'd used last year. The guys had done an outstanding job. There were even doors on the cupboards now and the windows had been caulked preventing insects and air from breezing in. She'd already seen all the upgrades from a previous trip this way when she'd watched them put in the additional dock earlier this year.

Yup, the roundup cabin was certainly getting into shape.

Brady grabbed the propane lantern, which was doing a decent job in casting off too much heat and headed for the door.

"Back in about fifteen minutes."

"Don't forget to put your boots back on and stay out of the lake! I don't want you to burn those magnificent balls of yours," she called out, hoping her way of putting it, might keep him out of harm's way. She doubted it, though. The man was stubborn, and she wouldn't be surprised if he did go for a swim.

He waved and then he left, his nice sexy bared ass disappearing into the darkness.

JJ turned to the new kitchen sink and turned on the tap. Happiness bubbled inside of her as she thought about her cowboys being closer to home and she began to hum as she went about her chore.

HIS BABY WAS DOING push ups.

That tidbit of news was still rocking his world as he got the water pump purring, then straightened and gazed out over to the other side of the lake where brilliant flashes of white lightning were forking across the dark sky. It seemed the thunderstorm had stalled as it hadn't moved much since they'd sat down to dinner.

Maybe they'd get lucky, and the storm would pass by. But a good rain would certainly cool things off for awhile and fill up the creeks with fresh water for the cattle.

He eyed the glass-like surface of the black water. It sure did look inviting to jump in, and he still was hot from the humid air. He was glad too that he'd listened to JJ and put his socks and boots back on because in the lamplight while walking to the water's edge, he'd stumbled over a couple of rocks. Had he been barefoot, he'd have had some aching toes tonight.

Instead, his feet were hot and probably smelly, but happy as he untied the apron and draped it over some nearby bushes. He was quite glad that all the mosquitoes had disappeared when the heat and humidity of the summer had hit, or he sure wouldn't be prancing around out here without any clothes on.

But he'd trade a swim in the lake for a sponge bath with JJ anytime. As he waited for the water to get pumped up to replace the water already in the tank in the cabin, he strolled along the shoreline toward the two docks they'd built last year. The docks were extremely wide and had been set parallel to each other and flanked the shore line.

The water was about eight feet deep in this area, and it had been easy enough to secure a setup that allowed JJ to angle the waterplane between the two docks. Last year they'd had one dock, and this year they'd added another one so the plane would be more secure.

The plane's pontoons were sheltered by the protective plastic lining on the sides of each dock leaving the plane little room for budging. In the winter, the docks would be lifted out of the water so they wouldn't get ripped away by the ice and then lowered again when spring came.

Unfortunately, there would be a short period of time when autumn changed to winter and when winter changed to spring that this cabin would be inaccessible by air due to the lake ice being unsafe to land on. If some emergency would happen to a worker during that time, then they'd have to go in on snowmobiles or atvs, depending on the weather.

But he was sure all would work out well.

Brady tugged on the ropes JJ had secured from areas on the plane to the dock as well as to the nearby thick tree trunks to make sure the floatplane wouldn't move if there was a fierce wind tonight.

He smiled. Baby mamma had some pretty good muscles.

Damn, she sure did know here stuff. Everything was nice and secure. She was a good mother to the plane just like she was a good mother to their daughter, who was doing freaking push ups.

Man, he still couldn't believe it. When she'd first told him, he'd been stunned, not believing his kid was already moving like that in such a short period of time. He'd expected his kid to continue to be a wobbly warm bundle for a little while longer.

A swell of emotions made him catch his breath. She was growing up and growing up too fast for him and there was nothing he could do to stop it. Except enjoy every day.

Shit. She'd never be a baby again. She'd be always changing. Why hadn't he been able to realize that fact until just now?

He guessed he shouldn't have teased JJ the way he had. He hadn't been able to resist in pretending to be a freaking out dad. Maybe he'd gone too far, especially after seeing her worried look, until he'd admitted he was joking. But had he really been joking? How was he going to protect Chrissy from unscrupulous boys who may want to take advantage of her when she got older?

And what about the baby JJ was carrying? Even if the baby weren't his, he knew without a doubt, he would be just as protective with a child belonging to JJ and one of his best friends.

Man, Chrissy would have a baby sister or a brother soon. It was all so surreal. He still hadn't been able to fully wrap his head around another kid in the mix so soon after Chrissy. It should be interesting to say the least.

He wondered what Dan and Rafe would think about getting people out this way to take care of the cattle. There had been previous discussions between them, but nothing had been done.

Knowing now that JJ was having trouble sleeping over them being away, just made it that much more real. He didn't want his woman to suffer. He would get this ball rolling and call his sister, Jenna, as soon as they got back home.

An owl hooted from somewhere nearby breaking Brady from his thoughts and returning him into the present.

His cock was aching for attention, and he would only find relief by being with JJ.

Excitement ripped through him as he thought about making love to his woman tonight. Suddenly, he just couldn't wait to get back to her because his cock was aching for attention, and he would only find relief by being with JJ.

Brady blew out a tense breath half and hour later when he entered the warm cabin with his rifle in one hand and the lantern in the other and suddenly remembered he'd forgotten the apron down at the water pump. He wasn't going back for it. At least not tonight.

Upon first arriving at the cabin earlier when he'd smelled the smoke, and seeing it was JJ and not hooligans squatting at the cabin, he'd left the rifle on the picnic table bench, where he'd sat down for supper, and he'd almost forgotten to bring it inside.

He'd also taken a few extra minutes making sure there hadn't been any remnants of food or anything else around the picnic table or on the grill that would attract the wildlife. But he was pretty sure animals in the vicinity would follow the scent that permeated the air from the barbecue and come to investigate the delicious aromas they'd smelled. The rifle was a good thing to have on such nights like tonight. He'd also discovered his clothes were gone from where he'd tossed them. JJ had brought them in.

After locking the door, he placed the rifle upon the nearby gun rack, then turned off the lantern, plunging him into semi-darkness. It was a good thing they'd put locks on the doors and windows too as some animals were quite clever and could turn doorknobs to gain entry to a residence. He noted all the screened windows were open though and lightning flashed brilliantly outside. Another rumble of thunder followed. This one sounding a bit louder. It appeared the storm was stalking toward them now.

He'd leave the windows open for a little while longer, not that there was a breeze or anything, but maybe there would be one when the storm finally broke. Fresh air would be so welcome in here.

He took off his boots and socks and strolled barefoot across the warm wood-planked floor into the main area of the cabin. The battery-operated lantern still hung on the hook above the sink splashing out some light. The dishes had been done already and stacked in the dish rack.

But there was no JJ.

Had she gone to bed?

Oh man, he hoped she was okay. He hadn't even thought that maybe she'd be tired because of the heat and humidity and cooking over a hot barbecue. Guilt made him move quietly toward the bedroom at the back of the cabin. If she'd climbed into bed and had fallen asleep, there was no way he was going to disturb her.

He peeked into the bedroom. The room was lit fairly well. Candles flickered in the rustic birch bark chandelier hanging from the ceiling, but she wasn't in any of the bunk beds.

So where was she?

He left the bedroom and stepped into the narrow hallway. That's when he noticed the back door was ajar. The smallest flicker of light caught his attention.

She'd gone outside. Probably because it was cooler out there and since there wasn't a bathroom or shower stall in the cabin, it made sense to sponge bathe outdoors.

Brady moved to the screen door. He peered around and found her standing on the deck to his left. Light from the candle chandelier was spilling out of the bedroom windows illuminating her. Beside her were two chairs with washcloths and towels and there were several pails of water on the deck.

And she was completely naked.

Wow. Yeah. This was going to be a hot night.

Brady's cock went into primal awareness mode as he watched her. She was standing him and, facing away from him, watching lightning flicker across the sky. She was wiping a washcloth along the back of her neck, her hand lifting her wet strands of hair.

It appeared she'd washed her hair and had gotten started with the sponge bath without him.

He swung his gaze downward over her growing breasts, to her baby bump, which he swore her breasts and pregnancy bump were bigger than the last time he'd seen her a few days earlier.

Just watching the delicious curve of her belly, knowing a baby was growing inside of her, made him feel incredibly protective for both mother and unborn child. Made him feel possessive of her too and he also wanted to make her happy and to pleasure her.

"About time you showed up. I thought you went swimming," JJ said softly.

He hadn't thought she'd heard him, but she had.

He opened the screen door and stepped outside to join her.

JJ'S HEART THUNDERED with awareness at the creak of the screen door as Brady came outside. She could hear his heavy, rapid breathing as he neared her. Felt her own pulse react as his body heat splashed against her warm flesh.

Lightning was really blinking all around them now, showing off all his yummy assets.

"I thought you didn't want me to get hit by lightning, so I saved myself for you," he said with a chuckle as he took the washcloth from her and dipped it into one of the cold-water buckets.

"I don't mind if you do, I just don't want anything to happen to your scrumptious balls," she teased and gasped as he wiped the wet cloth along the back of her shoulders. Although she'd already washed her hair and was feeling better after dousing water over herself, the coolness of the washcloth felt like heaven.

"Hmm, you like my balls do you?" he mumbled as he followed up the wet area on her shoulders with a few hot kisses.

"And other parts too, of course."

She nodded to the farthest bucket of water.

"That one there contains the warm water. I don't want you shrinking on me with chilly water, so I'll use that one when the time comes."

She let her gaze drop to his engorged penis to let him know what she meant and blew out an aroused breath as she surveyed his erection. It was long and thick, and his body was looking hard and tense as he watched her.

"I can see you didn't go for a swim in the cold water," she added.

A surprised expression flittered across his face at her comment and then he understood and burst out laughing. It was a loud booming laugh that echoed throughout the surrounding forest.

"Is that what this is about?" he finally asked after he'd finished laughing.

JJ nodded, holding back her own laughter, trying to keep a straight face.

"You were afraid my cock would shrink in the cold water, and I'd have polar penis? That's why you didn't want me to go for a swim?"

"The thought did cross my mind," she teased.

Truth be told, she seriously didn't want him to get hit by lightning while swimming in the lake, but she wanted to play with him for a bit.

"The lake water isn't *that* cold. But you are one selfish woman. I think I need to get some punishment going on you for being so self-interested," he growled.

JJ smiled, shook her head, and reached for a fresh washcloth. She dipped it into the cold-water bucket and then rubbed it against the bar of soap.

"Not before I punish you for taking so long to get back to me," she said.

He inhaled sharply as she slapped the cold wet washcloth across his broad chest.

She enjoyed the soft curses that followed and then she took her time to soap him. He moaned with gratitude as she smoothed over his taut muscles knowing he must have been quite heated from working in the sun today.

She dipped the cloth into the bucket several times, generously soaping it each time, telling him to lift his arms so she could lather him beneath his armpits too. His sharp intakes of breath made her believe he truly appreciated this intimate gesture and sensed he would feel quite refreshed.

When he was all sweet-smelling, she returned to washing his chest, enjoying the trembling of his chest muscles beneath the washcloth as she soaped him there.

She loved the way his nipples were beading as she gently cleaned his areoles.

"I think I'll get in on this action too," he said, his breaths getting louder.

He picked up a clean washcloth, dipped it into the water, soaped it and began to lather her chest. The coolness of the wet cloth seemed like a bolt of welcome ice against her increasingly hot flesh. He touched her gently as he smoothed the soapy cloth over the curves of her tender breasts.

They fell quiet, taking their time, just soaping each other while brilliant sparkles of lightning shot through the black sky above them. Thunder boomed close by.

But she didn't mind. Her breaths were coming faster too as Brady brushed the washcloth over her nipples at the same time she was tending to his nipples.

He was mirroring her, she realized.

This was fun.

After she rinsed the cloth, she wiped away the soap from his nipples. Then slowly leaned forward and lapped at the man boob on his right side. He groaned his approval. It was a guttural primal sound that shot spears of eagerness through her.

She took his taut warm nipple between her lips and began to play with it with her tongue, laving and bushing until he was moaning, and it was pebble hard. Then she moved to his other nipple, sucking on the hot bud until he was cursing softly.

"I'm glad you like that, Brady," JJ muttered, drawing her mouth from his chest.

She was about to dip a new washcloth into a nearby clean pail to continue washing him but gasped as his luscious lips enclosed her right nipple. His five o'clock bristles from his face rasped her sensitive flesh and the pressure of his mouth sucking on her shot arrows of pleasure deep down inside of her pussy. She moaned in approval.

"I'm glad you like that, baby mamma," he breathed against her nipple.

JJ couldn't help but giggle at him echoing her earlier words and then she moaned again as he quickly left her nipple to slurp her other nipple into his mouth.

"You sure do have a way with those lips," JJ gasped as she dropped the washcloth and smoothed her hands upward, over the hard, smooth curves of his biceps.

Brady tugged and sucked sending zips of pleasure to parts down south. She writhed, enjoying what he was doing to her.

Oh yes, she liked this kind of foreplay.

Excitement zapped into her, and she slapped her hands upon his hot shoulders as she braced herself.

She knew what was coming.

Once Brady started suckling, she was in for an intense ride.

He cupped her breasts and began a tender massage, and at the same time his teeth rasped over her throbbing nipple, his lips sucking. She was already a bra size bigger, and her nipples were getting larger too just like they had during her first pregnancy. They were getting darker also and oh, so sensitive.

He must have noticed her sharp inhales of breath because suddenly he eased a bit on the sucking. It felt good. So yummy to have his lips on her nipple. Her appreciative moans flew around the night air as his beautiful mouth tended to each of her aching peaks.

Excitement was rushing through her body as he finally let go. Then they collected the washcloths again, she dipping hers into the warm water bucket and then soaping it. She kneaded the warm cloth down his lower abdomen, feeling his muscles clench and listening to the hissing of his lips as he pursed them and inhaled.

"Easy there, baby. I'm really hot for you tonight," he warned as she plunged lower.

"I wouldn't have it any other way," she replied as she gently lathered his scrotum, watching his eyelids drop with arousal and his cock grow even harder.

"Oh, this must hurt beautifully," she mused as she washed along the base of his thick shaft, and moved along the length, feeling his penis thicken against her cloth.

"You don't know how much, baby," Brady grumbled.

As she soaped his shaft, he prepared a washcloth for her, and she inhaled in shock as he slid the soapy cool cloth between her spread legs and began an erotic rubbing along her quivering clitoris.

She swore softly as her vagina clenched and her clit throbbed intensely as he massaged.

"Oh, this must hurt so beautifully," he said, amusement etching his voice as he echoed her earlier words.

"You don't how much," she said between clenched teeth.

Oh yes, his touches were shooting flames of desire through her, and she could feel her juices flowing down her vagina, preparing herself for him. The heat of arousal was coursing like molten lava. Her bared breasts were heaving with her every quickening breath and her pussy was becoming fever hot.

Her body felt too tight, and she was surprised that she was able to continue washing Brady. She dipped the washcloth into the warm bucket again and soaped it, then continued stroking him, until his shaft was pulsing so hard, she could feel it moving like a serpent against the washcloth.

Her vagina clenched as she imagined him sliding his cock into her. Her lower abdomen became heavy with need, and her vagina felt like it was dropping open like a blossoming flower. The familiar shudders of an oncoming orgasm signalled a warning that she was going to climax soon. She sensed Brady was nearing his breaking point too as his harsh breathing boomed in her ears.

They would need to rinse off all this soap first though before they made love.

Just then she felt the first drops of rain and smiled. The rain would rinse them off.

She whipped her cloth away and grabbed the one from Brady's hand, letting it drop.

Ignoring his surprised look, she slapped her hands upon his warm shoulders, loving the flex of his hard rounded muscles beneath her fingers as she got up on her tippy toes and melded her lips against his. The impact of her mouth against his burned blazes of lightning throughout her brain.

Yeah, she'd been wanting to do this again since he'd first shown up tonight.

His hands curled around her waist, and he pulled her against him. She shuddered at the heavy length of his cock pressing against her right thigh.

The rain grew heavier, soaking them. Lightning flashed. Thunder cracked nearby.

She just wanted to keep kissing him.

"It's raining," he whispered as he broke the kiss.

He stared down at her, his eyes flashing with heat. His hot breaths fanned across her face like a fierce wind. But then she realized it was the breeze too. A nice, refreshing wind that made her very happy.

"Let it rain," she breathed and took his mouth again.

He kissed her back, his lips opening up taking her like she was his possession. She liked that. Liked belonging to him. His kisses made her feel so sensitive. So alive. All her nerve endings were firing in a searing way.

She kissed him harder, rougher, wanting a closer impact.

She gyrated her hips, feeling his cockhead now smoothing over her throbbing knot of nerves. He was using his hot cockhead as a clit stimulator, and it was sending shockwaves and shivers into her body, making her nuts with need.

The rain poured down. It felt like heaven had opened up and was making love to them with all this rain. The cool liquid felt so wonderful on her hot skin, and the watery rivulets washed over her hair and down her shoulders.

She massaged her wet breasts against his chest, inhaling harshly at the pinpricks of pain and pleasure as his hard muscles pushed against her sensitized nipples.

Oh man! He was exactly what she craved tonight.

Now, if he would just...

As if sensing what she needed just now, he thrust his velvet hard penis into her creamy vagina. His thick muscular shaft plunging deep within, caressing all her needy muscles and he just owned her.

Her pussy gripped hold of his rigid flesh, hugging him, loving him, but then he withdrew.

She cried into his mouth as he left her body and moaned as he stretched into her again. The painful pleasure was quickly building. It was racing through her at lightning speed. She was going to lose herself any second now.

A couple of more well-aimed thrusts from his luscious cock and she was shattering into a frenzy just like the storm thrashing around them.

The pleasure was bone-deep, and her climax was long and convulsive.

Oh, this was so good, and it went on and on, like beautiful waves of ecstasy cascading over her.

His cock was strong and pulsing as he kept pistoning. Then his body quivered, and she knew he was nearing his release and soon he was joining her, both of them spiraling into the world of thunder and lightning and shivers and spasms.

Chapter Six

Later, they lay spooned in each other's arms on two mattresses they'd thrown onto the floor from the bunk beds. Rain pummelled the roof and wind lashed the two slightly opened windows shooting in fresh air that chased away the humid heat in the room.

JJ was fast asleep, her soft naked curves tucked safely against Brady's front. Her sweet ass pushed against his cock. Her long legs pressed against his legs. His hand was splayed over her pregnancy, keeping baby protected.

He loved the feel of her warm baby bump, felt so emotional thinking the baby was probably sleeping just like his or her mamma. He couldn't wait to meet this new kid. Couldn't wait to introduce Chrissy to her new baby sister or baby brother. What would she think seeing a little kid around? How would she react? Would she be inquisitive? Jealous?

He remembered when he'd been a kid, he'd been curious whenever his mom and dad brought home a new baby. But then jealousy would kick in at times when the younger kids got more attention than he did. He was after all the oldest, and it should have occurred to him that he didn't need such undivided attention as the younger ones did.

Yeah, it had been immature of him to pout and be a brat. He knew that now, but back then, well...he'd been immature. He'd been a kid. That's what kids did.

But he'd give anything to have his mom and dad back alive and well so they could meet their grandkid or grandkids as the case might be. He knew without a doubt they would love all their grandchildren unconditionally. Mom would teach them all how to bake and dad would teach them hunting skills.

Brady snuggled closer to JJ. He should rest. Morning would come quickly. But they'd eaten a late supper, and he wasn't used to going to bed on a full stomach. He just couldn't fall asleep. Especially because he could hear snorting sounds drifting in along with the wind and knew instinctively the barbecue had drawn in a bear or possibly more.

After they'd made love in the downpour, they'd finally come inside, towel dried and gone around closing the windows to keep the rain out. They'd left the ones in the bedrooms cracked open just enough so not too much rain could blow in if the wind got bad.

The fresh air was heavenly, and Brady breathed in the pine scented air deeply as he listened to the bear or bears following their snorting noses to find out where that barbecue smell had come from.

At one point he thought he'd seen a shadow at the window, but he wasn't sure as when lightning blinked nothing had been there. But just imagining bears being around had his heart thumping pretty loudly in his ears. He knew JJ would have stored any left-over food in the cooler in the kitchen so the animals probably couldn't smell anything and wouldn't attempt a break in. If they did, he had the rifle, but it was at the other end of the cabin.

Come to think of it, it probably would have been a wise idea to bring it into the bedroom.

Well, too late now. He didn't want to move away and risk waking JJ.

The wind was pretty fierce though, howling through the trees. He could hear branches cracking and he was surprised she just kept on sleeping. He was glad she was in slumber land, or she'd be anxious about there being bears just outside these walls.

He wondered how many more trees would be blown over onto the trails again. He'd have to take the atv out and start cutting on the way back home. He had enough canned food on hand to keep him going for several weeks, but if the trails were bad, he'd just call JJ and she'd fly in and pick him up here at the round-up cabin.

Brady smiled as he thought about JJ coming to their rescue on several occasions with the floatplane. Rafe having his leg seriously cut by the axe, Dan getting trapped in an animal trap and Brady when he'd gotten tetanus at the secluded cabin.

She'd flown in like a hero with her plane and rescued each of them from their respective dangerous adventures. Had they not had a plane, things wouldn't have worked out so good for any of them.

Then he frowned and shivered as a cold sense of foreboding rippled through him.

His JJ. A freaking pilot. He'd never liked the idea of her being a pilot. Too damned dangerous. But she was a stubborn one, insisting that a plane would be good for Moose Ranch. She'd been right. It didn't mean he had to like it though.

She'd even gone down with the plane once when she'd run into mechanical difficulties. Man, that had been about a year ago when she'd been pregnant with Chrissy. She'd been with a friend, thankfully. But they'd been missing, and he and Rafe and Dan had been so damned worried.

But the women had walked out of the forest right in front of him, with him thinking they were bears at first and him coming close to shooting them.

Shit. He'd never been so happy to see anyone in his entire life. He'd hugged the shit out of her then and hugged JJ closer now and buried his face into her sweet-smelling hair.

Man, if anything ever happened to her, he would most likely lose his mind.

Another snorting sound zipped through the open windows and Brady stiffened. He waited a long time and listened to the rain and thunder and watched the lightning play at the windows.

After awhile he didn't hear anything anymore.

He slept.

THE DAYS FLEW BY SO fast that before JJ knew it, the weekend of Kelly's surprise wedding shower had arrived. So much had happened since that night she'd spent with Brady at the round-up cabin. That night she'd slept so wonderfully being cradled by Brady's strong arms and his powerful body. She'd felt so safe and loved.

The next morning had brought fresh, cool air and bright, beautiful sunshine and some storm damage.

She couldn't believe she'd slept through it. Large tree branches were strewn all around the cabin, thankfully nothing, aside from the trees, had been damaged. Her plane survived without a scratch and Brady had decided to return to Moose Ranch with her, leaving the checking of the trails for another time.

A few days later, Dr. Willie gave Dan the go ahead to get back to work full-time and he and Brady had headed out to ween calves from their mothers as well as to do some castrating and other work.

Rafe picked up the task of assessing the trails and fences. He reported the damage had been minimal and had fixed some of the major problems with fences down and he'd cleared some trails. But he hadn't checked everywhere because the weather was turning hot again, and the haying needed doing while the weather was good. He had also found that a couple more calves had been killed by wolves up that way.

Rafe had also taken inventory of what was needed to make the round-up cabin appropriate for long-time living. Then he'd returned to haying, leaving some fencing and chain sawing for Brady or Dan still to be done. All three men had agreed they would work on the cabin in any spare time.

The four of them had discussions about hiring new hands, making many notes and they'd agreed it was best to have them housed at the round-up cabin. They had then talked to Brady's sister, Jenna, at length, sending her all the requirements they needed in new hands, and she said she would put into motion a search for two eligible convicts through Cowboys Online.

The guys had come home every night, which JJ loved, and she showed her love by showering them with hearty meals and lots of attention in the bedroom, which made them and herself quite happy.

Her days were spent with Chrissy, who was tumbling around like a little beach ball. It wouldn't be long before she was crawling and then standing, and JJ couldn't wait to see that happen.

She loved every minute of her life, even the laundry and the dishes and especially the strolls down to the dock with her daughter in her arms to watch the beautiful sunsets.

Finally, the time arrived to go to the city, and she didn't want to go. She loved her routine here on Moose Ranch, but she also realized she should push past her comfort zone and go.

Just yesterday they'd received a phone call from Mitch, Brady's brother over at Snowy Creek Ranch, letting JJ know not to pick up Milena because she'd gone to the city with Daegen and would be spending a few days there. But Milena would meet her at the wedding shower this afternoon.

JJ smiled as she thought about Milena. Her friend had hooked up with all three men at Snowy Creek Ranch and JJ couldn't be more thrilled for her. She deserved all the happiness in the world, especially with being incarcerated in prison for so many years and not having a loving family to care for her during her teenage years. It appeared someone in heaven was now looking out for her.

This morning when JJ called in her flight plan, she'd been warned about possible severe weather conditions this afternoon, due to the increasing heat and humidity, but she'd flown in dangerous weather before, and she felt confident she could handle any storms that might pop up.

Besides, she'd be in Thunder Bay by the time storms burst anyway.

As she sat in the cockpit and looked out the windows, another intense longing to stay home snapped through her. She bit back a wave of tears as Dan stood on the dock and shouted to her letting her know all the ropes were untied and the plane was free.

She waved acknowledgment and goodbye. Halfway up the trail, Brady held Chrissy in his strong embrace, and he was holding her little hand up showing her how to wave.

JJ's heart clenched with such an intensity that she could only explain it as love. She smiled and waved back at them.

Adrenalin pumped through her as she started the plane. The roar of the engine crashed through the peaceful quiet of the early morning.

As the engine rattled, she checked all of the gauges. Everything appeared normal. She radioed in to air traffic control that she was ready to head out. She was cleared for takeoff almost immediately, with yet another reminder that severe weather could happen in the afternoon.

JJ acknowledged and then moved the plane away from the dock.

"Here we go," she said softly as she slowly maneuvered the plane toward the east end of the lake, watching for any signs of deadhead logs in the mirror flat water. Sometimes logs got pried loose from swampy areas due to the wind or waves or trees fell into the lake and began to float half submerged or just below the waterline. She was always cautious when it came to keeping an eye out for debris in the water. Any kind of damage to the pontoons could prove costly to her life and her unborn baby and to Moose Ranch's pocketbook.

Thankfully today she didn't feel anxious or panicky. Feeling calm was always a good thing when she went up in the plane because then flying was so much more enjoyable.

When she reached near the end of the lake, she made a wide turn and then increased the power. Sunlight glinted off the windshields. The plane roared louder. She began a fast pace forward down the middle of the lake, leaving a trail of white waves in the plane's wake.

Moments later the plane felt lighter, and she sighed in relief. She was airborne, sailing easily into the blue cloudless sky. Another successful takeoff. The idea of it filled her with glee.

She dipped the plane's wings in a way to say goodbye to those below. Then Moose Ranch and its scattering of outer buildings disappeared as she soared over the treetops of the nearby forest and angled the plane in a wide arc northward so she could take a peek at Rafe, which she'd promised to do when he'd left this morning.

"AND THERE GOES YOUR mom," Brady said in a quiet voice to Chrissy as she stared wide-eyed at the sky where JJ's plane had vanished. Soon the last putter of the plane's engine also disappeared, and Brady sighed.

Time had flown by so quickly since their night at the round-up cabin and now JJ was gone for the entire weekend. He hadn't told her about the bears that had been prowling around that night, because there was no need to scare her. But he had been surprised at seeing all the branches down around that cabin though, as he'd slept through it all himself. And he'd found her apron, nicely soaked, surprisingly exactly where he'd left it by the water pump.

He hugged his baby girl to his chest, pressing his cheek against her velvety cheek. She smelled so fresh and felt so warm and snuggly. He could hold onto her and this overwhelming emotion of love for her, forever. But she wasn't having anything to do with the hug for long, as she suddenly reached up and grabbed the tip of his nose and held tight.

"You've got a mighty fine grip on you, daughter," he laughed.

"Let's hope her dad has a good grip today. Your turn to do the northeast quarter. Remember what Rafe said, there are some fences down due to branches dropping on them," Dan said as he joined them.

"Yup, he drew me a map of the affected areas," Brady acknowledged.

"I can do it you know. I'm fine now," Dan prodded.

"Give it a few more days and then you can do what's left over. There's plenty of hard labor waiting for you," Brady said.

He was prepared for an argument from Dan, and he was relieved when he didn't get one.

Since the doctor had cleared Dan for full duties, Brady had let him do some lighter stuff, like castrating and tagging the cattle, assisting with births, ordering supplies, bookkeeping and other chores. He just wanted to ease his friend back into the ranch work gently after having such a long down time.

While Chrissy continued her fine grip on Brady's nose, they wandered back up to the ranch house. It was quiet as they entered the building. Rafe had left a couple of hours ago and JJ was now gone.

Brady wasn't a hundred percent comfortable leaving his daughter alone with Dan for the day, but the doctor had assured them that if anything bad were to happen to Dan it would have happened by now.

He wasn't willing yet to let Dan repair the fencing as it was a hard job. Besides, Rafe had also said he hadn't gotten all the new fallen trees off the trails in the area either, so Brady could get on to that job too.

When the new hands arrived, they'd be put to work widening the atv trails so there wouldn't be too many more issues in the future where fallen trees on the trails were concerned.

"Okay Chrissy, you stay with Uncle Dan. He'll entertain you."

She was staring at Brady, studying him and then her blue eyes sparkled, and he swore she understood that he was leaving her as a couple of tears dripped from her eyes.

"Shit, Brady. You're making her cry. Just don't look at her like that, man. All sad and sorry to go. She can read you like a book," Dan chastised.

Chrissy frowned and she let go of Brady's nose, a furrow dipping between her pretty eyebrows.

"Oh shit, she knows you're about to leave. Hand her over," Dan grumbled.

Brady wanted to tell Dan not to swear in front of Chrissy, but heck, she wasn't talking yet, so it didn't matter.

Reluctantly he gave Chrissy over to Dan who quickly started making faces at her and she began to giggle in his arms.

"You're already forgotten, Dad. Now grab your gear and sneak out," Dan mumbled as he made a cross-eyed look that made himself look crazy.

Chrissy laughed.

Brady shook his head. Had someone made a face like that to him when he'd been a kid, he would have run away screaming. His daughter must not scare easy. She was a tough little girl.

While Dan entertained her, Brady headed into the kitchen, grabbed the cooler filled with food off the counter and quickly strode down the hall.

His daughter's giggles chased him out the door.

RAFE WAVED HIS COWBOY hat to JJ as he watched her fly low over the meadow where he was haying. The white plane glistened beneath the early morning rays of golden sunshine.

He smiled and let out a giant whoop that had several nearby Angus mooing in the adjoining meadow, as the plane flew overhead.

Rafe didn't care that they were disturbed by the big white bird flying over their heads. The little buggers had kept him awake many nights with their mooing when he'd camped in the area. It was about time he got to disturb their peace.

He watched as JJ dipped her plane wings to show she'd seen him and then she was gone, flying low over the treeline arcing around and heading toward the city. The drone of the engine was soon gone, leaving him alone with a bunch of mooing cattle.

Rafe chuckled, slapped his cowboy hat back on his head and started up the tractor. As he began haying again he thought about JJ and the baby she was carrying.

He could not get over how lucky he was to have her. Few women would put up with taking care of three men, let alone have sex with them. He was glad she was getting off the property for a weekend with lady company. She would have fun and it was about time too. She deserved to have some alone time.

His smile turned upside down as he gazed up at the clear blue sky. He just hoped that the plane knew what precious cargo it carried.

THE FLIGHT PROCEEDED uneventfully, and JJ splashed down at the private airport just outside of the city a little over two hours later. She was thrilled to see several familiar water planes secured to the docks. Blue's blue float plane sparkled brilliantly under the hazy sunshine, JJ's midwife, Layla's beautiful yellow Cessna added to the colorful arrangement and Kayley, the pilot instructor who had taught JJ how to fly, had her new emerald-green bird secured at a slip.

But she didn't see Kelly's red plane, so either she had not arrived yet or Blue had flown her in.

There were numerous other planes here too, in a rainbow of colors. The sight made JJ swell with pride. To be a part of the pilot clan felt so humbling and also made her feel important in her achievement of attaining her goal of becoming a pilot despite all her mental health issues. She liked that feeling of accomplishment.

She climbed out of her plane and gasped as the humidity blasted against her face like a furnace and took her breath away. The sunshine burned her skin and JJ wished she were back home.

Mercy! It was really hot now compared to when she'd left Moose Ranch. Within a minute, perspiration popped out all over her skin as she worked quickly to secure her plane. Once her plane was tied down, her clothing, which were a pair of tan cotton shorts and a loose-fitting blue maternity blouse, felt like they were uncomfortably sticking to her skin. She climbed back inside her plane, grabbed her small knapsack, and slung it on her damp back.

She picked up her tiny suitcase, climbed outside, locked the door, and stepped back onto the dock. Then she hurried toward the check-in kiosk at the little airport. There she would find a taxi to take her to the inexpensive motel she'd picked close to the restaurant that Blue had reserved for the bridal shower.

Since her invitation to the shower, JJ and Blue had exchanged several emails where JJ had asked if Blue needed help decorating or if she needed some sort of financial contribution toward the party, but Blue had told her all was under control and to just bring herself and a present.

JJ hoped Kelly liked what she got her. The present was waiting for JJ when she checked into the motel a half an hour later. She had arranged everything online; the purchase of the bridal shower present, the gift wrapping and a beautiful card. She had paid by using her new online credit card and had arranged for the delivery to the motel where they'd agreed to hold onto it for her for a small fee.

The motel room was small but cozy and clean. It had one double bed, and the room was decorated in dark blue and sharp red tones. Framed photos of various tourist areas around the city of Thunder Bay decorated the walls which were old fashioned brown wood panelling. The air smelled a bit musty though. There was a television set that had seen better days, and the small bathroom contained a small shower stall with a window that did not have a working lock. Not good.

An air conditioner whirred noisily in the main room window, which kept the area nice and cool, and she was so thankful for it because she sure felt warm despite getting a ride over in an air-conditioned car.

JJ wasn't in the room more than five minutes when the motel phone rang.

"Hello," she said into the receiver.

"Hey, it's me. How did your flight go? How are you feeling? Everything alright?"

JJ smiled. It was Dan.

"Checking up on me already? I just got here actually, and all went well. How is Chrissy?" She opted not to confess to him how incredibly hot and humid it was in the city.

"She's having an early lunch. She's enjoying some mashed steak and potatoes, orange juice, and some squished up spinach."

JJ scrunched up her face at the mention of spinach. She had never been a fan. Had never even thought to try to see if Chrissy might enjoy it.

"How does she like it?" She cringed as she awaited his answer.

"So far she's loving it. You should see the face that she's making. Her baby blue eyes are wide with wonder, and she is asking me what is this delicious delight Uncle da da Dan is feeding me?"

JJ laughed.

"She certainly doesn't take after me in that regard," she said.

"Actually, I was just kidding. She hates the stuff. Spit it out faster then I could shove it in," he replied with a chuckle.

JJ stifled another laugh as she imagined her daughter spitting green and poor Dan probably being shocked at the sight.

"But I thought I would try anyway. Just so you know, she is having no problem eating her mashed carrots or that plum baby food in the jar she loves so much. I just want her to get her fruits and vegetables y'know," Dan said in a serious tone.

"Well, that's one less worry for us. I thought she might not eat if I wasn't around."

Chrissy went through phases like that. There was one period of time she refused to eat unless her dad was around, which had caused JJ a great deal of anxiety and lately her daughter had been acting that way when JJ wasn't there.

"Hey, can I help it if I'm a good cook? Hey, Chrissy wants to talk to you. I'm holding the phone to her ear. Talk to her," Dan instructed with eagerness.

"Hey baby girl, what are you doing with Uncle Dan? Do you miss mommy already? What are you going to do later today?"

JJ could hear her daughter's breathing quicken and she made some noises and gasps. Then she heard a little giggle that made her heart burst with pleasure.

"Are you going for a swim later? It's getting really hot out. I bet you'd enjoy a swim in the lake," JJ continued.

Her daughter was really breathing faster now, and JJ could hear her trying to say something.

"Okay, Mom, I've got to go because you've got her all excited. Her little feet are kicking up a storm. And I'm afraid she might tip over the high chair here, so I'll let you go. Have a fun time. I'll talk to you later. Okay, come on baby, let's settle down..." she heard Dan say in a gentle tone.

JJ laughed imagining her daughter sitting in the high chair. Her hands were probably curled into tight little fists, and she was most likely smashing all the food bowls on her tray, while she kicked her feet in glee. She did that when she got excited to see all the men come home every night.

"Okay talk to you later. I love you," she said softly, feeling her homesickness smash into her like a train. She hoped Dan hadn't heard her voice crack.

"Love you, too, sweet baby mamma. Enjoy your weekend!" Then the line went dead.

JJ blew out an emotional breath.

When she hung up, she almost decided to make her excuses and go home. She wanted to see her daughter. Wanted to be with her cowboys. She inhaled a deep breath and stared at the shower present on the bed.

She'd had the gift wrapped in a pretty country style floral paper. Red, white, and pink roses with sharp white background and a pretty pink ribbon and puffy bow. It looked even nicer in real life than it had on the online site where she'd bought the gift and the wrapping paper.

JJ sighed and settled her hands over her baby bump and caressed gently, feeling an incredible warmth of love embrace her heart.

"We're in this together, sweet baby. Mommy needs to stay strong and not be so selfish. We came for a bridal shower and by golly we're going to it!" But somewhere at the back of her mind, a little voice echoed saying maybe she could even leave the city late this afternoon right after the shower and surprise everyone by getting home tonight.

Having that thought suddenly made her very happy and she began laying out the clothing and makeup she would wear for the party. She had just a little under two hours to shower and change, order an uber, and to get to the venue.

So, she'd best get to it!

A COUPLE OF HOURS LATER, JJ walked into the restaurant where Blue had instructed they would all meet for the shower. When JJ told the red-haired hostess why she was here, the woman of about fifty, who wore the largest golden hoop earrings JJ had ever seen and was dressed up in an elegant plum colored dress that accented her shapely figure, became all smiles, introducing herself as Donna. Then she led JJ through the almost full restaurant where so many people were eating, talking, and laughing.

So much noise. It hurt her ears and made her nervous.

She was so thankful when Donna opened up a set of glass doors at the end of a hall and ushered JJ inside a large room, which was as quiet and cool as can be. Immediately, JJ felt relieved.

Gosh, she was so used to the nature and quiet of Moose Ranch that it appeared any loud people sounds were now overwhelming. But she shouldn't be reacting this way because the guys were a pretty loud and boisterous bunch. Then again, her cowboys were familiar. This place was not.

Another round of anxiety shifted through her, and she forced herself to focus on keeping her breathing even and to look at the decorations, which were quite lovely.

White, red, and gold streamers hung from the ceiling and white magnolia flowers and red roses and gold balloons were everywhere.

There were bunches tied together with white ribbons at various places on the three lovely red brick walls and on the one glass wall, of which consisted of the glass doors she had just entered.

"The other ladies are waiting in the next room. The door is just over there," Donna pointed to an open doorway and JJ could hear an occasional giggle and laugh coming from the other room.

Down the middle of this room was a long buffet table clad in white linen tablecloth with an assortment of party sandwiches displayed on various silver stands. There were salads in large glass bowls and glasses and thick slices of cakes and cupcakes arranged on serving trays, and at the beginning of the table there were stacks of gorgeous white plates with gold trim, gold cutlery and piles of pretty sky-blue colored napkins.

"Help yourself to some food and bring it into the other room where you can join the ladies. There are tables in there to set your food. There are beverages in the other room too. You can place your gift right over there." She pointed to a stand near the open doorway where more laughter was erupting.

Wow, that stand was overflowing with presents of all sizes and colorful wrapping paper. Some presents were even on the floor.

"The bride-to-be will be coming through another door, so she'll see all of you first and then later someone will bring in the presents. Now if you'll excuse me, I've got to wait for the bride-to-be and the maid of honor. Someone will let you all know before they arrive at your room. So, get ready to yell surprise when that happens. Have fun."

JJ thanked the woman, blew out a tense breath and quickly strolled over to the stand with the presents, her sandals quietly echoing on the pristine white ceramic tiled floor. She swallowed at her suddenly dry throat and placed her present amongst the pile of others.

Goodness, her present looked so small and plain compared to the other gifts that had extravagant bows and lavish colors of white, silver, gold, and other flashy decor. Nervousness splashed through her. This was her first ever bridal shower, and she hadn't had too much time to surf the internet to research the proper etiquette of what type of present to bring.

Had she screwed up with the gift she'd gotten for Kelly?

Suddenly she just wanted to leave.

"JJ!" came a woman's call from behind her.

JJ turned around to find her neighbour and friend, Milena, standing in the doorway to the room where all the ladies that had come to the bridal shower were seated.

Her face was full of excitement as she rushed over and embraced JJ in a warm hug that squeezed a lot of tension out of her. Her hug was long and oh so needed. When she pulled away she took JJ by her hands and stared at her.

"I'm so glad you're here. I've missed you. How is your pregnancy coming along? You look ravishing and obviously the baby is growing. He or she is going to be a big one," she said as her gaze dropped to JJ's baby bump.

JJ laughed. Lately, the two of them had met up a couple of times over at Moose Ranch when Mitch had come to visit his brother, Brady, and to use the Internet for orders as Snowy Creek Ranch didn't have Internet access.

Each time the two of them had visited, Milena asked all kinds of questions as to how JJ was feeling and how she was handling her anxiety issues while pregnant. Just talking to Milena always made JJ's day. Just like it was now.

"Baby is growing like a weed. Morning sickness is gone."

"Oh good. How is your anxiety? Better?"

JJ shrugged.

"It comes and it goes. I can handle it." Most of the time, she added silently.

Milena smiled warmly.

"I'm glad. Remember it's a work-in-progress trying to get a handle on your anxiety and remember what Layla said too, hormones has a lot to do with it."

She'd had anxiety way before she'd become pregnant, but JJ wasn't about to remind Milena about their prison years. Suddenly JJ just wanted the topic off herself.

"Well, you look really nice!" JJ complimented as she surveyed Milena.

Her friend wore makeup, which she rarely did, and it really made her look so different. She'd also curled her light brown hair, and it shone beautifully beneath the lights. She wore a sleeveless light green colored cotton dress that gave her a cool breezy look.

"Thanks, I just bought it yesterday. Hey, I am so glad you are here. Sorry for bailing on you but Daegen had an appointment here in the city and he asked if I'd like to come along with him, so I did. He's taking me out to dinner tonight and he's rented a plane for tomorrow, and he wants to show me the mountains they have up this way. And then the next day, we're going to a horse show. Oh my gosh, I had no idea we had mountains in Northern Ontario. Would you like to come along with us? It will be fun!" Milena gushed.

JJ stiffened at that request. She wanted to go back home. Possibly tonight. And she wanted Milena to enjoy herself with Daegen. He was such a nice man and most likely wanted some one-on-one time with her.

"Oh, no thanks. I've got other plans," JJ replied, hoping Milena wouldn't prod her any further.

Thankfully, she didn't.

"Okay, that's okay. Blue said she'd give us a lift back in a couple of days. So, don't worry about us. Hey, listen, everyone is here except

Blue and Kelly. And I might add you look so beautiful. You wear your pregnancy so well. And I love your dress. Turn around, girlfriend. Let me inspect."

JJ laughed, feeling self conscious as she did a slow turn.

She'd worn a floral print with butterflies maternity dress with a scalloped collar, and short sleeves.

"You look like a breath of fresh air," Milena gushed.

JJ wasn't used to getting compliments, except from her cowboys, so she felt her cheeks flush with heat.

"Come on over to the buffet. The food here is absolutely delicious," Milena said as she hooked her arm with JJ's, and they strolled over to the long table laden with the food.

"I've already had a little, but I was waiting for you. I saved you a seat beside me, so we can chat."

Relief poured through JJ. Although she did know several women, like Milena, Blue, Layla, Kelly, and Kayley, she'd been worried she'd end up sitting beside someone she didn't know. Usually she felt shy around strangers, and knowing Milena was being so kind and thoughtful in thinking about her, made her feel somewhat relaxed.

JJ took a moment to admire all the food, trying to commit items to memory so she could make treats for her guests when she threw her next party which would probably be Christmas, since Jay was going to be surprising Kelly with a Thanksgiving wedding and had invited everyone to be there. Had there been no wedding JJ would have thrown a Thanksgiving party on the October long weekend. She enjoyed planning such festivities, especially for the people she knew.

Milena pointed out that she'd found the pre-portioned salad in the huge margarita style glasses, which were a combination of iceberg lettuce, green leaf lettuce, sliced cucumbers, chopped cherry tomatoes and shavings of carrots, quite fresh and delicious. There was also an arrangement of toppings and dressings nearby for the salad.

She studied the several types of cold cuts, cooked meats, cheese, and other yummies so guests could help themselves to whatever they wanted to try.

JJ found the idea of pre-portioned salad in those type of glasses intriguing as she always made several types of salads in large bowls and let her guests help themselves to what they wanted. She sensed these pre-portioned salads with a display of different toppings and dressings might be a hit if she decided to go with it at her next party.

She followed Milena's lead and grabbed a large plate.

"There's more cutlery and napkins at the other end of the table, and trays there too."

JJ nodded, understanding that the setup of having cutlery, plates, napkins, and such were set on each end so the people could come at the goodies from both ends of the table.

She picked one of those glasses filled with salad and drenched it with mozzarella cheese shavings, grilled chicken bits and a dollop of crumbs of crisp bacon. Then she helped herself to a few finger sandwiches; cucumber-butter, curried egg salad, mortadella-watercress, and chocolate-raspberry.

"I could swear I would eat everything here if I didn't think I'd weigh a ton and make the plane Daegen is renting go lopsided and crash. Wait until you get to the dessert section, it is to die for," Milena laughed, her brown eyes sparkling with excitement, as they both proceeded further down the table.

"Yep, you are right about the dessert," JJ giggled when they reached that area.

"And everything is labelled so you know what you are getting. How cool is that?" Milena said as she used a cake lifter to lift a slice of chocolate ganache layer cake onto her plate. It was followed by a fresh fruit frangipane tart.

JJ helped herself to a luscious looking chocolate covered strawberry and a portion of orange-cranberry bundt cake. They both looked longingly at the vanilla raspberry truffles in the small glasses and JJ decided to go for it.

Milena laughed and helped herself to one too.

"I haven't seen so much gorgeous looking and delicious smelling food since your spring party, JJ," she praised.

JJ felt pride flow through her. She enjoyed cooking and she was happy at Milena's compliment.

"Come on, let's get back and wait for Kelly and Blue," Milena urged.

At the end of the table, they grabbed a tray, some utensils and placed their plates onto the trays.

Then JJ followed her into the other room.

She swore her mouth dropped open as she entered the room. There must have been about fifty women in here. No wonder there had been so many presents and so much food. Blue had truly outdone herself for her best friend.

Fancy white-cushioned chairs with small glass tables in between each chair had been placed in a huge semi circle in the large room that was similarly decorated like the buffet room with puffs of white magnolia, red roses, and gold balloons. It smelled nice in here too. Like the flowers.

Most of the women were sitting, nibbling on food, and chatting. Several women stood at a long table which had a couple of coffee machines and a hot water machine for tea drinkers. There were stacks of white mugs with gold rims, spoons, and napkins.

Beverages of all kinds were set in huge trays of ice on another table. Pop, water bottles, milk cartoons, and even red and white wine bottles and wine glasses.

Wow, this was awesome, JJ thought as she admired everything.

"Come on, this way. We can grab our drinks after we set our stuff down," Milena said as she headed toward the far end of the semi-circle of chairs.

"Hi JJ!" she heard someone call out. It was Kayley. She was waving from the beverage area and JJ wished she could wave back but her hands were full as she carried the tray she'd picked up.

"Hi! Kayley! I'll be over to chat in just a bit" she called back, admiring Kayley's gorgeous long-sleeved peach-colored linen pants suit. She looked so pretty with a new short bob haircut, which made her straight blonde hair flow like golden water as she turned to chat to the woman beside her.

Milena led her to a seat that was right beside Layla, her midwife.

"Hey, how are you? I'm so happy to see you," Layla gushed and immediately took the tray from JJ and set it upon a small table between them.

Wow, even Layla had gussied herself up for the event, wearing a plain midnight blue colored swing dress and matching blue shoes.

Suddenly JJ was really glad she'd come.

THE EVENT LASTED MORE than three hours and JJ was still reeling from everything when she let herself into the motel room.

All that nervousness this morning and the days leading up to Kelly's bridal shower had been for naught. When would she ever learn not to be anxious about things?

She remembered the surprise on Kelly's face when Blue and she had entered and heard all the women shout surprise! She had been truly shocked. Even her face had gone red. She'd been wearing a cute blue dress with white polka dots and Blue had worn a casual V-neck black T-shirt dress.

JJ had been able to chat with all her friends finding out that everyone was doing good. Half way through the opening of presents, her midwife Layla had been summoned away because of client of hers had gone into early labor. Kayley had left right at the end, stating she had a flight instruction class she had to do.

JJ shook her head. Kayley was still always on the go.

Kelly had loved the gift JJ had given her. It was a gift basket with sample packets of coffee from all around the world and two cute Mr. & Mrs. matching mugs. Blue had hinted that Kelly and Jay loved to drink coffee and that's when JJ had decided on what to get for her.

At the end of the shower, Jay had shown up to get Kelly to take her out for dinner. A few friends of theirs would be taking the gifts to Jay's place in the city. JJ had offered to help, but they'd said they were fine, and JJ had been glad because she didn't know any of the women anyways. Blue had been picked up by a date and Milena had been whisked off by Daegen.

That had left JJ all on her own. But she was still glad she'd come.

So, here she was at the motel seesawing between staying for the night in a room she'd paid for or going home.

Oddly enough she wasn't tired, probably because of all the delicious coffee she'd drank with the food and desserts, so she opted to sit down on the bed to watch television while she decided what her next course of action would be.

She reached for the remote and turned on the tv, but nothing happened. She checked to see if it was plugged in. It was. The remote battery was fine. All the attachments on the back of the set were fine.

Hmm, she almost reached for the phone to call the motel lobby and complain about the tv, but that air conditioner was getting on her nerves, it was so noisy. If she turned it off, it would be hot in this room in no time.

Her gaze drew to the bathroom. From here she could clearly see that window with the broken lock.

She looked at her travel clock. There was still several hours of sunlight.

Suddenly her mind was made up. She was going home tonight!

Chapter Seven

"**A**ren't the two of us so lucky that we can take a swim in the lake?" Dan said to Chrissy as he held her beneath her armpits and let her pudgy little legs dangle so she could splash her feet in the water. It was late afternoon, and it was incredibly hot.

He had a moose lasagna cooking in the oven, and he knew the guys would enjoy it after a long day working in this heat. Just thinking about the delicious meat drenched in noodles, mozzarella and parmesan cheeses and sizzling with a bunch of fresh herbs from their garden had Dan drooling.

He laughed as the little girl kicked her pudgy feet. The cool water splashed up like twinkling crystals spraying the both of them and she giggled and kicked some more. He moved further into the lake until the water reached her waist. She began to writhe like a mad woman, her feet kicking harder.

Dan grinned. She was probably wondering why she wasn't able to splash anymore.

Despite that, he knew she'd get a good workout strengthening her muscles. As she kept kicking, Dan gazed out across the sunshine drenched lake.

Haze wavered over the water and the lake shone like a glass mirror. There wasn't a hint of wind as the sun's rays arrowed wicked heat upon his naked back. He held Chrissy in such a way that his body kept her in the shade.

It felt good to be wearing his bathing suit and to be standing in the water with two feet instead of one foot as he'd feared might happen. He could have lost his foot because of that damned animal trap he'd been stuck in.

He was surely glad to be alive too. Hell, he still had nightmares of his foot being stuck in that trap and him having to cut into his ankle, slicing into muscle and sinew and sawing the bone with his jackknife to break himself free. Sometimes he even dreamed about having died from hypothermia and his lifeless corpse was rotting out there while JJ and everyone kept searching for him.

He always worried if there were more old rusty traps in that area. If there had been one, he figured there was a good possibility there were more. He sure did not want anyone else or any animal to experience the same horror he had gone through.

It was not something he would be writing home about either. His parents would just freak out if they found out. As far as they knew he was enjoying his life here on the ranch with Rafe and Brady. He had never told them about JJ or Chrissy or that JJ was pregnant again or about their unique foursome relationship. He had no idea what to say to them on that regard.

They wanted to come for a visit, but he had been putting them off ever since JJ had been here. It was a good thing his mother did not like to fly, nor did she like the desolate wilderness, especially because she thought he lived among the wolves and bears, or they might have actually dropped in unannounced.

He had taken short trips home to visit them. Each time he went his parents looked older. More fragile.

Dan frowned. What if one of them dropped dead? What would happen to the other? It was something he didn't like to think about.

A low rumble of thunder came from the north snapping Dan back to the present.

"Oh, oh, girl. Sounds like a storm is happening where your daddy is working today. I get the feeling they may not make it back tonight."

Dan hoisted little Chrissy from the water and held her wriggling body as he turned to face north. The sky appeared clear, but that did not mean anything. Clouds could be gathering behind the tree line and the storm could blow in quickly.

He wanted to indulge her in a little more play, but his instincts told him to get back to the ranch house. He was glad he had followed his instincts because a few minutes later he and Chrissy were inhaling the delicious scent of moose lasagna while they gazed out the north facing living room windows where ominous dark clouds were quickly stalking toward the sun.

It was a good thing JJ was booked into that motel until tomorrow. He wouldn't want her flying in this nasty weather.

BRADY GAZED OUT THE Misty Lake cabin window as he sipped on his hot coffee and watched the rain pour down in sheets of white. Although the canopy of pine trees and other trees surrounding the cabin was dense, lightning flashed bright light into the cabin windows illuminating the dark interior and he couldn't help but wince at the heavy pounding of rain on the sheet metal roof or tense at every crack of thunder that shook the floorboards and made the thin glass in the windows rattle. Even the wind was getting in on the action, wheezing through the odd cracks in the chinking of the logs holding the cabin together and making the trees dance at awkward angles.

As soon as he'd taken cover in the cabin, he'd called the ranch house and talked to Dan, who said he and Chrissy were tucked away safely inside. That was one less worry.

"Seriously, I did not think you would make it here when you called and said you were going to try and outrun the storm."

"Neither did I," Rafe chuckled from behind Brady.

He turned around and remained silent as Rafe sat at the kitchen table and towel dried his brown hair, his steaming mug of coffee untouched in front of him. He appeared seemingly oblivious at how he had ignored their protocol of taking cover at the first sign of thunder.

After a couple of minutes, Brady broke the silence.

"It was a bad risk, Rafe. You know how fast these summer storms can creep up on us," Brady scolded.

Rafe gazed up at Brady, his deep brown eyes twinkling with amusement.

"Hey, I've got a deck of cards."

Brady inhaled and rolled his eyes. It was like talking to a deaf man.

With this storm, it appeared they wouldn't be going home this evening to enjoy that moose lasagna that Dan had been bragging he'd be making for them for supper, so they may as well amuse themselves with some card games and canned pork and beans.

He was glad that Rafe made it here okay or he would have been worried.

And he was really glad that JJ wasn't coming back tonight.

He wouldn't want her flying in this nasty storm.

"OH CRAP!" JJ SHOUTED as she struggled to keep her float plane flying at an even pace.

She should have stayed at the motel for the night. Should have insisted on a room with a proper lock on the bathroom window, demanded a quiet air conditioner and a working television set. She would have been safe and because of her stubbornness in wanting to go home, she'd put herself and her unborn baby in jeopardy.

How stupid could she be? She should have known better.

She felt the panic rising inside of her like a looming monster as another gust of wind pummeled her plane almost ripping the yoke from her hands. For a moment she felt disoriented. She tried to peer through the dark stormy clouds, but she knew she should concentrate on the instrument panels. They would be her savior if she just didn't panic.

If she did the opposite to what she'd been taught and concentrated on going visual instead of trusting her instruments then she might actually make the plane go upside down or head straight toward the forest or the lake and not even know it, until it was too late.

She focused on what she'd been taught by Kayley, her flight instructor. Trust the instruments not the pilot.

Breathe. You can handle this. Just breathe and that will steady your nerves.

She remembered how happy she'd been after making her decision to go home. Happier than a pig in shit, was what Rafe sometimes said.

When she'd radioed in her flight plan, she'd been warned again that there was a severe weather warning just north of her destination. She should have paid attention to the warning and not thought herself some daredevil swooping low below the clouds, dodging lightning bolts and surprising everyone at home.

She should have turned around the instant she saw those billowing dark clouds on the horizon, but she was so close to home, and she thought she could make it. But the storm had burst like an explosion all around her.

Now she would pay the price and take her baby to his or her death with her.

Oh, stop with the morbid thoughts! You'll live to tell this story. You have to.

She rotated her tight shoulders. Forced herself to loosen up. She had flown in several rain storms since getting her pilot license and she'd handled them.

But none had been like this!

Icy shivers raced up and down her spine as another violent gust of wind smashed against the plane and lightning zipped at the windows. She knew she was almost home, but she also knew she needed to get out of this storm and fast. She reached out to press the microphone to start a mayday, but another burst of wind hit the plane at that second.

Damn! She needed both her hands on the yolk to land.

Anxiety rushed through her, and she began to shake from head to toe. Thankfully, she knew where she was and where she could land.

Once again she was breaking protocol in not radioing in a mayday with an adjustment of her co-ordinates. But she had no choice and angled her plane off course. She brought the plane lower, zipping right above the tree line.

She licked her dry lips and watched white lightning crack the gunmetal blue clouds above her. A sudden sheet of rain pelted the windshield and she saw nothing but rivulets of water.

Oh no! How was she going to see the lake? Suddenly the rain blew away and she could see again.

And her destination was right below.

She sensed she only had a small window of opportunity. She needed to put down now.

Lightning sizzled all around and thunder crashed. Another wave of wind bounced her plane. She checked her co-ordinates and thanked her memory for remembering where Lucas' cabin was on this lake. She'd go to him. She'd be safe at his cabin.

JJ angled the plane around and arrowed down the center of the lake, much in the same way she'd done that one time earlier this year when she'd had a panic attack and landed here in this very desolate lake with many bays only to have Lucas come puttering in his motorboat to see if she were okay.

Oh God, if only he would do that this time.

The sky was so dark now, she swore she'd never seen this color of blue before, and whitecaps were beginning to whip up from the wind. She realized the lake had been almost calm until just now.

Maybe she was at the edge of the storm? Or maybe it had been a lull. Or someone in heaven was parting the sky so she could land.

Suddenly JJ prayed like she'd never prayed before.

JJ held her breath as she splashed her float plane down upon the tumultuous waves. It was a rough landing, but she managed it pretty well. But now the plane bobbed madly on the waves and bounced with every gust of wind, making her feel queasy.

It was noisy in the cockpit. Rain pummeled the plane and windshields and the waves crashed into the pontoons with a vengeance. But she was down and out of the sky. Now she just needed to find refuge.

To her surprise a weird calm came over her as she angled south on the choppy lake toward the area where she remembered the rock outcrop with the towering white pine trees and that cabin she'd once seen.

Her praying must have worked because despite the sheets of rain splashing upon the windshield, the wipers were doing a pretty good job in letting her see the dark shoreline, which was rocky and cluttered with driftwood. She prayed there were no logs floating on the water because she wasn't able to see due to the tumultuous waves and would probably not be able to avert a collision.

She sighed in relief when she spied the rock outcrop and the wood dock. It was small and it appeared to be equipped with the appropriate equipment to protect the plane's pontoons. She took her time, getting pushed off course a couple of times due to the high wind and waves, but finally she was able to motor the plane against the dock.

For a split second she thought about reaching up and activating the Emergency Locator Transmitter that was strapped to the ceiling of the cockpit, but she also realized that the plane was being pushed away from the dock.

She made a split-second decision to not waste the few seconds to do it. She would do it later.

She moved fast, opening the door and stepping out into the howling wind which was so strong it almost tore the door off the plane and almost blew her off the ladder! She struggled to slam the door shut as the wild wind screamed all over her, ripping at her hair which she'd put up into a ponytail before coming on board back in the city. The cold rain drenched her in seconds as she grabbed weathered ropes attached to the dock and quickly began to tie down her plane. She spied another rope tied to a nearby tree, grabbed that one and secured it to her plane.

In this fierce wind, she'd need every available rope. She debated whether to get more from her plane, but that welcome weird calm she'd been experiencing shattered as lightning sizzled through the air too close for comfort. She literally could hear the crackling which made her hyper aware she was in extreme danger. Roaring thunder chased horrid goosebumps up her back.

For a split second she thought about defying her fear and climbing back into the plane and sending out a mayday, activating the Emergency Locator Transmitter, and grabbing her purse with cellphone inside, but another blade of lighting slammed into a nearby tree on the shoreline, slicing it right into two, causing pieces of wood to blow past her like shrapnel along with white sparks and puffs of grey smoke. Thankfully, she didn't get hit by flying pieces, but she heard some loud thunks against the hull of her plane. Unfortunately, she wasn't wasting any time to see if the plane suffered damage because she was out of here!

No time to send a mayday. She'd do it, if need be, when the storm was over.

Top priority was to get inside that cabin. She scrambled up the rocky outcrop, following a line of rock steps and screamed as yet another bolt of lightning sizzled through the air above her.

Oh, dear Lord! Was she about to get hit by lightning?

She called out Lucas' name. Actually shouted. Prayed he would appear at the top of the stony knoll like a hero, telling her it would be okay.

But nobody came.

She bit back a sob and moved faster, stubbing her toe on a rocky step, but she kept ascending the rustic steps. Thankfully, she had had the foresight to change out of her dress into shorts, a comfortable top and running shoes because if she'd been wearing her sandals, she most likely would have a big cut on said toe.

As she came over the crest of the rocky outcrop, the tiny log cabin was like a beacon nestled amongst towering white pine trees. She sensed something was wrong as she rushed toward the structure and scrambled up the wood steps beneath the small, covered porch. She knocked and shouted out Lucas' name.

No one answered.

Shit! Seriously? He said he lived here year-round!

She tried the doorknob. It turned and the door opened.

Thank God! It wasn't locked!

She rushed inside out of the storm, slamming the door shut behind her. To her surprise it was much quieter in here, but she also realized no one was home.

In that split second she also knew what she'd been sensing was wrong. There had been no boat at the dock. Nadda. Lucas was not here.

She was all alone.

She dared a gaze out a window, but it was raining so hard now she couldn't see anything but the downpour. So, she turned to inspect the cabin, instantly feeling welcome at the scent of pine which reminded her of Moose Ranch.

The cabin was just one large room.

All the walls were knotty pine panels. The ceiling was white-painted boards. There were a couple of oil lamps on shelves. No electrical light fixtures. No light switches.

No paintings or photos on the walls. There was one single bed with a couple of pillows without pillow cases, folded blankets and a rolled up sleeping bag. The bed was pushed up against the wall, right beside the window, which was lighting up every few seconds with flashes of lightning. Beside the bed was a wooden night table with flashlight set on top.

There were a couple of midnight blue-colored oval carpets on the floor. One in front of the only door that she'd come in and the other beside the bed.

She scanned the one room for landline phones and already had realized there was no electricity. It appeared Lucas, the hermit, lived in an old-fashioned completely off the grid setup.

But there was a kitchen area with a quaint white metal stove with claw type feet. Upon a closer look, it was a propane stove.

She would be able to cook. That is, if the stove had a propane tank, which from the look of the metal pipes that went out the side of the cabin, there should be a tank somewhere. She peeked out the window and could barely make out a couple of those white barbecue tanks set under an open picnic shelter like structure with just a roof. It seemed the tanks were tucked away from the elements but open, with no walls in case there was a leak. She turned on one of the stove knobs and smelled propane and quickly shut it off.

Whew, it stunk, that meant she had propane. At least she'd have a warm meal tonight because she was actually cold.

With a quick check of the cupboards, she discovered there was plenty of canned goods and drinks. One small oak table with two scarred up wooden chairs were set near a kitchen counter. There was a black cast-iron stove in the middle of the room with a black pipe that went up into the ceiling. Some firewood and some kindling was set nearby in a couple of aluminum pails.

The interior looked old as if the place had been here for many years.

Suddenly she realized that she was safe, and she could search for towels and undress. She would be okay here until the storm was gone. Yet she started to shake from being cold and then emotions came out of nowhere and attacked her.

JJ bit her bottom lip and began to cry.

DAN GAZED AT THE BATTERY-operated clock set on the fireplace mantle in the living room. It was exactly seven o'clock and usually it was quite light outside at this time. But tonight, the clouds continued to roll along the sky in ominously black puffs. White lightning zipped around the clouds, and thunder continued to boom. It was raining cats and dogs and pretty windy.

Dan wasn't worried though. The ranch house was sturdy.

He just wished he could hear JJ's voice and find out how she'd enjoyed that bridal shower and if she were going out to dinner with any of the girls tonight.

He gazed down at Chrissy who was transfixed with watching a giraffe mobile slowly turning over the playpen. She looked good and tired from her water workout. Her chubby cheeks were pink like two little rosebuds, and he had the feeling it would be an early night for her. The exercise had tuckered her out and the fresh air had made her hungry and she'd eaten all of her supper without protest. She'd enjoyed a bath and now she was in her cotton sleeper, still awake. But barely as her blue eyes were heavy lidded.

He bet she was keeping herself awake waiting for her mom to bring her down to watch the sunset. Too bad she didn't understand about her mommy being away for the weekend and the storm was preventing him from sticking to her routine.

He jumped when the landline phone rang and then he hurried to get it. Had to be JJ! He couldn't wait to hear how much fun she'd had!

But he did not recognize the number, or the area code on the call display and it wasn't the motel number where JJ was staying at either. He picked it up anyway.

"Hello. Moose Ranch," he said into the receiver.

There was nothing but dead air and then a disconnect. He shook his head and hung up. Probably some damn telemarketer.

When he returned to the playpen, he grinned.

Chrissy was rubbing her eyes. It was a sure sign she was ready to go under for the night. He would bring her up to bed, tuck her in, read her a story until she fell asleep and then he would give JJ a call.

He couldn't wait to hear her voice. He'd missed her like crazy today.

JJ FROWNED AT THE CELL phone she held in her hand. She had found it on a bookshelf in the living room area of the cabin. To her surprise and excitement, the cell phone had just a little bit of juice left in the battery. Enough that after many tries of getting a connection, she actually heard Dan's voice! But as she began to speak, the battery died, and the line had gone dead!

Darn it!

JJ was back to her only other ways of communication which were her cell phone or via radio which of course both were in the plane.

It was too gloomy and still too stormy to go outside now, especially since she was not familiar with her surroundings. With her luck she would fall and hurt the baby. No, she was not taking any more chances. She would just have to wait until daylight and fly home. Too bad she hadn't been smart back in the city and stayed put.

Earlier, she'd removed all her wet clothing, and bunched them into a fresh garbage bag that she'd found in a box on the floor. She had discovered clean towels too on a shelf and had dried herself with one of them and then wrapped herself in a blanket and went around searching the cabin for items she would need to spend the night.

She located some track suits and other men's clothing along with some thermal socks. They were neatly folded in a cubicle shelf. She picked a pair of baggy black track pants for herself to wear and thankfully it fit okay over her abdomen and around her waist compliments of a drawstring. She picked a red track top to wear. It was a bit too big, but it was warm.

Her running shoes were soaked, so she left them by the door. Hopefully, they would be semi-dry by morning from the warmth inside the cabin.

After examining her stubbed toe, which was a bit sore with only a bruise, she slipped on the warm socks.

Then she had gone about making supper.

She'd found a gas lantern hanging from a hook on the ceiling over the kitchen sink and several boxes of wooden matches on a shelf and moments later there was a friendly glow of lamplight chasing away the miserable shadows. She'd lit a burner on the stove and cooked up canned pasta and a can of green beans. She ate everything, mainly for her baby's sake, and she swore supper had never tasted so good.

She would brush her teeth before bed using a new toothbrush she'd found still in the package and some toothpaste on the kitchen counter where there had been shaving lather and a razor blade, along with several bottles of pain killers, and some other pill bottles, which she recognized as prescription bottles, all of which were nearly empty. Those had the labels ripped off. None of the pain killers were expired, so that must mean Lucas was still using this place. But why would he rip labels off his prescription bottles?

She sighed and sipped on a warm can of ginger ale, remembering how Lucas had come to her rescue with crackers and cold ginger ale after she'd made an emergency landing on his lake due to her panic attack which had been followed by a nasty bout of morning sickness. He'd said he kept the cans in the lake and that's why they were cold. She should have clued in with that remark that he had no electricity.

Goodness, was it only a month or so ago? She wondered where he might be. He had told her that he lived here year-round.

She found herself wondering why he was here in this cabin with only the bare essentials. She'd seen several cases of beer and several bottles of whiskey. Was he an alcoholic? Or had he just stockpiled? Did he carry demons from his past and was self-medicating? What kind of pills were in all those prescription bottles?

JJ frowned.

She certainly had her own demons from the past. Killing a man. Spending all those years in prison. While in prison, she'd been drugged up on anti-anxiety and anti-depression pills. Any and every complaint to the prison doctor that she was having yet another panic attack or anxiety issues was met with yet another prescription.

A sudden crack of thunder, and a brilliant flash of lightning snapped JJ from her thoughts. It appeared the storm was intensifying again.

Oh, how she wished she were safe and sound back at home with her daughter and her men. She lay a protective hand over her protruding belly and gasped as she felt a flutter low in her abdomen.

The baby was kicking already. Maybe he or she was pissed off at how stupid she'd been in not staying in the city.

Another small flutter came.

Excitement snapped through JJ.

Yes, the baby was awake and suddenly she didn't feel so alone anymore. She wished her men could feel the baby kicking. They would be so thrilled.

Layla had told her that she would most likely feel the baby kick earlier than with her first pregnancy. She'd been right.

JJ caressed her belly and the baby settled down. She really should get some rest.

She eyed the single bed in the corner of the cabin. There were no sheets.

However, a quick search of a far corner shelf had her finding a set of pale blue sheets in an unopened package. From what she could tell, there were no other sheets, clean or dirty. No dirty clothes. No dirty laundry whatsoever. Perhaps Lucas had gone to the city to do the laundry and grocery? Maybe a visit to the doctor for more prescription pills?

How long had he been gone? He certainly wasn't returning tonight in this storm. He had to have gone off with a plane, hadn't he?

But what about his boat? Had it pulled free from it's mooring in the storm? Or was Lucas stranded somewhere out there? Had he been out fishing or doing something else and had gotten caught out in the storm? Had the boat capsized, and he'd drowned?

Her tummy hollowed out in a really bad feeling.

Oh, she hoped he was okay.

JJ forced herself to push away the anxiety nibbling on her about Lucas being out there somewhere. No, there were no extra sheets, no dirty clothing. No dirty dish cloths. Yeah sure he might have washed them in the lake, but where were they? Hanging out on a clothesline somewhere? Maybe.

Okay, she was going nowhere with all these questions. All would be revealed at daylight. There was nothing she could do tonight.

She opened the package of sheets and within minutes had the bed made and to her delight there was a matching pillow case in there too. Normally, she would wash new sheets, however this was an emergency, and she had no choice but to use as is. She would of course take the sheets back home, launder them and get Lucas a present for the use of his cabin.

She may as well sleep in his clothing too and read by the lamplight until she got sleepy, which with all this cracking thunder once again roaring overhead might be an impossible task to get some shut eye.

She eyed the small bookshelf and strolled toward it.

Hopefully, she would find something good to read.

DAN FROWNED WHEN NO one answered in JJ's motel room. He had tried her cell earlier and no answer there either. Eventually it had gone to voice mail and so he'd left a message on her cell for her to call no matter how late she got in.

Geez. She must be having a great time with the girls. He was glad, but still it would have been nice to hear from her before he went to sleep tonight.

At least Brady and Rafe were together over at the Misty Lake cabin. Brady had gotten through to him on the satellite phone earlier letting Dan know all was good on their end.

He had teased Brady that they had missed a damn good moose lasagna and he had laughed when he'd heard both men groan their disapproval. Oh well, more leftovers for tomorrow.

Tomorrow night everyone would be back home again safe and sound.

On his way to the shower, he looked in on Chrissy. She was still fast asleep in her crib. His chest swelled with love as he watched her. Her pudgy hands were scrunched up beneath her chin and the pacifier hung from her slightly parted lips.

Quietly he removed the pacifier and added an extra thin blanket over her. Despite it being pretty warm in here with the windows closed, he figured it was best for her to be toasty instead of chilly.

He left her bedroom door partially open and crossed the hallway to peek into JJ's room, just because he missed her so much. Instantly he smelled her scent permeating the air. He experienced an emotional release of loneliness, which was quickly followed by a physical reaction.

He moaned as his cock engorged and his balls tightened with arousal. Man, his body was so tuned into JJ that just her scent turned him on.

In order to sleep tonight, he knew he would have to take a very cold shower.

"GONNA BE A LONG NIGHT," Rafe heard Brady murmur from the other bed nearby as lightning flashed its brilliance into the cabin.

Thunder rumbled for quite a long time overhead, and Rafe waited for it to subside before answering.

"What you need to do is count sheep," Rafe teased.

"What I need is JJ. I miss her. I'm glad she'll be back tomorrow," Brady replied from the bed.

Oh man, now Brady had gotten him thinking about her too.

Brady chuckled.

"What?" Rafe asked as he pounded the crap out of his pillow with his fist and then tried to get his head into a comfortable position.

"Bringing up JJ in conversation was pay back for telling me to count sheep. I'd rather count all the positions we put her in when we make love to her."

Rafe's entire body went tense as memories of making love to JJ danced in his head.

Rafe swore and tried to get the rest of his body into a contented position.

"Sweet dreams," Brady replied and chuckled again.

"Asshole," Rafe muttered as he reached under his sleeping bag and stroked his very erect shaft. He stifled a moan as pleasure zipped through him.

Brady was right. It was going to be one hell of a long night.

Chapter Eight

J J sat on the bed, her back pressed against the wall, the snug blankets pulled up over her abdomen, making sure to keep her unborn baby nice and warm.

She stared out the blackened window right beside the bed. It wasn't black for long as the lightning flashed every few seconds allowing her to catch glimpses of the silvery sheets of rain that poured down against the large trunks of the nearby pine trees. And she meant nearby. The tree trunks were literally only six feet away from the cabin windows.

From the thumping upon the roof, she could tell it was not a metal roof as those made quite a bit of noise when the rain hit, at least from her experience with Moose Ranch's ranch house, which had a metal roof, complete with lightning rods. She just hoped the shingles didn't fly away and the roof would start to leak with her in it!

She wondered if this little cabin had a lightning rod. It sure would have made her feel safer if it did. And blackout curtains would have been nice too. Then she wouldn't have to see all that lightning as it was making her nervous. She'd have to sew Lucas some colorful curtains to cheer this place up as it seemed kind of depressing in the gloom of the night.

The rain and bursts of wind smacking against the windows was another story. The windows were just single paned, and the wood frames had seen better days. The white paint on the panes was peeling in spots and there were a couple of areas where some animal had gnawed on the wood. She could literally see teeth marks!

Oh dear. She hoped there weren't any mice living in here. She hadn't seen any mouse traps. Hopefully, those gnawing marks were really old. They didn't look fresh. She hoped too that if a branch decided to get knocked loose from the nearby trees and smash through a window, she wouldn't have a heart attack.

JJ inhaled deeply counting to ten and then slowly exhaled.

She was making herself crazy with all these what if scenarios. Her wicked way of thinking was not helping with her situation. After all the research she'd done on anxiety and changing the way she thought, here she was right back to square one with the what if's.

Despite her anxiety due to being trapped here, she kept telling herself that yes, the windows looked old, and that meant nothing bad had happened to smash one...yet. The ceiling didn't have any water stains, so the roof must be solid. Those propane tanks outdoors were not going to get hit by lightning and explode because they were under that shelter and the cabin was not going to catch fire and force her out into the windy elements.

And of course, there was no bathroom in here. She'd found a pail that she would go in when the time came. There was a large stash of packaged toilet paper set beside all those cases of ginger ale, beer cases and liquor bottles, so that meant Lucas had to be coming back. People just didn't leave all these toiletries, food and expensive booze lying around in a cabin they didn't use, right?

There had to be an outhouse around too. That was top priority on her to do list in the morning. Find the outhouse.

JJ blew out a tense breath as she picked up the large hardcover book she'd found in the bedside night table drawer. She'd pulled it out moments earlier and had settled it upon her lap while she contemplated reading it.

Earlier, she had flipped it open and realized it was a journal. The pages were filled with handwriting. She had immediately closed it, feeling as if she had inadvertently stumbled across someone's deepest thoughts. Sure, she was curious about Lucas, but what he wrote in his journal certainly was not her business.

Yet, she still wasn't sleepy and the fiction and non-fiction books on his bookshelf appeared to be too technical, boring, or frightening. Some were books about firefighting, smoke jumping and paramedics. Others were murder mysteries. Some were thrillers. None were exactly what she wanted to read at the moment.

JJ bit her bottom lip.

Should she open his journal and start reading?

He would never have to know that she had read any of it. And there was enough light from the gas lamp that she could read without difficulty.

JJ smiled and placed her hand upon the cover of the journal. She was ready to flip it open when shards of lightning splashed ominously against the window, immediately followed by a bone jarring crack of thunder that made her swear. That damned storm was right on top of her!

It was as if the lightning and thunder snapping at the same time as she was about to open the journal was a warning not to open it.

Okay, if that wasn't a sign not to intrude on his privacy, then she didn't know what was. She shivered and placed the journal back into the night table drawer where she'd found it.

She would just have to force herself to fall asleep and try to ignore this awful storm.

She turned the gas lamp on a low setting, then slid down into a sleeping position on her back and drew the blankets right up under her neck nice and snug. She closed her eyes, dropped her arms, and cradled her baby bump.

Then she began to count sheep.

DAN AND CHRISSY HAD been up for hours.

The electricity as well as his cell phone and the landline phones had gone down last night during the storm and had been down most of the morning. Because they had standby generators, they'd kicked in and that hadn't been an issue with power. So, breakfast had been warm formula, mashed banana, and some mashed cooked egg, for Chrissy, which she'd eaten all without protest.

He was pretty proud that she was eating so heartily, and he couldn't wait to brag to JJ about it.

He'd made himself a hearty breakfast of steak and eggs, followed up with a couple of cups of coffee. He was good until lunch time, which was in about an hour.

The power had returned an hour ago. About half an hour ago, he'd checked the phones yet again, and the landline was finally working. He'd called JJ's motel room a few times since, but no answer. He'd texted but the signal wouldn't go through. He'd called her cell and left a message for her to call him right away when she got in.

He figured she'd most likely tried to contact him last night and this morning but hadn't been able to get through with the phones being down and maybe she was out with the girls this morning having brunch or shopping or something. He hoped she was having a really nice weekend. She deserved some fun away from here.

The morning was warm, windy, and sunny. It would be a perfect day for JJ to fly home.

He sighed heavily as he hung up and turned to Chrissy who looked expectantly at him from her high chair where he'd sat her down so he could make the calls to JJ. He'd hoped to hold the phone to Chrissy's ear so she could hear her mom's voice, like he'd done yesterday.

The kid had literally flipped out hearing JJ's voice on the phone. Her eyes had gone wide like saucers and her fists had banged down on the tray of her high chair so hard, all the empty bowls from her supper went flying into the air and onto the floor, which had made her laugh. Then her legs had gotten into the action, swinging like crazy, and he'd been afraid she'd tip the chair over.

And now, in the cute way she was staring at him, her head cocked slightly to one side, why did he get the feeling the little kid wanted to go to the lake and get immersed in water so she could kick her feet and splash just like yesterday.

"You want to go for a swim, don't you?" Dan asked, knowing full well that's what she wanted.

Chrissy smiled at him and swung her legs. Was it possible she understood him? Wouldn't that be something.

Dan laughed and lifted her from the high chair and hugged her warm body to his chest. Then he headed for the stairs.

"Time to get on our bathing suits and go swimming!" he shouted.

He hoped by playing with Chrissy it would keep his mind off JJ. She'd be home this afternoon sometime with all the fun news of her weekend adventure.

Hopefully, she would be back early, and it would get rid of that weird growing feeling deep down in his gut that was telling him that maybe something was wrong on JJ's end.

JJ'S HEART JUST ABOUT smashed through her chest as she stared at the area where she had tied her float plane. She stood at the top of the rocky outcrop and was looking downward. All she could see was water.

At first she'd thought maybe she had gone to the wrong side of the bluff?

Or maybe she was having a nightmare?

Or maybe she'd just gone insane?

But the dock and the tree she'd tied her float plane to...were gone.

And her plane was gone too!

Sunshine glistened like jewels off the choppy waves that splashed against the rock lined shoreline where she'd stepped off the dock onto land just yesterday late afternoon.

She didn't understand why she was so surprised that her plane had vanished. The winds had been fierce. The dock had been rickety and the ropes she'd used from the dock had been pretty weathered, but she'd thought they weren't *that* bad.

She'd most likely done a haphazard job securing the plane with all those lightning bolts whizzing over her head and the rain blinding her too.

She began a swearing mantra as she carefully descended the steep decline along the rock stairs, praying the plane would suddenly just reappear.

It didn't.

A couple of minutes later JJ stood on the shoreline staring at the tree that had been split in half by lightning. Wood was twisted every which way. Pieces were strewn on the land and shards were in the water crashing against the shoreline with each jolting wave.

Right now, the only things that kept her from screaming her head off for help was the hope that the owner of the cabin would be returning sooner rather than later and that there was probably nobody around for miles to hear her anyways. She tried to remember if there were any other buildings on this lake from looking at that topographical map back at Moose Ranch, but she really hadn't been searching for buildings at the time, just the size of the lake and the location of Lucas' cabin.

Besides, she needed to stay as calm as possible because of her baby. The last thing she wanted was for stress to increase her blood pressure to the point where she had a stroke out here with no help leaving Chrissy an orphan and her unborn child dead.

There was plenty of food in the cabin. An entire fresh-water lake of water to drink from and she had shelter.

She just needed to not freak out.

But where was her plane? She held her hand up above her eyes to shield them from the sunshine which was already very high in the sky. She could barely see the opposite shoreline. But nothing moved on the water out that way. There was no glint of sunshine off metal. Nothing but whitecapped waves, forests, and glistening sunshine.

She couldn't see anything but water where the lake stretched northward. It was long and she knew from looking at the topographical map that the lake was actually quite large with many bays. This area that Lucas' cabin sat on was a large bay and not actually the small lake she'd thought when she'd first landed here that first time.

So, just because she couldn't see her plane, didn't mean it wasn't out there somewhere.

But what if her plane had sunk?

Her tummy hollowed out in a really bad way.

Or was it damaged beyond repair crashing against the rocky shores in this stiff breeze?

Anxiety slithered through her, and she inhaled deeply and slowly.

Okay. Everything was okay.

No need to panic.

First things first. Breakfast.

She'd slept like a rock once the storm had quietened down and since there was no working clock in that cabin, and the sun was high in the sky, it was a safe bet she'd missed breakfast. But that wasn't going to stop her from having it. There had been a couple of unopened boxes of cereal and some condensed milk cans in the pantry.

And binoculars. She remembered seeing binoculars in the cabin too.

She would search for her plane with them. But what about all those other bays she'd seen on that map?

She'd just have to hope that Lucas was coming back today, and she could get a ride out with the pilot. But what if he didn't come back? Ever?

Don't go there, JJ.

Feeling dejected, she turned and started up the rickety rock steps again.

Why did she leave her phone in the damned plane? She should have risked it and gone back in and grabbed it. Should have activated the Emergency Locator Transmitter. Should have sent that mayday on the radio.

Stupid woman!

She had to find the plane. She could radio for help.

Hopefully, it wasn't at the bottom of the lake.

RAFE AND BRADY WERE surprised that the damage on the trails had not been severe. Only a few trees to clear, which Brady had taken care of while Rafe finished up the haying in the area.

By noon they were more than halfway home but decided on a pitstop for a lunch break. Now they were enjoying a much-deserved steaming hot cup of coffee they had brewed over a very small open fire on a rocky outcrop in one of the meadows beside a creek.

"Doesn't look or feel like any storms brewing today," Brady said as he gazed up at the cloudless sky.

Rafe nodded. He knew what Brady meant. It wasn't overly hot, and it was a good day for flying.

"Bit of a breeze," Rafe commented as he slipped the spatula beneath the large pancake he was cooking in the frying pan over his little portable propane stove. He easily flipped the pancake and his mouth watered at the delicious scent wafting beneath his nostrils.

"She has flown in worse," Brady acknowledged, his gaze still glued to the blue sky.

Rafe grinned. Brady was staring in the direction of home. Maybe he was hoping JJ had returned early and might fly up this way.

"Yeah, I guess she's pretty savvy with that plane," Rafe replied as he returned his attention to the pancake and watched it bubble and cook.

"She's a pro. I just wish she didn't have to fly so much," Brady said.

Brady didn't like the idea of her being up in the air just as much as Rafe didn't like the idea. It was just too dangerous.

"We can't tie her down," Rafe said and shrugged his shoulders.

Brady grinned and Rafe immediately understood why. Rafe rolled his eyes and shook his head.

"Don't go there, Brady. It's only torture and JJ is not here to bring us the relief we crave."

"Yeah, I guess you're right. Is the pancake done? I'm starved."

"Another couple of minutes. How are the blueberries?" Rafe asked.

He watched as Brady stood and strolled over to the single burner propane stove a few feet away. Each one of them carried a stove with extra propane canisters whenever they went out on the trails. They came in handy to brew up coffee or a quick meal.

Brady nodded and switched off the stove.

"Blueberries are done. I made a good sauce if I do say so myself."

Earlier they had discovered a nice batch of blueberry bushes and picked enough to make a sauce for their pancake lunch and a good amount to make a blueberry pie for JJ when they got back home.

"Good, let's eat," Rafe answered.

He swore he was drooling as he slid the spatula under the pancake and lifted it onto a plate. He cut the pancake in half and placed half onto another plate for Brady, then he put some more oil into the pan. In a moment, the oil would be hot enough so he could pour the remainder of the batter for another pancake for them to share.

"Here you go, Brady."

He was about to pass the plate to Brady where he had situated himself on the ground beside Rafe, readying the little pan of blueberry sauce for them to use, when a loud growl from a little too close for comfort made Rafe tense.

"Hear that?" Brady said in a low voice.

"Uhhuh," Rafe answered.

"No sudden movements," Brady warned.

"I'm pretty sure it's behind me. Can you see it? Wolf? Bear?" Had to be a bear. It must have smelled the blueberry sauce.

Brady was squinting his eyes like he needed glasses.

"Oh yeah. It's a big one. No way we can outrun it."

"Shit."

Rafe's stomach hollowed out with a sense of impending doom.

Was it a bear or a wolf? He was actually too scared to even ask that question.

Another growl had icy shivers crawling up Rafe's back and he resisted the urge to get up and run.

"My rifle is in the atv trailer. Where's yours?" he asked Brady.

"Too far for me to get to. I have an idea. Toss your pancake over your shoulder so it can have it. When I tell you to run. You run for your life like the dog from hell is on your heels."

Rafe shook his head jerkily.

"Running is not good, Brady. It makes us prey."

"We're already prey. Just do as I say, Rafe. I'll distract it. You go for the rifle."

Shit!

He grabbed his pancake which was so damn hot he could barely hold onto it and threw it behind him.

And then he ran like his life depended on it.

"Run, Rafe! Run!" Brady yelled.

Rafe moved his legs like he had never moved them before. He was at his trailer within the blink of an eye. He didn't look back to see if Brady was alright because it would just waste precious time. With trembling hands he unhooked the tarp, slid the rifle from the scabbard, released the safety, turned, and quickly took aim.

He had expected to see Brady being mauled by a bear or at the very least him fighting off a pack of wolves with rocks.

He did neither.

Instead, he just sat, quietly eating his half of the pancake. There was no bear. No wolf. At least none that he could see.

What the fuck?

Rafe wasn't sure if he swore out loud or to himself, but suddenly he caught movement of something about ten feet behind where Rafe had just been about to eat. He did a double take as a blur of black and white came slithering along in that tall grass heading toward Brady.

A skunk? Did skunk's growl?

"Did you like Rafe's pancake, little fellow?" He heard Brady say in a gentle voice.

Suddenly it came out of the tall grass, and Rafe let out a string of violent curses.

Not a bear. Not a wolf. Not even a damned skunk.

"A dog, Brady? You scared ten years off my life over a dog?" Rafe cursed as he held tight to the rifle and watched Brady toss the animal the last piece of his own pancake. The dog happily pounced on it like it was starving.

"Not just any dog. It's a border collie," Brady answered.

Unfreaking believable. A dog way out here in the middle of nowhere? The dog looked about forty pounds with black and white matted fur. It had a long bushy, very wagging white tail and it's black ears were perched high on its head, very erect ears and the tips were folded over in a really cool way.

"He really enjoyed your pancake, Rafe," Brady said, amusement twinkling in his blue eyes.

"I have a mind to shoot you, Brady."

Brady chuckled and shrugged.

"Hey, I didn't know if he was friendly or not, so I had to think fast."

"Fast my ass. You knew it was a dog," Rafe frowned as the dog gazed at him and growled.

"Well, I did warn you to run as if the dog from hell was on your tail."

"Funny, ha, ha." Rafe snapped.

He focused his attention to the dog who bared his teeth in a menacing way and growled at him.

"This is the thanks I get after giving you my lunch?" Rafe said between gritted teeth to the dog.

The animal tilted its head sideways as if trying to understand what Rafe was saying.

The dog had light brown colored oval shaped eyes. Despite the ominous growling, Rafe sensed the dog was scared, but in the way it's tail was wagging, it was also happy to find people and had enjoyed the pancake and wanted more.

"Where do you think he's from?" Rafe asked as he kept a close eye on the dog.

As he moved closer to inspect the animal, he kept his rifle on the ready. Its fur was tangled with burrs and the white areas of his fur appeared dirty. It looked like it had been out here for some time foraging for food. Poor little bugger.

"Probably lost. But I'll take a walk and call out and see if anyone is nearby. You get moving on making another pancake. I turned down the heat on the stove so the oil wouldn't burn so I'll just turn it up and by the way the blueberry syrup is absolutely delicious. Try some."

Rafe shook his head.

"After the stunt you just pulled, I don't feel like sharing my pancake with you or the dog,"

To Rafe's irritation, Brady laughed and turned up the heat on the stove and then stood and stretched.

"Yup, that was delicious. Hey, you should be happy it wasn't a bear or a wolf."

Ray swore at him and settled himself on the ground where he had previously sat before he had been so rudely interrupted. To his annoyance, the dog came over and sat down right beside him, his light brown eyes peering up at him with a pleading *give me some more* look.

Thankfully, it didn't growl anymore. But its entire body became tense a few moments later when Brady, who'd walked over to the trail, began to shout.

"Hello! Anyone lose a dog!"

The only answer was a chattering squirrel sitting on a nearby rock staring at them, probably waiting for a piece of pancake from himself.

Rafe poured the batter into the pan. The batter sizzled, bubbled, and smelled so good his mouth was watering again!

A sliver of sorrow whispered through Rafe as the dog focused its gaze upon the pancake in the pan.

"I am hungrier than you since you already ate my share of pancake. But I have an idea. How about I eat this entire pancake, not share it with Brady and I'll open up a can of corned beef for you?"

To Rafe's surprise, the dog gave out a sharp bark as if answering "it sounds like a good idea."

Rafe couldn't help but smile at the mutt and found himself hoping that the owner was nearby. He doubted it because the dog didn't look like it was being looked after.

If he was lost, then they would have to take the dog home with them.

JJ and Chrissy would absolutely love this cute creature. After he got checked by a vet and had a bath of course.

JJ LOWERED THE BINOCULARS and sighed.

After a big bowl of cereal and condensed milk, she'd hung up her wet clothing on a clothesline she had found near the cabin. Then she'd spent hours standing in the shadows of the towering pine trees surveying the far away and close by shorelines looking for any sign of her plane or Lucas' motorboat, a lifeless body floating in the water, as well as any other planes that she might be able to wave down.

The area around the cabin had a magnificent view of the entire bay. But she didn't see her plane or any sign of life. No boats, no dead people, no docks, no buildings. Nothing but wilderness, wild driftwood entangled shoreline, and the occasional lonesome wail of a loon somewhere out on the water.

Too bad Lucas' motorboat had disappeared right along with the dock and the plane. That boat would have made life so much easier.

Oh well, it was time to hang up the binoculars because her arms were getting sore, and she was feeling way too hot out here in the increasing heat. From the look of the sun, it was probably late afternoon, and she would have to get supper too, despite not being hungry.

Surely the guys knew she was missing by now and a search and rescue was ongoing. Especially if she hadn't called them this morning. The problem was, she'd gone off the flight plan she'd submitted.

No one knew where she was.

A wave of dread zipped through her, but she clamped down on it.

No. There was no need to panic. At least not yet.

She figured she had three options.

Option one. She could stay here high on the rocky knoll and build a smoky fire in Lucas' firepit that was close to the edge of the cliffs and try to attract attention. But that was a long shot, and it was too windy. A stray spark could start a forest fire, which would certainly attract attention, but she couldn't do that to all the wildlife in the area and she'd get burned up right along with everything else.

Option two, she could begin to walk along the shoreline around the lake of bays, following the direction of the wind, looking for her plane. That option would be dumb if her plane had sunk, and it would take her days to walk around the entire lake. She could die of exposure, have a deadly encounter with wildlife or get seriously injured on the unfamiliar rugged terrain.

And then there was option three.

Stay calm and stay right here until help arrived. Here she could go for a nice leisurely swim and just relax and wait for Lucas to return. If he hadn't drowned or become stranded, he might be coming back in a day or two. Or tonight. All would be well.

JJ opted for option three. And since she didn't have a bathing suit and there wasn't anyone around...

A few minutes later she stood once again where the tree had been hit by lightning down on the shoreline and surveyed the sandy beach area near where the dock and her plane had been. Despite it being wavy, the water was clear, and she could see to the bottom. There didn't appear to be any broken glass or rusty tins. Just plain sand. And best of all, the area was in the shade.

She sighed. Lucas just had to be coming back. It was just a matter of when. Unless of course, he'd gone out with his motorboat and had had an accident.

JJ shook her head.

No, she wouldn't go there, despite her mind always going there.

Right now, she just wanted to relax. Destress. Clear her mind. Out with the negative shit and in with the positive vibes.

She kicked off her shoes and socks, which were now nice and dry because she'd laid them in the hot sunshine on the rocky ground while having breakfast.

Then she began to peel off Lucas' top followed by his track bottoms, which were now uncomfortably hot with the increasing humidity.

The warm wind breezed against her bare skin and the sensations made JJ smile despite her awful circumstances. It felt nice to feel something other than anxiety and panic.

As she walked further into the water, the warm liquid gently caressed the backs of her legs, and the soothing laps of the waves encouraged her to go deeper and soon, because of a very steep drop off, she was almost up to her neck.

The water embraced her and made her feel safe.

She stood there, almost neck deep, closed her eyes and just felt the rough waves play against her.

She inhaled the pine scented air, which smelled of a tinge of fish. Enjoyed the touch of the wind and spray of water on her face. The sounds of water splashing against the nearby rocky shoreline. The forlorn loon cries in the distance.

It was as if she'd just been dipped into a nature spa.

Yeah, this was nice.

"WHAT DO YOU MEAN SHE checked out yesterday?"

That uneasy feeling Dan had been experiencing at the pit of his gut had just turned into an avalanche of fear. He double checked his call display to make sure he had called the right motel. But he had because this person had just told him JJ had checked out.

"What time yesterday?" he asked.

"Around four o'clock, sir."

Oh man.

"Did she give you any idea where she was going?"

"She said she was going home. She seemed quite happy."

Dan's gut clenched in panic.

"Is Blue there? Or Kelly? Kaylee? Or Layla? Daegen?"

"Blue? Sir? Last names?" The receptionist sounded confused.

Dan shook his head.

"I don't remember last names. There was a wedding shower."

He couldn't think straight. His mind was a blank.

"Hold on," the receptionist said.

If JJ had checked out yesterday, it was almost twenty-four hours since she had left the motel. Where the hell could she have gone?

The receptionist said she was going home.

Icy shivers threatened to shatter what was left of his composure.

That storm.

Holy shit! If she was coming home then she must have gotten caught in that storm!

The wait for the receptionist to return was indescribably horrible. All kinds of scenarios screwed into his head. Maybe she had been kidnapped like once before, or maybe she had seen a cockroach and just told the motel she was going home so as not to hurt their feelings? Or maybe she really had started for home and something bad had happened.

Damn! Where was that receptionist?

Dan glanced over at the playpen where Chrissy had fallen asleep.

After their morning splashing and then lunch, he'd kept her entertained outside while he'd worked in the vegetable garden, pulling the portable play pen here and there so she could watch him, and he could talk to her. He'd taken her from the playpen numerous times to show her the tomatoes, or cucumbers or whatever he'd been weeding. All of this was going on while JJ might be lying injured somewhere after a crash.

Or...

Don't go there, Dan. Don't.

"Hello, sir?"

Thank God, the receptionist was back.

Dan's grip tightened on the phone. Please be good news. Please.

"I've checked and no one with those first names were here. I'm sorry. Can I help you in any other way?"

In other words, get lost so you can continue to do your job? He almost hung up on her, but he said a quick thanks. He needed to get in touch with each of the girls and see if they knew something. Maybe she was with one of them?

But first, he needed to call Brady and Rafe and tell them what was unfolding.

Oh man, they were going to freak right out.

Chapter Nine

JJ tossed another piece of split wood onto the fire she had made in a second fire pit. This one was located near the shoreline not too far from where she'd gone for a leisurely swim. She'd also found a nice sized woodpile of split wood and dry kindling beneath a tarp nearby.

The day had dragged on as she'd waited for the wind to subside. She'd eaten some rice that she'd cooked up from a package. Some canned vegetables and canned fruit had followed. An afternoon nap in the warm cabin had followed that.

She'd slept surprisingly well, awakening feel fresh and relaxed.

About two hours before twilight, the wind had died and she started a fire, trying to keep it smoky by pouring bits of water on it. Grey smoke trailed high into the air and billowed over the bay. She doubted anyone would be flying overhead. She'd heard no planes all day which wasn't unusual back at Moose Ranch. But she dared not give up hope.

Her clothes had dried on the line, and she was wearing them again, but as darkness began to fall there was a bit of a chill in the air. The sunset was spectacular, bright orange clouds tinged with red and yellow made it look like the sky was on fire. Chrissy would have loved it, she was sure.

Homesickness wrenched her heart at the thought she was missing such a gorgeous sunset with her little girl. She wondered how Chrissy was feeling. Was she wondering why her mother had abandoned her? Was she crying and sad because she wasn't around to feed her, bathe her and tuck her into bed tonight?

She held back tears as white blades of lightning flickered ominously along the billowing clouds as the sun set and the forest and lake grew black and spooky.

Despite the warmth from the fire, she felt cold. She really should head up the trail and get back to the cabin, but she didn't want to leave the fire. She should put the fire out now and get inside before the storm hit, but some weird loneliness kept her outside watching the darkening sky, praying that someone would come for her.

All day long she had hoped Lucas would return from wherever he'd gone. Her mind kept flip flopping to had he drowned via a horrific accident with his boat to had he been picked up by a float plane because the sheets were missing on the bed and the only ones she'd found were the ones in a package. Unless he didn't use sheets.

She should read his journal. Surely there was a clue in there as to where he had gone? She seriously should have done that last night, but she'd been so rattled. And today her hopes had been pinned on someone coming here, and she'd forgotten about that journal.

At least by now the guys would know she was missing. She hated that they were worrying about her. She had destroyed their peace and had once again stirred up their belief that she should not be flying a plane as it was too dangerous.

JJ sighed and stared at the yellow sparks shooting up into the air as the log crackled and caught fire. Watching the orange flames relaxed her in the same way swimming in the lake and the afternoon nap had relaxed her.

She jumped when an owl hooted from a nearby tree branch. It took a moment to blink through the darkness toward the sound and then she spied the dark silhouette of a big bird perched on a dead branch of a tree about ten feet up. She could easily make out the markings from the light of the fireplace splashing against it.

It was a barred owl. The guys had a book on birds at the ranch house and sometimes she would look through it. She could tell this one was a barred owl because it had smears of brown and white coloring. Its underparts were deep brown with white vertical stripes, and its feathery wings were a barred white and dark brown. It had the blackest eyes as it stared down at her. She wondered how long it had been sitting up there watching her. Usually, she didn't pay much attention to owls, but tonight she was glad to have its company.

"Hey little owl. Can you go and find my cowboys and bring them to me?" she called up to the feathery creature.

It remained silent and stared back at her with his wide black eyes. Then it slowly blinked, and JJ shook her head.

Good grief, she was talking to a bird.

Off in the distance came the soft rumble of thunder. The sound chased chills up her spine as she remembered what she had gone through just yesterday.

Man, she really was lucky she had made it here without crashing. It had been so windy and so hard to control the plane. She hoped she didn't lose her pilot's license due to deviating from the flight plan. This had been an emergency landing and the threat of getting hit by lightning had chased her into the cabin for safety without following protocol in radioing a mayday.

But now as she had a clear head she realized she could have sat in her plane without fear of getting hit. The plane was equipped with lightning protection.

Damn, in her panic state, she hadn't really thought things through. She could have gone into the plane, radioed in her coordinates, grabbed her emergency pack and cell phone, and then run for the cabin. But everything had happened so incredibly fast.

Why was she so stupid?

You're not stupid, JJ. You were trying to save your life and the life of your baby. Nothing wrong with that.

Sure, she wasn't the calmest of people when it came to anxiety-provoking situations. She knew she still had a lot of work to do to think better about herself and to heal her inner trauma wounds. She was a work-in-progress, and she and her baby were still alive. That accounted for something.

The owl hooted again and smacked JJ back to reality. From across the lake in the direction of the oncoming storm she heard a swish sound she didn't like. She knew what it was. Either rain or wind or both.

Following instincts, JJ heaved up the heavy metal bucket she had filled earlier with water and dumped the contents on the fire. Grabbing the flashlight off the ground beside where she was sitting, she stood and moved quickly to the lake and filled the bucket a couple more times dousing the lingering flames of the fire and stirring the remnants until there was no smoke. Then she dumped another bucket of water onto it, making sure it was dead.

JJ laughed with glee as she ran up the rocky trail using the flashlight as a beacon. She could hear that wind or rain or whatever it was coming closer. The towering trees above her started to sigh as the wind began to blow through their branches.

A couple of minutes later she rushed into the cabin. Moments after she was in safely, the wind and rain slashed all around outside, pummeling the roof and battering the windows and door.

Lightning flashed and thunder crashed.

The owl hooted from somewhere nearby. Had it followed her up?

For some crazy reason she was not afraid of spending another night here. It was better than being out there. Besides, she was not alone. She had the owl for company, and she had her baby. She placed her hand over her swelling abdomen and headed for the lantern. Time for a nice cup of hot coffee.

BRADY WAS SO GLAD TO be home.

After Rafe had fed that ungrateful border collie dog some canned corned beef and they'd given it tons of water, the damned dog had taken off and disappeared. They'd called it for hours, but it hadn't come back.

Brady had finally given up, but Rafe had decided to hang back and keep calling.

On the way back to the ranch house, Brady had had to cut through several more trees that had fallen over the trails. He'd hoped to get back before nightfall, but he hadn't been able to make it.

Now the sky was blinking with lightning and thunder was roaring somewhere to the south and the sight of the buttery glow of lights flowing out of the windows and the brightness of the porch light spilling into the yard in welcome had him smiling.

He was here now and the first thing he did was gaze down at the lake so he could see JJ's white plane but frowned when her plane was not there.

What the heck? Where was she? Had she decided to stay another night in the city?

Suddenly Dan was rushing out of the ranch house, Chrissy cradled in his arms.

The serious expression on his pale face made Brady's stomach clench with dread.

"What's wrong?" he asked Dan, knowing instinctively it had to do with JJ.

"Why weren't you and Rafe answering your phones?" Dan growled.

"The battery died on the satellite phone, and we were in the dead zone. What's wrong?" he asked again.

"JJ's missing," Dan said.

"What do you mean she's missing?" he asked, trying to keep his voice low so as not to frighten his baby girl. Dan held out Chrissy to him. She was giggling up a storm obviously happy to see him.

Quickly he took her into his arms and held his soft bundle of a daughter against his chest seeking some sort of comfort from what Dan had just said.

"She checked out of the motel yesterday afternoon. She told them she was going home. I haven't heard from her since yesterday morning when she got there. Been trying yesterday to get ahold of her. Figured because the lines were done last night and this morning, that's why she wasn't calling. Today I called reception. I should have called reception yesterday when I didn't get an answer on her cell or her room. I thought she was just having fun. How the hell did I know she was coming home yesterday?"

Dan was talking so fast as they headed back toward the ranch house that Brady couldn't get a word in edgewise. Not that he could say anything as his head was spinning.

Yesterday? Why would she come home early without letting them know?

"Coffee. Let's grab coffee and you can tell me everything."

Dan nodded. His head reminded Brady of one of those bobbleheads.

Brady tried to smile as Chrissy suddenly looked up at him. To his surprise, she had a little furrow between her eyebrows, like she suddenly knew something was wrong.

Oh God, please keep an eye on JJ, Brady said silently, and he hoped God was listening.

JJ FELT PRETTY GOOD after a nice warm sponge bath and a late snack of canned mushroom soup and crackers. Now she was situated on the bed, just like last night. The blankets were tucked over her baby while wind and rain pummeled the windows and the roof.

Lightning flashed and thunder roared, but the storm was so much better than the one she'd gone through yesterday. And just like yesterday, she was not in the least bit sleepy.

What she needed was to read. When she had been in prison she'd always been able to relax before bedtime reading a decent romance novel she would get from the prison library. The library had tons of them. But none of those romance novels ever gave the heroine three hot sexy cowboy lovers like she had gotten.

JJ frowned. What was Chrissy doing tonight. Did she feel abandoned? Feeling abandoned was not a nice feeling. She'd experienced that when she'd been put on trial and then dumped into prison with no way out and no one coming to visit her.

What were the guys doing now that they knew she was missing. They would be frantic with worry. They didn't like that she was a pilot. This misadventure was just one more notch for them to dislike her flying. But despite what had happened, JJ knew she would always fly. She felt so free up in the air. Like she was high on a drug.

Flying made her feel so important too. She used the plane to make the guys life easier by flying out to the city to get parts for the numerous machines they used to run the ranch. She flew out to get groceries. She flew to do airdrops of hay or supplements for the cattle in the winter months and so many other things.

If they so much as dared to suggest she give up flying because of what had happened, they would get an earful when she got out of here...if she got out of here.

Her gaze strayed to Lucas' journal where she had said set it on her lap. Maybe if she just checked the last page? It might give her an indication when he would be returning?

Excitement rushed through her as she snapped up the diary. She swallowed and quickly swept through the written pages and stopped at the last entry which to her horror wasn't even dated.

Heading out tomorrow. Not sure when I will be back or if I will be back.

JJ hopes disintegrated into a zillion pieces.

Oh my God. If he'll be back?

But I need to do this new therapy as soon as possible. If I can get my shit together before she gets married, then maybe she'll give me another chance...

JJ couldn't stop the swell of emotions from bubbling up.

Lucas might never come back. Her heart began a frantic beating.

She might be here forever? Who would deliver her baby? What about her prenatal vitamins? She could not exist on canned food forever. Eventually it would run out.

OK, JJ. Just calm down. You still have options.

She could still make smoky fires. Write out an SOS with rocks in a clearing somewhere nearby. She could start looking for her plane. Maybe it hadn't sunk. Maybe it was just drifting around out there? Maybe everything would workout okay?

JJ swallowed and bit her bottom lip with a sudden bout of worry.

But what if it didn't?

RAFE COULDN'T GET BACK to the ranch house fast enough after Dan's cryptic text message had come through on his cell phone the minute he'd left the dead zone area of their ranch.

You need to get your ass back here right away. It's an emergency. Just don't kill yourself on the way back. Stay calm.

After feeding that damn dog a can of corned beef it had disappeared. His gut had clenched thinking it was lost yet again but

Rafe had given it his all in looking for it. Still, he couldn't help but feel guilty for leaving it behind.

As he motored along the trail, his headlights slashing through the darkness, and lightning blazing through the sky above him, he wondered if maybe Brady had had some sort of accident on the way back. He'd come across several trees that had been freshly cut and pushed to the side of the trails.

That meant Brady had come through here. If he'd encountered a medical emergency, at least he was at home. They would deal with it. If it were bad, JJ could fly them to the hospital in the city or they could call Will, the bush doctor.

Thankfully, the rain had held off as he made his way into the yard. The ranch house was ablaze with lights and his first instinct was to gaze down at the lake for JJ's white plane. He couldn't wait to see her. He had missed her so much.

He frowned and his gut clenched in a really bad way. Nothing was there. No plane.

That's when he knew.

The emergency had something to do with JJ and his entire world came crashing down around him.

As he entered the ranch house, on rather shaky legs, Chrissy's cries echoed down the hallway prompting Rafe to hurry. As he entered the open concept kitchen living room area he found Chrissy in her playpen.

Her face was red, tears splashed from her beautiful blue eyes, and she had her arms reaching out to Rafe when she saw him.

His heart filled with sympathy as he rushed over and swooped her out of the playpen. She wrapped her arms around his neck and pressed her wet hot cheek against his and she just kept crying, breaking Rafe's heart.

"Oh, baby girl. It's alright."

Both Brady and Dan were on their phones. Each man pacing back and forth like caged lions as they spoke to whomever.

"What the fuck is going on here?" Rafe called out. He was so pissed off at them for ignoring Chrissy that he literally saw red.

To his surprise the men completely ignored him.

Rafe hugged Chrissy tighter and thankfully she stopped crying.

"Hey!" he shouted. Not impressed at how nuts they were behaving.

Brady waved him away.

Dan covered the receiver.

"I'll fill you in later. I've got search and rescue on the phone. They've got me on hold. Can you change Chrissy and get her ready for bed?"

Search and rescue.

Oh man, this was so not good.

Rafe nodded and tried really hard not to ask what had happened to JJ. He truly didn't think he could handle any bad news about her.

So, he focused his entire attention onto Chrissy who hadn't let go of his neck and she continued pressing her cheek against his as he headed upstairs.

Something really bad was going down and the kid was picking up on it.

"Damn assholes for scaring you like that," he muttered.

He did not care that he was swearing in front of her. He felt really bad for her. He hoped she wasn't too traumatized by being ignored like that. Thankfully when he brought her into her room, he felt her entire body relax. She lifted his arms from his neck and moved her head away from his cheek. Then she began to rub her eyes indicating she was tired.

"Okay, sweetie pie. Let's get you cleaned up, changed and ready for bed."

He was going to stay up here with Chrissy until she was fast asleep. There was no way he was going to traumatise her again by leaving her alone and inconsolable.

Damned assholes.

JJ AWOKE WITH A START. For several seconds she didn't know where she was as a dimly lit area rolled into focus and then she remembered. She'd been reading Lucas' journal and had dozed off in his bed after a good cry.

Now, knowing she had only herself to rely on in getting out of here, she felt determined, and her thoughts were beginning to focus.

She and her baby would be okay. No matter what. She would make sure of it.

Tomorrow she would begin to figure out how to build some sort of raft. She would be like a pioneer. Hell, if she could set her mind to learning how to fly a plane, then she would set her mind to finding a way to get home. Building a raft was now top priority.

With renewed courage, JJ reached out and made sure the flashlight was within reach. Then she turned off the gas lantern beside the bed, where she'd placed it on the night table. The room fell into complete darkness, which was quickly interrupted by flashes of lightning.

JJ snuggled deeper beneath the blankets. From here on out the lantern would only be used in emergency.

She had limited supplies now that she knew Lucas might not be returning. She could handle this. She had no other choice.

DAWN BROKE, BRINGING sunshine, a stiff wind, heat, and humidity. Brady stood on the dock; his forehead already dotted with perspiration as he watched the two float planes come roaring down upon the choppy waves one after the other. Brady recognized the black one as being the wilderness doctor, Will, and the bright yellow plane would be Layla, JJ's midwife.

The phones had been ringing off the hook all night as plans were made to go looking for JJ. Search and rescue had been scouring JJ's flight plan the instant the storm had moved out of the area early this morning and Brady was grateful someone was looking for her.

As Dr. Will's plane neared the dock, Brady rushed over ready to tie down the plane.

Moments later, Will was descending the plane ladder and stepped onto the dock. The guy was a bit shorter than Brady, clean-shaven and he had a full head of chestnut colored curly hair. He wore black pants and a light blue colored cotton shirt that had a nametag on the breast pocket that said Dr. William Brown on it.

He looked a bit stressed, and for some insane feeling Brady felt relieved to see him. He barely knew the guy, meeting him only on a couple of other occasions when he had flown in to check on Dan.

"Hey Brady, how are you holding up?" Will asked as they shook hands. He sounded concerned and the question almost unraveled Brady's self composure.

Will must have sensed his distraught because suddenly Brady was being engulfed in a mighty big bear hug. Then he let go, giving Brady an encouraging smile.

Fuck! Had the guy hugged him one second more, he would have lost it, most likely breaking down into a washer full of tears.

"Any news?" Will asked as they waited for Layla to maneuver her plane in behind Will's plane.

"Nothing. Still missing."

"Hey, no news is good news. Keep it positive. That's the best for the kid, am I right?" the doctor asked with a smile.

Just thinking of his daughter did bring a ray of sunlight into the gloom Brady was feeling.

The doctor nodded toward Layla's plane.

"Come on. Let's help Layla. She's babysitting so we all can go out for the morning to search. The more eyes on the plane, the better the chances of seeing something."

Brady did a double take.

"But you've got patients to see. We don't want to take you away from people who need you."

"Layla and I have cleared our schedules for the ones who can wait and for me just one stop for us as we search. I'm on call for emergencies, so there might be interruptions. And in my opinion this is an emergency. Blue and Kelly are coming this afternoon to take over. All is good, my man."

Will slapped Brady's shoulder and ushered him toward the end of the dock where the yellow plane was quickly approaching.

Brady recognized the midwife and gratitude enveloped him that these two people would come all the way out here to help look for JJ.

For a split second he felt like the luckiest man in the world and quickly sobered remembering the reason why they were here.

JJ STARED AT THE YELLOW kayak she'd found and began to laugh, not believing her good luck.

She had awoken early this morning, feeling surprisingly refreshed and calm. It had been cool in the cabin, perfect for sleeping.

After dressing in Lucas' warm track clothes, she'd opened the door and instantly realized from the mugginess of the air outside it was going to be a hot, humid day. She detested hot, humid days.

It wouldn't be long before the cabin got warm, and she had no access to fans or air-conditioning to keep her comfortable. A tinge of anxiety swept over her at the thought of dying of heat exposure, but then she remembered she did have an entire lake to swim in. That would keep her and baby cool and happy.

When she'd taken a quick trip to the rustic old wood outhouse out back of the cabin a few minutes ago she'd spied the trail. It went behind the outhouse. She hadn't noticed it on prior trips to the bathroom, maybe because she'd been distraught and mentally preoccupied.

Curiosity lured her along the winding path, which left the shade of the towering pine trees and into the hot sunshine. The trail meandered between small saplings and bushes. After a few minutes, the trail forked, one went straight ahead toward a small treeless area and the other went to the right which she sensed would eventually lead downward to the lake.

She went right.

Anticipation snapped through her as the trail led to a little enclave in the lake. Out there, foot high waves shimmered like white diamonds beneath the bright sunlight. It was windy but nothing compared to when she'd first arrived in that storm.

Here, in the enclave, the shoreline was very shallow, swampy, devoid of trees and no driftwood. Instead, it gave way to lush green ferns. Lily pads laced the area. Some had pretty white flowers and others had bunched yellow flowers. Small green frogs were lounging on top of the lily pads and when they saw her, most jumped into the water leaving little splashes in their wake.

To her surprise, she found a dock here. A giant turtle was sunbathing at the end, and when it saw her coming, it jumped into the water with a giant splash and vanished beneath the surface.

The dock appeared to be relatively new, extending about ten feet out and maybe six feet wide. This dock was much smaller than the other one that had been dragged off with her plane. An aluminum lawn chair was set beneath a lone tree and JJ found it funny that it hadn't blown away in the winds.

Nearby she'd spied a green tarp secured by logs and beneath the tarp was the kayak. She would have wished for a motor boat, but hey, this little boat would save her from making a raft. She had never been in a kayak before but in prison she had sometimes watched kayak races on tv. She noted the required plastic paddle was nestled in beside the kayak.

"Okay, newbie. We can do this," she whispered to her baby bump.

To her surprise, she felt the slightest little flutter. The baby was kicking, letting her know he or she was ready for the journey.

Giddy with excitement, JJ returned to the cabin. She had breakfast which consisted of a big bowl of bran cereal, watered-down condensed milk, a small can of fruit cocktail, which was followed up by two coffees and a granola bar, of which Lucas had many packages, thankfully none were expired.

A quick search of the cabin produced a man's baseball cap, and a small knapsack.

She'd packed the knapsack with several cans of ginger ale, bottles of water, matches which she wrapped inside tin foil in case it rained, one tiny burner stove with small propane tank that she had located in a box in the cabin, a couple of cans of pasta in case she got hungry and some crackers...also just in case. Although she was pretty sure all her morning sickness was gone, with her luck it just might come back and bite her on the butt.

She found an elastic, tied up her hair into a ponytail, and tucked her hair beneath the baseball cap.

JJ looked into the small mirror that was set on the kitchen counter and smiled. She looked like a guy. But at least it would be cooler with her hair up and the wind wouldn't be whipping it into her eyes.

She changed out of the warm track clothes and into her shorts, bra and a large white T-shirt that belonged to Lucas. The white color of the shirt would hopefully not attract the heat as much and the material was quite thin. If she got too hot, she could bunch the material beneath her breasts. It felt very comfortable and cool at the moment, so she kept it loose.

After brushing her teeth, she lathered on some suntan lotion. Lucas had plenty of it and mosquito spray on hand. She stuffed a small bottle of mosquito spray into the knapsack but shoved the suntan lotion into her shorts pocket.

She blew out an excited breath and caressed her pregnancy bump.

"Newbie, we're going on an adventure. I want you to stay calm and all will be well. I promise," she whispered. She awaited a flutter of acknowledgement, but nothing came. Newbie must have gone back to sleep.

Confidence raced through her. She would find her plane today; she just knew it, but if she didn't, she would come back here and rest, then head out again if help didn't arrive.

She grabbed the small knapsack, and stepped outdoors into the bright sunshine, and tried to ignore the heat and humidity that blasted against her.

Down by the lake, the kayak was heavier than she expected as she dragged it over the land and onto the dock, but she managed.

The knapsack fit perfectly inside the back of the kayak and as she straightened and stood on the dock, her white top billowing in the wind, she stared at the boat, and frowned.

There was just one problem. She had no idea how to get into the contraption!

DAN HADN'T LIKED LEAVING Chrissy with Layla. Yeah sure, the baby had been really excited to see the midwife when she had strolled into the kitchen too damned cheerful with the doctor and Brady, but JJ had left Chrissy in *his* care when she'd left for that damned wedding shower. He should be staying here, but it appeared the doctor wanted all eyes in the sky.

He hadn't been proud of the way Brady, and he had behaved yesterday evening either where Chrissy was concerned. He knew she'd been tired; knew that's why she was crying. But he'd been held up with Search and Rescue and Brady had been contacting some of the girls that had attended the wedding shower trying to find out if they knew about JJ and if she had stayed, despite what that motel receptionist had told Dan. But nobody knew anything. Just that she had been at the shower, had enjoyed herself and left alone telling Milena that she had plans.

He'd been thankful when Rafe had shown up to rescue the crying little girl.

Shit! He'd wanted JJ to have fun, not disappear off the face of the earth.

He refocused his attention to watching the montage of green trees, lush meadows, glimmering blue lakes and winding rivers down below. A few times his hopes soared as he spied movement in a meadow or on a shoreline, but they had been animals.

Everyone was quiet as they looked out their respective windows. It smelled lightly of oil and fuel in the float plane, kind of like how it smelled in JJ's plane. As he gazed out the window he willed himself that he was flying with JJ in her plane. JJ in the cockpit, flying them to a drop off point in the east section or the north quarter where they kept a bunch of machinery to use in those areas. But all his wishful dreaming didn't work. He was still sitting in the doctor's plane searching for JJ.

Brady sat in the cockpit with Will and Rafe sat opposite Dan peering out that window. None of them had gotten any sleep last night as they'd called around for help and now he wondered how useful they were in not being well rested. Would they miss a sign that an alert person might not miss?

Hell, better to be up here in the air than on the ground doing squat.

He had gotten irritated when Will had mentioned he needed to check on a patient that was several miles off JJ's flight plan, but guilt assailed him at being so selfish. The doctor had volunteered to give his valuable time and he had no right to want the doctor's undivided attention on searching for JJ.

But still...he was both angry and devastated at JJ going missing...again.

Man, when was she going to give up being a pilot? By now she must realize how dangerous flying a plane could be? Pilots disappeared without a trace every year in the dense forests of Northern Ontario.

The good news was she'd phoned in a flight plan before leaving the city and at least they knew where to search.

"Down there," Will suddenly said.

Dan's head snapped up. Rafe gazed at him; his face going white as a sheet.

"That's the lake my patient lives on," Will continued, totally oblivious that he had scared the shit out of both himself and Rafe as Dan was sure in Rafe's expression that he'd thought Will had seen some kind of wreckage.

Rafe shook his head and turn to look out the window again.

Dan did the same.

Hell, JJ just might have had to go off the flight plan if she hadn't been able to fly in the storm. So, where the hell was she if she'd landed safely? She had a radio and her cell phone. Why hadn't she called in a mayday? Unless whatever happened had happened so fast, that it had been catastrophic, and she hadn't been able to call for help.

And why the hell didn't they have a GPS system on that plane? He did remember JJ had looked into it at one point and she'd said it was expensive and that because of the isolation of the area, tracking software would be spotty at best, so she'd come to the conclusion that Moose Ranch would not invest in it.

Dan blew out a tense breath as the plane began to descend toward the lake.

Man, JJ was a smart lady when it came to her plane. Why had she not called anyone?

No, he wasn't going to think about any other possibilities except that she was safe...somewhere. Any alternative ideas would just drive him nuts.

JJ STOPPED PADDLING and listened.

Was that a plane she could hear? She could barely hear something, but she wasn't sure what it might be. But because of the loud thumping of the waves against the hollow kayak, she couldn't hear properly. Then the odd sound was gone.

Had she just wishfully imagined the sound?

JJ frowned.

Yeah, it had probably been her imagination.

She began to paddle again, always making sure to keep her torso in the middle of the kayak for balance. She'd learned rather quickly that leaning too much to one side or to the other side would tip the kayak and her over. She had the wet clothes to prove it. She had fallen in twice, but thankfully she'd had the foresight to remove the knapsack before putting the kayak into the water and practicing getting in and out close to the dock.

Now, an estimated two hours out, perspiration swept across her forehead and down her back. The air was sticky, and she felt hot beneath the harsh rays of the sun but dipping her hand into the cool water once in awhile and splashing herself, brought temporary relief. Because she'd stuffed all the drinks into the knapsack and there didn't seem to be anywhere she could stop and get out of the tippy boat to retrieve the knapsack and get at the drinks, she'd resorted to scooping water up with her hat and drinking quickly from it.

Every once in awhile, she also plunged the hat into the water and then dumped the contents over her head, inhaling with shock at the coolness of the water splashing all over her heated body.

Despite not having access to her drinks, she felt like a pro as she leisurely paddled, pacing herself, keeping about twenty feet from the shoreline. The wind was coming in from the west today, splashing against the side of the kayak, sending sprays of cool water against her.

She purposefully didn't think about the guys or her daughter because the last thing she wanted to do was start bawling in the lake and tip over. So, she kept her focus on her surroundings.

The mixed forest of conifers and deciduous trees gave a palette of gorgeous colors of green. Emerald, yellow green, olive, blue greens. It all looked so pretty with the backdrop of a brilliant powder blue sky and the rolling blue waves.

The forest trees hugged grey rocky shorelines. Dead trees had fallen into the lake, their creepy narrow branches reaching up to the sky like big bony fingers of the dead.

She remembered the last time she'd landed on this lake; panic stricken and nauseated with morning sickness. Everything had looked so desolate.

It still did. Kind of.

She'd been paddling so long now her arms were beginning to get really sore. She knew she should turn around and head back. Realized also that she would not make it to wherever this lake of bays ended in a day of paddling. It might take days.

Despair brushed over her and JJ stop paddling. This excursion was a failure.

It was time to turn around and head back to Lucas' cabin.

Chapter Ten

The cabin looked in pretty good shape as the four men meandered toward it along a fern enshrouded trail that led from the lake where the doctor had landed his float plane.

Rafe had been the first one out when the doctor had brought his plane against the dock, right behind a chocolate-colored float plane with a huge white daisy painted on it's side. Rafe had secured the doctor's plane with the help of Dan while Brady had chatted in the cockpit with Dr. Will.

The patient's cabin was a brown painted wooden A-frame style building set beneath an arrangement of giant white oak trees. It's green leaves fluttered crazily in the brisk wind along with a Canadian red and white flag perched on a flag pole to one side of the A-frame.

An elderly gentleman, with tufts of white hair, a white handlebar moustache and bushy white eyebrows set above squinty eyes, sat in a white rocking chair on the wide porch, waiting and watching as the four of them drew closer.

"Hey, Will! Did you bring me my boys? Where did you find them damn city dwellers." The old man called out in a raspy voice. He was dressed in dark blue coveralls and no shirt underneath.

His boys? Rafe wondered if maybe the old guy didn't possess all of his faculties.

"Sorry, Gus. These here are not your boys. How is that head injury you called me about?"

Rafe, Brady, and Dan waved at the old man, who lifted a cane in salute. The three of them remained at the bottom of the stairs giving Dr. Will and his patient some privacy as the doctor ascended the steps toward the elderly man.

"Damned widow maker tree didn't kill me, but it hurts like a son of a bitch! I hope you brought some pain killers cause I am plum out," the old man complained.

Rafe could see from here the injury on the man's forehead didn't look so good. Blood smeared the old guy's cheeks and there were several cuts, bruises, and a large goose egg sized lump across his forehead.

"Was walking along in back from the outhouse and heard the crack. Looked up and saw the branch dropping and bang, right in the head. Knocked me clean off my feet and knocked me out for a bit. Damned branch has been hanging there for going on near twenty years and picked just that time to drop. Who did you bring with you if they are not my boys?"

Will dropped his black bag onto the veranda and bent over Gus now taking a closer look at the injury and Rafe didn't hear the conversation or the doctor's answer.

Truth be told he ached to get back into the sky and keep looking for JJ.

"He looks kind of familiar," Brady said as he waved them away from the bottom of the stairs to allow Dr. Will more privacy with his patient. Then he stopped and turned to stare at the old man.

Rafe didn't give two shits if the guy looked familiar. He wanted out of here.

"Now that you mention it, yeah he does look like someone I might have seen before," Dan said from the other side of Rafe.

"I think I'm going to go for a pilot license," Rafe suddenly blurted, his patience dissolving.

Dan and Brady snapped their heads around and stared at him like he had grown two horns out of his head.

"If I can fly the plane then JJ can stay home where it's safe," Rafe said as his idea began to gather like a storm.

To his irritation, Brady chuckled.

"JJ's not going to stay on the ground just because you get a pilot license. If you think so then you don't know JJ."

"Yeah, you don't even like to fly, Rafe," Dan said in a much too soothing tone.

"She's going to stay on the fucking ground. I won't go through this again," Rafe snapped as the anger he'd been holding inside him suddenly unleashed its full force.

"Hey, man she's her own lady. We can't tell her what to do, no matter how much we want to keep her safe," Brady replied.

"And you wouldn't want to make her a prisoner. She's had too much of that, in prison. It would kill her." Dan's words felt like a splash of ice water on Rafe's face.

"Unless she's already fucking dead." Rafe spat as anger surged.

Dan shook his head.

"She's not dead," he stated.

"Yeah, right. Why haven't we heard from her? Huh, Mr. Positive? She has a radio in her plane."

"Maybe the radio died," Dan replied with a shrug to his shoulders.

Silence hung in the air between the three of them. What else could they say? There was no proof she was alive or dead.

"I'm heading back to the plane" Rafe said. He needed some alone time to gather his composure.

"Don't go there, man" he heard Dan say as Rafe turned and headed back down the trail toward the lake.

Don't go there.

Rafe knew exactly what Dan meant. Don't go in your mind where she's dead.

Too fucking funny because he was already there.

JJ COULD NOT STOP THE dread from beginning to overwhelm her as she paddled the kayak around and began to head back. She thought she had travelled for miles, but if she squinted hard enough through the shimmering haze, she could see the cabin.

It was a spec on the outcrop of rocks and pine trees in the distance.

However, as she paddled, another idea was forming. She had come this far on her first day out. How far could she go if she didn't turn around and just kept paddling? Twice as far that's how far.

She could make camp somewhere. She could keep going around the entire lake until she found her plane. She could stay overnight in the creepy woods. Mosquitoes might kill her if she had no tent if they came out at dusk. But there hadn't been any last night and she had mosquito spray, in case.

Maybe Lucas had a tent? She would have to check around the cabin. Some lip balm would be good because her lips were feeling dry and windburn. Sunglasses would be nice too because she was beginning to get a bit of a headache and her eyes were sore from all her squinting into the sunlight.

White sparkling giant diamonds glistened on the waves, blinding her and boy she swore it was getting hotter. The sun hung high overhead, so she figured it was maybe early afternoon and she was starting to get hungry. Perspiration beaded her forehead as the sun cruelly beat down upon her baseball cap, the back of her neck and all exposed skin. She was beginning to feel a bit too uncomfortable on her butt too.

She tensed as something black suddenly appeared in her vision to her right, lake side.

She did a double take when not more than six feet away, a loon paddled, keeping pace with her.

"Wow aren't you a cutie," JJ said softly as she examined the bird.

It was big. Probably ten pounds with a long body and a short tail. It's red eye peered at her and it's black dagger-like bill was slightly open. It's feathers were a spotty black and white and its rounded black head shone with a greenish tinge.

She was used to seeing loons back at the ranch as they swam by the dock, but never had she experienced one swimming right alongside her.

She would have to invest in a kayak. She liked the quietness of it and how close to the water she could be. She could also imagine how strong her arms would get if she went out kayaking every day. It made her wonder what other kind of wildlife she might be able to sneak up on if she quietly kayaked along the shoreline instead of puttering along in a noisy motor boat.

The loon kept pace with her for quite some time. Probably fifteen minutes.

JJ spoke softly to it, telling it how beautiful and handsome he looked. She told the bird about her family. About how she missed them so much and then she laughed when she realized she was talking to a loon.

Gosh, last night she'd talked to an owl, today a loon. Would she end up going mad out here with no one to talk to?

Suddenly the bird flew off ahead of her, it's wings fluttering noisily close to the waves as it went. To her surprise the loon joined another loon about fifty feet away and then they both paddled further out into the lake and away from her.

Wow. This was something she would never forget. Being so close to a loon for so long without it even being afraid of her.

Such a lucky loon to have a companion. A sudden well of emotions had her about to break down into tears when that noise she thought she had heard earlier, started again.

JJ frowned and stopped paddling.

She listened, and tried to orient where it was coming from. But the thuds of the choppy waves crashing against her kayak prevented her from fully getting a direction.

North? West?

She could barely hear it, but if she were to guess it might be a plane.

Were they widening their search for her? Or was it just any random plane? She just couldn't be sure where the sound was coming from, then it was gone.

Frustration rushed through her, and JJ began to paddle faster.

Shoot! She should have stayed at the cabin and made a huge ass smoky fire to catch the attention of any planes. But darn it, she couldn't be in two places at the same time! And certainly, didn't want to burn down the forest in this wind.

She brightened as another idea took hold. A smoky fire in the cast iron stove inside the cabin might be doable. Why hadn't she thought about that before? If a plane saw smoke in this heat coming from a cabin, they might investigate.

Maybe she was just imagining that sound? It may have been nothing but some sort of echo of the water crashing against a certain area of the shoreline. Maybe no one was even looking for her, presuming her dead?

JJ blew out a pissed off breath and glared into the distance where she could no longer see the cabin due to the haze.

Nope, she wasn't going down without one hell of a fight.

She had to find out if her plane was out there. She needed to at least search. She needed to make some sort of a plan.

She wanted to go home.

She didn't want to wait around here for a possible rescue. Emphasis on possible.

She needed to hug her baby. Craved to see her cowboys. Wanted to find out who the baby daddy was.

Gosh, she missed everyone so much.

She ached with hurt.

But boy, her arms hurt too. She just hoped she could make it back to the cabin.

BRADY HAD NOTICED RAFE'S continued silence as they got back underway in Dr. Will's floatplane. Sitting up here in front with the pilot had him thinking about JJ and how he usually sat with her in the cockpit when she was flying because Dan didn't care where he sat, and Rafe preferred to sit near an exit.

That Rafe was pissed off was understandable. Brady felt angry too. Not at JJ though.

He was angry because something bad always seemed to be happening lately. JJ's depression following Chrissy. His sister Jenna's husband's unexpected death. Dan's foot caught in an animal trap with him almost dying of exposure and now this.

That was life, he understood that. But he didn't have to like it.

Keeping his gaze on the tapestry of trees, lakes, and meadows, checking for any signs of a downed plane, he decided a bit of small talk would be beneficial and crack through the disturbing crypt-like silent atmosphere in the plane.

"Is your patient going to be okay?" Brady asked Dr. Will.

He understood that the doctor wouldn't be able to divulge any important medical information, so he figured this question was harmless.

"He should be. He took a big hit to the head, and I patched him up. Gave him some painkillers. I want him to get a CT scan, but he's refused. I'm thinking of contacting a next of kin and letting him know."

"Would that be one of his boys?" Brady asked.

"Yeah, he has three sons actually. Foster sons. They are around your age so for him to confuse you all from a distance for his three sons is not alarming."

"He looks familiar," Dan blurted from behind them.

Brady noted Dr. Will smile.

"I asked him if I could tell you if you guys recognized him and he said I could as long as you don't show up at his door asking for autographs. He values his privacy. Do I have your word?"

Brady refocused his attention to the search and nodded. Probably some actor.

"Sure," Dan replied.

"No problem," came Rafe's reply.

Well at least Rafe was now listening and talking. Hopefully, it was a good sign.

"You recognize him from the pictures on the back of his teen boy mystery books."

"Gus G. Gusterfersone! Author of the Sullivan Triplet Mysteries! That's why he looks familiar," Dan suddenly shouted.

Brady chuckled as he now understood why he and Dan thought they had seen the guy somewhere before. The pictures on the back of his books gave a much younger version of him.

"I should have known. My brothers and sisters and I were raised on his books," Brady said.

"Never heard of him," Rafe mumbled.

"You never heard of Gus G. Gusterfersone!" Dan chimed. "He's like only one of the most famous authors in the world, man. I have a bunch of his books on my shelf. You know, the dark green covers with the three teenage boys on them. You gotta read them, Rafe. All teenage kids should read them. There's survival, camping, and the boys are always stumbling into some sort of trouble. You know similar to the Hardy Boy and Nancy Drew Mysteries," Dan said.

"I promise to read them if you just keep your attention focused to the task at hand, okay?" Rafe growled.

"You are on. JJ will be found, and you will be reading every last one," Dan teased.

"Last count there was well over a hundred books," Dr. Will chimed in.

"Wow you read them too?" Brady commented, feeling guilty for his brief focus off worrying about JJ.

"Yes, I did. They are very well written. You can imagine my surprise when I first met him on a previous visit."

"I bet," Brady grinned and returned to looking out the window.

When they found JJ, he was going to reread every last one of those books to Chrissy. She might not understand what he was saying, but he'd love to read them again, especially now that he knew the author was living in the vicinity.

Suddenly the radio crackled, and Layla's voice erupted into the plane.

"Will, are you there? Over."

A deep sinking feeling shot over Brady. He heard Rafe swear softly and Dan inhale a deep breath as if bracing for bad news.

Will pushed on the radio microphone.

"Will here. What have you got for me. Over."

"An update from Search and Rescue. Wish I had better news. They saw a no sign of a downed plane along the flight path. No emergency beacon or any other signals. Search and Rescue said it could be the result of a catastrophic failure of the plane, or the plane is submerged, and the radio and emergency beacons were compromised due to the water. They would have liked to expand the search but unfortunately they need to send their team further north to assist in locating and treating a fire crew trapped in behind forest fire lines. Blue and Kelly are on route to Moose Ranch. ETA about one hour. Tell the guys we'll just keep looking until we find her. Over"

Brady didn't like the grim look on Will's face or the awful feeling in the pit of his gut.

"Okay, thanks for the update. We'll circle around soon and start heading back. ETA about an hour and a half. Over."

"Okay, Will. We will have lunch ready for all of you. Talk later. Over and out."

Brady's head was spinning.

Was this it? Search and Rescue was leaving them to their own devices? Were JJ and the newbie gone?

"We'll keep looking. We'll charter a plane and a pilot and totally find her," Dan said from behind them.

"Right, we'll keep looking," Rafe grumbled. But Brady picked up the undertone of despair in Rafe's voice.

"Sorry, guys. I wish we had had better news. I'll see about coordinating my schedule so I can take you up again tomorrow. Maybe in the afternoon this time, so I can see patients in the morning," the doctor said.

He sounded dejected. Did he also believe there was no hope?

Brady fought the well of tears that began to blind his vision. Then just as quickly as his despair threatened to overwhelm him, defiance raged within.

No way were JJ and the baby dead. If her plane had gone down during that storm, they would find her. She hadn't survived years in prison just to end up dead.

Using his renewed defiance, Brady smiled and refocused on searching for anything out of the ordinary within his view out the window.

They would find her alive. Suddenly he had no doubt.

JJ HAD BEEN PADDLING for what felt like ever when she finally made it back to the dock. The wind had shifted from the west and was now coming straight at her from the south, so the last hour or so, she had to paddle harder against its increasing force and against the larger waves that cascaded over the bobbing kayak.

Thankfully, this kayak had a protective cape that kept out most of the water, but her arms ached like they had never ached before, and she could barely stop herself from crying as she paddled in beside the dock.

She was so stiff, she could barely get out of the kayak, almost tipping it over with her in it twice. But she made it. Then came the hard part, lifting the kayak onto the dock. But she managed with surprising ease.

Despite feeling so tired that she could literally sleep while standing, she forced herself to pull the kayak along the dock onto land. If it got much windier she was sure that the kayak could blow off the dock and sail away just like her plane.

Moving slowly, as her back, butt and legs hurt, she leaned over and pulled out the knapsack with sore arms. The knapsack seemed to weigh a ton compared to when she'd left. She dropped it onto the ground, straightened and winced at her aching back, looking out at the hazy lake as it shimmered beneath the hot sunshine.

Man, she was glad to be on land again.

Just then a menacing growl erupted from right behind her.

JJ froze. Her heart crashed against her chest as intense fear took hold.

Oh, come on. Seriously?

What was growling? A bear? A wolf? Could she somehow get the kayak back into the water and leave until the threatening animal was gone?

Another growl had icy shivers shimmying up and down her spine, prompting her to search the ground for a fallen branch or anything she could use as a weapon of defense.

There was nothing except...the paddle.

Moving slowly so as not to cause the animal any alarm, JJ squatted and grabbed the paddle. She held it tightly, stood and then cautiously began to turn around to face her would be attacker.

Hopefully yelling and screaming and waving the paddle would frighten the animal away. If worst came to worst, and the animal came too close, she'd smack it over its snout.

Terror raged within, yet her grip was rock solid. She would protect her baby and herself as if their lives depended on it, which it did.

The growl came again, from a nearby low hanging patch of juniper bushes.

She gasped as the bushes moved and suddenly a black and white dog crawled out on all fours. Its pink tongue dangled from its open mouth and the cutest brown eyes stared back at her.

"Oh my gosh! What are you doing here?"

JJ ignored a voice inside her head warning her that the animal looked unkempt and could have rabies, and immediately crouched onto her haunches into a non threatening position.

The dog stood and gave out a couple of barks as if approving. Then, with a madly wagging tail, it scampered over to where JJ had dropped the knapsack. It's black wet nose sniffed fiercely at the knapsack, and it then looked up at her, its head tilting to the left in a most endearing way, as if to say, can I have what's in there?

"You're hungry," she said.

She didn't dare reach for the knapsack. For all she knew the dog could bite her.

Then suddenly she realized if there was a dog here, people were here too!

Her hopes soared.

JJ left the knapsack near the shoreline, kept a firm grip on the paddle, just in case the dog got violent, and hurriedly ascended the trail. To her delight, the dog passed her and raced up the trail ahead of her.

Oh my gosh, it must be going to its owners.

When she reached the cabin, she was huffing and puffing from the exertion and perspiring from the heat. The dog stood there, panting, waiting for her. No sounds came from within the building. There were no signs of any boats on the nearby shoreline. No planes. Nothing. Just a sunny haze.

She began to shout as frustration grabbed hold.

"Help! Is anyone around! I need help!"

Her answer was a little bark from the dog.

She yelled a few more times. No response.

All she could hear was the wind whipping through the boughs of the overhead pine branches and the clunk clunk of waves slamming against the rocky shoreline below.

She shouted a few more times. Nobody answered.

"Where is your family?" she asked the dog, who had moved to sit beneath the shade of a towering pine tree.

It just stared at her.

Although she'd already realized that the animal was unkempt, she now noted it had no collar and its black and white fur appeared tangled and dirty. It was obvious no one had run a comb or brush through its hair in quite some time.

Devastation rocked her.

"Oh, crap. You are on your own too, just like me," she said to the dog.

The dog tilted its head in that endearing gesture as if trying to understand what she was saying.

"Okay, let's get you some food and water."

She stepped into the warm cabin, left the door open and grinned as the dog strolled up the small steps onto the porch, sat and gazed in the doorway at her. But it didn't come in.

As she searched the pantry, she kept peeking out the window looking for signs of people. Maybe the dog came from interior campers? Or hikers?

Gosh, what kind of food did dogs like? Probably meat and there were plenty of meat tins. Maybe the dog belonged to Lucas? No, she doubted it. There didn't appear to be any canned dog food.

"Want some corned beef?" she asked the dog.

The dog barked in answer.

"Okay, corned beef it is!" Oh great, now she was talking to a dog.

JJ laughed as the dog lay down in a crouched position and settled its head upon its front paws, watched her and patiently waited while she began to open the tin.

Truth be told, she was so grateful for the company and hoped the dog would stick around but she hoped even more that the dog wasn't lost, and people would soon be looking for it and come here too.

THE INSTANT LAYLA HEARD the purr of an incoming plane, she knew it was her ex-husband, Willie. Blue and Kelly had arrived on schedule and were currently upstairs with Chrissy as they got her ready for an afternoon nap. She'd had no problem feeding the little girl, but Layla could tell in the way Chrissy's brow would sometimes furrow that she knew something was wrong.

Layla gazed at the food she'd made for the men. She realized they wouldn't be hungry due to being despaired over JJ, but they needed to eat.

She vividly remembered when JJ had confided in her that she did not know who the father of her baby might be, and that Brady and she had an open relationship, and the other man knew about it and that neither man was jealous of the other.

She wondered if Dan or Rafe was the other man?

All three of them had looked like they'd been run over by a truck this morning when she'd come into the ranch house, so it had been hard to tell which other man could be the father of her baby. The few times she had met the three men, they had all been harmonious and they gazed at JJ with love in their eyes.

Her ex-husband Will would never approve of a situation for her like JJ had. And it wasn't something Layla would even think of trying.

But in the way the three men had looked this morning, she wouldn't be surprised if JJ were sleeping with all three of them. She held no judgment over their situation. All she wished was for them to find JJ alive and well and the baby in good shape.

She nibbled on her lower lip as she wondered where JJ's plane had gone down.

She tensed as the men stomped up the outside stairs and entered the mud room. No one spoke. Their silence was profound as they entered the kitchen one by one.

First, Brady, then Rafe, and finally Dan. They looked even worse now than this morning before they'd left, and her heart clenched with sympathy for them. She was not surprised that Will had not come inside as he tried to avoid her like the plague if he could.

Today, he had been civil. So, she had been civil. It had been amazing that he agreed to put his patients aside and fly out here to help out Moose Ranch. It had felt like old times. In the past, they'd worked well together, that is until everything had fallen apart.

"The doctor said he'll call you later, to co-ordinate a time to go back up again to search for JJ," Brady said as he headed for the kitchen sink.

"Yeah, on our way back, he got a call, so he couldn't stay for lunch," Dan added.

"How's the kid?" Rafe asked as he grabbed a mug from the counter where she had placed a bunch of them beside the coffee maker.

"She's doing good. All fed. I followed the routine you guys wrote up. Blue and Kelly are up there with her now."

"Actually, Blue is with her now, reading a nursery rhyme to her. I'm heading down to my plane to do a flight check. Do you think you guys can be ready in half an hour? Severe weather is brewing so the faster we get up, the more time we have," Kelly said as she came rushing down the stairs.

The men mumbled affirmations.

Kelly smiled grimly and left.

The men fell silent again as they each took turns washing their hands at the kitchen sink and then sat at the table.

"Eat up, gentlemen. You need to keep up your strength for JJ. Am I right?" Layla asked, trying to give them a reason to eat.

They nodded and slowly began to help themselves to the assortment of salads and meat dishes. She would stick around a while longer to make sure each of them ate their fill. Gosh she could see how wiped out and devastated each man looked, and it made her want to cry. She prayed they would find JJ alive this afternoon.

Layla grabbed the steaming coffee pot and headed to the table. She knew the men would need good strong black coffee to help keep them awake and focus for the afternoon search. Lots and lots of coffee. She began topping up their mugs.

RAFE ACTUALLY FELT better after downing some food, several cups of black coffee and having the fastest shower he had ever taken.

Then the three of them met Kelly down at the dock within half an hour. He'd noticed instantly that it was hotter and more humid, the air smelled of ozone. It was going to storm at some point this afternoon or tonight and he was grateful that Kelly decided to go up anyway.

Now they'd been airborne for over an hour, with Kelly expanding the search area. Dr. Will had slipped a note onto Kelly's cockpit seat with the area they'd already covered. When she'd read the paper, she'd placed it on her lap and nodded.

Renewed hope had flowed through Rafe as he kept his gaze riveted out the window and scanned the dense wilderness dotted with lakes below.

Man, so many trees. So many lakes. So many places for a plane to go down. As he kept his gaze searching, his thoughts turned to more pleasant times.

Rafe smiled as he remembered that one time JJ and he had set out one evening for a walk after supper leaving Dan to clean up the dishes and giving Brady some quality time with his daughter on the dock as they waited for the sun to set.

If the baby JJ was carrying was his, that evening would have been the time newbie would have been conceived. He should have known better to carry condoms when he was around JJ.

But he had been so happy that she'd been feeling so much better after her bout with postpartum depression that he had not expected she would be the one to make the move on him.

They had been holding hands talking about their upcoming alone night together, and she'd casually turned the conversation to telling him she wanted him to make love to her while she was tied up. She'd removed the very long red ribbon that she had used to tie her hair into a ponytail and had dangled it in front of him like a matador teasingly dangling a red flag in front of an angry bull.

Except Rafe hadn't been angry. He had been hornier than hell the instant he had gotten her meaning.

"Come on, Rafe, I dare you to catch me, strip me naked, tie me to a tree and make me scream for you."

Her brown eyes had twinkled with such happiness and excitement that he had been momentarily mesmerized by her beauty. Then she was running, her long hair lifting in the breeze like a brown waterfall and that naughty red ribbon flowing from her hand like a target.

He'd easily caught her and had stripped her right there out in the wilderness at the side of the trail, tying her to a tree with that red ribbon and then he'd made love to her until she was crying out his name. He hadn't worn a condom that one time.

His heart clenched as if someone were squeezing it so tight that he feared it would explode. He couldn't lose JJ or that baby.

His thoughts disintegrated as the radio crackled and Blue's voice erupted into the plane.

Shit! He could not endure any more bad news.

"Kelly, are you there, over."

"I'm here, Blue. What have you got for me? Over," Kelly asked.

"Bad weather popping up all around you. They're saying a severe weather alert with violent winds and pop-up thunderstorms. Happening now. To your east heading westward at a slow pace. Over. You'll need to get back so we can avoid it," Blue said.

Rafe blinked as he gazed out the window. Way to his left he spied the dark blue thunderclouds amassing. He was pretty sure Kelly and Brady must have already seen them and had remained quiet, maybe hoping for a little extra time to search.

"OK, thanks. We'll start heading back. Over," Kelly answered.

"Roger that, see you soon. Over and out."

Rafe silently cursed. They hadn't even been up in the air for very long this time around. He had hoped for at least another hour before they had to go back. But he knew Blue didn't like storms and she needed to get back to her daughter who was with an elderly babysitter. He should be grateful that they had come out, but he just couldn't put aside his disappointment.

"Brady can you write down the coordinates where we turn so the next pilot knows where to pick up?" Kelly asked.

"On it," Brady replied.

He could tell in Brady's tight tone that he was just as disappointed as Rafe.

He glanced over at Dan who was looking toward the cockpit and frowning. He was probably thinking the same thing as he was thinking. If they saw nothing on the way back home then JJ would have to spend another night out there.

Alone.

The four of them were finally alone once again despite Brady inviting Blue and Kelly to stay the night in order to avoid the storms. The last thing he wanted was for something bad to happen to them because they'd come out to help find JJ.

But Kelly said she knew how to fly in storms and Blue needed to get back to her daughter.

Brady shook his head as he stared out across the frothy lake. What was it with these daredevil women pilots? He just didn't see the need to put their lives in danger flying around storms or ending up like JJ.

He didn't argue with the women. Just said thanks and wished them well and if they would please call and let them know they'd made it home safe. They said they would.

Truth was, he felt like a zombie as he cradled his warm, sweet daughter in his arms while he stood with her on the dock. She was staring out across the lake, into the sky, and for the first time ever, she was ignoring the sunset.

He knew what she was doing. She was searching those puffy dark storm clouds that were billowing in the southeast where they had just come from earlier with Kelly's float plane. The clouds were moving in their direction with a tardy slowness.

Chrissy was searching for her mother. Expecting to see that sparkling white float plane burst out of those black clouds like a flying super hero.

Brady nuzzled his cheek against her pudgy cheek, but he had to be careful. He hadn't shaved in a couple of days and the bristles would give his baby a rash. When she nuzzled him back a thick well of emotions clutched at his breaking heart.

He knew they should head up to the safety of the ranch house, but he just couldn't make himself move from this spot. Maybe because he was hoping he'd see JJ's white plane coming out of those clouds too.

JJ, where the hell are you? His inner voice shouted the question over and over in his mind like a mantra.

Then wetness splashed down his cheeks and for a moment he thought it had begun to rain, but then he realized he was crying and as he moved his face away from Chrissy's so she wouldn't see his distress, he saw tears rolling down her cheeks too.

Ah, man.

JJ, where the hell are you?

Chapter Eleven

J J stared out the open door as the sheets of rain fell and hindered her view of the lake.

Well, so much for making a signal fire. No one would be looking for her in this miserable weather.

Thankfully though, she had company. After feeding the dog, she had decided to leave the door open so he would come in. But he just lay there right outside the doorway, watching her.

Did he want more food? Probably, but she would wait until supper was ready.

On the propane stove, she had spaghetti boiling on one burner, and on the other burner in a frying pan there were a couple of sizzling slices of corned beef that she had not given to the dog. Vegetables for supper included green bean salad. The green beans came from a can, and she'd sprinkled pepper and salt over the beans and dribbled some oil and vinegar. All she had to do was toss the beans when she was ready to eat.

She was impressed with Lucas' set up. He had simple foods. There were packages of dry goods such as rice, cornmeal, pasta, an arrangement of dried beans and lentils, ready-mix mashed potatoes among other foods. Canned goods included an abundance of peach, fruit cocktails, pears as well as an assortment of canned vegetables. There were plenty of canned pop and juices in cartons as well as dry drink mixes. It appeared the got the water from the lake as there were several steel galvanized empty pails stacked beside the doorway.

She'd used a couple of bottles of water to boil the spaghetti this time. If she were stuck here long-term, she'd of course turn to pails and carry the water up from the lake.

Suddenly lightning flashed and thunder cracked and to JJ's amusement, the dog scampered inside and dove under the bed.

"Oh dear! Little fellow, it's all right."

Just saying that to the dog kind of made her feel better herself. Quickly she closed the door, wincing at her sore shoulders.

Outside the wind intensified and rain blasted against those delicate window panes but for the first time since being stranded here she felt like humming. She ignored the storm and went about stirring the noodles and flipping the corned beef in the pan, which smelled so delicious that it had her mouth watering.

It continued to rain and thunder and lightning but with the dog here, she really did feel okay.

Ha! Who would have thought a dog would help keep her anxiety in check?

A little while later she set a bowl of water and a bowl filled with noodles and pieces of cooked corned beef upon the floor near the bed where the dog was hiding and then she set the table for herself. The scent of corned beef and the dry cheese she sprinkled on top of the noodles had her mouth watering.

Gosh, it smelled so good. She was famished!

The dog finally crept out from under the bed and noisily lapped up the contents of the food bowl, completely ignoring the water. Her heart smiled as she watched the dog gobble the food and lick the bowl clean.

"It looks like I don't need to wash the dishes with you doing such a thorough job," she complimented.

Again, as the dog listened to her, it tilted its head in that charming way that made emotions clutch at her heart. She wanted to hug the sweet bundle of black and white fur as it gazed at her with such compassion in its brown eyes, but she didn't dare. At least not until they both felt more comfortable around each other.

The thought of rabies once again crossed her thoughts, so she needed to be mindful of that possibility.

"You are so cute when you do that with your head. It makes me wonder, are you a girl or a boy?" she asked the dog.

It began to wag its tail. A tail full of burrs and leaves.

"How long have you been on your own, sweetie?" JJ asked as it watched her sit at the table and begin to eat her meal.

"And you don't even drool," she added.

"I had a friend when I was a little girl, and her family had a Saint Bernard. All that dog did was slobber this sticky drool that stuck to my clothes like glue. It was so gross that I got turned off to dogs ever since."

JJ smiled.

"But I think you're the one who is going to change my mind."

She laughed heartily as the dog once again tilted its head to one side as it listened to her.

Yes, tonight was certainly going to be enjoyable compared to the previous two nights.

"WE'RE GOING TO HAVE to figure out how to take care of the ranch and keep searching for JJ," Dan murmured as Rafe washed the dishes and he rinsed.

Dan noted Rafe tense beside him.

"You and Brady take care of the ranch. I'll charter a pilot to take me out to look for her. We can't take advantage of everyone for too long, they have jobs to do," Rafe said.

Dan nodded. Rafe had a point.

Layla and Will had patients to attend to and Kelly and Blue had their contract jobs with North Country Air. Everyone had bills to pay so they needed to work.

A low rumble of thunder sifted through the open kitchen window.

"Why isn't Brady coming in? When thunder roars, go indoors. How many times has he drilled that saying into us?" Rafe complained.

Just then the landline phone rang, and Dan's heart began to beat frantically as he hurried to get it.

Hell, it was twilight, with storms popping up all over because of the heat and humidity. The search and rescue people had gone off on another emergency, and no one was looking for JJ at the moment. Despite that, he prayed it was good news about her.

He frowned at the number on the call display. It seemed familiar and yet he had no idea of whom it could be.

"Moose Ranch," Dan spoke into the phone.

There was nothing. Crap! Another telemarketer?

"Hello? Is anyone there? JJ?"

Why the hell would he even think that it might be her? It wasn't even her freaking number.

The line crackled. He thought he heard a voice, but it sounded mechanical and far away. Then the line went dead. Anger rushed through him, and he slammed the phone onto the receiver.

"Who was it?" Rafe asked as he slipped another dish into Dan's side of the sink to rinse.

Dan returned to his station at the sink, furious at being bothered.

"Probably some telemarketer. They called the other night too, but no one was there, just no sound and then the line crackling and then the line goes dead. This time I thought I heard a voice, but the connection is so bad I couldn't tell them off."

Rafe frowned.

"Why did you say JJ?" he asked.

Dan began rinsing the dishes and shook his head.

"I don't know. She's just on my freaking mind. She's the only thing I can think of," Dan explained.

"Yeah. Same here."

An uncomfortable silence hung heavy in the air between them. Usually, Dan knew what to say to cheer up his friend, but no amount of joking with the guy with what ailed him this time around would help.

Rafe broke the silence.

"We should shout down to Brady and tell him to get Chrissy back inside before it starts to rain. The last thing we need is a sick little girl, especially without JJ and her expertise with the plane if things go south."

Dan sighed. He had to agree with Rafe. Without JJ they were helpless in an emergency situation relying on pilots to come in from far away or wait for Dr. Will to get here.

"You're right. JJ is the glue who keeps us all feeling safe, especially that she flies a plane."

To Dan's surprise, Rafe chuckled.

"Yeah, she's tough. I think she would have been able to handle whatever happened to make her disappear."

"We just have to find her," Dan replied.

Rafe nibbled on his bottom lip, strolled to the nearby kitchen window, and looked out.

"Yeah, wherever she is," he said softly.

JJ CURSED LUCAS' STUPID cell phone.

Earlier, after she'd eaten, there had been a break in the storm, so she'd ventured out to get the knapsack she'd left near the shoreline when she'd returned from the kayaking trip. The dog had decided to hide under the bed again, so she'd left it in the cabin, leaving the door open in case it wanted to go outside.

To her excitement, the air wasn't muggy anymore. Instead, it smelled fresh and clean, but the sky remained dark grey and heavy with rain clouds. The wind had died down, but she heard grumblings of more thunder in the distance and knew there would be another storm coming. It was just a matter of time.

On her way back up the trail with the knapsack, she'd decided to explore the other trail she'd seen this morning. Along that trail she'd found herself on a little treeless hill. There, to her utmost surprise and exhilaration, she'd discovered a small solar panel. Beside it, a tarp. Beneath the tarp was some kind of a contraption that would allow her to plug in the cell phone's battery charger, which she remembered being on that shelf beside the cell phone in the cabin.

In her elation, she'd almost fallen over several times on the muddy trail as she'd rushed back to the cabin to retrieve the items she'd need.

Despite being sore and tired from all that paddling, she'd literally danced with anticipation as she plugged in the phone fully expecting to be able to call out without delay. Or even text. But the texts all got hung and never got sent. The power wasn't enough to call and so she'd waited, anxiety nibbling on her. While she waited, she did some more exploring and found a little fenced in vegetable garden nearby. There were hardly any weeds around the numerous plants, so she figured Lucas must have left only a few days ago.

She'd laughed as she spied tons of vegetables ready to be picked! Bright red tomatoes, healthy green cucumbers, and luscious looking fresh crisp lettuce. Purple, green, and yellow beans dangled from vines beneath leaves on poles and there were small thatches of carrots, onions, and more vegetables.

Oh my God! She had fresh vegetables! And there were berry patches too. Strawberries, raspberries, and blueberries!

Happiness soared as she'd collected tomato, cucumber, and some lettuce. She would make herself a salad tonight and in the morning, she'd come back for some berries.

While she waited for the cell phone to charge beneath the tarp, she'd returned to the cabin, made her salad while the dog slept under the bed, and she swore it was the most delicious, crunchy, bursting with flavor salad she had ever eaten in her life.

She would have waited many more hours to charge the phone, but the sky was darkening with thunderclouds and lightning began to flash, so she'd quickly retrieved the phone only to discover it had only charged to one percent.

Obviously, there was a problem with the phone and that's why Lucas had left it behind.

Despite the shortage of power, she'd tried once again to call Moose Ranch and when she'd heard Dan's voice, she started crying and talking, but it appeared he wasn't able to hear her at all!

Just like the last time! The line had quickly gone silent, followed by crackling and then the line went dead. She'd tried texting again, but nothing got sent.

Despair crushed her hopes of being rescued, and she cursed so loudly the dog came out from beneath the bed and began to bark at her, not in a menacing way, but one in which it appeared the dog was upset too.

"Oh dear, I'm so sorry," she spoke softly, and the dog immediately calmed down, its tail wagging wildly as it stopped barking.

"Okay go back to sleep," JJ instructed in a calm voice, and she was surprised when the dog returned to its position beneath the bed.

Wow, smart dog. It appeared the dog didn't like her to be angry or upset.

As twilight descended lightning blinked at the windows and an ominous rumble of thunder shot shivers up JJ's spine, but then she smiled and caressed her baby bump, wincing at her sore shoulders.

"At least the two of us have some company tonight, and such a good watchdog he or she appears to be," she whispered and then she went about getting ready for bed.

She was exhausted.

BRADY WAS IN SUCH A deep sleep that when he heard his cell phone ringing loudly beside him, he almost decided to just let it ring, but then he remembered JJ was missing and in the darkness, he hurriedly reached over and picked up the receiver.

"Moose Ranch," he automatically mumbled, fighting to clear the cobwebs from his thoughts.

"Morning, Brady." It was his brother, Mitch.

Brady blinked.

Morning? Why was it so dark in his bedroom? He stared at the drapes. They'd been drawn.

What the heck was going on? He never slept with the curtains closed. Who the hell had closed the curtains? He glanced at the alarm clock and did a double take. It was seven o'clock. His alarm should have gone off two hours ago.

"Daegen let us know about what happened to JJ. Has she been found?" Mitch asked with tension quite obvious in his voice.

"No. I didn't think she'd be gone so long. Thought we would have found her by now."

Those same emotions that had clutched his chest last evening while he had held his daughter on the dock rushed through him again. He swallowed hard, trying to supress them. He didn't want to break down and cry like some damn baby, like he had done on the dock.

"Okay. Here's the plan. Daegen has rented a floatplane, but he can't get access to it until late this afternoon. It's high season for rentals so a plane has been hard to find. Anyways he and Milena will be flying back here from the city and then we will be there tomorrow morning first thing. Rain or shine. Blue and Kelly will be coming to your place for today's morning shift. Will and Layla in the afternoon. We'll co-ordinate so someone is in the air as much as possible. We'll keep looking until she's found.

Brady just about lost it. He felt delirious with relief from everyone's support. He couldn't speak and thankfully Mitch just kept on talking.

"If you need to attend to urgent stuff on the ranch, then one or two of you stay and tend to the work. But if things can wait, the more eyes in the sky, the better. Am I right?"

Brady nodded as his eyes teared up and the room blurred.

"Are you there?"

He cleared the emotions out of his throat.

"Um, yeah. Yeah. Thanks."

"Cool. All will be well, bro. Just hold on," Mitch said.

"Yeah. Will do. Thanks, Mitch."

"No problem. Let me know if anything changes. If not, we'll be there tomorrow. See you soon."

The line went dead.

Brady closed his eyes and sent up a huge thanks to God. Why hadn't he thought about Daegen, over at his brother's ranch? Mitch had once mentioned the guy had been in the military and had flown all kinds of planes in all kinds of weather.

Man, with Daegen involved, they could keep the search going for like ever.

Brady blew out a tense breath. No, not forever. They would find JJ. There was no other option.

RAFE KNEW THAT BRADY would be pissed off when he came downstairs this morning, and he wasn't wrong.

"Who the fuck shut the curtains and turned off my alarm?" Brady snapped at Rafe as he entered the kitchen area, grabbed a mug, and poured himself some coffee.

"And where is my kid? She gets up before her own dad. That's not right."

Rafe smiled as he flipped over the eggs he'd been frying up for Brady.

Last night when Brady and Chrissy had returned, he had noticed they had both been crying. Brady had brought her directly upstairs saying he would bathe her and tuck her in. The man had looked exhausted.

Hell, they all were mentally exhausted.

"You were dead to the world, so I turned off your alarm and drew the curtains early this morning," Rafe admitted.

Brady glared at him.

Wow, if looks could kill, Rafe would be dead right now. He needed to figure out a way to lighten the doomy mood.

"The little one is entertaining Dan in the garden. Blue and Kelly will be here within the hour. Who was on the phone? I was on the throne, and I couldn't be disturbed if you know what I mean."

Rafe hoped the joke would loosen Brady up but nope, Brady just shook his head at him.

"Information like that I don't need to know," he growled.

"Okay then. Bacon and eggs coming right up. I guess it was another telemarketer on the phone?" Rafe asked as he began working the bacon onto the waiting paper towels on the plate.

"Huh? What? Telemarketer?" Brady grimaced as he sipped the hot coffee.

"Dan mentioned a couple of evening prank calls. No one on the line. Just static. Same number."

"Block the bastards. We don't have time for that. We need to keep the phone lines open. It was Mitch who called when you were in the john. Daegen rented a plane. He'll be getting the plane tonight and they'll be here tomorrow. Said rain or shine, Daegen is going up. Says they'll keep the plane up for as long as it takes."

Rafe's hopes soared at this unexpected news.

"No freaking way."

Brady smiled and that alleviated some of Rafe's stress about the guy.

"Yes, freaking way. Now where's my breakfast? I'm suddenly hungry." Brady replied.

"You know what? So am I," Rafe said and winced as Brady slapped him on the back.

"Sorry for biting your head off. I know you're just looking out for me," Brady murmured as he snapped a piece of bacon off the paper towel and shoved it into his mouth. His blue eyes were suddenly twinkling, and Rafe was glad that Brady was feeling a bit better, even if for just a second or two.

"Well, JJ would kill Dan and I if something happened to you on our watch," Rafe admitted.

Brady's grin widened.

"We are going to find her. I just know it."

Rafe nodded. He'd had the same feeling just yesterday. Not as much this morning, but having Brady saying it and feeling it, made Rafe's doubts fade away.

"Yeah, we will find her," he agreed.

DESPAIR CRUSHED JJ. She could see her plane. Could clearly make out the white silhouette of the wings, the windshield glinting in the sunshine, the floats. Everything.

The wind had died down and the early morning sun shone brightly. There were no more waves to obscure her view. She could see her plane from where she stood on the rocky hill in front of Lucas' cabin.

Her plane was below the blue shimmering water, deep in the lake.

She could see it so plainly that her heart just about exploded out of her chest, and she realized she was never going to be rescued. The emergency signal, the radio, and her cell phone, all were underwater. She would be here forever, a stranded Robinson Crusoe with her little baby. The two of them all alone and at the mercy of the wildlife and the vast wilderness.

JJ awoke on a tortured moan. Her heart crashed against her chest as she opened her eyes, and she realized it had been a nightmare. She was safe in Lucas' cabin and her plane wasn't submerged...unless it had been a premonition?

She was laying on her back and the blankets were tucked under her chin. She'd slept so soundly throughout the entire night she'd felt no aches and pains from all that kayaking until she tried to shift her body. She moaned at her throbbing shoulders as she moved her arms to push down the blankets.

She winced at the soreness in her lower back as she tried to wiggle her butt into a more comfortable position. What the heck had she been thinking going out in a kayak for so long? Her body ached and not in an enjoyable way.

She tried to move her legs but couldn't because something heavy lay across her them. For a split-second anxiety rushed over her. Why couldn't she move her legs? Had the cabin fallen in on her during the night and now she lay pinned beneath a beam of wood?

Panic hit her and she looked down and discovered that the dog had climbed onto the bed sometime during the night and now it lay sleeping on her. The sight of the sweet black and white dog chased away her panic and disintegrated the rest of the devastation she'd brought out of that horrible nightmare.

Oh dear. Maybe she should just forget about the idea of kayaking along the lakeshore in search of her plane. At least if she stayed here, there was hope that maybe someone would come looking for the dog, or that Lucas might eventually return. She could keep a smoky fire going on the off chance of someone flying by. But would they even explore it?

But sitting around here feeding a smoky fire to attract someone's attention didn't feel right to her. Today she would stay here and rest her body and give that phone another chance at charging. She would keep calling home. And continue to text in the hopes some messages might get through. It was a long shot, but she would at least try.

In the meantime, she would make preparations to go out with the kayak, but this time she would not return. This time she would take many long breaks so she wouldn't get sore. She'd step out of the kayak in shallow areas along the shoreline. She'd camp overnight in the wilderness. She'd found a knife, bear spray, a whistle, and a one-man survival tent in a box in the cabin. The tent was in good condition. If no one came today, she would head out tomorrow to search for her plane.

Having a plan made her feel in control and she liked that feeling. She smiled as she watched the dog sleep. Such a sweet little creature all alone in this desolate wilderness.

How had it survived? Where had it come from?

Suddenly her gut hollowed out in a really bad feeling.

How in the world could she leave this dog behind? But she had to. She had no other choice.

THEY HAD SPENT THE entire morning crisscrossing along JJ's flight plan and nothing out of the ordinary had shown up. Of course, it didn't help that sudden bouts of rain from occasional rain-laden clouds blocked some of their view making dejection swamp Dan.

Blue had remained quiet as she flew the plane, and they had all kept watch out the windows. She'd broken the silence only once in awhile with questions about the ranch. He knew it was small talk, a momentary distraction. He knew too that she wanted to start a sheep ranch similar to the one their elderly hermit neighbor, Jane Sunflower, was running.

Blue had told him that's what she wanted awhile back when she had been nursing him after he'd been struck over the head and knocked out by JJ's stepbrother who'd come out here to Moose Ranch after learning JJ had been released from prison. He'd come to exact revenge on her for killing his violent father.

Dan shivered in remembrance.

Man, that son of a bitch had kidnapped JJ and Dan had thought he was going to lose her then. That same chilling gut-wrenching feeling he'd felt then was hanging around him today. He knew the longer it took for them to find her, the less chance she and the baby would be found alive.

After lunch, Layla and Will had come to relieve Blue and Kelly. Blue and Kelly had said they would be back tomorrow afternoon to help again in the search for JJ despite assurances that Daegen was coming with the plane. They'd also found out that Kaley, the woman who'd been JJ's flight instructor was away on vacation, hiking somewhere in the Rocky Mountains, without cell service. Kelly was trying to contact her as Kayley had many hours of night flying and would want to help in the search. But so far they hadn't been able to reach her.

Dan stifled the well of emotions that clenched his chest. JJ had such good friends who cared so much about her.

This afternoon Layla had taken them up in her yellow bush plane leaving Dr. Will to care for Chrissy. Layla was the opposite of Blue. She liked to chat. She tried to keep their spirits up as they expanded their search.

It was a lot of wilderness and lakes to cover and for all they knew, they could have already passed over JJ and not seen her. This afternoon there had been a couple of sightings of light smoke. Layla had swooped in low to check them out and they'd discovered campers and canoes along a river shoreline. A quick look at one of the interior camping maps had shown these were canoe routes.

So, interior campers. No JJ.

To Dan's surprise, Layla never mentioned JJ's pregnancy. Perhaps she thought it was a touchy subject with JJ missing. Another fear kept rattling around in Dan's thoughts too. Had JJ crashed and survived? What about the baby? Had she lost it?

Dan inhaled slowly at those thoughts and refocused his mind to peering out past some gentle raindrops that spattered against the plane's window.

Damnit! JJ, where are you?

RAFE BLEW OUT A TENSE breath as he sipped on his hot coffee and kept his gaze on the map of the area they had covered today. It was really quiet tonight as he sat in the living room. Quiet and hot. All the fans were whirring at top speed, and the windows were open. There wasn't a hint of a breeze, but lightning was once again flashing at the dark screens and the distant sound of thunder made Rafe grimace at thinking JJ was somewhere out there in this. But he couldn't think about her being out there because he would literally go nuts.

So, he focused on the events of the day, replaying things in his head.

Today had been a dud. No sign of JJ. But he continued to cling to hope. Actually, he was seesawing between hope and despair. It felt better to be on the hope side, but then dread would rear its ugly head and Rafe would once again face reality. She might never be found.

Kelly had supplied a hearty lunch for them, frying up steak and potatoes and bowls of salad. All three of them had forced themselves to eat, knowing that they needed to keep up their strength for JJ and Chrissy, despite not being hungry.

Then when they'd returned from the afternoon search, Dr. Will had supplied an assortment of sandwiches and tons of black coffee. He told them he wasn't much of a cook, but he sure did make a mean egg salad sandwich. Once again, they'd forced themselves to eat and make friendly conversation with their guests, feeling relief once they were gone.

Brady had brought Chrissy up to bed awhile ago, saying once his daughter was tucked in, he was going to take a shower and turn in.

Dan was taking a shower in the bathroom down the hall and Rafe was hanging out in the living room, nestled snugly on the sofa, the map in his lap. Tomorrow Daegen, Mitch, and Milena were coming in a rented float plane. He wished it were already tomorrow.

He closed his eyes and sent up what was probably his hundredth prayer of the night, that tomorrow would be a good day and they would finally find her.

Man, he felt so damned tired. Mentally exhausted.

The three of them had literally abandoned running the ranch to search for JJ. But they couldn't neglect the ranch forever. They would have to make some really tough decisions and soon. Like who was going up in the plane and who was staying on the ground to make the rounds on the ranch.

He felt his eyes begin to close, knew he should go up to bed, but he'd just sit here for awhile longer. It felt so peaceful in this land between awake and sleep. So nice.

The sharp shrill of the landline telephone had Rafe opening his eyes. He felt disoriented.

The phone rang again, and he jumped out of the couch and raced to answer it. A quick look at the call display and he knew Dr. Will was calling, which was weird because he'd just left like an hour or so ago. Rafe swept up the receiver and mumbled a hello, seriously not wanting to deal with any small talk with the doctor who was probably just checking up on them.

"Rafe, it's Will. I've got some news," came the doctor's rushed voice.

Rafe's hand tightened so hard on the phone receiver he thought he heard it crack or maybe it was his hand that cracked.

"What kind of news?" Good? Bad? He sure didn't want any unwelcome news. It would completely wreck him.

"I got a phone call from Gus. Remember him? The author?" Dr. Will asked.

"Yes I remember him." Seriously? What the hell? Had the old man decided he wanted to give autographs after all? Oh, come on. He would tell Will off if that was why he was calling.

"Gus says he thinks he remembers a low flying plane roaring over his place the afternoon of the big weekend storm, the Saturday JJ went missing. He was about to take a nap and was just nodding off when he thinks he heard the plane.

He didn't remember until just earlier today. At first he figured it might have been a dream, but then he thought it might not be. He thought it best to say something just in case it was real. I have to tell you that it could just be his head injury scattering his thoughts, but the head injury occurred after JJ went missing. I had mentioned to him on the day of our visit that we were looking for a missing plane, so his thoughts might be jumbled from what I said.

He sends his apologies for not saying something earlier. Got a pen and paper so I can give you the co-ordinates to Gus' place? He said he thinks the plane was flying in an easterly direction and flying really low. It was right in the middle of the thunderstorm."

Rafe's mind whirled. He couldn't believe what he was hearing. Was it possible that plane could have been JJ? It *had* to be her.

He grabbed a pen and paper from beside the phone and started scribbling down what Dr. Will told him.

He didn't even remember if he thanked the guy when he hung up. He looked up and saw Dan standing in the hallway staring at him with concern. His hair was wet, and he only wore his underwear. Brady was rushing down the stairs in his underwear too, his hair also wet. He looked troubled as well.

"What's going on? Why the big shout?" Dan asked.

"Man, you're going to wake up the kid! I just put her down!" Brady complained.

Rafe stared at the two men. He didn't even remember shouting, but his adrenalin was pumping now.

"Where's the map? Where did I put the map?" Rafe shouted.

He'd been looking at it when he'd nodded off.

"It's there on the floor by the sofa. Who was on the phone? What's going on?" Brady asked, his face contorted into an irritated grimace.

"The lake where Gus lives. We need to get out there."

"I thought you didn't even know the author? He asked for us not to hound him for autographs," Dan said with a frown.

"Get the fucking map," Rafe spat as he read the paper he'd just written on. He couldn't think straight. He needed to collect his thoughts as to what Dr. Will had just said.

For a brief instant he wondered if maybe he'd fallen asleep and was now dreaming? No, this was too real. This was happening.

"What's wrong? Who was on the phone?" Brady swept up the map and splayed it out on the coffee table, in the process tipping over Rafe's coffee mug. Thankfully, it was now empty.

"Was it that telemarketer again?" Dan asked.

Rafe ignored his question and produced the paper with the coordinates. He immediately located the lake that Gus lived on. He pointed to it.

"Here. We need to go here first thing tomorrow," he said and then he began to explain everything the doctor had told him.

"Okay so, she was flying low, and she was off her flight plan. Maybe she was looking for a place to land. But why would she not just land on Gus's lake?" Dan asked.

"His cabin is about a quarter mile from the lake. Maybe she didn't see it?" Rafe explained.

"Which way was she going?" Brady asked.

"Gus thinks the plane was heading in an easterly direction. But he's not a hundred percent sure as he was just nodding off. He said he could have been dreaming."

Rafe noted how both Brady and Dan frowned, their excitement disintegrating.

"A dream?" Dan mumbled.

"He's not sure. At first he thought maybe, but the more he thought about it, he wanted to let us know, in case it wasn't a dream," Rafe explained. Rafe knew he was rambling, maybe even making stuff up to make sure the guys would take this seriously. He also realized they were grasping at straws with all the dream talk, but hell it was a lead and was not about to ignore it.

"It's about fifteen minutes off her flight plan." Brady chirped in.

"Just under half an hour plane ride from here. She was almost home and got caught in the storm," Dan was still frowning, concern rippling wrinkles into his forehead. His green eyes appeared too bright. Rafe knew Dan was now getting seriously emotional.

"And a shitload of lakes to check, just look at this map. She could be on any of those big or little lakes, and most of those lakes are uninhabited," Brady said.

"The good thing we've got going for us is that she was flying low, most likely looking for a place to land," Dan replied.

"Or she had engine trouble or might have been flying low to avoid most of the storm?" Brady surmised.

"Too bad Snowy Creek's cell service sucks so bad or I'd call and ask Daegen to get us in the air tonight. But the instant he gets here tomorrow morning we are air bound. Go get your rest gentlemen. We've got a long day ahead of us. We're gonna find JJ," Rafe said eagerly.

"Unless the guy really was dreaming," Brady reminded, breaking down Rafe's excitement and pulling him back to reality.

"But at least we've gotta lead now. We'll definitely ask Daegen to take us there first," Dan added.

Rafe nodded. He doubted he would get any sleep tonight. Morning wouldn't come soon enough.

Hold on, JJ. We're coming for you.

DAN LAY IN BED LISTENING to the rain pelt the steel roof on the ranch house. It was damned noisy, and he could not sleep. Hot tears kept seeping from his eyes, and he angrily brushed them away.

JJ was out there somewhere in yet another storm. She could be hurt. Suffering. Starving. The baby, if he or she was still alive, would be missing out on prenatal vitamins.

Oh man, and another heatwave was starting tomorrow. Another swell of emotions clutched at his chest.

He clenched his jaw in frustration and forced himself to banish all bad thoughts about her being helpless and scared from his mind. He realized it was just his imagination playing with him. JJ was a strong woman. He needed to stay Mr. Positive as Rafe had so eloquently put it the other day.

Better to be positive than to let his mind run amok with unpleasant crap.

Dan blew out a tense breath and turned over onto his side. He forced himself to slow down his breathing. Forced good memories about JJ to flood his mind.

Memories of how pretty she had looked when she'd first arrived at Moose Ranch. Her innocent looking very dark brown eyes with gold flecks in them had caught his attention rather quickly. The light spattering of brown freckles across her cheeks and then those delicious dimples that popped whenever she smiled deeply at them, sure did a number on him. Not to mention all that velvety brown hair curling over her shoulders. So soft and feathery as he ran his fingers through them.

He'd fantasized right from the start about teaching her how good sexual pleasure could be at the hands of three men. But he couldn't go into a sexual fantasy about her. Not now. Not with her out there somewhere, suffering, maybe injured and hungry or worse.

He smiled and turned into Mr. Positive.

Yeah, they would find her tomorrow. He had no doubt.

Dan slept.

Chapter Twelve

JJ had worked long into the night getting ready for her excursion to search for her plane. The dog watched her every move. Every once in awhile it tilted its head one way and then the next, making JJ laugh at how cute it looked. But when it began to rain and thunder, the dog once again dove under the bed. Despite the stormy night, she'd slept well and had awoken at daybreak with the dog sleeping on her legs again.

Regardless of all her aches and pains, she was ready to go.

She wasn't going to waste another day on keeping a smoky fire going that made the cabin so hot that she'd had to sit outside and rush in every once in awhile to grab what she needed or to place another log in the cast iron stove.

Lucas' cell phone was defective as it refused to charge beyond one percent. She'd tried 911 many times, but nothing went through, and no one could even hear her the one time she'd actually made a connection to Moose Ranch. Her texts remained unsent.

No, she was leaving and that was all there was to it.

Earlier, she'd dragged the kayak to the edge of the dock, and then she made several trips from her cabin with the items she needed and placed them beside the boat. She'd put the tent, a lightweight raincoat, bear spray and other weapons, plus a warm blanket inside a plastic bag and shoved it far back into the hollow guts of the kayak, tying a rope to the top of the bag so she could pull the bag out when needed. That was followed by the bag with canned goods, cutlery, waterproof matches, a pot, a can opener and one burner stove with propane cannister which left room for drinks immediately in behind her.

On top of the kayak, directly in front of her, she strapped the small knapsack to the kayak, placing the knapsack right in the middle, so the kayak would have an even distribution and hopefully not tip. In the knapsack were vegetables and berries from Lucas' garden, crackers, and granola bars.

She brought a cup so she could drink from the lake when needed.

The dog, who she'd discovered was a girl after she'd watched the little lady squat to go pee, she named Katie, because that's the first girl name that had popped into her head, and she looked like a Katie too.

Her heart broke as she fed the dog another can of corned beef on the porch and then on her final trip down the trail, she'd broken into tears at leaving Katie behind. Sure, she could have put the dog in the kayak with her, but there was really no room. Besides, Katie would simply tip the boat if she so much as leaned over to drink from the lake. She had survived this long in the wild, surely she could handle herself on her own again.

JJ managed to push the packed kayak into the water with relative ease despite its heaviness and in spite of her continued aching arms and lower back. And since she'd practiced off and on all day yesterday getting in and out of the kayak, on the shoreline, at the dock and also in knee deep water, she felt like she was now a pro as she paddled away from the safety of land, forcing all thoughts of abandoning Katie from her mind.

It was really early in the morning.

The air felt stuffy, and JJ knew it was going to be a very hot day. Instincts told her to stay here, but she wasn't going to listen to her instincts. Not this time. She would just have to deal with the heat by taking breaks and doing some swimming.

For now, the sun was still behind the towering pine trees, which cast cool shadows over the mirror-like lake. Despite her wearing a baseball cap and a red long sleeved flannel cotton shirt that flowed warmly over her unborn baby, the curls of white mist that cloaked the surface of the dark water, brought dampness splashing against her body which sent chills through her.

In order to warm up, she began to go faster, dipping one paddle and then the other paddle into the water. Before long she was going at a good speed, the heavy kayak slicing through the lake with ease and her arms protesting already with soreness.

She ignored the aches. This trip was something she needed to do. Waiting around for someone to find her was unacceptable as well as anxiety provoking. She didn't like that she wasn't in control of this situation. Didn't like that she and her baby were at the mercy of fate. That's why she enjoyed a routine back home because it kept her grounded.

She should never have gone to that bridal shower in the first place. She should have stayed within her comfort level. She should have known better. But it was what it was and now she had to deal with it.

Back at the cabin, she'd left a note nailed to the front door and placed a note on the table inside in case Lucas returned, giving him directions of where she was heading and to please send help.

She'd also grabbed as many vegetables and berries as she could carry from that little garden. She'd put them into storage containers and then into the knapsack, along with some toilet paper, mosquito spray and suntan lotion. Using two yellow rachet straps that she'd found in the cabin, she secured the knapsack on the top of the kayak, right in front of her and directly in the middle so as to keep the kayak weighted evenly so she could go straight like an arrow.

She smiled. It was kind of like how she made sure any weight in her plane was evenly distributed in order to avoid any issues flying.

After what she figured was an hour of paddling, she slowed, cautiously reached into the knapsack, and dug out a cucumber. As she crunched on the crispy treat, she stared straight ahead into the swirls of white mist. It was starting to lift as she caught glimpses of the blue sky. To her right the shoreline was within sight and the wind was nonexistent.

Suddenly the sun broke through at the top of the nearby trees, streaming rays of heat upon her. The warmth felt good. It cheered her up and after she finished the cucumber she drank some bottled water, which was awfully warm.

She planned on taking many breaks, going slow from here on out and remaining optimistic.

Easier said than done though as many hours later, she felt close to tears as she headed for land for yet another break and another swim in her birthday suit in an effort to cool down her heated body. She figured she must have been paddling for many hours, still no end to the lake and still no sign of her plane.

She'd removed the red flannel shirt a long time ago and had spread it out upon the knapsack. She wore another of Lucas' oversized t-shirts which unfortunately due to no wind, did little to protect her skin beneath, making her feel horribly hot. She'd also been experiencing increasing amounts of fluttering from the baby. She hoped he or she wasn't in distress, but how couldn't her baby not be, especially when she didn't feel well herself.

Her arms and her back were ultra sore now, and her legs felt as stiff as boards, despite having had several short breaks and swims near the rocky shoreline.

While paddling she'd passed several loons, none of them followed her like the loon had the other day and that made her sad for some unknown reason. She'd spied large snapping turtles lounging on logs and many green frogs sunning themselves on lily pads near the shore. Awhile back, a black snake had slithered right by her just below the surface of the water sending chills up her spine.

She'd even seen a couple of beavers chewing on sticks along the shoreline and she'd spied one deer drinking from the lake. The instant it had seen her, it had disappeared into the forest, it's white tail raised in alarm.

Cicadas shrieked everywhere promising more heat and an occasional dragonfly or butterfly settled on the kayak for a rest before flying away again. Woodpeckers clacked their strong beaks against trees here and there, and bluejays chatted with one another in the trees.

Now, as she struggled to bring the kayak close to shore, she managed to grab some bushes, noted the water was shallow enough and steadied herself. Wearily she got out, thankfully without tipping over which she noticed the chances of that happening were increasing.

She was tired. She should stop and make camp, but adrenalin and hope that she would find her plane just kept urging her to keep going.

The afternoon sun shone strong in the cloudless blue sky and beat down upon her in an unmerciful manner as she stepped onto the dead branches littered land. Her wet running shoes sloshed uncomfortably as she roughly pulled the front half of the kayak over the rocks, grimacing at the scraping sounds against the hull.

Okay, so maybe heading out like this wasn't such an innovative idea. Maybe she should go back to the cabin?

Her view of the lake blurred by her tears of anguish, and she shook her head.

No. She needed to rely on herself now. There was no turning back. No matter what.

If she felt worse, she'd just have to find a spot to pitch the tent in the shade and sleep. Maybe even travel during the night, which she now figured she should have done in the first place.

This trip could very well be the only chance she had to find her plane, because she could feel her baby growing inside of her every day and soon she'd be too big and feel too awkward to manage kayaking let alone walking over rough terrain.

What she needed was to eat some food because she was hungry and depressed. Hopefully, food would cheer her up. What she wouldn't give for some bacon and eggs or a banana-soaked chocolate ice-cream sundae or better yet, a pancake drenched with Brady's delicious home-made maple syrup.

Instead of a pancake, she dug out a fresh but ultra hot tomato from the knapsack. After washing it in the lake, she enjoyed the delicious treat, savoring the sweetness and letting the juices dribble down her chin. She followed it up with some mushy, hot raspberries, then crackers and a granola bar.

She was debating if she should open a can of tuna when sounds of snapping branches and some sort of heavy breathing shot through the air.

JJ froze.

Oh my God! Something was rushing through the bushes, right along the shoreline. It was coming fast, and it was coming toward her!

Panic paralyzed her and she did not dare move, hoping the animal would somehow pass her by without noticing her. The paddle was on the other side of the kayak and not within reach, and neither was a knife that she'd placed in a side pocket of the knapsack.

She should have known better. This was the wilderness. There were hungry black bears, beavers with long teeth, wolves who would love to munch on a stranded lady and her unborn baby, and moose with long legs that could kill you with one swift kick.

They all roamed the woods and drank from the lakes. This was their territory. She didn't belong here. She just wanted to go home.

Icy creepy crawly shippers shot through JJ as the animal kept rushing toward her and then she screamed.

Not in fear but with gratitude as the little black and white dog, burst through the bushes, her pink tongue rolling out the side of her mouth as she panted and rushed right up to JJ.

She let out a couple of sharp barks, her tail waving at such a speed that JJ was sure the tail would snap and fly off into the sky like a flying windmill. She didn't even stop the dog from jumping into her lap as it reached up and slapped her wet tongue all over JJ's face. She grabbed the dog and hugged her, beginning to cry as guilt assailed her.

"Oh Katie! I am so sorry for abandoning you! Will you ever forgive me! I have never been so happy to see anyone in my life! What are you doing here? Why did you follow me? I would have come back for you, eventually."

The dog kept kissing her and then a far-off noise captured JJ's attention. The dog tensed and stopped licking her, its ears perked up as she gazed south, down along the shoreline from where JJ had come from.

JJ held her breath and listened. A half minute later she could make out the distinct rumble of a far-off plane. She could tell almost right away it was not coming her way. She couldn't see anything either because she'd paddled into an inlet.

Oh crap!

"Over here!" she shouted.

Despite knowing it was useless, she rushed to the kayak, grabbed the paddle, and stumbled into the water, trotting out as far as she dare, slipping this way and that way, on the muddy bottom. She held up the paddle in a vertical position and waved it around, but she didn't see the plane.

She must have frightened the dog because suddenly it ran away, scampering into the bushes and heading back to where it had come. The rumbling of the plane died away.

JJ swore.

Emotions, thick and raw, clutched at her chest. She wanted to cry but she would probably dehydrate. That thought got her laughing. She did after all have an entire freshwater lake to drink from.

This was great. Just freaking great.

With her luck the plane probably went right over the cabin. Had she been there she would have been able to flag them down.

Nonetheless, her opportunity was gone. She decided it was best to push on with her plan and immediately felt better.

"Onward and upward," she mumbled and stumbled back to the shore. Since she was already wet, she'd forgo a swim.

It was time to get back into the kayak and shove off. Tears streamed down her face at the loss of the dog.

"THERE IT IS!" BRADY just about passed out from the excitement raging through him as he spotted JJ's white plane gleaming brightly in the sunlight at the north end of a swampy area of a very long lake. It was listing a little.

"Probably got caught up on some logs or rocks or the pontoon might be damaged," Daegen said from beside him as he angled their plane around for a closer look.

Dan and Rafe scrambled toward the cockpit and Daegen yelled at them to get back to their seats. They complied and fell silent. Probably thinking the same thing Brady was thinking. Was JJ in the plane? Was she dead? Or alive? So far he'd seen no movement from inside the plane.

He blew out a tense breath and tried to prepare himself for the worst.

"I'm going down. Everyone just stay put," Deagen said as he began to circle the plane and just like that Brady spotted someone sitting in a yellow kayak slowly waving a paddle in a vertical position. Back and forth. There was a red cloth draped over the top of the paddle.

Obviously, the person was trying to get their attention.

The person in the kayak was almost half a mile south of them and just as far away from JJ's plane.

It looked like some guy. He was wearing a baseball cap, white T-shirt and—

Brady did a double take as the guy removed his baseball cap and a moment later a waterfall of familiar auburn hair fell down around the person's shoulders.

"Holy cow! I think I'm hallucinating," Brady mumbled. He must have had a stroke or something because the guy looked like JJ.

"What's wrong?" Rafe called from his seat.

"My side. Three o'clock. Along the shoreline."

Dan swore.

"What?" Rafe asked.

"Look!" Dan answered.

Ignoring Daegen's shout to stay seated, Rafe scrambled to Dan's side where both men gazed out and began to laugh and swear at the same time.

"It has to be JJ! She's alive!" Dan shouted.

Beside Brady, Daegen chuckled as he looked out the window to where Brady pointed and swore softly.

"She's quite the resilient woman. Got herself a kayak. Okay we'll be down in just a couple of minutes. Rafe back to your seat please. We're going down," Daegen instructed.

Rafe did as Daegen asked and went back to his seat. Dan and Rafe just kept swearing and laughing and Brady joined them.

Man, he'd never seen a more beautiful sight. But his laughter died as a wave of emotions hit him like a ton of bricks and he felt tears streaming down his cheeks. He brushed them away and kept staring out the window at her.

Daegen had been flying them around since dawn, almost ten hours non-stop. They'd checked Gus' lake and then they'd begun checking other lakes in the area. Brady's eyes burned from all that watching and searching over the hours, but man, she was a sight for sore eyes. Was he ever glad she appeared okay, and that the search was finally over.

Daegen looked tired yet happy beside him, his eyes were glistening cheerfully as he easily began to make the descent. He picked up the radio and called into Moose Ranch.

Mitch answered.

"We've got JJ in our sights. We're just going down to get her. Here are the coordinates. Over," Daegen announced.

"How is she? Over," Mitch asked after Daegen relayed their location.

"She seems okay. But I'm not sure. Might be best to contact that bush doctor and ask him to get over to Moose Ranch to check her and the baby out. Over."

Brady barely heard anything else. He remained focused on his beautiful JJ for fear if he so much as blinked, she would disappear.

Oh man, he sure hoped he wasn't having a dream.

JJ COULDN'T STOP SENDING up thank you prayers as she kept slowly waving the paddle with Lucas' bright red flannel shirt perched on top. Because the beak of the baseball hat had been in her way, and she hadn't been able to look up due to a very sore neck, she had torn the hat off her head, breaking the elastic in the process, allowing her hair to fall down.

Now she could see the plane clearly. It was bright orange and they had seen her because someone was waving out the passenger side of the cockpit window. She wondered who they were. Sightseers? Or someone maybe looking for her?

A moment later the plane was down upon the lake. Silver splashes of water shot up from the sides of the black floats as the plane drew closer to her.

Oh, such noise from the plane. Such a wonderful feeling to hear a plane coming to her rescue. She wished she could cover her ears, but she just kept waving the paddle with her arms that were so tired that she swore they were now permanently damaged.

It was already quite awhile ago she'd spied her plane nestled far ahead in a swamp beckoning to her like a beautiful beacon. It had not sunk like she had seen in that frightening dream. Despite feeling awful, she'd forced herself to keep paddling along the shoreline toward her plane.

But now, sweet mercy! Her nightmare was over!

On the shoreline, she heard barking.

Katie was back! That sweet dog was thankfully safe.

"Katie! Stay!" She yelled, having the sudden urge to get to her.

To her surprise, the dog sat on the shoreline, its tail wagging up a storm and she watched as JJ turned the kayak around and paddled toward her. Suddenly, she just wanted to get her feet onto solid ground.

Wearily she got out of the kayak, pulled it to the shore, fell down upon the bushy shoreline and embraced Katie. The dog's tail was once again twirling like a windmill, and she was eagerly kissing JJ.

JJ held the dog tight and stared at the orange plane as it roared closer.

The sun was going down in the west, a giant ball of red hovering over the treeline and the orange plane was silhouetted right in the middle of the red.

Gosh, it was like a gorgeous mirage, wavering in the heat of the sunshine. The plane slowed and because the sun was in her eyes and she had no idea where her baseball cap had gone and she was just too tired to lift her sore arms to give her gaze some shade so she could see, she just sat there and waited.

She saw figures jumping into the water. Counted three of them. Heard splashing as they swam toward her. The plane went quiet.

She thought she heard Brady calling her name, but she didn't dare hope it was him because then she had to be dreaming, didn't she? She was so unbelievably tired, and she had such a wicked headache. She just couldn't call back. Couldn't even raise an arm to wave. All she could do was hold onto Katie for dear life for fear she would once again run away.

Then she heard Rafe shouting that they were coming. Heard Dan happily cursing.

She must have heat stroke or something because she really didn't feel so good.

She watched numbly as all three of her cowboys suddenly rose out of the calm lake. They looked like golden gods with the red sunset behind them. Then her men were embracing her, asking if she and the baby were okay.

Suddenly she just wanted to sleep, and everything went black.

"SHE'S EXHAUSTED." SHE heard Daegen's voice and suddenly remembered she'd been rescued.

She should be thrilled, but she just felt tired, and her head ached. She felt hot too. She forced herself to open her eyes and realized she was on a plane. She didn't remember them bringing her on board. She must have passed out. But the plane wasn't moving, and twilight was descending.

Daegen was hoovering over her. Taking her pulse. Placing a hand over her forehead.

"JJ, can you hear me?" he asked.

"Yes," she whispered.

"You passed out for a few minutes but you're going to be okay. You have heat exhaustion and mild heat stroke. We're going to put some cool cloths on various parts of your body to cool you down."

She didn't answer. Too tired.

She wasn't surprised she had heat stroke. It was incredibly hot out, but she had just kept paddling, figuring all those dips in the cool water, and drinking fluids would keep her going. She'd seen her plane and despite feeling awful she'd just started paddling toward it, knowing she could call for help when she got there. That was probably the wrong thing to do. What she should have done was get back into the lake to cool herself down and rest. Instead, she'd been stubborn and now she was paying for it.

"The baby. Is it dangerous for the baby?" she asked, struggling to get the words out in a whisper, knowing it had to be bad for her baby.

"It can be. You're too hot so we'll just get you cooled down. The doctor and your midwife are heading to Moose Ranch to check you and the baby out," Daegen said and squeezed her shoulder in a reassuring way.

"Chrissy?" She needed to know her other baby was okay.

Suddenly Dan hovered into view and crouched beside JJ. They'd laid her down upon some sort of fold out seat near the back of the plane and JJ literally drowned in Dan's forest green eyes and his comforting smile.

"Chrissy is doing good, baby mama. She's a strong little girl. She's with Mitch and Milena. Blue and Kelly are there too. Don't worry about her for one minute. I've got cool cloths for you. Soaked them in the cold water from the melting ice in the coolers."

He wrapped chilly cloths around her wrists, upon the back of her neck, along her groin area and other parts. The coolness felt heavenly.

"Katie?" she whispered.

"Who is Katie?" Dan asked with a concerned smile. A weird look passed between Daegen and Dan. They probably thought she was hallucinating.

"Dog."

Relief swept over their faces.

"She's here," Daegen replied with a chuckle.

"She dog paddled her way out to the plane," Dan replied. "She didn't want to leave your side, but I coaxed her away with a sandwich. She's sitting in the copilot seat looking out the window watching Brady and Rafe secure the plane and the kayak. We'll be underway in just a few minutes. Then we're going home."

Home. The most beautiful word she'd ever heard in her life.

Relief poured through her and for the first time in awhile, she was able to relax. She was so glad that Chrissy and Katie were okay.

She must have drifted off, because suddenly the plane roared to life and Rafe, and Brady's excited voices were nearby. She opened her eyes to find them staring down at her, huge smiles on their faces.

Goodness, but they looked so tired, their eyes had haunted looks. She could tell they'd lost weight too and had worried about her. Her heart clenched in sympathy for what she'd put them through.

"Welcome back, Sleeping Beauty," Rafe said with a grin.

"Your plane isn't going anywhere. We've also brought the kayak on shore and removed all the items. I bet there's one hell of story behind all that," Brady said, his blue eyes twinkling with amusement.

JJ could only smile. Even that little movement hurt her very dry lips.

Wow was she ever tired.

"Okay guys take your seats so I can start moving. JJ is all buckled in. She'll be okay." Daegen called out. His voice was loud and booming and then the guys were saying their farewells and left her.

She slept.

RAFE COULDN'T STOP staring at JJ as Daegen took them up into the air again. Her face appeared red, and her lips looked pretty chapped. Her breathing seemed too fast for his comfort but thankfully Dr. Will and Layla were on their way to Moose Ranch. They'd know what to do.

What the hell had she been through? Why was she kayaking around with a ton of food stashed in the boat on a sweltering day like this? Why hadn't she called for help from the plane? She should have been sticking to the shade of the trees and not moving. He prayed that baby and mamma were both okay. He hadn't heard good things about heat stroke in pregnant women and that's what Daegen had said she had.

He gazed over at Dan who was turned around in his seat, staring at her, while she slept. He was frowning, not looking happy at all. Rafe figured Dan didn't like the look of her either. Seeing her fast asleep like this when she was normally bubbly. It just felt so wrong.

Fuck! Why did this have to happen to her? She didn't deserve to be sick. He wanted her healthy and back to her normal self. He was getting the same useless feeling he' d experienced when she'd had the post partum depression after Chrissy was born. He hated that feeling of helplessness and he had no idea how to help her feel better, except to just be there for her, follow any directions from the doctor and midwife and support her in any way he could.

He knew the guys felt the same way.

His gaze dropped to the black and white dog who was lying down on the floor right beside JJ. How the hell had that dog ended up with her? It must have done a good bit of travelling on his little legs after running away from Brady and himself a few days ago.

As if sensing it was being watched, it's ears perked up, the tips flopping over as it looked up at him with big brown eyes. It must have sensed Rafe's foul mood because it suddenly growled at him.

"Oh, shut up, dog. No pancakes or corned beef for you anymore. You are so ungrateful running off the way you did," Rafe said to it.

"Name is Katie. She's a girl, according to JJ," Dan replied.

Rafe nodded.

Huh. Katie. That was a nice name. Truth be told he was glad the dog was okay. He'd tried not to worry about her, but he'd felt guilty at having to leave her in the woods when she'd run off the way she had.

Daegen had suggested that they not let the dog near JJ, until Paul, the veterinarian, over at Snowy Creek Ranch had a look at her. He said he'd bring the dog home with him, and he sensed JJ wouldn't want to be parted from that dog for long.

But everything would turn out okay.

Rafe frowned.

He hoped.

"SHOULD WE WAKE HER up? Or just carry her in?" JJ heard Dan ask.

They must be back home. Excitement made her rally and she forced herself to open her eyes. It was dark in the plane. Night time. The air felt so muggy. She didn't like it.

Dear Lord, had her guys not come to her rescue, she would still be back there in this heat. Maybe she might not even have made it to the plane tonight to call for help. That was why she'd been hugging the shoreline with the kayak just in case she fell asleep and tipped over. She'd hoped the shock of the water would wake her. Had she gone straight across the lake, toward her plane, she might very well have fallen in and drowned, and they would have found her lifeless body with her unborn baby, bobbing in the water.

She trembled. Oh God, she couldn't think that way. She must not think that way.

She remembered shortly after taking off, Dan had forced her to drink some cool water. She'd felt a bit queasy, but it seemed to have subsided. Then she'd slept again.

It appeared while she'd been sleeping someone had been refreshing the wet clothes draped on parts of her body, because they felt so invigorating and cool. She didn't want to lose them.

"I'm awake. Help me up," she reluctantly whispered. She tried to reach up an arm, but it felt way too heavy and hurt too much.

Gosh, nothing on her moved without pain. It was scary.

Brady got to her first and he swept her off the reclining seat in a powerful swoop, lifting her into his arms. Wow, he smelled the same as always. Like Brady. Like her man. Her cowboy.

"Put me down, Brady," she whispered.

She didn't want him to hurt himself. Especially since he still had occasional bouts of pain in his legs left over from that tetanus scare last year.

"Do you deny one of your three princes in carrying you to your castle, Ms. Sleeping Beauty?" Brady murmured. He was gazing down at her and despite it being dark inside the plane, she had no problem making out the amusement lifting his luscious lips.

JJ could not stop a giggle.

"That's our princess. She's already on the mend," Rafe said from somewhere behind them as Brady carried her in his arms down the isle.

"She's going to be just fine and so is the baby," Dan commented and winked at her as Brady and her passed him.

I hope so, she silently thought, trying to stop the swell of tears in thinking she'd put her baby at such a horrible risk. Had she stayed at the cabin, the guys would eventually have found her, wouldn't they have? But she'd just wanted to go home and nothing else had mattered. She'd been so selfish in putting their lives at risk and now her baby might pay.

She emitted a whimper of distress at the thought of losing her baby and Brady quickly nuzzled his raspy bearded face against her cheek. The beard tickled her skin and she felt safe in his arms. She melted against his warm muscular body, inhaling his man scent and grateful that she didn't have to climb down the plane's ladder in her enfeebled state.

Daegen instructed Dan to grab hold of the dog as he didn't want her getting out of the plane and would be taking her to Snowy Creek with him to get checked out by Paul. When Dan picked her up and stuffed a piece of a sandwich in her face, Katie happily chowed it down.

"Bye, Katie," JJ whispered, and the dog gave her a sharp bark in response and then eagerly accepted another piece of sandwich.

With the dog distracted, Daegen quickly opened the door to the plane and Brady carried JJ down the ladder with ease. How he did it, she had no idea. Apparently he was stronger than she'd thought.

The air was muggy, and the night air felt so hot that she just wanted to ask Brady to throw her into the lake. As he carried her up along the dock, a gas lantern splashed light upon Mitch and Milena as they waited at the other end of the dock. One special figure was cradled in her friend Milena's arms.

Chrissy was watching her with wide eyes and then suddenly she smiled in recognition. JJ's heart burst with love and she couldn't stop herself from crying and sobbing. It was like a dam broke inside of her and all the emotions about never seeing Chrissy again that she'd been stuffing deep down inside of her while being stranded, just gushed out. She just couldn't stop weeping.

"See, she's okay, and she's thrilled to see her momma back home," Brady's deep soothing voice whispered into her ear and JJ forced herself to stop crying. She didn't want to frighten Chrissy.

Brady brought JJ right up against her baby and JJ could barely stretch out her tired arms to her. She ached to take her daughter into her embrace.

"I want to hold her," JJ said.

"Is she strong enough?" Milena asked, concern quite evident on her face.

"Just place her on top of JJ, I can carry them both up to the ranch house," Brady said.

Before JJ could protest about him carrying both of them, Milena was smiling at her and gently placed her baby upon her chest area. Then JJ was wrapping her leaden arms around her baby and kissing Chrissy's warm pudgy cheeks, holding her tightly for fear she might drop off. But there was no chance of that happening as Chrissy wrapped her arms around JJ's neck and pressed her smooth cheek against hers.

"Ma ma," Chrissy blurted against her ear.

Shock shot through her.

"She just talked! She just said ma ma!" JJ gasped.

Cheers erupted and then Brady quickly carried JJ, with Chrissy upon her, up the trail toward the ranch house.

Bright buttery lights flowed out from every window of the two-story building that she feared she would never see again, welcoming her home.

"Will and Layla are on their way. ETA fifteen minutes for the doctor and thirty minutes for Layla," she heard Mitch reporting.

"Okay, thanks," Dan replied.

"There's food ready for you on the table. I made a light chicken sandwich for JJ and some cool broth as per Layla's instructions," Milena was saying.

She heard Dan say thank you again.

"The doctor said you'll need to keep her cool and hydrated with cool drinks," Mitch continued.

She felt disoriented with everyone talking and tuned it all out as she cuddled Chrissy.

Her baby had just said ma ma to her. How cool was that? She wanted to hear her say it again, but Chrissy seemed quite content snuggling against her. So, JJ just quietly wept some more.

Brady carried them up the stairs and into their home.

Chapter Thirteen

Rafe couldn't believe JJ was back home safe and sound as he watched her sleep in the king-sized bed with cool towels draped upon her wrists, neck, and other body parts. She had fallen asleep while cradling Chrissy after Rafe had put her on JJ's chest. Now he lifted the little rascal off her mother and settled her in beside JJ. In seconds, Chrissy was nuzzling JJ's neck with her face.

Now he was just waiting until the baby fell asleep before carrying her back to her crib.

Dr. Will had brought his portable air conditioner directly from his own home instructing them to install the exhaust hose or whatever they called it, out a window in the room where JJ would be recuperating. The beauty of the machine was it could be moved from room to room as it had wheels.

Earlier, Dan and Daegen had installed the air conditioner into this room, removing the screen, cutting pieces of wood and insulation to accommodate the pipe that went out the window. They'd picked the room with the king-sized bed where she could spread out her legs and arms and they could take turns draping fresh wet clothes over her throughout the night and for as long as she needed.

It was pleasantly cool in this room now with the air conditioner humming and the overhead fan whirring away, and he was grateful to Dr. Will for thinking of the aircon as it would probably have taken a few more days to get one flown out here because he sensed none of the guys were going to let JJ out of their sight to go solo flying anytime soon. And placing an order through North Country Air took time, especially during their busy summer months.

This was the first summer that the house had been so incredibly hot. Usually the summers weren't this bad, but with global warming it appeared they were finally being affected here in the northern wilderness as well as the rest of Canada. They should have been prepared and he mentally kicked himself that they hadn't been.

Hell, they should have invested in air conditioning long before now, especially for JJ. Earlier tonight, Dan had volunteered to look into getting a central air unit installed as soon as possible.

The doctor said they could use his air cooler for as long as they needed it. He'd said she was lucky that her heat stroke hadn't gotten any worse for it could have caused JJ to lose the baby or caused developmental issues for the baby. Her body temperature was higher than it should be, and he said with keeping her cool as well as keeping her hydrated, she should feel much better soon.

Layla had brought along a fetal monitor, and she discovered the baby had developed an arrythmia. The heart rate was too high, but she'd said that was expected under the circumstances. She'd reassured them once JJ was rehydrated, her electrolytes once again in balance, took her prenatal vitamins and began eating, the baby's heart rate should go back to normal.

He didn't like the word, should.

Layla said at this point there was no need for hospitalization, but she'd drop by sometime tomorrow to check on the baby and JJ and then reassess.

Man, what had JJ been thinking being out in the heat like that?

Despite his momentary burst of anger and his concern for her and the baby, Rafe grinned.

She did appear to be quite the resourceful woman. He and everyone had wanted to ask her tons of questions about her misadventure, but they all figured plying her with fluids, some light food and a restful sleep was more important.

According to Milena and Mitch, Kelly and Blue had left before JJ returned. They'd been ecstatic upon learning JJ had been rescued, stating that the less people around the better for her and they would visit in a few days when JJ felt better.

Milena and Mitch had whipped up a light meal for JJ and a delicious supper for the rest of them. When Rafe had spied her nodding off at the table, after sipping on some of the soup and eating only half her sandwich, he'd brought her up to bed and then gone back down to get Chrissy for her at her request.

She looked so serene now, a smile on her lip-balmed lips, as she slept in the light pink cotton nightgown he'd helped her into. The baby was watching her with sleepy blue eyes and a smile. It was so obvious now that she'd missed her mom. And it was so cool when she'd said mama. She had the sweetest voice he'd ever heard.

Man, it was all surreal at how things had finally come together late this afternoon and he could not wait until he told her how they had located her. But that could wait. They could tell her when she was ready to hear it.

Flashes of lightning suddenly blinked at the dark windows and Rafe heard a low rumble of thunder.

A really bad feeling swung through him. If they hadn't rescued JJ when they had, she would be caught out in another storm tonight. Maybe in the plane, or maybe stranded on the shore with that growly dog. Maybe even losing the baby.

Rafe blew out a tense breath.

They had dodged one hell of a big bullet this time around with that damned plane she enjoyed so much. A part of him hoped what had happened would knock some sense into her and she would decide never to fly again, but another part hoped she wouldn't be afraid of flying because of what she had gone through. He didn't want her to experience lingering anxiety over this mishap.

He had a new respect for JJ. She had made the best out of a potentially very bad situation. Somehow she'd gotten separated from her plane and had found shelter at Lucas' cabin. He still needed answers from her, but she'd been so tired that everything was on hold.

He watched Chrissy rub her eyes. She would be asleep soon and then he could go to bed. He was physically and emotionally exhausted, but tomorrow it was back to work.

It was pretty quiet downstairs now, so he figured everyone had left.

He was so grateful for how everyone had come together to help find JJ. The thought of how they had all been so helpful almost brought him to tears. He was really thankful for Blue, Kelly, Layla, the doctor, Mitch, Milena, and Gus for all their help and he was thankful Daegen had gone out of his way to rent a plane to take them up today in this godawful record heatwave.

He hadn't felt comfortable accepting everyone's help at first as he preferred to do stuff himself. But in this case, he couldn't, so maybe that's why he'd been exceptionally grouchy, but yeah, he was really happy everyone had come to their rescue. They were true friends and true friends always came through for you in a crisis no matter how inconvenient it was for them.

"HOW IS SHE DOING?" Brady asked as Rafe entered the kitchen where Brady was finishing washing the dinner dishes.

Man did Rafe ever look tired.

"Fast asleep. So is Chrissy," he answered.

"Good. Where is Dan?"

"Taking a shower. He stinks," Rafe teased.

"So, do you!" Brady teased back.

"How rude," Rafe laughed.

Brady was glad to hear Rafe's laughter once again. They all felt so much better with JJ back home.

But they had been warned by the midwife as well as by Dr. Will to make sure JJ didn't get exposed to any more hot conditions throughout the rest of her pregnancy. Layla had said that heat exhaustion and heat stroke could be a very serious issue for the baby during its development. It could also cause premature labour. There were other things she had pointed out and Brady shuddered just thinking about them.

He'd had no idea that heat would have such an impact on a pregnant woman and her baby. It also appeared JJ had had no idea that a heat wave was about to break upon them. He was sure if she'd known, she would have stayed at that cabin, in the shade and tried to keep cool.

"With JJ back home we're going to have to have someone with her for awhile to make sure mom and baby are okay," Rafe said.

Brady had been thinking the same thing.

"There's lots of work to catch up on," Brady stated. He sure as hell didn't want to leave JJ on her own. At least not anytime soon.

"We can take turns staying with her. Dan is good to work. Dr Will gave him another checkup after he checked JJ. He said Dan is good to go. Chances of him having a stroke or other issues are now extremely minimal, thanks to the meds he's taking."

Brady sighed, realizing they didn't have much of a choice anymore. They'd neglected the ranch and cattle for too long.

"The optimum word minimal, but the possibility still does exist," Brady pointed out. He didn't want to risk Dan though.

"Dan said he is willing to chance it. He wants to get back to full time work. I agree with him. We've talked and we decided you can stay home with JJ and Chrissy tomorrow."

Relief splashed over Brady. He was glad he would be on the first watch. If he so much as sensed JJ was hiding any health issues from him, he would be on the phone to the doctor and Layla faster than JJ could snap her fingers.

"By the smile on your face, you approve?" Rafe said with a chuckle, his dark eyebrows raising in question as he awaited Brady's answer.

Brady nodded.

"Good. He is a big boy, you know. He'll be fine," Rafe assured.

Despite the doctor, Rafe and Dan thinking Dan was okay, Brady was still worried something bad could happen.

"Keep in touch with him throughout the day. Maybe give him some light stuff. The last thing Dan needs is to cut himself being on those blood thinners. If you can work together, the better. We'll go over where you'll be working in the morning. The heatwave is continuing, so keep hydrated and take lots of breaks in the shade"

"Yes, mother," Rafe answered.

Brady rolled his eyes in answer.

Rafe laughed.

"Need help with the dishes?" he asked.

"No. Go up to bed."

"Okay, but just so you know Dan and I talked before, and we came up with a plan for tonight. He's taking first watch with JJ. I'll take second watch. We'll keep the cool compresses going until her temperature gets back into the normal range. Doable?"

"As long as you don't sneak in and turn off my alarm clock and screw around with my curtains," Brady warned.

Rafe grinned.

"Okay that's a promise. I'm heading up."

"Right behind you. I'll just finish cleaning up and will be up in a few minutes."

Brady watched Rafe slowly ascend the stairs to the second floor and then he returned to the dishes.

He'd had a tight knot in the pit of his gut since bringing JJ home. How in hell was he ever going to survive if something bad happened to her again. He knew it could because he had no doubt she would want to fly again, and he knew he couldn't stop her. It would be like clipping the wings off a bird who wanted so badly to be free to fly.

Brady cursed softly beneath his breath. There really wasn't anything he could do about it.

In the meantime, though, he would make sure their days were productive and enjoyable and their nights even more so.

DAN BLEW OUT A TENSE breath as he stood beneath the harsh spray of water gushing out of the shower head. Since first realizing it had been JJ in that tiny kayak, slowly waving that paddle on that big lake of bays, something inside of him had changed.

Something, some protective male instinct that up until that exact moment had been very active toward JJ and the baby, but right when he'd seen her, realizing she was alive and seemingly okay, he'd felt punch drunk. The need to protect her, and the newbie, had grown exponentially. That feeling had squashed the positive attitude he'd been harbouring to keep him sane and going.

Perhaps it was a primal instinct that told him that baby she was carrying belonged to him, despite having no proof, or that he'd almost lost the most precious person in his life, and he was seriously lucky to have her back.

He just could not put a name to it, but one thing he knew for sure, he had to know if that baby was his and he needed to know soon.

Yes, his close brush with death, being stranded on that lonely shoreline on Misty Lake a few weeks back had been the precursor to that moment of change when he had seen her in that kayak.

He was a jumble of other emotions as well. They were see-sawing through him like painful blades.

Anger at her for not staying safe and remaining back at the motel. Had she done that, she would have answered the damned phone, and he would have told her severe storms were popping in the area. He was also deliriously happy that she and the baby would hopefully be okay and damn it he couldn't help it, but he just had to cry.

And so, he did, and he let the tears stream down his face.

He was so thankful for the people who came out to help them search for her. He was doubly thankful that the shower was so loud it would hopefully conceal the chest wrenching sobs that escaped him.

Man had he known it would hurt so much to think that he could have lost her and the baby, he might never have signed on to asking JJ to stay with them at Moose Ranch. But that thought disappeared as quickly as it had appeared and Dan simply allowed the poison of fear, and anger to leave his body through his sobs and his hot tears.

He prayed he would never have to go through such a scare again, but deep down he also knew that this was the wilderness life and bad things happened here, just like they did in the city.

It also meant; he didn't have to like it.

When his sobs were finally free of him, he felt better.

He chuckled to himself remembering what his mom used to say when she was sad about something or another thing and on a few occasions he'd caught her crying.

"Whether you are a man or a woman, a good cry is always a good thing to set you straight. It isn't healthy to keep things bottled up," she'd say.

Well, mom, I took your advice tonight, he silently thought.

He nodded and stepped out of the shower. He was first watch on JJ tonight, so he'd best hurry.

JJ WANTED TO STAY IN this cocoon of relaxation forever. But something far away was signaling for her to wake up.

Slowly she migrated through the layers of sleep and heard the low hum of an engine of some sort, and a luscious cool breeze blew across her face and arms. Something cold and wet was laying on her forehead, her wrists and even on her feet.

Had she set up the tent? It didn't seem hot anymore. Was it raining and the tent was leaking water on her? Whatever it was, she liked it and it felt really good.

Her thoughts whirled in confusion. Finding her sunk plane...no, that had been a dream. The dog, Katie. She had run away when JJ had shouted or had she? What had happened to the dog?

It had been so incredibly hot in the sunshine while she'd been paddling. She'd taken many breaks, many swims, drank water from the lake and ate salty crackers and granola bars, but then she'd begun to sweat profusely.

She'd used the cup, dipped it into the lake, and splashed water all over her clothing. But there hadn't been so much as a breeze to help cool her down. Determination had kept her paddling. She had one thought. To find her plane, get to her phone and the radio and call for help.

She'd thought she'd had it all planned out perfectly. But the intense heat she had not anticipated. It had become relentless, but she must have found a good spot for the tent because the ground was so soft and cozy beneath her sore body.

Mentally, she did a body check. Aside from a headache and sore arms and back, she felt...alive.

Wait a minute. Had the orange plane been a dream?

JJ inhaled the cool air and smelled something familiar. Freshly scented sheets. But she didn't have sheets in the tent.

Why was she so confused? Why had she hugged her daughter if she was stranded?

JJ smiled and her heart clenched with love as she remembered Chrissy saying the word ma ma. Had that been a dream? It had seemed so real.

A floorboard creaked somewhere.

Wait. What? Floorboard?

No, she had to be dreaming. If she was dreaming, she needed to wake up and get to her plane. She had seen it, hadn't she? She needed to open her eyes and get back to reality.

She opened her eyes and blinked as a room rolled into focus. Not any room but the one with the king-sized bed that the four of them shared on their foursome nights together.

Mercy, she suddenly felt hot too. And not in a bad way. In a normal, pregnancy hormone, she wanted sex, kind of way.

She moaned softly as she tried to move the cool sheets off of her.

A floorboard creaked again and then she turned her head and saw Brady standing in front of one of the windows. It was sunny outside and he was gazing out in the direction of the lake. The firm set of his jaw made her believe he was in worry mode. He held Chrissy in his strong arms, and their daughter's chin was cradled upon his shoulder. She was staring at JJ with the sweetest blue eyes.

JJ smiled at her. She smiled back.

"Mama," she said sweetly, and JJ burst with happiness. Chrissy had put the two words of ma ma together!

"Mama is right there, honey," Brady replied in a soft voice that she heard him use only for Chrissy.

He turned and then his eyes widened as he realized she was awake and watching them.

Brady's face seemed to relax, and JJ noticed all the tension leaving his body. His shoulders slumped, the tautness hugging his jaw loosened and his eyes began to sparkle.

She could tell by the dark circles beneath his eyes that he had not gotten much sleep while she was away. She could see the hollowness in his cheeks, that he hadn't eaten as much as he should have eaten, and it had all been her fault.

Guilt assailed her.

"Hey," she whispered, trying really hard to crack a smile.

She wanted to get out of bed and go to them, to hug them both to her and tell them she was so sorry, but before she could even move, Brady strolled over to stand beside the bed.

He looked down at her, his luscious lips slanted in a half smile, and it made her heart go pitter patter.

"Hey yourself and I know what you're thinking. Don't you dare move a muscle, JJ. Don't get out of bed. Not without assistance."

Chrissy gazed down at her, blowing spit bubbles. She looked healthy and happy. Her cheeks were blushed with a pretty pink colour and her eyes sparkled blue just like Brady's eyes and just like the clear blue sky outside their windows. She was dressed in a cute white cotton dress with light pink hearts scattered all over it and a matching pink bow.

"Don't you look so pretty. How's my little girl?" JJ asked, wondering how in the world had she and Brady created such a beautiful baby.

"She is a rascal as usual," he replied. He lowered her so JJ could hug her and give her a kiss.

Chrissy giggled as with her shaky hands, JJ framed her squirming daughter's cheeks and kissed her warm, spitty lips. Then Chrissy became active, grabbing some of JJ's hair and giving it a hard tug.

"Ouch," JJ laughed.

"Okay, leave mama alone. She needs rest," Brady lifted her baby away and JJ wanted to ask Brady where was *her* kiss from him, but then Chrissy suddenly began kicking her legs, trying to squirm out of Brady's embrace, obviously wanting JJ to play with her.

"Hold on, kiddo. You're too rough for mommy right now. You can hang out with her when you get tired."

Chrissy kept kicking and giggling as Brady held her out at arm's length gazing at her, a huge grin on his face.

"What? Are you going to become a kick boxer or something? Hmm, that might not be such a bad idea. It will make any boyfriends think twice before asking you out on a date."

JJ laughed. She remembered their discussion back at the cabin when he'd pretended to be panicked about their daughter having boyfriends. Gosh, had that only been three weeks or so ago? It felt as if it had been years since that night when they'd been alone together and made love outside of the roundup cabin in the storm. Naughty heat burned brightly through her as she remembered how sexually needy she'd been that night and how she'd enjoyed sponge bathing him with lightning flashing all around them.

Goodness, she, and her baby had probably been very close to death because of the heat, and here she was thinking about sex. She should have her head examined.

"And the baby?" It was a question she wished she didn't have to ask but she remembered the doctor and then Layla checking her over after Milena had helped her take a quick shower to get her refreshed before their arrival.

Just doing the shower and having the checkups had tired her out to the point where she'd been unable to eat much and lifting her arm to feed herself had been such a chore. But right now, she needed to be informed that her baby was okay because despite both Dr. Will and her midwife reassuring her all was fine; she had read concern in their gazes.

"Fine. No worries," he replied, trying to act low key, keeping his attention on Chrissy.

Instantly she knew he was lying. There was something in his gaze. A concern. Something, he just could not hide.

An awful feeling of foreboding snapped through her. Although she didn't want to know if there was a problem, she knew she needed to deal with whatever might be wrong.

"Brady. Tell me the truth," she said firmly, wishing he would simply tell her she was making things up.

He didn't.

"They were concerned because your temperature was too high. Now it's almost back to normal. It's why we've been keeping you cool with the wet cloths, ceiling fan and compliments of the air conditioner Dr. Will loaned us."

He moved away and she saw the tall white unit on the floor and a tube going out the boarded up lower part of the window. That was where that motor sound had been coming from and why she felt so refreshed.

Thank you, Dr. Will!

"That was very nice of him. So, it's still hot outside then?" she asked.

"Will be for the near future. You slept right through the thunderstorm last night. It was a doozy, but it didn't bring any relief. We've got a heatwave, it has stalled right over us, and you headed out onto that lake on day one of it, sweetheart. Humidex forty-five plus Celsius or over one hundred Fahrenheit. That's why it's so hot. You sure know how to pick a day to go kayaking," he chuckled.

"You're avoiding my question about the baby, aren't you? Just because I'm feeling better, doesn't necessarily mean the newbie is feeling better, am I right?"

She *was* feeling better, but far from normal. And she hadn't felt any flutters from the baby since yesterday early afternoon and she wasn't feeling anything now.

Oh God. She hoped her baby was just sleeping.

"Layla is coming later to check on you and the baby because the newbie's heart rate was a little bit too high for her comfort."

Damn! She knew it! Anxiety sliced through her like a knife, and she watched Brady bounce Chrissy up and down trying to distract her from all that kicking. Or was he just avoiding eye contact with JJ on purpose?

"Brady? Is there more?"

Thankfully, he looked at her and she could read in his eyes he wasn't hiding anything else. Or at least she hoped she was reading him right. Or maybe she was just getting paranoid because that's what she did when she got anxious. Started imagining things and that usually set her up for panic attacks. She needed to nip this anxiety in the bud because she could feel it building.

He must have sensed her increasing nervousness because he slowly shook his head.

"Nothing we can't handle. And don't look at me like you're going to freak out. Don't go there, JJ. Look at it this way. You would be in the hospital right now if things were really serious. Right?"

His words, really serious, grabbed hold in her mind, meaning it *was* serious. She nodded jerkily as tears began to well in her eyes.

Brady's face softened with sympathy.

"Baby, it'll be fine. Let's not panic unless there is something to panic about and right now all is good. Layla will check out the baby and newbie will be okay. You'll see. Trust me on this."

Okay. Okay. He had a point about her not being in the hospital. She needed to stay calm for the baby. But still...

"And you? How are you? Are you mad at me?" she whispered.

He sighed heavily.

"JJ, mad wouldn't even begin to cover my feelings. I'm pissed that you left the motel without so much as a word to us that you were coming home. Look what happened," he growled.

Yep, he was not happy. She worried her bottom lip and bit back a retort. She wanted to tell him that she'd missed them all so much and that she'd wanted to surprise them and that cheap motel she'd thought she'd save money on, was a broken-down piece of crap. But she kept silent. He had every right to be mad.

He sighed and hoisted Chrissy higher in his arms. Gosh, they looked so cute together. Two sets of identical blue eyes gazing at her. It just melted her heart.

"Are you hungry? I'm going to get you breakfast in bed. Pancakes with maple syrup, prenatal vitamins, and decaf coffee to start. Orange juice and fruit. But before that, do you need to use the bathroom?"

Actually, she did have to go, but she would wait until he was gone then she could go to her bathroom down the hall by herself. She just wanted some alone time to process what he'd said about the baby's heartrate being too fast. That was not a good sign.

"Bathroom can wait. I am a little hungry," she admitted.

He smiled and suddenly all her guilt at leaving the city and about him being mad just sailed away. She was sure they all would have some sort of argument or fights over it sometime in the days to come. Right now, was really not the time.

"Okay, baby mama. You just rest. We'll be back soon."

Just hearing Brady's voice return to normal without that edge of anger in it, had JJ relaxing.

"Say bye bye to mama," Brady said. He grinned at JJ as he lifted Chrissy's arm and waved.

JJ waved back.

Gosh, her daughter was so adorable!

Chrissy didn't say bye or mama, but she did grab onto Brady's nose with her free hand, looking to JJ for approval, which had both JJ and Chrissy laughing as he rolled his eyes. Then he strolled out of the room telling Chrissy that she was going to turn his nose into a long one and he would soon look like Pinocchio.

JJ blew out a deep breath as he closed the door behind them.

She wasn't dreaming. She really was home. Her survival nightmare was actually over or was it? What had she done to her baby?

Gosh! If she could take it all back, she would. She should have just asked for another motel room and stayed put and enjoyed some alone time. Now her unborn baby was suffering. She was such a reckless, bad mother.

She sighed with frustration and stared up at the ceiling fan. It went round and round, just like her thoughts about her baby. She should have done this or that. Should. Should. Should. Shit!

Hot tears of guilt and frustration streamed down her cheeks, and she tried to steady her breathing.

She waited until she heard the clatter of dishes in the kitchen downstairs before she dared to move. Unbelievable soreness raged through her as she slowly pushed aside the sheets and delicately swung her feet out of the bed. Her legs were ultra stiff, and she felt woozy.

Oh dear. Maybe it was best if she waited for assistance.

She didn't have to wait long as the door suddenly swung open and Dan and Rafe burst into the room, both rushed over to her. Rafe was fully dressed in his work clothes, but Dan wore only his underwear.

They both looked as tired and haggard as Brady and more guilt assaulted her at what she'd put them through.

Suddenly she was being swept off the bed by Dan and he twirled her around like she was a rag doll, her bare feet lifting into the air.

"She's back! She's beautiful! She's mine!" he said.

His green eyes were cheerful, and his hot lips melted over hers in such a bold kiss, she couldn't help but wrap her arms around his neck and kiss him back, despite knowing she probably had bad breath.

But it appeared he didn't care as his lips smoothed over hers in such a sultry way she thought she just might self-combust.

"Man, Dan, she's not ready for all this hot loving. Be careful with her," Rafe warned.

Dan pulled away, his kiss leaving her lightheaded and quite aware of that thick knot of an erection she'd felt pressing against her lower abdomen.

"Well, this is certainly a welcome home greeting," JJ said as she unwound her arms from Dan's neck and laughed as he set her upon her wobbly feet.

"Glad you are back, baby mama. Man, I can't wait until you feel better so I can show you how much I missed you," Dan said with a wink.

"Hey, she's mine," Rafe teased as he sidled in at the other side of her, his hand sliding around her waist, steadying her.

"Goodness, I don't want a duel over me," JJ giggled.

"Good idea! A duel at sundown, for the hand of this fair lady. I challenge you," Dan growled to Rafe who howled.

"You are on! You die at sundown, my man!" Rafe shot back.

"Guys, please, no fighting over me. At least not at the moment. I need to go somewhere," she hinted.

"I'll take you, JJ," Rafe growled, and Dan let her go.

"I still have to get dressed, my fair lady. Until we meet again," Dan said, and he bowed to her like those gentlemen in the historical movies she'd watched in prison.

"Until we meet again, sir," she agreed.

And then Dan slipped away, leaving her with Rafe who told her to lean on him, which she happily did because she felt pretty tired. Going to the bathroom alone was not going to be in the cards today.

Rafe was so strong, and he smelled so nice as he asked her how she was doing and letting her know that Brady was staying home with her and Chrissy today. He just kept chatting away telling her how much he'd missed her and how glad he was that she and the baby were okay.

And the way he just kept talking, she was almost convinced her baby was going to be fine.

In moments, he had her down the hall, and into her bedroom, then to her bathroom, all of the rooms were notably warmer than the room with the air conditioner and she felt a light sheen of perspiration dot her forehead.

Thankfully, he let her go into the powder room by herself and he waited on the other side of the door, remaining quiet as she went about her business.

A little while later, when she came back out, she was trembling slightly from fatigue, after having washed her face and brushed her teeth. Now she felt as if she were closer to what a human being should feel like, but she was still awfully tired.

"This way, my lady," Rafe said as he held out his elbow like a gentleman for her to take.

"Chivalry is not dead," she teased as she took his arm and held tight.

He shuffled her out of her bedroom into the hallway and turned her toward the room she had just been sleeping in, but she pulled on his arm, indicating she wanted to stop.

The succulent scent of Brady's pancakes wafted through the air and her mouth watered. Then her tummy growled.

"Bring me down to the kitchen. I would rather eat down there. Besides, I need some exercise."

Secretly she wanted to do some movements, to maybe wake up the baby so she could feel the flutter. To make sure he or she was okay. She just needed a sign.

Rafe groaned. That idea did not sit well with him.

"Please? I just want things to get back to normal as fast as I can."

Rafe sighed.

"You can't erase what happened, JJ. Brady won't like it. But let's try."

She could barely make the stairs as Rafe held her waist and supported her.

Gosh, she hoped she wouldn't be exhausted like this forever.

As they quietly entered the kitchen area, Chrissy spotted her from the highchair and giggled.

"What's got you laughing, sweetie," Brady asked as he flipped over a pancake.

"She's happy because her mommy came home. Aren't you my sweet baby?" JJ cooed.

Brady whirled around, crushing JJ's happiness. He looked absolutely livid.

Chapter Fourteen

"**D**amn it, Rafe. I told you to keep an eye on her!" he shouted. Surprise washed through JJ at his fury.

"Hey man, the lady needs to get some exercise," Rafe replied coming to her rescue.

"She can get exercise when she is stronger. Now get her back into bed before something happens!"

Irritation at his command made JJ stand firm.

"Since when are you my prison guard?" She snapped angrily and realized instantly that she should not have said those words. But she had put her prison years behind her, and she didn't want Brady or anyone else to start putting her behind bars again.

Brady's cheeks went red as he glowered at her.

"Okay, that's our que to leave so you two can work this out," Dan said as he joined them, now fully dressed in his work clothes. He hoisted a suddenly quiet Chrissy out of the high chair.

"The three of us will be out in the barn for a little while. Call on the baby monitor if you need us," Rafe said as he began to follow Dan and Chrissy.

"Thank you, Rafe, for assisting me. You are a knight in shining armor, especially now when I need one," she said and glared at Brady.

Brady remained silent until the mud room door slammed shut.

Then he moved swiftly toward her, and JJ cried out in surprise as her feet left the floor and he swept her into his arms. His body heat embraced her like a torch, and she'd expected him to remain furious, but as he carried her toward the stairs, he smiled at her, making her frown at this sudden mood change.

She'd been prepared for a fight, but his luscious lips were mere inches from hers. Suddenly she wanted him to kiss her, but that would defeat the purpose of being mad at him.

"I thought they would never leave," Brady whispered in a husky voice. It appeared he was trying to lighten the atmosphere.

JJ opted not to put up a fight, so she remained silent as he carried her up the stairs two at a time with her in his arms. That he'd carried her and Chrissy last night, and now he was carrying her again, suddenly made her happy. It appeared he had the confidence that his legs were finally strong after that tetanus he'd gotten last year. Since then, he'd been having trembling, nerve pain and weakness now and again in his legs.

"How's that for your knight in shining armor?" he asked as he brought her into the cool bedroom, kicked the door shut with his foot, carried her to the bed, then gently placed her onto the mattress and splashed the covers over her.

She ignored his self praise. She wasn't about to reward what she felt was a total disregard for what she wanted, which had been to sit and have breakfast with her family.

But in the way he was gazing down at her with his smoky blue eyes, she knew that look. He was aroused. Just as she was aroused, just being in his arms.

Her stupid body was deceiving her.

"Where is my dog?" she asked tightly, forcing herself to get mad at him again.

He frowned, perhaps realizing he'd gone too far with his reaction.

"At Snowy Creek. Paul is keeping her in quarantine until he is sure she doesn't have any rabies or other issues. We don't want her biting you. We're going to place ads in the lost and found areas of the internet and in the city paper. She must belong to someone."

She belongs to me. We belong together, JJ said silently. She missed her little black and white friend.

But Brady was right. They should look for Katie's rightful owner. She was being selfish about the dog, wasn't she? She didn't want Katie's owners to be found. They had been reckless in losing her. They didn't deserve her.

"If she was going to bite me, she had many chances," JJ said feeling the need to protect Katie.

"Better safe than sorry sweetheart. We have to watch for Chrissy too."

"And what about the plane?" she asked.

He stiffened at her question. Perhaps now was not the time to discuss how to get her plane back.

"Your plane is being looked at by Daegen today. He said he'd call when he knew the situation. I'll be back in a few minutes with your breakfast. Promise me you will stay in bed. Just until Layla checks you and the baby. Remember you are thinking for two of you," Brady said gently.

Wow. She certainly did feel admonished.

He didn't leave. But continued to stare at her, probably trying to see if he could trust her.

"Promise me, JJ, "he said again.

Reluctantly JJ nodded. She knew he was concerned for her, but it just felt so restrictive having to stay in bed.

"I'll be right back, sweetheart."

She watched him leave. Loved how his jeans hugged the curve of his ass and his long, muscular legs. Legs that she wanted intertwined with hers.

She moaned softly as heat cascaded through her and gasped as she felt the familiar flutter of her baby in her womb. The flutter felt the same as before. Newbie was letting her know he or she was still alive.

Thank God! The sense of relief was overwhelming. She closed her eyes and concentrated on the beautiful flutter kicks, making sure they didn't feel different. They didn't and suddenly she was very happy that her baby was kicking. It had to be a good sign.

While feeling the lullaby of the lightest of kicks, she must have drifted off to sleep because she suddenly came awake at the delightful scent of maple syrup.

Early this spring Brady had tapped a bunch of sugar maple trees within snowshoeing distance of the ranch house. He had harvested a good amount of maple juice in tin buckets and boiled the juice down until it was a sweet, thick amber syrup.

In prison, they'd had pancakes every Sunday morning with sugary syrup that came in small packages, which said maple flavored, but it didn't even have any maple syrup in it. What Brady made was organic, delicious, and naturally sweet. She could never get enough of eating pancakes drenched with his syrup.

"I'm sorry you felt that I was your prison guard, JJ. That wasn't my intention. I just want you and the baby to be safe," Brady said in a soft tone.

Obviously, he knew she was awake, so she opened her eyes to find him standing beside her bed holding a tray and a big smile on his face.

"Words won't cut it, Brady. You are going to have to work for forgiveness," she said. She just couldn't help but tease him.

His eyes widened in surprise but then those eyes went smoky hot blue, and he pursed his lips. Lips she wanted to kiss.

"Oh, woman, you are so hard on me." Brady growled as he set the tray upon the night table.

"Hard, being the dominant word, I hope," JJ teased, needing Brady to touch her, kiss her, make love to her.

But she knew she was too weak for sex. She wasn't too weak for a kiss.

"Doesn't breakfast in bed usually come with a kiss?" she asked.

JJ pursed her lips indicating to Brady that she wanted a kiss.

He grinned, swooped over, and gave her a quick peck on the cheek.

"Brady!" she guffawed.

"No kisses for you, until you eat your breakfast. Now let's make you comfortable, so I can put the tray over your lap," he instructed.

Disappointment washed over her. Why was he being so mean?

"Fine, your pancakes are better than your kisses anyways" she teased.

Brady chuckled.

"Flattery about my cooking will get you nowhere. Scoot up, and then lean forward so I can put pillows in behind your back."

She did as he asked, inhaling his masculine scent, and wanting that kiss bad.

A moment later, with the pillows nice and cozy behind her, she watched him place the tray on her lap like she was some disabled person. Which, she guessed she was at the moment.

Everything on the tray looked so delicious. There were sliced up ripe red strawberries and whole raspberries from their garden, which were piled in a bowl with sugar sprinkled on top. A big glass of orange juice. There was a hard-boiled egg, peeled and cut in half with salt and pepper sprinkled on top, just the way she liked it. Steaming coffee and a fluffy pancake that was already chopped into bite-sized portions and maple syrup glowing amber in the glass maple syrup dispenser.

He had no idea how grateful she was that she wouldn't have to cut the pancake with her sore arms. He poured the amber liquid upon the steaming pancake pieces and her mouth just watered as she remembered how badly she'd wanted pancakes drenched with Brady's homemade maple syrup while she'd been stranded.

Now, she was getting her wish, and she could not wait to dig in.

The savory scents of her breakfast had her forgetting about Brady and despite her sore arms she stabbed a fork into a piece of syrup-soaked pancake and shoved it into her mouth. Heavenly flavours burst against her taste buds making her moan with appreciation, and she certainly enjoyed listening to the quickening of Brady's breaths.

"I'm going to head outside to get the guys so they can have breakfast and get to work. Stay put, for the baby's sake. Okay?" he ordered.

She eagerly nodded. She wasn't going anywhere. She was suddenly hungry, and this breakfast tasted way too good to make an escape attempt.

BRADY COULDN'T GET out of the room fast enough.

Hell, yes, he'd wanted to kiss her when she'd asked. It had taken everything inside of him just to give her an innocent peck on the cheek. Under any other circumstances, he'd have been shoving his hands through the strands of her silky hair, holding her head hostage, and kissing her luscious, sweet lips, drowning in her sweetness. Then he'd have gotten both of them naked as sin and made love to her right there and then, letting her know exactly how much he'd missed her, needed her and how grateful he was that she was okay.

But he'd also realized withholding a kiss and everything else he wanted to do to her, especially after hearing her moan the way she had, was the leverage he needed to keep her in bed.

Blowing out a tense breath and admonishing his quite alert and swollen cock for pushing too hard against the tight restraints of his pants, he headed downstairs and made his way out of the ranch house smack dab into a furnace.

Man, it was hotter than hell out here. And it wasn't even seven o'clock in the morning! The sun shone bright and strong as it came over the eastern horizon blazing streams of sunrays over the serene blue lake and Brady knew it was going to be another brutal hot day. He had no doubt had JJ been out in this kind of dangerous weather again today, she would have surely lost the baby and probably died herself of heatstroke, never even making it to the plane.

It was why he'd reacted so strongly upon finding her in the kitchen earlier. He'd just seen red, and he meant that literally. She was being too reckless. Rafe was too, in assisting her down the stairs in her weakened state. She could have fallen. That they didn't even appear to be thinking about what might be happening to the baby inside of her with her walking around, well, it just pissed him off.

Maybe he was being overprotective, but he just couldn't help it.

They'd just gotten her back and now everyone was pretending it was just like life as usual.

Well, shit. It wasn't life as usual, and he was going to make sure everyone knew that.

He found Rafe and Dan in the barn, which wasn't too hot yet, but it would be as the day went on. They were in the tool room. Dan was holding Chrissy in his arms and Rafe was holding up a branding iron, showing it to his inquisitive daughter, who seemed mesmerized by it.

"And that's how we brand our cattle," he heard Rafe saying as Brady stepped into the room.

Like seriously? She was just about seven months old and had just said mama yesterday for the first time, which he was still trying to process, and they were talking about branding cattle to her. She wouldn't know what a branding iron was, at least not for a hell of a long time.

"Guys, we need to talk," he said as he held out his arms for his daughter. Suddenly he just wanted to hold her and prevent them from making her grow up with all this information about their ranch.

"Oh, oh, we're in trouble, just like JJ is," Dan chortled as he handed Chrissy over to Brady.

He snuggled her into the crook of his left arm and thankfully she just sat there like a nice little girl.

"No one's in trouble. JJ is enjoying breakfast in bed as we speak. I know you want to please her. Hell, we all do. But we need to corral her just until she's gotten enough rest, and until we find out that the baby she is carrying is okay. Are you getting my drift?"

Dan and Rafe chuckled.

"And no stinky jokes, please. I'm serious. We were really lucky we found her when we did. You heard what Dr. Will said about heat stroke and what Layla said about the baby's too fast heartrate and all the other shit that might happen to JJ and the baby if we aren't too careful with the heat. I need for you guys to take this as serious as shit."

Brady liked that the two men suddenly sobered up. Thankfully, he was getting through to them. They usually paid attention when he swore a lot. Maybe now that the kid was learning to talk, he should stop swearing, though. Well, it was too late in this instance.

"Okay, message received," Dan replied.

"Loud and clear," Rafe added.

"Good. Thanks. Now let's get back inside so you guys can eat your breakfast and get out to work. We've got a ranch to run!"

Brady loosened up when the two men grumbled and left the tool room.

He peered down at Chrissy who was looking around the room, her gaze settling on this instrument or that device, like she wanted to know what they were all for.

"No way, baby. You're not growing up on my watch. Today, you are a baby. My baby. You like that don't you?"

At the sound of his voice, she turned her head and looked up at him. A mischievous grin flared in her blue eyes and before Brady knew what was happening, she was once again grabbing hold of his nose.

Oh great, his daughter had a nose fetish.

He shook his head, smiled, and carried her out of the barn into the heat and hurried to the house.

Time to check on JJ and then make breakfast for everyone else!

THE FOOD TASTED EXCELLENT. Brady had popped his head in to do a quick check on her, found her in bed, grinned, gave her a thumbs up sign, and then closed the door again.

As she ate the delicious meal, in the delightful cool room, she smiled as she listened to Rafe or Dan laughing about something downstairs. The mouth-watering scent of fast fry Angus steaks drifted along the air and JJ wished she could have some too, but half way thru her meal she'd wanted to do nothing but fall back asleep. She'd fought the weariness and forced herself to finish everything. Then she drifted off, sailing into a dreamworld of kayaks, thunderstorms, drowned airplanes. Of Katie tilting her head this way and that and Chrissy saying mama.

"JJ, can I wake you up?" came a familiar woman's voice.

At first she thought she was dreaming and then the soft voice came again.

She blinked open her eyes and discovered her midwife, Layla, standing beside her bed with a big smile on her face.

She looked so pretty and healthy, dressed in a lightweight navy-blue V-neck top and matching kaki shorts. Envy spilled through JJ. She wanted to be healthy like Layla. She wanted to get back to making meals for her cowboys and her daughter. To have the energy to hang up the laundry on the line outside and to fly her plane.

Immediately she noted the breakfast tray was gone, and she vaguely remembered Rafe removing it along with the pillows behind her, and him telling her to scoot down so she could sleep properly. She'd felt a featherlight kiss upon her lips, but she'd been too sleepy to enjoy it.

"Good afternoon, sleepy head. How are you feeling?" she asked.

"Afternoon?" JJ mumbled.

"According to Brady you've been sleeping since just after breakfast. He decided to let you sleep, so he didn't wake you for lunch. It's now one and he's making lunch for you as we speak."

"Oh my gosh. I was sleeping like the dead," JJ said and shivered at that last word. But she did feel a bit better than this morning and struggled into a seated position.

Layla quickly placed pillows behind her lower back making sure she was comfortable.

"You are tired and sleepy because it's your body trying to recuperate from the heat stroke. The tiredness could last up to a week, so don't worry about it. Just listen to your body and do very light exercises like walking up and down the hallway or to or from the bathroom. No stairs yet. I've brought the fetal heart monitor, mind if I hook you up so we can take a listen?"

No stairs yet. It appeared Brady had ratted her out.

JJ's gaze strayed to the dark blue tote bag set near the doorway. At the sight of the bag and the mention of the fetal heart monitor, JJ fought back a sudden swell of tears, and Layla being too observant, sat down on the bed beside JJ, a caring expression on her face.

She reached for JJ's left hand, gently squeezing her fingers as JJ just started to sob. It was another dam bursting, just like she'd broken down yesterday when she'd seen Chrissy.

"It's okay, just let it all out," Layla soothed.

And JJ did.

She heaved sobs and wiped tears away with tissues that Layla kept handing her and the tears just kept coming, gushing out of her like a river, splashing over her cheeks. Layla just kept smiling with such reassurance that JJ wondered if maybe she was over reacting? Maybe her baby was going to be okay? Or maybe not. Then she began to cry even harder. She hoped Brady and Chrissy couldn't hear. She didn't want them to worry, but she just couldn't stop.

JJ didn't know how long she cried, but it tired her right out again. Although, she did feel better afterwards, despite her eyes now feeling hot and puffy.

Gosh, she must look an awful mess.

Thankfully, she was finally able to manage some form of self-control.

"I know the baby has you worried. That's why I'm here. Let's take a look and put our minds at ease," Layla said in the softest most reassuring voice that JJ had ever heard.

JJ nodded, but she was terrified that the news was going to be devastating.

DAN HAD SPENT SOME of the morning riding tractor, finishing up the haying that needed doing. Rafe had been in charge of this section of land and when he'd asked Dan to do the haying today, he'd agreed. He understood that Brady and Rafe were still worried about him and would continue to break him in slowly. He appreciated their concern, but their worry felt a bit stifling. That was okay now, because today he was finally back to work on his ranch. Unfortunately, he wasn't able to fully enjoy the hot, muggy sunshine, the smell of freshly cut grass, and being alive because JJ and the newbie were on his mind.

When she had gone missing, everything had stopped, and Dan realized that she was now the glue that held the entire ranch together. When she was down, they were all down. He wished he hadn't joined the others in encouraging her to go to that wedding shower for Kelly. But he'd hoped she would enjoy herself. She must not have, because she'd tried to return a day early.

Oh well, no one could have anticipated that she'd have to do an emergency landing with the plane and that a heatwave would be upon her. Last night she hadn't said much about her ordeal as she'd been exhausted. She had said she'd headed to Lucas' cabin because the storm had been too intense for her to handle, and she thought he'd be there. But he hadn't been and thankfully the door was unlocked, so she'd taken refuge inside. The next morning, her plane was missing, and she'd found the kayak and had started to look for the plane.

She was one resourceful lady.

Despite a growing need that he should head back to the ranch house, he forced himself to stick with the planned chores. So, after finishing the haying, he'd driven the atv to check on the new red Angus herd of cattle they'd started early this spring. The group of fifty head all seemed strong and healthy. The heatwave didn't appear to be bothering them despite research saying they were less heat resistant than the black Angus. Most of the cattle were grazing on the special nutritious grass they'd planted last year in anticipation for these new arrivals.

The cattle didn't seem to be shying away from the sunshine. There was only a handful that were hanging around the river and a couple lounging in the shade at the treeline.

When Brady, Rafe and himself had started the ranch, they'd planned it to make sure all the cattle had access to shelter and shade in the forests, lush meadows to graze, and drinking water from the fresh-water rivers and creeks that meandered throughout the meadows and forests. So far it had all worked out according to plan as all the cattle appeared to enjoy their lives on the range.

In this section of the ranch, there were no signs of the wolves. No carcasses. No cattle missing.

These cattle were resilient. Old enough to run away if a predator dared approach. They were young, brought in early this spring by train, on the old track that ran along the northern edge of the property. Up until recently they'd used the southern railway access on their property, but it was fairly far.

After cutting a good-sized trail, which had taken several years during their down-time, plus putting up the roundup cabin last year, they'd moved the roundup area to the northern railway track, which was still quite a distance to get to, but less work gathering the cattle that were going to market.

Purchasing the red Angus had been a hefty price, but after their breeding program got started and they expanded the herd and the cattle were fattened up, these animals would be worth the monetary expense. They'd researched that the red Angus were easier to handle, and the marbling was better than the black Angus, meaning their was more streaks of fat through the steak which was more sought after than with the black Angus.

But they would keep both black and red Angus giving the buyers a choice.

After checking on the new crop of red, Dan forced himself to return to Misty Lake, which was nearby. After brewing up some coffee in the cabin, he'd headed directly to the area where he swore he'd never return to after he'd been set free from that damned rusty metal animal trap.

Now he was back, coffee cup in hand, just like the last time, standing right where he'd been trapped, gazing out across the lake. He allowed the memories to wash over him in waves. The despair. The pain. The panic. Back to when he'd thought he would never see

JJ or Chrissy again. To the day he thought he would never get the chance to welcome the newbie into the world.

That day, with pain searing his foot, he remembered JJ flying her white plane over the lake, then splashing down. She came in like a hero. He'd probably be dead now, if she and Brady, along with Chrissy, hadn't decided to fly onto this lake that day to help look for him when he'd gone missing.

He owed JJ in having the necessary items on board the plane to help with his hypothermia. He owed Rafe his life for finding him that day and he owed both men for their strength in getting that trap open and off his ankle. He knew had it been much longer, his foot would have been severely compromised and the doctor would have had to amputate. Had he not been found when he had, he would most likely have been dead from hypothermia by the next day.

When JJ had gone missing, all those emotions of despair, panic, of not seeing her again, had resurfaced, but he'd pushed those away, trying to be Mr. Positive. Deep down inside though, he'd been dying. Thoughts of never seeing JJ again, or not seeing the newbie being born, had been killing him.

After they'd found her, he'd had that meltdown in the shower last night. Had taken first watch over her, placing cool cloths over parts of her body while she'd been in a deep, almost comatose, sleep. Even the violent thunderstorm that had shuddered the house last night, hadn't woken her, or Chrissy for that matter. He had checked on the baby a few times, but she'd been oblivious. Probably content to know her mother was home again.

Dan grinned. Both lovely ladies had been happy in their sleep with smiles on their faces. He liked that they felt so safe here on the ranch.

Truth be told, he was in love with JJ. It went much deep than caring.

He. Was. In. Love. With. JJ.

Now as he stood here, he gazed at the large grey rock where the metal stake had been pounded into. The rock that had held the trap via a long chain. He was pretty sure he would come back one day and explode it to smithereens. He smiled at that thought and then gazed at the black charcoal remnants of the small fire he'd built here on the shoreline while trying to stay warm and waiting for help.

He thought he'd be a nervous wreck in reliving the memories of being imprisoned here in these pristine surroundings. Surprisingly, he wasn't in the least bit uneasy.

He'd had rough nightmares of still being here, trapped. Dreams of being a zombie, desperately trying to escape the shackle of captivity by gnawing on his ankle. He'd woken with anxiety screaming through him and sweat drenching his body many a night since then.

Dan chuckled.

Man, he sure did have an imagination.

Coming here was cathartic. There was no threat here, he realized that now. He was glad he'd pushed through his fear and was now here.

His gaze strayed from the black charcoal, back to the lake.

It looked peaceful. Sky blue in color. A mirror flat surface beneath the bright sunshine. The only thing cutting through the lake was a white arrow of water where a beaver leisurely swam to Dan's left close to the sandy shoreline. The beaver hadn't seen him, and Dan kept quiet as it swam past, its wet brown furry head above water, black eyes staring straight ahead, black nose pointed to the sky and a long flat tail floating behind it. The only sounds he heard was the breathing of the animal, an occasional snort and trickling water as it swam.

It was amazing that the beaver hadn't been caught in the trap. He knew that maybe there were more traps left here in the nearby woods, but it was just too much ground to cover to search and they now knew not to venture into the forest around here anyways.

Now that he was here, and the sky hadn't fallen, so to speak, and the coffee tasted pretty good, he allowed his thoughts to focus yet again on the baby JJ was carrying. Today the midwife was coming to check up on JJ and the newbie.

Dan had been telling himself all morning while haying, then while checking the red Angus and then on the journey here that the newbie would be okay.

But if the baby weren't okay, he knew they would have to find some way to handle any bad news. If something were wrong, he knew JJ would blame herself and it would take a toll on her. He, too, would blame himself for encouraging her to go to the city.

He should have been there today, he realized, in case there was bad news. But Rafe and he had discussed it last night that it was best that Brady be there. He was the father of Chrissy and having Brady there for JJ in case of bad news would be best. She was bonded to Brady because of Chrissy and JJ would most likely feel better having her little family there with her.

Now that he was back here though, he remembered thinking about building a nice dock here so JJ could park the plane. It would be another getaway for her so she could come up this way and they could have lunch at the Misty Lake cabin. Misty Lake had a nice sandy shoreline, where they could go swimming.

He could go for a swim now, as he was sweating bricks standing beneath the hot sun. But he wasn't quite prepared to take a swim alone in a place where he'd almost died. With his luck he'd step in a trap in the water. Maybe if there was someone here with him, then yeah, he'd do an intense search via mask and snorkel to make sure the lake was safe. It would be a project for him to accomplish in the future. Swimming here and building a dock.

Last night, he'd also checked the emails. Nothing from Jenna about bringing in a couple of convicts to work out of the roundup cabin. But these things took time.

He did get some news back about getting central air in at Moose Ranch. Last night, after Dr. Will had suggested they put in central air for JJ as soon as possible, Dan had contacted via email the same company who'd put in their furnace. He hadn't been surprised to receive a reply email early this morning from the owner, Tony.

Dan knew from their previous interactions that Tony was a workaholic. The man had said they were pretty busy, but he would try to clear some time in his own schedule sometime in the next two weeks due to the medical nature of Dan's request. Since Tony had all the information from their previous work at the house, he'd attached a couple of different central air units that would be suitable to hook up with the existing furnace system along with prices.

He'd mentioned Tony's quick reply to Brady and Rafe at breakfast this morning, and they'd agreed to look at everything tonight after supper, if they had the time. No one at breakfast had mentioned Layla coming today. It had been a happy breakfast knowing JJ was okay.

Dan frowned, suddenly feeling sad. But what about the newbie? That poor little kid must not have felt good being without prenatal vitamins and having a fast heart rate while being tucked away in JJ's tummy. He sure did hope the baby was okay.

Suddenly he had the urge to play hooky for the rest of the day and just get back home and be with JJ. Within minutes he was on his atv, heading back to the ranch.

RAFE HADN'T BEEN ABLE to fully concentrate on work all morning. He'd checked the fence lines along the west quarter meadows, found a few that needed mending. It was brutal work in the heat, but he'd managed.

Then he'd checked on the cattle in the area, making sure they were healthy. One hadn't been standing correctly and upon closer inspection, he'd found a stone caught in its hoof. He knew it wasn't advisable to examine a hoof while alone, as a cow was unpredictable and could kick and injure Rafe or even itself.

The hoof trimming chute, of which they had many in each section of the large ranch, was a bit too far for Rafe to get the cow to on his own, so after a bit of coaxing with a few pieces of apple, he'd managed to distract it, and quickly pried out the stone. Thankfully, it hadn't caused any damage to the hoof.

They usually did a semi-annual check on the hooves of each cow. Once in the spring and then in the autumn. It was quite the chore, rounding them up, and getting them into a chute, one by one, tying up a leg at a time and inspecting and treating the hoof, if needed. But sometimes, a cow ended up lame due to some injury. An injury caused anxiety to the cow, and he wanted their cows to be happy.

Happy cows made healthy cows and that made good, delicious organic steak for their buyers.

He was glad they'd finally decided on getting some more hands from Cowboys Online. After the hands were trained, that should alleviate some manual labor burdens off Brady, Dan, and himself.

Beneath this scorching heat, he'd forced himself to move slowly. He took many breaks in the shade and drank plenty of water as well as electrolyte infused water and some salty snacks. He'd even taken a couple of swims in a river along the route he'd been checking.

But his mind had been on JJ and the baby. He knew that Dan and he had discussed getting back to work today as the cattle had to be checked on, fences mended and all the other things that they wanted to catch up on, but he felt like he needed to be back home with JJ, especially if the baby news turned out to be bad.

Many times, he'd resisted the urge to head back, but suddenly he wasn't struggling anymore. It was time to cave and give in to what he desired to do and that was to go home and be with JJ. Good or bad news, he would support her in any way he could.

Moments later, Rafe was straddling his atv. He was heading home.

A LITTLE WHILE AGO, the midwife had shown up and Brady had been fast asleep on the couch in the living room. He hadn't heard Layla's plane arriving, hadn't even heard her knocking. Hadn't heard a thing until she had been standing over him, gently calling out his name.

Man had he ever been embarrassed. He'd just been so exhausted since finding JJ and worrying about the unborn baby. Earlier he had checked in on JJ and found her still fast asleep. Then he'd put Chrissy into her playpen and watched her go to sleep as well.

It had been so quiet, and warm in the ranch house, it had made him feel really sleepy.

He'd figured he'd just lay down for a few minutes, and poof, two hours had sailed by when Layla had woken him up.

Chrissy must have heard Layla because she'd woken up shortly after her arrival.

Layla had asked to go up to see JJ privately and he'd taken the time to whip up a meal for Chrissy.

Some housekeeper and cook he'd turned out to be, Brady thought as he fed Chrissy. She was happy and hungry, her cheeks flushed like the color of pink rosebuds due to their early excursion down to the lake for some splashing in the water. Of course, their fun hadn't been in the hot sun, but in the shade of the nearby towering pine trees.

He'd even had her floating naked as a jaybird on her back, while supporting her backside and neck with his hands. She'd stared up at the sky with wonder and she had kicked her chubby little legs, happy to be free of her diapers, while he'd moved her around and around. She'd giggled and laughed up a storm. She'd really enjoyed it and he'd been happy, forgetting for brief moments that something might be wrong with the newbie.

Then he'd taken her to the garden showing her all the vegetables that were growing; the green and yellow beans dangling from the beanstalks, the small green cucumbers hiding beneath the leaves, the bright red tomatoes, and different varieties of lettuce, among other vegetables.

Then the two of them had dined on the delicious, sweet, warm strawberries and raspberries from the garden and he'd brought her inside when she'd scrunched her fists against her eyes, indicating she was sleepy.

All that fresh air had her eagerly eating the food now as he spoon fed her. He frowned as he thought he heard JJ sobbing upstairs, but he hadn't been too sure. He hoped the news from Layla wasn't bad news about the baby and if it were, he'd force himself to remain calm, for JJ's sake.

He should be up there with JJ, but Layla had said she wanted privacy with her, so Brady hadn't seen fit to push his way into the bedroom, which is what he really wanted to do. He just didn't understand this turnaround for privacy, as Layla hadn't had a problem with him, Rafe and Dan being there in the bedroom last night, and they'd been able to listen to the rapid heartbeat of the fetus.

It had sounded so fast, but Layla had reassured them that a fetus' heartrate was normally fast...just not *that* fast as what she was hearing. It hadn't been an emergency fast, but she'd seemed concerned and had said if the heartrate hadn't gone into normal range by today, then she would have to hospitalize JJ and they'd administer meds to get the heart rate slowed. Thankfully, Layla hadn't said anything about taking her to the hospital in front of JJ. That would have just caused added anxiety.

After getting a decent amount of food into his little girl, he left the leftovers in the bowls on the tray for her to play with. That would keep her occupied as she liked to mush her fingers into the bowls. Her being busy playing would allow him to get something ready for JJ.

He opted for making a large amount of tuna salad for sandwiches, putting in chopped onions and chives, a dash of yellow mustard, oil, vinegar, salt, and pepper. JJ liked it that way.

He placed the prepared tuna into the fridge for now. He figured when Layla was finished with JJ he'd bring up sandwiches, some yogurt, fruit, and a slice of that raspberry pie he'd found frozen in the freezer. JJ must have baked it and a couple of other pies earlier this month and stashed them for another time.

Before falling asleep, he'd left the pie on the counter top to defrost and as he jabbed it now with a fork to make sure it was defrosted all the way through, he heard an atv enter the yard and his gut did a really wicked twist of concern.

Had something bad happened that had sent one of the guys back home so early? It was barely one o'clock. He glanced out the kitchen window and spied Dan removing his helmet. A moment later, Rafe entered the yard on his atv. Thankfully both men appeared to be okay as moments later, they hurried into kitchen.

DESPITE THE SOFT WHIRR of the portable air conditioner, JJ and Layla had been able to hear the atvs roaring into the yard. Layla had taken a quick look out one of the windows, telling her that Rafe and Dan were here.

"Looks like the troops have arrived. I told them I'd be by sometime this afternoon," Layla chuckled as she turned away from the window and headed toward her bag near the door.

"They were supposed to work today. That's what they told me. I don't understand why they're here. They've already fallen behind on the ranch work because of me," JJ complained, feeling quite nervous now at having potentially bad news coming about her baby.

Layla shook her head. Her eyes flashed with what JJ could only guess was compassion.

"They were very distraught when you were missing, JJ. All three of them. They didn't want to eat. We had to coax them to have something. It was apparent to us that they hadn't slept much either. I hope you don't mind me saying, but they were virtual basket cases when you were gone. All they wanted to do was stay in the air and keep looking for you."

Well, Layla's confession certainly didn't make JJ feel better as guilt once again assailed her for putting them through everything that she had put them through. How would she ever be able to make it up to them?

"Now that we've had our private chat. Would you like them to come up and listen to the heartbeat?"

JJ nodded eagerly.

She was glad that Brady had given them a bit of privacy as after her crying, she'd been able to confide in Layla that there was a possibility that any of *three* men could be the father.

Layla had kept a poker face at that confession, just as she'd kept a straight face when JJ had admitted the other time that she didn't know who the father was. She was thankful that Layla was not the judging kind of woman and her midwife had reassured JJ that DNA paternity testing was available to find out who the father of her baby was, and they didn't even have to touch her baby.

Now with all three of her men back in the house, it was time for her cowboys to know exactly what she wanted, and Layla had agreed to execute JJ's wishes. But first, JJ wanted to know how her baby was doing.

Layla was just about to open the door to call the men, when a knock erupted on the other side.

She grinned at JJ.

"Impatient bunch aren't they?" Layla giggled and then she opened the door.

JJ bit her bottom lip as she spied all three of her men standing in the doorway, gazing in. Brady held Chrissy and all of them, including Chrissy, looked ultra-worried.

"Come on in, gentlemen. I was just about to call you. We were just about to begin," Layla said.

"We didn't mean to intrude," Rafe said quickly as he stepped in first.

"Actually, we did mean to intrude. Brady mentioned you wanted privacy, but we didn't want JJ to face this alone," Dan said as he entered the room and winked at JJ.

"Chrissy wanted to make sure her mom was okay too," Brady replied sheepishly as he held up Chrissy's hand and waved.

"Mama," Chrissy suddenly said and JJ's heart burst with love as her daughter grinned at her. JJ eagerly waved back.

"Oh, my goodness, she's already talking. That's wonderful," Layla gushed and gave Chrissy a kiss on her pudgy cheek.

"She talked when she saw me last night," JJ boasted. With everything that had been going on, she'd forgotten to tell Layla about the baby saying mama.

"She's a smart little girl," Layla said as she placed the fetal heart monitor onto the bed.

At the sight of the machine, JJ's breathing began to speed up and anxiety snapped through her like a live wire.

"Hey, everything is going to be okay," Rafe gently said, picking up on JJ's uneasiness. To her delight, he went around to the other side of the king-sized bed, hopped onto the mattress, and scooted right over beside her, his warm shoulder melting against hers.

Rafe was followed by Dan, who sidled up beside Rafe on the bed, reached over and took JJ's hand into his, gently squeezing her fingers.

"Rafe's right. The newbie is going to be okay," he said.

Both Rafe and Dan gave her reassuring smiles and as her gaze swept to Brady, who remained on the other side of Layla, gave her a nod and a wink, while Chrissy stared in fascination at the fetal heart monitor machine that Layla had placed on the night table right beside JJ.

"Okay, now that everyone is settled, let's see how the baby is doing," Layla said softly.

She delicately lifted JJ's nightgown over her swelling belly and then tucked the sheet over her lower abdomen.

JJ almost wanted to joke to her that the men had already seen everything there was to see down there, therefore Layla didn't need to cover her up, but she figured that might embarrass Layla, and so she remained silent.

A moment later, Layla squeezed a couple of generous dollops of warm ultrasound gel onto her belly.

"Okay, you know the drill. Keep very still. Here we go," Layla said, and JJ held her breath as she felt the round end of the doppler smear the gel along a swath beneath her belly button.

Everyone grew quiet and almost instantly; they could hear something.

"That swooshing sound is your placenta," Layla explained.

JJ nodded and anxiously awaited to hear her baby's heartbeat.

Layla kept moving the wand, pressing a little harder as she went. There were other noises as well and Layla described them as the baby moving around, which brought great relief to JJ. At least her baby was alive.

Layla kept her gaze glued to her monitor, and then suddenly stopped moving the wand.

"Hear it? That's the baby's heartbeat."

JJ swallowed as she could barely hear a heart beating. It was going so fast. But Layla had already explained last night that a fetus' heartrate was pretty fast.

The guys remained silent, watching. Even Chrissy appeared fascinated with what Layla was doing. She was quiet as well, her eyes round like little saucers.

About three minutes went by and Layla kept the wand at the same place. JJ fixed her gaze on Layla's face trying to garner her reactions. It was a time like this she wished that Layla didn't have a poker face. Her midwife just kept staring at the monitor, her look quite intense and it was at that moment JJ realized that her midwife was extremely serious about her job.

Layla truly had their backs, and it gave JJ an added feeling of support.

Finally, Layla nodded and smiled at JJ.

"The heartrate has returned to normal."

Suddenly all three of her men were hooting and hollering. Even Chrissy was getting in on the action, kicking her legs into Brady's belly emitting an oomph from him.

"Oh, thank God. I was so worried," JJ whispered, feeling as if a huge weight had just been lifted from her body.

"We were all worried. We were just trying not to show it," Dan confessed.

JJ noticed his green eyes were twinkling like emeralds and she knew he was fighting back tears of relief. Rafe too looked quite relieved as she heard him give out a heavy sigh.

"I'll come back in a couple of days and check on the two of you again. But everything sounds good. I want you to rest for at least another two days. Just light walking up and down the hallway. To the bathroom. Someone will need to assist you. I don't want you wandering around by yourself because you will continue to feel weak for at least a few more days. So, no walking around without assistance. No stairs. No going outside in this heat. Is that clear?"

JJ nodded and Layla looked from one cowboy to the other cowboy to the other.

All her men were nodding.

"We'll take turns staying with her," Rafe reassured.

"Good."

"Is JJ's temperature normal now?" Dan asked.

"Almost back to normal. You won't need to put any more cool compresses on her. But if she begins to feel warm, take her temperature and if its elevated, I want you to begin the cool compresses again and call me as there might be an infection starting somewhere. She was taking many swims and sitting in wet clothing. Infections can occur."

Oh no. Something else to worry about.

Layla stared directly at JJ; her gaze appeared serious.

"And I want you to stay calm, no matter what because we can treat everything that might come up. And I am saying to keep an eye out for an infection as a precaution. It doesn't mean it will happen, but it is something you need to look out for. As of now, there is no need for any hospitalization. The baby is moving, and the heartrate is back within the normal range. Everything else sounds normal. Okay?"

JJ nodded.

Layla smiled and turned her attention to the guys.

"Now there's something JJ and I have discussed, and she has asked me to bring up the subject of DNA testing. She would like to find out who the father might be as soon as possible."

JJ swore each man's face went a bit red. All three of them got quiet. They were most likely surprised and maybe even embarrassed that she had confided intimate details of their foursome relationship to Layla.

"I assure you everything that is said to me in this house, remains confidential. I have everything we need for testing right here in my bag. I can take cheek swabs from all three of you and then I can draw JJ's blood. We could have results in a few days, depending how busy the lab is."

"You don't have to jab the baby with a needle?" Brady asked.

"No. Those days are over. They have non-invasive techniques now. There is enough of the baby's DNA floating in the mother's blood that the lab can easily compare to the father's DNA, which will be from the cheek swabs."

JJ swallowed nervously as three sets of eager eyes stared at her.

Dark brown eyes of Rafe. Forest green eyes of Dan. And sky-blue eyes of Brady.

Instinctively she knew they wanted to know the baby's paternity and they may not have known how to broach the topic either.

Maybe she shouldn't have been such a coward in hiding behind Layla and asking her to bring up the subject. Maybe she should have brought up the subject herself? She hoped they didn't think she had betrayed them in some way by telling Layla. For an unknown reason, she just hadn't been able to do it herself and after her misadventure with the plane, she just wanted to know her baby's paternity.

"Is everyone in agreement?" Layla asked.

There came a swift round of affirmations and nods.

JJ relaxed.

Soon they would all know who the baby daddy was. She had also been given the option of finding out the sex of the baby from the DNA profile and she had declined. She was being old fashioned and maybe even selfish, she knew that, but she didn't want to know the sex until the baby was born.

Of course, whoever the baby daddy turned out to be, she would ask if he wanted to know and if he did, she would ask him not to tell her.

"Okay, let's get to work," Layla said and slid the wand off JJ's belly and quickly wiped away the gel with some wet naps.

For the first time since this nightmare misadventure had begun, JJ felt at peace. Soon she would know the father of her baby and she realized too that she was feeling so much stronger this afternoon than this morning.

Soon she would be back to normal, and she could once again take care of her loved ones.

THE NEXT TWO WEEKS flew by quickly and JJ grew stronger every day. For one week, each of the guys took a day off and took care of her and Chrissy. It was wonderful to have alone time with each of them. She'd finally explained why she'd decided to leave early, mainly because she was homesick and missed her family.

Daegen had called and said her plane had not suffered any damage. A pontoon had gotten caught on a log and Mitch, Blue, Kelly, Milena and himself had been able to free the plane. There had only been paint damage as well as a couple of dents in the plane. She figured that was from when the lightning had hit the tree and wood had shot all around like shrapnel.

They'd returned the kayak to Lucas' cabin, and removed her notes from the cabin in case Lucas returned and didn't know she was okay.

The return of her plane happened the day after Layla's second visit, when Layla had given her permission to do the stairs with assistance.

She'd been thrilled when Kelly had flown JJ's plane to Moose Ranch. To see her beautiful white float plane moored at the dock had brought her both excitement and anxiety. She just hoped the next time she went up she didn't have flashbacks and panic attacks from what had happened during and after that storm. For the time being, she was quite content to stay on land.

Daegen, Milena, and Blue had flown over with Blue's plane to pick up Kelly. Daegen hung out with Rafe in the barn and the four girls had a wonderful afternoon of chatting about Kelly's upcoming wedding, of which Kelly admitted she still had no idea what Jay had planned or when it would be. She'd confided in them that she preferred not knowing when the event was happening as she was so nervous about something horrible occurring before the wedding as it had happened to her first fiancé just before they were to get married.

The guys had wanted to talk about her rescue several times, and the unique way they'd found her, but she'd shut them down. She didn't want to hear it, at least not until she was ready. Talking about it, brought her great apprehension. To think if they hadn't shown when they did, brought chills of terror. Thankfully, they quickly dropped the subject.

Central air conditioning was put in the day before JJ was allowed to wander throughout the house on her own and she absolutely loved the coolness. Sleeping was so much better too. But she continued to sleep alone, because the guys insisted they wanted baby and mama to be in tip top shape when they resumed pleasuring her.

JJ's cravings for sex were once again alive and well and she couldn't wait to have her guys make love to her again. Layla had given her permission to do so, but not only were the guys holding back, JJ was holding out on them too.

She wanted to wait until she knew who her baby's father might be. She had no preference. She loved all her cowboys equally and any of them would be an excellent dad, just as they all were to Chrissy.

It was a just a little after two weeks since returning home, with no problems regarding infections and JJ was feeling back to normal.

The heatwave had ended bringing some cooler early August days. The guys were back to work full-time, and she felt wonderful today, albeit on edge because she hadn't heard from Layla, except a few days ago when she'd called to say that the lab was backed up and it would take longer than anticipated regarding the paternity results.

It was getting late in the day, and the ranch house smelled delicious. Aromas of spices and roast beef wafted through the air and JJ was sure the guys were going to love a hot home-cooked meal of mashed potatoes, garden salad and of course delicious roast beef.

Dessert was to be a raspberry layer cake which she'd layered with delicious whipping cream and garnished with raspberries from the garden. She had placed the cake into the refrigerator until it was time for them to eat it.

Her misadventure was in the rearview mirror, so-to-speak and while entertaining her daughter, by blowing baby safe bubbles into the air with a wand while she and Chrissy sat on the living room blanket, the phone suddenly rang.

JJ glanced over at the call display and her heart began to pound a mile a minute.

It was Layla.

JJ blew another round of bubbles for Chrissy to watch and while keeping an eye on her daughter, she reached over to pick up the receiver.

"Hi Layla," she said as calmly as she could. But her insides were going haywire. Was Layla calling her with the paternity results?

"Hi yourself. Just calling to see how you're doing?" Layla asked in her normal cheerful self.

Disappointment shot through JJ. Maybe no results yet.

"Doing good, actually. I still haven't felt any of those flutters from the baby I mentioned that I'd felt when I was stranded and then when I first got back. But like you said, I shouldn't read anything into it. I'm on the baby's timetable, right?"

Layla laughed.

"You're learning. He or she will start it up again, don't you worry. Have you heard anything more about your dog, Katie?"

JJ smiled as she thought about the little black and white border collie. She so wanted to see her again badly.

"So far, so good. Paul is keeping a close eye on her and Brady put all those ads into the lost and found but no one has answered. We've searched previous lost ads, but nothing fitting Katie."

"So, it looks like the dog will be yours?"

"She doesn't have a chip, a tattoo, or a collar, so we have no way of locating the owner. I'm trying not to get my hopes up too high," she admitted. But it was already too late. In her heart the dog belonged to her.

"I think that dog was so lucky she came across you when she did. And I bet you enjoyed her company," Layla said with a chuckle.

"She was my guardian angel," JJ admitted, remembering how much better she felt having Katie there with her. Kind of like an emotional support dog or something.

"That's a lovely way of looking at it, JJ. Now, listen, the reason I called. I have the paternity results and I have sent the link to them directly to your email address."

JJ blinked. What had Layla just said?

"You did?"

"Yes, I did. I hope that's okay? I figured you'd like to see the results in private unless you want me to tell you over the phone?"

JJ's thoughts swirled and her fingers tightened around the receiver.

The results were in.

Oh, my goodness. The paternity results were finally in!

"No, I can check the email. Thank you, so much, Layla. Thank you so much for everything you have done for our baby and for us. We really appreciate it," JJ gushed.

The freaking paternity results were in!

"Not a problem sweetheart. You just let me know if there is anything else I can do to help. You have my number," Layla replied.

JJ nodded.

They said their good-byes and she hung up.

"What am I going to do? How am I going to handle this?" she muttered out loud, feeling off balance and all flustered.

What was the appropriate etiquette in telling the father when there were three potential fathers involved?

She blew out a tense breath and stared at Chrissy, who was sitting upright and gazing back at her, her eyes twinkling mischievously.

JJ's mommy alert antenna went up.

"Okay, what did you do?" JJ asked.

She leaned closer to her daughter, sniffed the air, and had her answer.

Checking her email was just going to have to wait until her mommy duties were out of the way.

Chapter Fifteen

"Just in time!" JJ called out as she heard Dan's atv zooming into the yard. Rafe, Brady, and Chrissy were already seated at the table for dinner, the two men deep in ranch discussion as they poured themselves coffee.

Dan was the last one to arrive and she still hadn't had a chance to check the email that Layla had sent regarding the paternity results. She hadn't mentioned it to anyone yet either.

This would be their last meal together before another big change would come to their family and she wasn't one for change. She liked the current dynamics of their foursome relationship. Loved the comradery between the three cowboys, and she hoped when the baby daddy was revealed they wouldn't be too upset at the news, especially since this had been an unexpected pregnancy, and the guys hadn't been too thrilled about the surprising news in the beginning.

But they certainly had warmed up to the idea of having another baby in the family. So maybe she was just reading too much into nothing. She realized she had a bad habit of doing that.

Moments later, the mudroom door squeaked open, and JJ heard a strange sound rushing down the hallway. A black and white blur raced into the kitchen where she was standing and started dancing around her feet.

"Oh my God! Katie! What are you doing here?" she gasped not believing her eyes.

Immediately she crouched and the dog began whining and licking her face. JJ gathered her into her arms and hugged her so hard that she hoped she wasn't hurting the animal.

"Found her on the trail heading for the ranch house, so I picked her up a few miles back. She loves riding in the atv trailer," Dan said as he entered the kitchen.

"She must have escaped Snowy Creek!" JJ gasped.

"Well, let's put another plate at the table for the newcomer," Rafe said with a chuckle.

Just then the phone rang, and Brady rose from the table.

"I guess we all know that might be Snowy Creek looking for the dog," he called out and hurried to answer the phone.

"Oh, Katie. I missed you so much. How have you been? How did you know where to find me? Snowy Creek is so far away," JJ asked when the dog finally stopped with her kisses and began to gaze around the room with her pretty brown eyes.

JJ couldn't get enough of looking at her. She loved the white blaze that streaked down the middle of her face and then arrowed down her neck and across her chest to meet with her black fur.

"Dogs can travel many miles, some more than thirty miles in one day, which it appears this one just did," Rafe said.

At the sound of Rafe's voice, Katie's gaze fixated on him. Rafe stared back at her with a big smile. JJ figured he must be happy to see the dog too.

Katie let out a little growl.

"I guess you remember me, eh? I'm the one who let you eat my pancake and then I gave you some corned beef," he said to the dog, whose head was tilted at an angle as if trying to figure out what Rafe was saying.

"I gave her corned beef too when we were stranded," JJ admitted, remembering that Rafe and Brady had told her about meeting Katie on the trails and that Brady had jokingly pretended to Rafe that the dog was a bear or wolf, scaring him to the point where he'd abandoned his pancake which Brady had fed to the dog.

"It's Paul," Brady called out. "He said not to be afraid of Katie. She's got all her shots, and he was going to take her out of quarantine tomorrow but when he went get her to take her for a walk, she had dug her way under the barn door and escaped. They've been searching for her ever since. I let him know she's here."

Then he returned to speaking on the phone.

"Oh, Katie, I hope you aren't going to start disappearing from here, sweetie," JJ said and hugged the dog some more.

Gosh, she was so happy now. So incredibly happy. She had a new family member.

"I tried to keep her outside, but she squeezed in the door before I could even keep her out. She's quite insistent, aren't you, Katie?" Dan asked.

The dog gave him a bark.

"I'm just going to clean up, baby mama and then I'll be right back. By the way, you look so hot tonight!" Dan said.

He grinned and then headed back down the hallway to the bathroom.

JJ smiled feeling warmed at Dan's compliment, but what about her hello kiss? Or maybe he just wasn't into kissing a woman who'd just been kissed by a dog?

"Want some roast beef, girl?" Rafe called out.

Despite the dog growling at him in answer, Rafe just shook his head. He stood, came around to the other side of the table and held up a giant piece of roast beef. He crouched and Katie let out another growl, then sniffed the air with her black, wet nose. Her floppy black ears went up and she wiggled in JJ's arms, so JJ quickly put her down. The border collie raced over to Rafe.

"Sit," Rafe commanded in a firm, voice.

The dog sat and waited patiently.

"Good girl," Rafe complimented, and he hand fed her the slice of roast beef. She gulped it down and then waited eagerly for more.

JJ filled up a bowl of water and placed it to the side, showing Katie where the water was by calling her. But she just gave JJ a quick look and then ignored her.

"Well, how rude, Katie. It appears you have switched alliances already," JJ said.

She just loved the way her dog was madly waving its tail. She appeared to be quite happy, and she looked so well looked after too. Her fur was shiny and well-groomed, despite her being out in the forest for hours and she even had a nice black leather collar. She would have to thank Paul for it.

Rafe laughed as Katie followed him back to his seat where she waited patiently beside him as he began to eat again.

JJ gazed over at Chrissy who sat in the highchair a couple of seats down from Rafe. She was transfixed by the dog, staring wide-eyed down at it and JJ laughed, realizing this was Chrissy's first ever dog that she'd seen. She would have no idea what Katie was.

Oh, my goodness, this had turned out to be quite an evening and she sensed it was going to be even more so as soon as she told the guys that the paternity results were in. But the news would wait until dessert because she had put a surprise for them on the cake.

After several minutes Dan and Brady returned to the table. Brady leaned over and gave the dog a few welcome pats on her head.

"Hey, Katie. Nice to see you again. Glad you could make it to dinner," he said with a chuckle.

Then everything fell back to normal as the three men started chatting about work, laughing, and joking as they passed around the serving plates filled with roast beef, mashed potatoes as well as the bowls of salad.

JJ washed her hands, warmed up Chrissy's food, then settled in beside her and began to feed her.

Compliments about the roast beef were flying around as they ate heartily. It warmed her heart, watching her guys enjoy the meal she'd created for them. She noticed too that Chrissy had the cutest little smile on her face as she gazed from her dad, to Rafe, to Dan and then back to her dad again.

"Dada" Chrissy suddenly said.

"Shh, listen," Brady whispered.

Everyone grew quiet and watched Chrissy.

"Dada," she said again in the cutest little voice, staring at Brady.

JJ's heart just melted.

"Holy cow, did you hear that? My kid just said dada to me," Brady roared.

Dan and Rafe laughed and congratulated the old man, warning him his daughter was going to be talking his ear off. Then she'd be having boyfriends, going off to college and the joking just continued.

Brady caught JJ's gaze, and she could tell he was very pleased that his daughter recognized him as her father. Pride shone in his blue eyes as he reached out and softly brushed his thumb over Chrissy's right cheek.

"That's right, my baby. I am your dada. For now, and forever."

Chrissy grinned in response and JJ pushed some more mashed potatoes against her lips. She opened up and thankfully ate it.

"I have a really smart kid, don't you think?" Brady asked Rafe and Dan. Both men nodded and then they joked about him being an old man.

Soon the three of them were once again laughing and playful with each other, casting glances with huge smiles at JJ and at Chrissy.

Chrissy was once again looking at her dad, then at Rafe, then at Dan, and back to her dad again. Soon the three men were talking ranch talk again. and JJ knew what Chrissy was thinking. Her dads were a loud, friendly bunch and they made her feel happy and safe, just like they made JJ feel happy and safe.

To have been stranded for several days not knowing if she would ever see any of them again had been rough. But she had learned something about herself. She was tough when things got rough. That she'd been able to pull herself together where her anxiety was concerned had been a miracle. A miracle she doubted would last, but for right now, she was feeling good, and she planned on holding onto her peace for as long as she could.

After supper, JJ tried to keep her nervousness at bay as she set the table for dessert. The guys gave whistles of appreciation when she brought out her raspberry layer cake.

But that all stopped, and they grew very quiet when they read the message she'd scrawled in black icing across the white whipping cream on top of the cake.

The Results Are In.

Her three cowboys looked up from inspecting the message she'd written on the cake and stared at JJ. She read shock and surprise in their gazes.

Brady was the first to break the silence.

"Seriously? You got the results?"

JJ nodded.

"So, who is the baby daddy?" Rafe asked, his voice a bit on the nervous side.

Heck, she didn't blame him. This was serious stuff.

"I don't know," she admitted.

Dan frowned.

"What do you mean, you don't know?"

"It means Layla called late this afternoon and told me the results are in. She asked if I wanted her to tell me over the phone and I said no."

All three men cursed softly.

"She sent me a link to the results in an email," JJ elaborated. This wasn't going as well as she'd planned. Perhaps she should get straight to the point and stop teasing these poor men.

"I thought we should open the email and get the news all together. We are after all a family, am I right?" she asked, hoping she was using the right approach.

Sure, an email was an impersonal way to get the information, but with all of them getting the news together like a family, it was the best personal way she could think. And it wouldn't put her on the spot trying to figure out how to break it to the men individually of who was the father of her baby.

"Huh, she has a point," Dan said.

"She is a smart woman," Rafe added.

"Let's go see," Brady urged.

All three men suddenly rose from their chairs, and Katie began to bark as she sensed something unusual was happening.

"Hold on! What about the cake?" JJ asked as the men suddenly stopped. Now she was teasing. She knew they were as eager as she was to look at the results.

"We'll use the cake to celebrate. Come on, let's go see who the daddy is of your future sibling" Brady said to Chrissy. Then he laughed as he swept Chrissy out of the highchair.

Chrissy had picked up on the enthusiasm and began to babble. She'd been doing that a lot lately and Layla said it was her way of trying to speak.

"You see, I told you, Brady. Dada was just the beginning. Now she's already talking your ear off," Rafe joked to Brady as they all headed down the hall to the office where they kept the main computer. JJ trailed behind them, and she was thrilled that the dog followed the men, her tail wagging a mile a minute.

She couldn't believe how excited the guys were when she entered the office. She'd expected them to be somber and serious, but they were boisterous and joyful, and Katie was happily barking. It was quite a different atmosphere from when she'd first told them she was pregnant in the barn over two months ago. Then they'd been shocked and solemn at the unexpected news.

Rafe had the computer running in a minute. Dan pulled up a chair in front of the computer and asked JJ to sit. Then he told Katie to sit and be quiet, which she did. Meanwhile, Brady was tossing Chrissy up into the air and catching her. Thankfully not too high or JJ would have had an anxiety attack.

"Okay, here goes," JJ whispered as everyone got quiet and she entered the password into her email account.

Sure enough, there was an unopened email from Layla. In the subject heading, it read, *The Results Are In.*

"Goodness, I couldn't have said it any better myself on that cake," JJ laughed.

She thought the guys would get the joke, but she got no reaction. Their gazes were glued to the computer screen.

"Oh, maybe we should just wait until tomorrow to get the results," she teased.

That got them talking.

"No way!" Brady laughed and hoisted their daughter into the air again. Chrissy giggled and began to babel again.

"Now please. I feel like it's Christmas," Rafe chuckled, and JJ noticed he was wringing his hands with eagerness. Wow, she'd never seen him do that before.

"I'd really like to know now, JJ," Dan said in a serious tone, his eyebrows arched in anticipation.

"Okay, now it is," she said.

Without further hesitation, JJ hovered the mouse over the email and clicked. The email opened and there was the link.

She held her breath. Their lives were about to change with the press of a button.

"Ready?" she couldn't help but tease some more.

No one answered. She could hear their breathing. Rough and heavy. Fast. Their expectations hung heavy in the air.

She took a moment to just feel. She couldn't believe how lucky she was to have these three men in her life. They looked out for each other and cared deeply for one another. She knew that two of the guys would probably be disappointed, because she'd read in their eyes over the past weeks, they truly loved the newbie.

She swallowed and hovered the mouse over the link and slowly clicked. A few seconds went by, and the screen went blank.

Then the results popped up. Everyone was quiet as they read the results on the computer screen.

Dan broke the silence first.

"I'm going to be a dad," he whispered.

JJ turned and smiled up at him. He looked quite pleased, but his gaze was transfixed to the screen.

Suddenly Rafe and Brady were pounding him on the back, congratulating him.

"Hey man, breathe, or you'll faint," Rafe joked.

"Congratulations, baby mamma," Brady whispered into her ear.

He'd crouched beside her with Chrissy, and he kissed her on her cheek. Just feeling his lips on her skin had her hurting. She wanted more. Before she could reach out to him, he pulled away.

Brady's blue eyes were beaming as he gazed at her. Instinctively she knew he was happy for her. For her and for Dan.

Rafe looked a little sad, but when he caught her watching him, he grinned.

"I couldn't have picked a nicer dad for newbie," he said. He bent down and gave her a quick peck on her cheek. He pulled away before she could reach out to him.

Hmm, she was going to have to rectify all these lukewarm kisses.

But despite Rafe's disappointment, warmth flooded through her.

Her baby had a daddy. Now she finally knew who it was, and relief poured through her. Now they could move forward with their lives.

She couldn't resist to smooth her hand over her belly and just at that moment, the baby kicked.

Finally! Her baby was letting her know that he or she was okay.

"Dan, give me your hand," JJ whispered.

He didn't seem to hear her as he just kept staring at the computer screen.

"Dan, your baby is kicking up a storm. Would you like to say hi to him or her?" she asked as the kicks grew tougher. They weren't flutters, like before. These were robust, healthy kicks.

Suddenly Dan's hand was there, strong, and warm and she guided him to where she was feeling the kicking.

"Oh my God, it's gotta be a boy. It is kicking so hard," Dan chuckled after a moment.

"Hey, girls can kick ass just as hard as boys," JJ protested.

"Oh man, that feels awesome," Dan replied.

"Not as awesome as JJ's cake! Let's have some to celebrate! Woohoo! Congratulations, guys! Come on, Katie!" Rafe shouted as he rushed toward the door with Katie hot on his heels.

"Hey! Leave some for us!" Brady called out as he carried Chrissy out of the room.

"What do you think about the news, JJ? Are you happy?" Dan asked when they left.

He squatted beside her. He looked different. Not his usual easygoing self. He appeared pretty serious.

"Dan, I am very happy. Your baby is very happy. And the guys have left us alone for a reason. You owe me a kiss. You didn't give me one after you came home," she hinted.

"Woman, I owe you a lifetime of kisses. When I came home I had bad breath as Katie and I both had corned beef out of the can when I picked her up. Figured she'd be hungry after escaping Snowy Creek."

JJ laughed as she imagined the dog and Dan eating out of a tin can together. She was so happy Katie was okay and so excited she finally knew the results.

"JJ, you've made me the happiest man in the world. You have no idea how much I want this baby with you. I love you," he said.

"I love you, too, Dan," she whispered, thrilled to hear what he'd just said.

His green eyes were twinkling, and she swore there were tears in them. Then his face was nearing hers and she closed her eyes as his warm lips gently melted over hers like ribbons of silk.

She shuddered as arousal coursed through her, strong and insistent, and she found herself moaning as she kissed him back. Her baby kicked even harder, and Dan ripped his mouth from hers, his eyes wide with surprise.

"Did you feel that?" he said with such excitement, as his warm hand began to caress her belly in a gentle soothing way. JJ knew without a doubt, that Dan would be the best father to their baby.

"Yes," she laughed. How could she not feel her baby kick? Silly man.

"JJ, I feel like I have hit some kind of jackpot. I feel delirious. Like I want to shout to the world that I am going to be a dad. How crazy is that?" he whispered.

"Not crazy at all, sweetheart," she whispered back.

She wanted his lips back on hers. She wanted him to make love to her. But all that could wait. It was time for them to celebrate with some raspberry layer cake!

"ARE YOU DISAPPOINTED you aren't the baby daddy?" Brady asked in a low voice as Rafe put on a fresh pot of coffee in the kitchen. He stood beside his friend, holding Chrissy in his arms as she watched with curiosity what Rafe was doing.

Brady was pretty disappointed that the newbie wasn't going to be his and he was interested if Rafe felt the same way.

"I am. But don't tell JJ. I was hoping this baby was mine, but he or she will be ours just like Chrissy is ours. Right, baby girl?" Rafe reached out and pressed his finger on her lower lip in a teasing way.

She giggled and Brady loved that she was such a happy baby.

"Well, think of it this way. We got the consolation prize," Brady said and nodded to the dog who was gazing up at Rafe with big brown eyes.

Rafe looked down at the dog and laughed.

"Yup, we did at that. I think she'll be getting pancakes tomorrow morning for breakfast. We have to solidify our friendship, don't we girl?" Rafe said and Brady enjoyed the smile he gave to the dog. It seemed Rafe genuinely liked the newcomer.

"Dan looked like he was going to pass out. He got all quiet and his face got a bit pale. I think he was in shock for a minute," Rafe said with a chuckle.

"Well, one day, it will be your turn to be in shock," Brady teased.

He swore Rafe's face went a bit pale.

"I don't know if JJ would want me to be a baby daddy. I'm too rough around the edges," Rafe remarked.

"You will make an excellent daddy," JJ's voice shot through the room and both Rafe and Brady as well as Chrissy turned to watch JJ and Dan walk into the kitchen.

Dan looked pleased, and Brady was happy for him.

It was pretty cool what they had here at Moose Ranch. They had a unique family with three men in love with the same woman. He wouldn't change it for the world.

"And as soon as we can, we'll be making a baby of our own," she said to Rafe and winked at him.

Brady enjoyed the way Rafe's eyes widened and his face went even more pale. Maybe it was best that Dan had been the dad this time around, because Rafe would probably have passed right out, if just talking about it was an indication.

"Thanks, guys for agreeing to look at the results with all of us together and for not getting mad that I let Layla tell you that I wanted to have the paternity tests done. I think I was just too weak to actually ask you myself."

JJ looked worried and Brady realized she truly was bothered in the way she had approached it with Layla. He'd been stunned that she would confide in the midwife, but he also understood. She had needed someone to talk to and she had reached out to Layla.

The midwife was a nice lady and he sensed she wouldn't go gossiping about their situation. It had made him feel better too when Layla let them know anything said under this roof was confidential.

"We'd never be mad at you, JJ. You know that," Rafe reassured.

"Well, actually..." Brady teased.

JJ's gaze snapped to Brady, and he laughed at her firm look.

"Just kidding, baby mamma," he confessed.

"You best be, if you know what's good for you," she shot back.

Brady was glad to see she was now back to her old self. She was not taking any guff from him, and she wasn't feeling weak and vulnerable.

She smiled at Brady and then she reached out her arms.

"Can I have Chrissy? I didn't realize it was so late. I'm going to take her down to watch the sunset."

Everyone's gazes flew to the kitchen clock.

Yup, time had gotten away from them.

He handed Chrissy to JJ.

"It's all Dan's fault," Rafe nudged his friend and Dan chuckled.

"It's not my fault I'm the only one working around here," he joked.

Rafe laughed.

They'd held off on eating supper, waiting on Dan's return as he'd been the farthest away from the ranch house while doing the chores today.

"Dan? Will you come down with Chrissy and me?" JJ suddenly asked as she headed for the hallway.

"Ooooh, someone's in trouble already," Rafe teased.

"You'd better be on your best behavior," Brady called out as he watched the three of them leave.

Suddenly he felt nostalgic, remembering when he and JJ would sneak off alone while she was pregnant with his child. Those recollections were so heartwarming and now it was Dan's turn to experience similar memories.

Brady swung his attention to Rafe as he began pouring coffee into a couple of mugs.

"Come on, let's see how much raspberry cake we can eat before they come back," Brady smacked Rafe on the back and laughed when Rafe cursed him for almost spilling the coffee.

Katie let out a bark reminding them she was here too.

"Okay, girl, you get some too," Rafe said with a smile.

Moments later, they were seated at the table with steaming cups of coffee along with plates filled with huge slices of cake.

Katie sat in Rafe's lap, her snout plastered with whipped cream as she enjoyed the occasional piece of dessert that Rafe fed to her while both men drowned their sorrows with JJ's delicious, whipped cream and raspberry infused cake.

WHEN JJ AND DAN REACHED the mud room, Dan grabbed Chrissy's little fleece jacket and opened the door for them.

"Gee, such chivalry," JJ laughed.

"Are you okay with Chrissy? Can I take her?" he asked as they went down the stairs.

He was following her so closely that she wondered if he thought she was some fragile China doll or something. She would have to rectify that situation tonight and she would need his help. But she would ask him her favor in a little while.

Right now, she just wanted to enjoy some private time with Dan and Chrissy and digest the news that Dan was her baby's father.

"I'm fine," she replied as she swung Chrissy onto her hip.

Her baby was growing fast, and she was getting heavy. And JJ noticed that she herself, was getting bigger. Newbie was sprouting and she could hardly wait until the baby was born.

The pain of childbirth though, she was not looking forward to. She pushed that thought aside as they strolled silently down the trail toward the dock.

JJ inhaled deeply, loving the fresh scent of pine trees wafting in the air. The days were getting shorter now, and the yellow sun hung low near the horizon basting the clouds with orange and red colors. Tendrils of white mist curled over the mirror-like water and the forest across the lake was already hidden in black shadows.

Her white plane was silhouetted right in front of the sunset and suddenly there was a spark bursting inside of her of wanting to fly again. It had been gone while she'd been recuperating. Then there had also been anxiety about getting back into the sky again. So, she'd forced herself to rest and to wait for that excitement to return. And now it had.

She said a silent prayer of thanks.

Out on the lake, a loon cried out. The long mournful sound sent shivers along her spine as she remembered the big loon that swam right beside her in the kayak. She wondered what that loon and its mate were doing tonight. Were they leisurely swimming and fishing in that long lake of bays or had they gone off to another lake.

Now that she was feeling better and the paternity of her baby was put to rest, her mind was a whirlwind regarding the day she was rescued. And that's one of the reasons why she'd asked Dan to come out with her.

He would answer her questions. He was an easygoing guy and she trusted that he would tell her in such a way that it wouldn't freak her out, because the guys had been hinting that it had been quite the interesting turn of events that had led them to find her.

As they stepped onto the dock and strolled toward the end, a giant splash erupted about twenty feet beside them. A beaver was smacking its flat tail against the surface of the water, trying to scare them away.

Chrissy noticed the animal pop up its head and then she began to kick her legs with so much enthusiasm that Dan quickly rescued JJ's thigh from further impact by lifting Chrissy away. He slung her into his arms, and she giggled as Dan nuzzled his bristly cheek against hers. They remained silent and watched as the beaver continued splashing for several minutes and then it did a disappearing act beneath the water only to pop up a minute later further out on the lake.

When the beaver left, Dan quickly wrestled the fleece jacket onto Chrissy and then her attention drew to the sunset.

JJ was impressed. He'd noticed it was cool out and he had made sure her daughter was warm. He was good father material, for sure.

"She's going to be walking soon. I'll mention to the guys we need to get to babyproofing the house. Once she starts exploring who knows what she'll get into," Dan suddenly said breaking the silence.

"It will be quite fun keeping her out of trouble," JJ replied. She could only imagine how she would get any work done chasing after a free spirit.

Dan grinned.

"Then when our baby starts walking, there will be hell on wheels with the both of them," JJ teased. And she was going to love every minute of it.

"Hopefully by then Jenna will come through for us with a couple of extra hands and then we can help you out more around the house," he said as he caught her watching him.

"What? Why are you looking at me like that?" he asked.

"I don't know. You seem different since I've been back."

"How so?"

JJ shrugged her shoulders.

"More serious. Less joking. I really am sorry for leaving early that weekend when I did, like I've told you and the guys I just missed everyone so much. If I had my way, I'd never leave here again."

Dan frowned and slowly shook his head.

"I hope that's not your anxiety talking?"

JJ nodded.

"It is," she acknowledged.

She heard him inhale deeply and a sad expression crossed his face. She didn't like that look; it made her feel bad that her reckless decision had caused them so much distress.

"What happened shocked us all, JJ. It must have been a thousand times worse for you. It's going to take some time to get over it. And you will get over it. I'm just glad we found you when we did."

And this was her queue to bring up the subject that was now forefront in her imagination.

"I think I'm ready to find out what happened on the day you guys found me. Can you tell me the short and sweet side of it?"

His lips raised into a tender smile.

"Short and sweet, eh? Are you sure?"

JJ nodded.

"Yes, I think the time is right and it will finally put my mind to rest. My mind has been pre-occupied with wondering which of you guys was the father and now that we know, it's like I need to know what happened. How did you find me?"

His eyes narrowed and JJ followed his gaze as he looked out across their lake. Not in the direction of the sunset, but toward the way where Lucas' lake was located, which was many miles southeast of Moose Ranch. That area of the sky was now a midnight black.

She swallowed as a shiver of fear rippled through her. Would she have still been out there? Alone. Waiting for help?

"The short and sweet version is you got found that day because two things happened," Dan began.

"The first was a call the night before we found you. It was from an elderly gentleman, a patient of Dr. Will. He wasn't sure but he thought he had heard a plane flying low over his place in the late afternoon that you went missing. Unfortunately, he had suffered a head injury shortly after. Dr. Will was flying us around the morning of his head injury, and we stopped by his place so the doctor could look after his head wound.

While we were there the doctor mentioned to him we were searching for a missing pilot. The man was out of it due to pain, and he didn't think about what he'd heard until days later. He actually thought it might have been a dream as he was just nodding off to sleep at the time. But he mentioned it to Dr. Will, and he called us."

"Had he not called the doctor, would you still be looking for me?" JJ asked.

"Well, I personally think we would have found you that same day or for sure the next day, because had Gus not called, there was a second thing that happened."

"Oh?" she asked, her curiosity piqued.

"Yup. One of the mornings when Kelly was flying us around while we were looking for you, Blue was babysitting Chrissy, and the phone rang. Blue recognized the number as being from Lucas' cell phone. She picked up but there was no one there. Just static."

"That would have been me. I tried so many times, but it took hours for the phone just to get the slightest charge and then the phone eventually became completely useless."

"I'm so proud of you for trying so hard. It must have been very frustrating," Dan said as he gazed at her.

His words and his compassionate expression injected her with some much-needed support and validation. But she still felt guilty for screwing up so royally.

"It was quite the experience and not fun. So, what happened?" she asked, suddenly needing to know everything.

Dan nodded.

"Blue thought it was odd that Lucas was calling because when she had flown him to the city days earlier, he had told her he would be gone for weeks, if not longer. During small talk on the ride, he'd mentioned he had to pick up a new cell phone because his old one, which he had left back at the cabin, was pretty much useless. He was very frustrated with it because it was his only way out of the wilderness and he'd been having a lot of trouble getting hold of North Country Air for a ride out. Blue found it weird that he was calling Moose Ranch in the first place but didn't think much more about it because she figured maybe she had heard wrong about him leaving his phone behind. She was focused on taking care of Chrissy who was pretty fussy since you were gone and then when she got home, she had to take care of her daughter who had gotten sick, so she pushed Lucas and his phone issue to the back of her mind and then forgot."

JJ's heart clenched with sympathy for Blue's daughter being ill and for her own daughter. Her poor baby thought JJ had abandoned her. She knew from personal experience how devasting it felt at the sudden loss of a mother, and she'd wanted to shield such trauma from her daughter. Unfortunately, due to her carelessness, she had failed Chrissy.

Dan continued.

"Then earlier on that afternoon that we found you, Blue said she was thinking once again about that mysterious phone call from Lucas' number. She had no idea why it popped back into her mind, because she thought there was no way he would forget to get another phone. She said it was a gut feeling that something was wrong. Said it was so strong, she couldn't stop thinking about it.

She wondered if maybe Lucas had returned to his cabin via another pilot or airline and hadn't picked up a new phone in the city. If that had been the case then Lucas might be stranded out there. And since Daegen was in the area of Gus' lake which was several miles away from Lucas' cabin, she radioed to Daegen and asked him to go and check in on Lucas. Daegen thought Lucas was still away, and then figured maybe he had returned. He agreed with Blue that we would go and do a quick check just in case he had come back and needed help. We were heading to Lucas' cabin when we saw your plane and you in the kayak."

JJ's mind whirled at what Dan had just revealed.

She would have been found had she stayed at that damned cabin!

"I wonder why that phone was working at all. If he was getting a new phone, then that one you were using would have been disconnected. Unless he decided to save some money and not get a new SIM card," Dan mused.

JJ shivered at what Dan had just said. She didn't know much about cell phones but knew enough they didn't work without a card if one didn't have internet access.

Blue's gut instinct telling her something was wrong out Lucas' way would have saved her. And once again because of JJ's homesickness, she'd headed out with a mission of getting home no matter what. First with her plane, which hadn't turned out well and then with the kayak, which hadn't turned out so great either.

"Then Daegen recognized the yellow kayak you were in as belonging to Lucas. When we got you to the plane he asked you if you had been at Lucas' cabin and you'd said yes, but Lucas wasn't there."

JJ shook her head. She didn't remember Daegen asking her. She didn't remember much after passing out when she realized she'd been rescued by her cowboys. Just waking up in the plane, then drifting off and on.

"I cannot believe what an idiot I am. Had I just stayed put both times, I would have been fine. I put our baby into so much danger because of wanting to go home. I am so sorry, Dan."

"Hey, you are being way too hard on yourself, JJ. Everything worked out. And just remember that there's no place like home, Dorothy," Dan suddenly joked.

JJ couldn't resist but punch him in the arm.

"Ouch," he grumbled.

"Oh, stop it. There's little comparison to Dorthy and The Wizard of Oz," JJ admonished.

Well, maybe there was some comparison. The young girl, Dorothy had run away from home, then had gone through such an ordeal trying to get back home because she'd realized there truly was no place like home.

"Just trying to make a point, baby. You love it here so much; you were willing to move heaven and earth to get back to us. We can't fault you for that."

"I was imagining myself there alone, delivering the baby by myself. Never being found. Running out of food. Getting lost in the wilderness had I tried to make it home on foot. My imagination was wild and when I found that kayak, it was a chance I was willing to take to find my plane and call home and then Katie came along, and she made me feel better and—"

Dan hoisted Chrissy into one arm and curled his free arm around JJ's waist pulling her close to him. She melted into the security his strong body gave out so wonderfully.

Sexual heat fused through her and she stifled a moan as her pussy clenched when she imagined how good Dan's cock would feel sliding deep into her aching vagina.

Oh yeah, she was fully physically healed from her ordeal now. Mentally, not so much, but as Dan had said it would take time to feel better.

"Hey, we can't predict the future, you know. We just have to stay in the present as best we can," he said softly as he gazed down at her, a sweet smile on his lips.

Lips she wanted to so bad to have on her mouth again and on other parts as well.

She couldn't help but feel unsettled as to the misadventure she had gone through. She needed to get back into her routine now more than ever. Especially tonight. Especially after what he'd just told her. She needed her cowboys to remind her why she'd risked her life to get back home to them.

"Dan, I need for you to do me a huge favor."

His grin widened.

"Anything for you, baby mamma. Ask me anything, because I am in love with the most beautiful woman in the world and she is carrying my beautiful baby."

JJ couldn't help but giggle.

"Flattery, baby daddy, will get you everywhere," she teased and then she told him what she wanted him to do.

DAN GRINNED AS HE STACKED the last of the dishes into the dish rack. JJ, Chrissy, and he had returned to the ranch house shortly after the sun had set and discovered Brady and Rafe engaged in a rowdy card game with the two of them seated on the living room sofa with Katie lying on the couch beside Rafe, fast asleep. The dishes had been cleared from the dining room table and piled neatly beside the kitchen sink ready to be washed.

Dan had sent JJ upstairs with Chrissy, telling her he would wash the dishes and she could get Chrissy and herself ready for bed. He would execute her plan when the guys least expected it.

She'd been thrilled and had quickly done his bidding. Then he'd started in on the dishes, taking ribbing from both Rafe and Brady who'd teased him that he was looking for brownie points where JJ was concerned by washing the dishes and would he need some help from them.

But Dan just smiled inwardly and told them no, he was pretty high from the news of being newbie's dad. There had been another round of congratulations from them and while he'd washed the dishes, they'd chatted about JJ, and he'd told them that JJ now knew how she'd been rescued, and she had taken the information pretty well. He'd suggested it might be best if they didn't bring up the subject unless she did, because she was being pretty hard on herself.

They had agreed.

He'd also told them that if they were tired, they could head up to bed now because JJ was putting Chrissy down and she was going to turn in early as she was pretty tired.

By the time Dan was half way through rinsing the dishes, the guys had disappeared, leaving Katie still fast asleep on the couch.

He stayed with his thoughts for awhile. Wondering if he was going to have a girl or a boy. Those kicks he'd felt had been quite different than the ones he'd felt when JJ had been at five months with Chrissy.

It had to be a boy. He knew JJ didn't want to know the sex until the baby was born, so he would wait on finding out for now. But it really didn't matter because he wanted the newbie to be healthy. That was top priority. Now with the house having air conditioning, they were all set for the next heatwave, and he wouldn't have to worry about JJ and the newbie. At least not as much.

Man, he was going to be a freaking dad. How in the hell was he going to break that news to his traditional parents and his siblings?

He shook his head. It was just going to have to wait. He pushed dealing with his family to the back of his mind and brought himself to the present.

All was quiet upstairs. He would give it a little while longer and then he would go up and execute the plan.

RAFE HAD JUST SETTLED into bed with one of those kid mystery books written by that Gus fellow, in order to try to distract himself from the disappointment he felt regarding not being newbie's dad, when a brisk knock shattered the silence of his room.

"Yeah!" he called out, knowing by the knock that it was Dan.

He whipped the book under his pillow. He didn't want Dan knowing that he'd snuck another one of those books from Brady's shelf and quite truthfully had been enjoying reading the stories about the three brothers who sure did have a knack for getting into trouble. He had to admit that Gus character was a cool author.

"JJ needs to see you right away," Dan called out from the other side of the door.

What in the world?

Dan sounded pretty tense. He hoped JJ wasn't having an anxiety attack now that Dan had told her how they'd found her. Rafe frowned as he quickly climbed out of bed.

BRADY HAD JUST STEPPED out of the shower moments earlier and was in the process of towel drying himself while thinking about how sad he felt that the newbie wasn't his, when a brisk knock came at the bathroom door.

"Yeah!" he called out.

"JJ needs to see you. She says it's urgent," came Dan's voice.

Brady stopped drying himself and wrapped his towel around his waist.

"Is she okay?" he called out.

"She needs to talk to you. You'll find her in the big room."

"Be there in a minute."

"No time to get dressed. She needs you now," came Dan's reply.

What the fuck?

Now?

Must be something quite serious. He hoped she was not having an anxiety attack, especially after what Dan had revealed to her about how they'd found her.

He headed for the door.

There was a soft knock at the bedroom door. That was Dan's queue to JJ that the guys were coming. Her pulse kicked into fast gear as excitement rocked her. He was such a sweetheart for doing this for her. She had been grateful he hadn't talked her out of being so selfish in wanting sex tonight without so much as giving the guys a heads up.

Sometimes she liked to surprise them. It kept the relationship hopping so to speak.

Both Will and Layla had reassured her the baby was safe and was doing well. She'd been told a couple of days ago by Layla that sexual relations could resume.

She felt good too. Ready. Willing and able.

She also wanted to push away the memories of her misadventure and get back into the routine she loved, especially her nighttime routine.

Tonight, she wanted all three of her cowboys in bed with her.

Whether they thought it was too early was not an option. Her cravings for a ménage were kicking in big time lately and her cowboys better be up to the task of pleasuring her until she went out of her mind.

She pulled on the restraints that Dan had secured her into just a few minutes earlier before he'd left to get the guys. He'd snapped velvet lined handcuffs around her wrists and her ankles and attached them to black bondage straps that were hooked onto concealed eyelets on various areas of the headboard and footboard of the king-sized bed. She'd been positioned right in the middle of the bed, spreadeagled.

She hoped the men liked what they saw. Dan certainly had liked it if that tented bulge against his pants between his thighs were an indication after he'd tied her down.

She'd been saving this outfit that she wore for a special occasion, and she figured this was it. The instant she'd seen it while online shopping a couple of months ago she knew she had to have it for herself.

The two-piece outfit was a sheer mesh midnight black material with a glittering gold stars pattern. The top was halter, and the skirt was filmy and knee length and tucked beneath her growing abdomen, illuminating her pregnancy.

Everything was transparent, allowing the men to gaze upon the curves of her breasts, her dark nipples, areola, and her pussy.

Her breaths came faster as she heard several sets of footsteps hurrying down the hallway. They stopped at the closed bedroom door.

She heard Brady and Rafe's concerned voices and giggled as she wondered what kind of excuse Dan had used to get the guys here so fast. She swallowed against her suddenly dry throat. And waited.

A knock sounded at the door.

"Permission to enter," Dan called out.

She heard Rafe and Brady questioning why they would need permission to go in.

Dan had done a good job. They didn't have an inkling that she was up for being naughty tonight.

The door swung inward, and a hard, delightful knot of need pulsed in her pussy, clenching her vaginal walls, and making her breath inhale as the three men entered the dimly lit room.

The pine-scented candles she'd placed on the shelves near the door, flickered, the yellow flames writhing and casting sexy shadows over her partially nude men.

"I thought she was having a panic attack or something. What's going on here?" Rafe asked as his gaze became riveted to her.

His eyes widened with appreciation.

"You need to ask?" Brady whispered.

Rafe turned to Dan, a scowl on his face.

"Earlier, you said she was tired," Rafe growled.

"Don't believe everything I tell you," Dan replied with a wink.

Rafe swore softly.

Dan grinned and waved an arm of introduction her way.

"Gentlemen slaves, I present to you the Queen of Moose Ranch."

Dan, then turned around and closed the door behind them.

"Gentleman slaves, our queen wishes to be pleasured in every way possible tonight. She has missed all her slaves and demands immediate attention. No refusals are allowed. The queen has spoken. Her wish is our command."

The firm way Dan spoke left no room for arguments.

JJ enjoyed the sultry way all three men gazed upon her.

"You. In the middle. Undress yourself, my slave," she commanded to Brady.

Brady let his towel drop. His blue eyes flashed with need in the candlelight. She could hear his breathing quicken as she let her gaze roam along the contours of his muscular body. She felt her nipples harden as she watched his erection grow quick and hard in a matter of seconds. Brady's shaft engorged and elongated, and she moaned softly as every nerve in her body ignited.

"Caress yourself," she demanded.

Tanned, rounded muscles flexed in Brady's chest and biceps as he reached down with both hands. One hand curled around the base of his shaft and with the other he began leisurely stroking his thick erection.

"You, to his left, undress," she commanded Rafe.

Rafe grinned crookedly, amused at her playing with him. His fingers slipped beneath the elastic band of his underwear, and he slowly slid his undergarment over his hips and down.

Rafe's cock sprang free, elongating like a serpent, arrowing upward to his abdomen. He was furiously aroused.

"Down, boy," she teased him.

"Kind of hard, now that you have me going, my Queen," Rafe said between gritted teeth.

"Stroke yourself, slave," she commanded enjoying the way his brown eyes glittered while he glared at her with a scorching stare.

He did her bidding. Tanned muscles exploded in his biceps as he reached up and began to caress his swollen length with his long, calloused fingers.

Her attention drew to Dan who seemed to enjoy seeing her all trussed up like one of his calves on branding day.

"Slave, your turn. Undress for your pregnant Queen," she commanded to Dan.

"I'd much rather make love to my pregnant Queen," he growled.

"Damn you, slave for being defiant!" she snapped.

Rafe and Brady seemed amused as they watched their interaction and thankfully they sustained her bidding and continued to arouse themselves.

But Dan, it appeared, did not wish to play along. Instead, he remained fully clothed, and strolled toward her.

"Now that I've got you in restraints, my Queen. I think I will have a little fun teasing you," he said as he sat down beside her.

"Don't you dare, slave," she teased him back, yanking on her restraints.

But oh yes, he would dare, she knew that. Could see it in his green eyes, which were darkening and sparking with excitement. When he leaned closer, he smiled at her, and her heart suspended in her chest with such a freeing feeling of love for him.

"Slaves, keep arousing yourselves as you watch me tease our Queen," Dan muttered to Rafe and Brady as he lowered his head to within a few inches from her face.

He smelled nice. A delicate spicy scent and she knew he'd put on some aftershave lotion. She breathed him into her lungs, letting herself savour his scent. His face was clean shaven, and the tip of his pink tongue poked out from between his luscious lips.

"Does it turn you on when I am being disobedient, my Queen?" he whispered, his warm breath teasing her mouth.

"It pisses me off, slave. But proceed," she goaded, her vagina creaming hot and wet for him.

He chuckled, the sultry sound sinking deep into her senses.

Anticipation pounded into her as his head descended. His warm mouth feathered along her left jawbone, leaving a hot trail of awareness inside of her. Then his cheek tenderly brushed hers, making her hiss with need.

Then his lips sucked in her earlobe and his tongue caressed her flesh.

Shivery arousal arrowed along her neck, and down her spine. She wanted his mouth upon hers and she wanted it now. It was as if he knew what she was thinking, for his lips moved away from her earlobe and his beautiful mouth took hers.

Immediately he thrust his tongue past her lips, and she eagerly obeyed, opening to him, accepting his sensual mating with her own tongue. His warm body heat enveloped her, and she felt safe and loved near him.

Desire raged in her as his hot hand settled over her right breast, his fingers tweaking her tender nipple through the mesh halter top.

Suddenly he broke the kiss.

"Slaves, orally pleasure your Queen," Dan suddenly called out and he let go of her nipple and moved away, watching Rafe and Brady.

Her mind whirled with excitement as she watched Rafe come around to the other side of the bed. His dark brown eyes were filled with heat and his lower lip had a sexual droop. His chin was dark with stubble.

He came upon the bed on all fours, giving her an intimate view of his long penis as it hung strongly from between his thighs. As he drew nearer, she gazed along the thick column of his neck, and along the large expanse of his shoulders, her fingers craving to reach out and run her hands along his muscular chest. She forgot she was bound and found herself cursing softly as she yanked at her restraints.

Dan chuckled.

"Easy, my Queen. Just lie there and enjoy," he muttered.

Rafe drew closer. The mattress dipped as he lay upon his erection, hiding it from her view.

"Damn shame to hide such a fine sight," she admitted to Rafe.

"Ditto," he replied.

She watched as Rafe lifted her halter top up and her breasts burst free for all of her cowboys to see.

"Damn fine sight," Rafe growled as he dipped his head over her right breast.

JJ cried out as his hot lips sucked her engorged nipple right into his mouth. Want raged through her as Rafe began to suckle.

"Oh!" she cried out as she felt the bed dip between her spread thighs. She stared down and found Brady crawling up the bed amid her legs.

Brady's blue eyes appeared so dark as he gazed up at her. His expression was filled with sensuality and lust. And promise. A promise of pleasure, as he licked his luscious lips and dipped his head between her thighs.

She jerked against her restraints as he slurped his tongue between her labia and lapped on her clitoris. She moaned as Rafe's lips sucked and sipped on her tender nipple. Cried out as Dan's mouth nestled over her other breast and he took her nipple between his lips and began to suck.

With both men suckling on her nipples, and Brady leisurely slurping on her engorged clitoris, her entire body stiffened with helpless pleasure.

She arched as Dan's hand smoothed over her baby bump. His hand was wide and calloused, boiling, and tender as he caressed their baby. It was such a sensual gesture, so intimate and private even amongst the other two men.

Calloused, hot hands were suddenly cupping her breasts, massaging, and kneading. She figured it had to be Rafe. Oh, it felt so good to have her breasts handled while mouths made love to her nipples.

She felt Brady's lips sucking on her labia, then swiping his tongue between them to lick on her clit. Warm juices gushed down her vagina, and Brady's mouth fused over her opening. He sucked on her aching core, drawing her cream into his mouth.

He moaned in appreciation and her thighs quivered as she tried to bring her legs against his head but failed due to her restraints. Brady moved his lips slowly back to her labia, drawing one pussy lip into his mouth, nipping on it with his teeth and laving the soreness with his tongue before letting go and then tending the other in the same way until they both burned.

Then he lapped at her clit once more going on to circle the throbbing bud like a vulture, making her keen from the pleasure he created deep inside her.

All three men moved so tenderly, their mouths loving her body, making love to her senses. It wasn't a torturous pleasure but an all-consuming mindless arousal. She writhed beneath the flooding heat, whimpered as the flames of need slowly grew more intense.

Hands slid beneath her buttocks and Brady lifted her bottom up a few inches and began to drink more deeply from her pussy.

The only sounds in the bedroom were that of her alternating keening and whimpering, an occasional man's groan, and the voracious slurps as they feasted upon her intimate body parts.

Their charismatic ministrations had her body humming so sweetly and she didn't want it to ever end. It seemed like it went on forever and before she knew it she was mindless, feeling the tightening, the clenching as they moved her slowly into the realm of needing more.

Before long she was aching, her body tense, her cravings mounting.

The three men must have sensed the changing needs in her body, because the mouths at her nipples became more forceful in their sucks. Teeth sparked pain as they nipped at her tender buds. Bristly tongues made her nipples ache, encouraging them to become as hard as glass marbles.

Her hips jerked as Brady began a slow thrust into her vagina with a finger and his mouth eagerly sipped from her well.

Soon she couldn't bare the anticipation any longer. Her body had grown so tight, she wanted them to bring her satisfaction. She also knew there was more to come.

She clenched her hands and pulled at her restraints, the mind-numbing pleasure suddenly too intense. She began to gyrate her hips, indicating she wanted to come.

"Hey baby, relax," Brady chuckled from between her legs. He lowered her ass, and his hands and mouth left her body.

"I need to come," she gasped.

She wanted Brady's mouth back on her pussy again.

"All in good time, sweet baby mamma. All in good time," he cooed.

Thankfully, Rafe and Dan eased off on their suckling and nipping, making her relax as best she could under the circumstances of having three men intimately touching her body parts.

Suddenly she heard the slurp of lube zip through the air, and she trembled as Brady told her to lift her ass, which wasn't easy as the restraints were pretty tight. But Dan had left just enough give to allow Brady to push a pillow beneath her buttocks, raising her up again.

"You're creaming so much, I just couldn't stop drinking," Brady murmured as he slipped a lubed finger against her sphincter.

"Let's just get you all nice and prepared back here, and then we can take this to the next level," he continued.

She moaned and quivered as his lubed finger tenderly moved against her internal anal muscles.

"You're nice and tight. Just the way we like you," he muttered.

More slurps of lube followed, and JJ's pussy clenched as Brady kept lubing her ass. He was always so generous with the lube, making sure that whoever entered her back there would slide in easily enough so as not to hurt her.

When Brady was finished, his mouth melted over her pussy again and he sucked and sucked until she was trembling and crying out from the powerful heat and pleasure pain.

Rafe and Dan had restarted their intense ministrations too.

After awhile she wasn't even mentally here anymore. She felt like she was hanging on a wall of pleasure. She was two big breasts, two throbbing nipples, a scorching hot pussy, and a clenching ass.

And to make things insanely interesting, she couldn't even form coherent thoughts or verbally say anything. They'd turned her into a wanton wild woman capable of only making sexy moans, whimpers, and keens.

She was so enthralled and rolled within the endless agony of need, she barely heard Dan order them to untie the Queen from her bondage. It was time to pleasure themselves as well, he said.

Suddenly the restraints she'd been unconsciously pulling on, disappeared and she was being asked to stand. With their help, she was ushered off the bed. They removed her outfit and mild air whispered against her nakedness.

Through heavy lidded eyes she managed to make out Dan quickly undressing. Muscles bulged across his chest as he removed his T-shirt and pants. Then his engorged shaft exploded from between his thighs as he dropped his underwear.

JJ trembled at the delicious sight.

Dan lay down on the bed near the edge, and Brady and Rafe assisted her in climbing on top of Dan on all fours.

"We'll just have you lay down on him," Brady instructed.

His voice was guttural as he spoke. She did his bidding and began to lower herself over Dan's body. Dan held the base of his shaft, and she hissed as his cockhead smoothed against her clitoris sending jolts of pleasure through her. She felt his cockhead slid into her, its immense swollen size pressing against her tender vaginal walls as he slowly sank into her. He slid deep inside and filled her to perfection, her pussy eagerly clenching around his velvet strength.

Her baby bump settled over Dan's stomach and her breasts and engorged nipples melted against his rock-hard chest, igniting pleasure pain, making her gasp at the scorching impact.

Dan's hands found hers and their fingers intertwined. He gently squeezed her fingers.

"Turn your head this way, so you can take Rafe into your mouth," Brady instructed.

Dan turned his head sideways allowing JJ to nestle her face upon the side of Dan's face. They were ear to ear and Rafe's cockhead was suddenly right there in front of her mouth. She parted her lips and Rafe moaned as his jerking penis slipped into her at a sideways angle. He slid in until he hit the back of her throat, then he pulled back an inch and wrapped his hand along the shaft so he wouldn't enter her mouth any further, preventing his cock from going down her throat when he lost control.

When they *all* lost control.

JJ was perspiring now as she tightened her mouth around Rafe's shaft, and he began a slow pistoning, which sent erotic shock waves around her clenched lips.

Then the bed moved. Brady's body heat washed over her as he came down upon her. His cockhead pressed against her sphincter, causing her to hiss at the intense pressure. He pushed his swollen shaft into her, and she moaned as her lubed anus eagerly accepted him. Cried out as the impact pushed her clitoris against Dan's pubic bone creating an awesome friction.

"So tight," Brady groaned.

How could she not be? She had two cocks inside her at the same time and one in her mouth and she absolutely loved it!

All their shafts were pulsing, and she was creaming up a storm.

She whimpered as Brady withdrew and then he entered her again, slowly, beautifully. Perfectly. His thrusts were well-aimed, making her clitoris rub against Dan.

Dan's penis pulsed inside her and his swollen length pushed against her sensitive vaginal walls.

JJ could feel an orgasm building. Heck, it had been building since they started.

But now, her cowboys weren't reigning her in. Their rods were pistoning into her like they were demons possessed and within seconds an explosion shattered her.

The naughty orgasm raged through her, fully igniting her already sensitized nerve endings, and making already tight muscles spasm beautifully.

Pleasure swarmed all over her, driving into every nook and cranny and into parts she didn't even know existed. She was a ball of fire. A ball of frenzy. The waves of pleasure and searing spasms had her keening over and over and then the men's grunts and groans joined her in an erotic symphony as they came one by one by one, spurting their semen into her.

Was it worth everything she'd gone through to get back to this? The question popped into her head with such suddenness, she instantly knew the answer.

Oh yes. A thousand times yes.

There *was* no place like home.

Having her men pleasuring her like this was worth all the torment of trying to get home and certainly worth being rescued by her cowboys.

The End

Spunky Girl Publishing Catalog

Jan Springer ~ Erotic Romance ~

Cowboys For Christmas
Cowboys Online 1 ~ Moose Ranch #1
Jan Springer
A Canadian Contemporary Ménage Romance m/f/m/m Series

Jennifer Jane (JJ) Watson has spent the past ten Christmases in a
maximum-security prison.

The last thing she expects is to get early parole, along with a job on a remote Canadian cattle ranch serving Christmas holiday dinners to three of the sexiest cowboys she's ever met!

Rafe, Brady and Dan thought they were getting a couple of male ex-cons to help out around their secluded ranch, but instead they get an attractive and very appealing female.

In the snowbound wilds of Northern Ontario, female companionship is rare.

It's a good thing the three men like to share...

They're dominating, sexy-as-sin and they fill JJ with the hottest ménage fantasies she's ever had. Suddenly she's craving cowboys for Christmas and wishing for something she knows she can never have...a happily ever after.

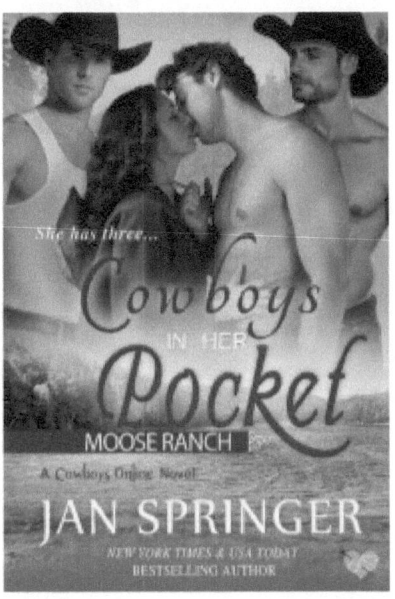

Cowboys In Her Pocket
Cowboys Online 2 ~ Moose Ranch #2
Jan Springer

After spending ten years in a maximum-security prison Jennifer Jane (JJ) Watson got early parole and a job on a remote Canadian cattle ranch playing housekeeper to three of the sexiest cowboys she's ever met...

Spring has finally arrived at Moose Ranch, and a single woman fresh out of prison shouldn't be experiencing scorching ménages with her three sexy-as-sin cowboys. But JJ's love for her men continues to grow as she gives into the fevered heat and scorching passions she feels for each of them.

Life is perfect.

Until her new life is tested when mysterious happenings occur on the ranch and then one of her cowboys is viciously attacked and injured. Will JJ's newfound freedom and happiness be ripped away?

Rafe, Brady and Dan never expected to find an attractive and very appealing female to help them out at their secluded ranch. But in the wilds of Northern Ontario, female companionship is rare. It's a good thing the three men like to share...

Brady, Dan and Rafe have never been happier. Their cattle ranch is flourishing and their continued desire to share the sexy woman who cares for them makes their life complete. Until danger threatens to rip everything apart...

Loving Her Cowboys
Cowboys Online 3 ~ Moose Ranch #3
Jan Springer

AFTER SPENDING TEN years in a maximum-security prison Jennifer Jane (JJ) Watson got early parole and a job on a remote Canadian cattle ranch playing housekeeper to three of the sexiest cowboys she's ever met...

Her love for her cowboys continues to grow as she gives into fevered heat. But JJ's simmering restlessness explodes and she's seriously making up for lost time by pursuing her dreams. There's only one little problem. She hasn't revealed to her bosses what she's been up to while they're away tending to the cattle. She knows when they discover her secret, there will be hell to pay.

Ranchers Rafe, Dan and Brady have found the woman who completes them. She makes their secluded ranch a home-sweet-home. She's vulnerable, sweet and willing to share her bed with all three of them. But when JJ's secret is unwittingly revealed, they're stunned and angry. They figure it's time to dole out some fiery punishment in some mighty naughty ways...

Cowboys In Her Heart
Cowboys Online 4 Moose Ranch #4

AFTER SPENDING TEN years in a maximum-security prison, JJ gets unexpected parole and a job on a Canadian ranch serving up scrumptious dinners and lots of hot love to three of the sexiest cowboys she's ever met.

Jennifer Jane "JJ" Watson has never been happier. She's going to have a baby!

Thankfully their wilderness ranch is a nice distraction for her three sexy cowboys while she's away flying her plane. But when she's home, her dominant hunks are tending to her naughty pregnant cravings and that includes plenty of sizzling ménages.

Rafe, Brady and Dan don't much like the idea of their woman flying the Canadian skies and being at the mercy of the unpredictable Northern Ontario weather. They would prefer having her warming their beds twenty-four seven. But she has a way of getting what she wants and right now she needs her new-found freedom.

Worst fears are realized when JJ, her friend and JJ's plane suddenly go missing and she doesn't come back home to them.

Always Her Cowboys
Cowboys Online 5 ~ Moose Ranch #5

1

A Canadian Contemporary Ménage Romance m/f/m/m

JENNIFER JANE (JJ) Watson has spent ten Christmases in a maximum-security prison. The last thing she expected was to get early parole, along with a job on a remote Canadian cattle ranch serving Christmas holiday dinners to three of the sexiest cowboys she's ever met!

Rafe, Brady and Dan thought they were getting male ex-cons to help out around their secluded ranch, but instead they got an attractive and very appealing female. In the snowbound wilds of Northern Ontario, female companionship is rare. It's a good thing the three men like to share...

Christmas is coming once again to Moose Ranch and with JJ's due date approaching, she's distracting herself from anxiety attacks

---

1. https://janspringerauthor.files.wordpress.com/2017/11/alwayshercowboys_ebook-1new.jpg

by keeping herself ultra-busy preparing for the arrival of her baby and planning Moose Ranch's first annual Christmas party!

In having a wee baby on the way, there's a lot of stress for Brady, Rafe and Dan. Especially due to JJ's decision on having a wilderness mid-wife deliver the baby *at their secluded ranch* - with *all* of them present for the birth! But their concerns don't stop the men from showing JJ how much they love her...out of bed and in!

With wicked snowstorms, a grounded bush plane, a cheerful holiday party and a sweet baby on the way, the owners of Moose Ranch know this will be one sparkling Christmas season they won't soon forget...

Her Forever Cowboys
Cowboys Online 6 ~ Snowy Creek Ranch #1 (mfmm)
AFTER SPENDING YEARS in prison, Milena Allen is conditionally released and given a job at a secluded Canadian horse ranch where she's instantly attracted to her three sexy cowboy bosses!

When Cowboys Online sends Mitch, Daegen and Paul, a female ex-con to help out around their wilderness ranch, they realize life has been lonely without female companionship. Despite being without women for so long, they vow Milena is off limits.

When violence threatens her cowboys, Milena's nursing skills are put to the test, and she realizes she's falling head over straw hats for her sexy bosses. Soon she discovers all three men are interested in her too! But they keep treating her like one of the guys!

She's always wanted someone to love her and for a place that she can call home. Can Mitch, Daegen and Paul, make her dreams come true? Or will a horrific mistake by Cowboys Online unravel everything?

Claiming Her Cowboys
Cowboys Online # 7 Moose Ranch #6 (m/f/m/m)
Jennifer Jane (JJ) Watson spent ten years in a maximum-security prison.
The last thing she expected was to get an early release, along with a job on a remote Canadian cattle ranch caring for three of the sexiest cowboys she's ever met!

Rafe, Brady and Dan thought they were getting a couple of male ex-cons to help out around their secluded ranch, but instead they get an attractive and very appealing female.
In the wilds of Northern Ontario, female companionship is rare so it's a good thing the three men like to share...

They're dominating, sexy-as-sin and they give JJ the hottest ménages plus one adorable baby!

But her second pregnancy comes as one giant surprise, and JJ's anxiety overwhelms her when she doesn't know who the father is. Is it Rafe, Dan or Brady?

Spring days on this ranch are bursting with hard work, danger and emergencies but nights are filled with scorching passions and naughty pleasures as JJ lays claim to her three sexy cowboys.

Here are some more Jan Springer stories

Risqué Girl Delights Boxed Set
(Contemporary Erotic Romance)

2

...a touch of romance, a ménage or both?

Edible Delights

YEARS AGO ALLIE MASTERS lost herself in the scorching passion of a ménage a trois relationship with her two bosses. In order to regain her independence, she walked away.

Max and Nick were very fulfilled with their gorgeous assistant. The lovemaking was breathtaking and both men willingly shared the woman they wanted to spend the rest of their lives with. Then she left.

Now Max and Nick have decided it's time to seduce Allie back into their lives.

---

2. https://janspringerauthor.files.wordpress.com/2015/02/
rgdelights_box_js_3d_noshadow-1.jpg

Toygasm

IT'S A CASE OF MISTAKEN identity when the two owners of Sexy Toys, show up for an erotic several day photo shoot of their toys with famous nude model Cammie Creek.

Cammie believes the two hunks are the male models she's supposed to work with. Usually she doesn't mix business with pleasure, but when they're seducing her right there in front of the camera, she can't resist turning them into her own personal naughty toys.

Josh and Jode are enjoying the perks of being male models; hot lust, sizzling toys and the best pleasure they've ever had. But how will Cammie react when she discovers they're actually her bosses and not just male models?

Shy Girl

FINALLY FREE OF AN abusive relationship, "Shy Girl" Emma McCall sheds her inhibitions and explores her sensual side at Club Rendezvous, a club specializing in the Alternate Lifestyle.

At the club she's surprised to find Logan Masters, a sexy hunk she's secretly fantasized about since college. With Logan's help, Emma will experience her ultimate fantasy - a scorching ménage a trois.

Roman and Julietta

HER PERFECT LOVER...

Modern day pirate Julietta Black's life has always been immersed in the violent and traditional ways of piracy. When her family's arch enemy puts a hit out on her family, Julietta knows there's only one way to lift the hit; she must kidnap the enemy's sexy grandson and force a union between the two warring families. Night after night, wrapped in Roman's strong arms, she can't deny the searing attraction blazing between them. Nor can she deny he now holds her heart as well as her life in his hands.

His dream angel...

When Roman Prince's mysterious captor offers him a luscious woman to bed, fierce desire ignites, melting his usually tight self-control. Lust quickly turns to love as he enjoys their naughty trysts more than he should. How will he react when he discovers he's been kidnapped, not for a ransom, but captured for his sperm?

Alpha Outlaws Boxed Set (Books 1-5 Outlaw Lovers)
5 Books!!

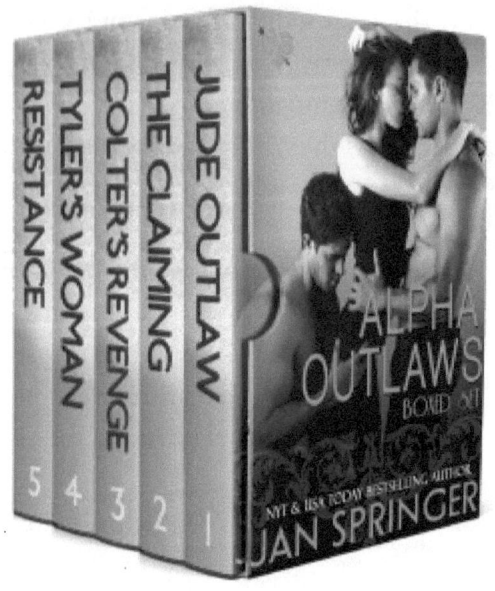

3

IN A WORLD GONE MAD...

A fast-acting virus has killed a majority of the world's female population. With the creation of The Claiming Law, groups of men suddenly have the right to claim a female as their sensual property and the sexy Outlaw brothers are going to declare ownership of the women they love...any way they can.

Jude Outlaw

When Cate Callahan learns Jude is coming home from the Terrorist Wars and is ready to claim her under the new law—with the help of his four brothers—she steals their boat and escapes to the high seas. Unfortunately, her runaway bid for freedom doesn't last long.

Quickly capturing his lover, Jude rekindles the flames and seduces Cate back into his bed.

But Jude holds a secret that could make him lose Cate forever...

PLUS

The Claiming

Seeking refuge from the Claiming Law, Callie Callahan hides in a deserted cabin in the Maine woods and is shocked when her ex-flame finds her. She's always craved being in Luke Outlaw's arms. Tasting him. Touching him. Taking him deeply within her. So, what's a girl to do but to delve into the sinful delights he offers.

Luke has finally reunited with the love of his life. He knows there is only one way to keep Callie safe and with him forever. He'll do it with the help of his three brothers and an assortment of naughty toys. Rekindling the flames between them, he unleashes Callie's sensual side, taking her in ways she never dreamed possible, all with the ultimate goal of introducing her to the Outlaw Lovers and The Claiming.

Colter's Revenge

Revenge belongs to Dr. Colter Outlaw when he unexpectedly reunites with the beautiful woman who broke his heart during the Terrorist Wars. Capturing her, collaring her and holding her against her will, he seduces her, fills her with wicked desires and naughty cravings for a delicious ménage. Fully intent on breaking her heart and walking away, Colter's plans unravel when he submits to the carnal pleasures Ashley gives him so freely.

Colter had told her he loved her. He'd whispered promises of rescue from her life as a slave, but when he'd suddenly disappeared, she'd been devastated. Infected with a version of the X-virus that leaves Ashley Blakely sexually excited on a daily basis, she has come to Pleasure Palace to bid on a cure for her illness. She never expected her Outlaw Lover to be there and screw her plans. Nor did she expect to give him her heart and body so easily...

Tyler's Woman

For years Tyler Outlaw and his best friend, Hunter Brown, endured brutal torture and worse in an overseas terrorist prison. Finally, free of their hell, they return home intent on seducing Laurie into their erotic-filled fantasies.

Laurie Callahan has always experienced red-hot pleasure and passionate love in Tyler Outlaw's arms. But when he's pronounced MIA, presumed dead in the Terrorist Wars, Laurie's world is shattered, and her heart is broken.

Shocked to discover Tyler is alive and he's taken a male lover, Laurie is thrust into a sensual world of sizzling seductions, scorching ménages and the carnal desires that both scarred men crave. But she fears Tyler won't want her when he discovers she's not the same woman he left behind...

****READER CAUTION IS ADVISED (m/m forced scenes) ****

Resistance

In the near future, a virus has been unleashed, killing a majority of the world's female population, forcing the introduction of the Claiming Law. A law that states men have all the rights and women are sexual property claimable by groups of men.

Fugitive female...

Renegade Resistance leader Reena "Red" Wilde is in for the fight of her life when she experiences an erotic attraction to the two most dangerous men she's ever met.

Black ops assassin...

Months ago, Will "Blade" Smith spent one sizzling evening in the arms of a red-haired seductress. Now she's his next assignment. One look into her gorgeous eyes and he's wrestling his heated cravings for her all over again.

Bounty Hunter...

When Cade Outlaw nabs his bounty, sexy-as-sin Reena Wilde, his profession dictates she's hands-off. But he can't ignore the magnetic sparks between them...or that she is the biggest temptation of his life.

Resistance is futile...

After Reena escapes Cade and Will and falls prey to a band of evil hunters, she's grateful her sexy hunks come to her rescue...and in return, saves their lives. Trapped in a solitary cabin during a wicked snowstorm, she can't resist her two, well-hung studs, nor can she deny they've claimed her heart.

Jasmine Black ~Erotica

(a.k.a. Jan Springer writing as Jasmine Black)
Here are some Jasmine Black stories.

Taken by Two Prison Guards

TWENTY-THREE-YEAR-OLD Madeline "Mad" Madison has quite the temper. She got ten to life in prison due to her getting mad at her late boyfriend and there's only one naughty way she knows of to keep herself calm and she's not getting *that* type of rehabilitation in prison. That is, until she's assigned hard labor on a chain gang and is taken by two prison guards.

Taken by Two Cowboys

Sierra Allan works hard at her late-father's horse ranch. When her step-brother adds her handy girl services to a private auction to help raise money for the failing ranch, she figures there's no harm...but she's stunned when her services are sold to two sexy cowboys who give her an erotic way to save the ranch—submitting to their dark desires..

Taken by Three Billionaires

Billionaire friends, Liam, Theo and Elijah have just won Princess Isabella in a billionaire card game. Isabella knows exactly what the three men will want from her...she just hadn't expected to have all three of them at once!

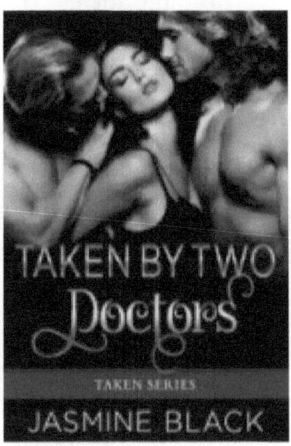

Taken by Two Doctors
A BDSM Medical Fetish Erotica Quickie MFM

Waitress Jean Spelling visits her controversial doctor once a month for some much-needed...stress relief. She looks forward to putting her feet up in the stirrups and enjoys Dr. Ball's naughty unconventional treatments. This time when she arrives, she's surprised to discover that she'll be physically examined by two doctors and they'll prescribe her some much-needed release right there on the examination table!

Ménage series
Taken by Three Bodyguards
Taken by Three Bikers
Taken by Three Billionaires
Taken by Three Doctors
Taken by Three Cowboys
Taken by Three Prison Guards

Taken series.
Taken by Two X-Husbands
Taken by Two Sugar Daddies
Taken by Two Prison Guards
Taken by Two Elves
Taken by Two Mountain Men
Taken by Two Cops
Taken by Two Santas
Taken by Two Lifeguards
Taken by Two Firefighters
Taken by Two Bikers
Taken by Two Billionaires
Taken by Two Bosses
Taken by Two Cowboys
Taken by Two Personal Trainers
Taken by Two Carpenters

Jasmine Black Website ~ http://www.jasmine-black.com
Twitter ~ @blackerotica1

Many more Jasmine Black and Jan Springer digital books, print books, audiobooks plus translated digital books and print books can be found at http://www.janspringer.com and http://www.jasmine-black.com

Here are ways we can connect:

JASMINE BLACK WEBSITE at http://janspringerauthor.wordpress.com/jasmine-black/

Jan Springer Website at http://www.janspringer.com[1]

Instagram – http://www.instagram.com/janspringerauthor

Facebook - https://www.facebook.com/janspringereroticromance

Twitter Jan Springer- https://twitter.com/janspringer @janspringer

Twitter Jasmine Black - https://twitter.com/blackerotica1 @blackerotica1

Pinterest - http://www.pinterest.com/janspringer1/

Jan's Blog - http://janspringerauthor.wordpress.com/blog-2/

Happy Reading,

Jasmine Black / Jan Springer

---

1. http://www.janspringer.com/

Next story in this series:

Wrangling Her Cowboys ~ Is it a boy or a girl?

Holidays, a birthday and a Thanksgiving wedding are upon Moose Ranch, and a very busy and very pregnant JJ finds herself hosting dinners and a wedding at Moose Ranch.

When Christmas draws close, an unexpected snowstorm strands her cowboys and its up to JJ to wrangle her cowboys together just in time for her to give birth. Will she have a baby boy or a baby girl? Find out in Wrangling Her Cowboys.

Cowboys Online Series

Book One ~ Cowboys for Christmas – Moose Ranch

Book Two ~ Cowboys In her Pocket – Moose Ranch

Book Three ~ Loving her Cowboys – Moose Ranch

Book Four ~ Cowboys in Her Heart – Moose Ranch

Book Five ~ Always Her Cowboys – Moose Ranch

Book Six ~ Her Forever Cowboys – Snowy Creek Ranch (Milena's story)

Book Seven ~ Claiming Her Cowboys – Moose Ranch

Book Eight ~ Rescued by Her Cowboys ~ Moose Ranch

Book Nine ~ Wrangling Her Cowboys ~ Moose Ranch

Don't miss out!

Visit the website below and you can sign up to receive emails whenever Jan Springer publishes a new book. There's no charge and no obligation.

https://books2read.com/r/B-A-WGQ-ZJNPD

BOOKS 2 READ

Connecting independent readers to independent writers.